S0-AEZ-396

What the
Spell

What the Spell

A **LIFE'S A WITCH** BOOK

BRITTANY GERAGOTELIS

SIMON & SCHUSTER BFYR

NEW YORK LONDON TORONTO SYDNEY NEW DELHI

SIMON & SCHUSTER BFYR

An imprint of Simon & Schuster Children's Publishing Division

1230 Avenue of the Americas, New York, New York 10020

This book is a work of fiction. Any references to historical events, real people, or real places are used fictitiously. Other names, characters, places, and events are products of the author's imagination, and any resemblance to actual events or places or persons, living or dead, is entirely coincidental.

Copyright © 2012 by Brittany Lyn Geragotelis

This book was previously published in electronic serial form in 2012.

All rights reserved, including the right of reproduction in whole or in part in any form.

SIMON & SCHUSTER BFYR is a trademark of Simon & Schuster, Inc.

For information about special discounts for bulk purchases, please contact Simon & Schuster Special Sales at 1-866-506-1949 or business@simonandschuster.com.

The Simon & Schuster Speakers Bureau can bring authors to your live event. For more information or to book an event, contact the Simon & Schuster Speakers Bureau at 1-866-248-3049 or visit our website at www.simonspeakers.com.

Book design by Krista Vossen

The text for this book is set in Granjon.

Manufactured in the United States of America

2 4 6 8 10 9 7 5 3 1

Library of Congress Cataloging-in-Publication Data

Geragotelis, Brittany.

What the spell / Brittany Geragotelis.

p. cm. — (Life's a witch)

Summary: When Brooklyn, a witch, turns sixteen, her conservative parents finally unbind her powers, bringing her newfound popularity and the attention of her long-time crush, Asher, but using spells may endanger her and, unless she uses her special ability to magically match couples, she may lose Asher.

ISBN 978-1-4424-6815-3 (hardback) — ISBN 978-1-4424-6708-8 (eBook) — ISBN 978-1-4424-6707-1 (paperback) [1. Witches—Fiction. 2. Magic—Fiction. 3. Love—Fiction. 4. Peer pressure—Fiction. 5. Cliques (Sociology)—Fiction. 6. Popularity—Fiction.] I. Title.

PZ7.G29348Wh 2013

[Fic]—dc23

2012025114

To all the dreamers out there who refuse to give up—
we can achieve the impossible.

Chapter One

It totally sucks being invisible.

Sure, if you had your pick of superpowers, you might *wish* for invisibility, but when you actually *are* invisible, the novelty of it all wears off pretty fast. Take my word for it. I've been invisible for the past fifteen years of my life.

Not physically invisible, of course—that would be a different story entirely—though I'm sure there's a spell for that. No, my ability to walk through life practically undetected is more of a social curse. And the truth is, being so average that you don't fit in with the nerds *or* the popular kids sometimes sucks beyond belief. Because in that case, you don't fit in *anywhere*.

But tonight my non-life as I know it will be over and everything will change.

"Ooof," I choked as my shoulder was nearly taken off by a member of our school's football team slamming past me. "Hey!"

Brad Pinkerton, who'd scored more than half the team's

points at last week's football game, looked back at me curiously before turning around and continuing on his way. My mouth fell open as I realized his eyes had focused on the space right above my head and not even on *me*. Chances are, he forgot about running into me almost as soon as it happened; I wasn't even a blip on his radar.

Figures.

I rubbed my shoulder and thought about how there was a reason football players wore padding. That bump was really going to leave a mark.

Awesome.

Happy birthday to me.

Turning back around, I shuffled on down the hallway, listening to the lively chatter coming from the cafeteria. The mixture of conversation and laughter made my heart race as I got closer and closer to the hub of the school. I stopped just outside the door and surveyed the scene.

There were all my classmates, having fun with their friends, eating their lunches, catching up on gossip. Each table was like its own little stereotype. There were the jocks, the alterna-kids, the drama group, the band geeks, the metrosexuals, the losers—every type was represented, and everyone fit somewhere. Only, one group in particular stood out above them all.

The Elite.

Just the name alone was enough to make you wish you could be a part of it. They were the ones who ruled the school, set the status quo, decided who was popular and who would be social outcasts. The Elite were both revered and feared. It was a widely accepted fact that its members were as dangerous as they were beautiful. Whatever they wanted, they got—no matter what rules or laws stood in their way. Of course, no one knew anything for sure, but there were enough rumors floating around—blackmail, cheating, and stealing, to name a few—that I couldn't assume they were all made up.

But their supposed run-ins with authority seemed to only add to the attraction, because they were put up on pedestals around here. Literally. Their table was the only one located on a slightly raised section at the back of the caf, which was probably a makeshift stage at one point but now acted as prime lunch real estate. The Elite were like teen royalty, and just like Kate and William, they had a loyal following.

I studied the group's two leaders, Gigi and Camden. They were Clearview High's golden couple. Both were seniors, both were ridiculously good-looking, and both were from wealthy and powerful families. The two even looked alike. It was almost narcissistic—like they'd sought out the opposite-sex version of themselves. Blond hair, big blue eyes, amazing bodies—if they weren't always locking lips, you'd wonder if they were related.

The Queen G herself looked every bit the part. She had perfect posture and walked around with her head held higher than anyone around her. This not only made her seem like she was about ten feet tall, but it gave the feeling that she was always watching over you. She was impeccably dressed and perfectly coiffed, and when she smiled, you couldn't tell if she was truly happy or planning something devious. As the head of the debate team, Gigi could argue anything—and you didn't want to be on the other side of that disagreement.

And of course every queen has her king, and Camden was it. He was president of the student council, played on the school's lacrosse team, and apparently planned to go into politics one day. Either that or he'd follow in his father's footsteps and end up running his own Fortune 500 company or something. The fact that he looked like he'd just stepped out of an

Abercrombie & Fitch catalog didn't hurt his cause either.

I was still watching them when Camden leaned over and planted a kiss on Gigi's cheek, causing the whole student body to let out a collective "Awwww."

The moment was immediately broken up by the two guys to Camden's right, Rhodes and Wheatley, who exchanged a comment under their breath and then laughed loudly. Wheatley used to be on the football team but was kicked off for being too rough on the field. Apparently he'd averaged at least two concussions per game—giving, not receiving. Standing an intimidating six foot three, he was considered the muscle in the group, which meant that most people left him and the other Elite alone. And if they didn't, Wheatley took care of them.

He and Rhodes were a package deal, though the two were complete opposites. Where Wheatley was aggressive, Rhodes was easygoing—and definitely the brains in the group. He had a photographic memory and could recall just about every fact he'd ever learned. People around school called him the walking computer, because there wasn't a single topic he didn't know about. Word was that Harvard had been recruiting him since he was a freshman, and if you'd ever seen the guy in action, you'd know why. This was probably why he was a part of the group—being able to hack into any system on the web no doubt came in handy. And the fact that he was as good-looking as he was smart didn't hurt either.

My eyes swept over to the only other girl in the group: Eliza. It was hard not to envy Eliza. Her dad was the bona fide movie star Kyle Rivers; sure, he seemed to be doing more behind-the-camera work these days, but he had his own star on the Walk of Fame for God's sake. As Kyle Rivers's only daughter, Eliza was your typical rich kid. She always had the newest Louis Vuitton and upgraded her sports car every year. What she lacked in brains, she made up for in dramatic interpretation. The girl was obviously her father's daughter and could cry on a dime, which made it difficult to trust any emotion Eliza showed to the rest of us.

Together, the five of them reigned over the student body. They were treated better than anyone else because they'd convinced us they *were* better than everyone else. And of course no one challenged them for the throne. To be honest, why would you want to? They were pretty, popular, and powerful. They were elite.

And I wanted desperately to be a part of their group.

Sighing, I headed toward the cafeteria's shake station to pick up my drink of choice: the Monkey Business. A combination of banana, chocolate, peanut butter, and fro-yo. It was the opposite of healthy, but it was the epitome of deliciousness. And it was my daily treat to myself for weathering another day at this school. Besides, I didn't exactly have anyone to impress.

Been there, tried that.

The first couple of weeks of my freshman year, I'd had the misguided impression that I was going to be able to start fresh in a new school. Middle school hadn't been entirely good to me; I'd had a friend for half the time I was there, but Kai was an exchange student who barely spoke English. And if I was really honest with myself, we were more like loners who chose to be alone together rather than friends. But when she returned to Europe, I went back to being on my own.

I was hoping that graduating to a new school, one where only a quarter of the people there had any chance of knowing who I was before, would be my chance to reinvent myself. During the first few weeks, I tried my best to dress like the other kids in my class, fix my hair like the girls in *Seventeen* magazine, and mimic the actions I thought would gain me a gaggle of friends.

It was when nobody noticed the change in me and I was left with no more friends than I'd had before that I made my biggest discovery thus far in my short life.

You can't will yourself into popularity. It is bestowed upon you if you are found worthy enough to have it. You either are or you aren't. And it had been decided by the powers that be that I wasn't.

After that, I sort of gave up trying. What was the point if things weren't going to change?

And the alternative was worse as far as I was concerned. Other wannabes tried to force themselves into the circles of popular kids at our school, and it was like watching a train wreck. They tried too hard, offering to do the bidding of those with a higher social standing in the hopes that they'd edge their way in. But all they did was embarrass themselves as the popular kids treated them like slaves and then laughed at them behind their backs.

So, in a way, I guess there *was* a fate worse than invisibility.

I paid for my shake and then began to walk back across the cafeteria, taking a huge slurp of my Monkey Business. My eyes gravitated toward The Elite. Eliza was cutting an apple into smaller and smaller halves, and Gigi was sipping her Diet Coke out of a straw. I bet neither of them had ever had a shake in their lives.

How sad is that?

I was so focused on The Elite that I wasn't paying attention to where I was walking, and before I knew it I was falling. Moments like this always seemed to happen in slow motion in movies, but for me, it all happened incredibly fast. I let go of my Monkey Business and reached out in front of me. A second before my hands hit the floor, the shake made impact and exploded. All over me. It was like a chocolate tsunami and there were no survivors.

As I attempted to lift my upper body from the linoleum, I could hear people laughing around me. Without opening my eyes, I knew that they were probably pointing, cell phones out, ready to capture the moment and then post it on the web later.

"Omigod, who is that?" someone asked not so quietly.

"Hard to tell now," another responded.

"What a loser."

The conversation grew around me and I wanted to curl up into a ball and disappear. If there was ever a time when I'd welcome invisibility, this would be it.

I pushed myself up onto my knees and wiped at my eyes. Monkey Business dripped off my lashes and onto my lap. I looked around to see that everyone was still staring, some in horror and others with amusement.

I had to get out of there.

Leaving the remaining contents of my shake on the caf floor, I grabbed my bag and ran out the door as people began to clap behind me.

I went back and forth between walking fast and jogging, not wanting to get stopped along the way by any teachers before I reached my safe haven. In less than a minute, I burst through the guidance counselor's door and tossed my bag onto a nearby chair before sitting down in the other.

"Oh. My. God," Ms. Zia said as she hopped up out of her chair and reached for the box of tissues on the edge of her desk. She took a few out and handed them to me.

"Thanks," I said grudgingly. There was chocolate everywhere. In my hair, my ears, down the front of my shirt—I'd be cleaning it off me for the rest of the day. Starting with my face,

I sopped up the brown liquid the best I could and then looked at her miserably.

"Who did this to you?" Ms. Z. asked, handing me a few more tissues. I placed the used ones in a pile on the corner of her desk.

"Me," I said. "*I* did this to me. My clumsiness struck again."

She looked at me sympathetically. "Oh, Brooklyn. What happened?"

"I wasn't watching where I was going and tripped over something. Maybe a chair, or it's possible it was over my own feet. Lord knows that happens often enough." This was just one more way that I seemed to be socially cursed.

Ms. Zia leaned forward and wiped a bit of banana off my cheek. "And this is . . . ?"

"Monkey Business."

"Oh." Ms. Zia handed me the box and then went back behind her desk and sat down. "Sounds like you're having a rough day."

"Aren't I always?" I grumbled, taking off my stained shirt to reveal a significantly drier tank top underneath. Reaching into my backpack, I grabbed the clean tee I kept in there for emergencies—believe it or not, spilling on myself happened more frequently than I'd like to admit—and pulled it over my head. I used the ruined shirt to soak up the rest of the milk shake from my hair before twisting it into a messy bun.

"I'm guessing this was just the tip of the iceberg, then?" Ms. Zia asked.

She pulled out a Tupperware container full of what I knew without looking was some sort of elaborate, healthy salad. I'd never seen her eat anything *but* a salad for lunch. Sometimes it had walnuts and fruit in it, other times it was heavy on the veggies. But it was always a salad. I looked down at my own sack lunch, which contained a PB&J and chips. It wasn't exactly the lunch of champions, but Ms. Zia never judged. That's why I always spent my lunch hour in her office. That and the fact that she was my only friend at Clearview High. Lame, I know, having a teacher for a friend, but Ms. Zia was actually really cool. Unlike the rest of the student body, I felt like she really got me.

She was like the older sister I never had.

"Brad Pinkerton practically tackled me in the hallway, and it was like he didn't even *feel* it. I swear, it's like I'm—"

"You're not invisible, Brooklyn," Ms. Zia said firmly.

"How can you be sure?"

"Um, because I can see you."

"Yeah, but how do you know that you don't just have special powers that let you see invisible people like me? Or maybe I'm a ghost and you're the whisperer. I bet this place is full of them. Kids are probably dying of boredom all the time," I said.

"Ha, ha," Ms. Zia said sarcastically, placing her salad container on the desktop. "Look, we've talked about this. High school isn't really *reality*. All the people who are popular now and all the things that seem important won't be when you leave this place. I know you think life would be better if you had different friends—"

"If I had *any* friends."

"—but none of that's going to matter once you graduate and go out into the *real* world. I've told you what happened to me," she said, lowering her voice a bit. "Please just trust me. Popularity isn't all it's cracked up to be, and in the end, nobody's going to care *who* you were in high school. And by this time tomorrow, everyone will have forgotten about your milk shake mishap."

That was easy for her to say. She had no idea what high school was like for me.

Ms. Zia picked up her lunch again and took a dainty green bite. Silently, I unwrapped my sandwich. I knew this topic was a personal one for her, since she'd experienced it herself. Only, she'd *been* popular growing up. Quite possibly the most popular girl in her school. With gorgeous dark hair and a figure to die for, Katerina Zia turned heads everywhere she went. She'd been the homecoming queen, had the athletic boyfriend, dictated what was cool, and pretty much ran her school.

And then she graduated.

When she got to college, nobody cared who Katerina Zia was. Suddenly, her good looks weren't enough to let her continue coasting through life, and people no longer focused on a social hierarchy in which she was at the top. After a tough transition freshman year, Katerina decided to study education and psychology and eventually became a guidance counselor. Now, as Ms. Zia, she's come to look at high school differently.

And she was constantly trying to get me to do the same. Sometimes she took the older sister thing a little too far and I couldn't help but get annoyed. But in the end, I knew she did it because she cared. And the thing we argued about most often? My school situation. She thought she knew better because she'd lived the life I wanted.

But I wanted the chance to be popular on my own terms.

"It matters to me," I said quietly. "You of all people should understand."

Ms. Zia remained silent as my statement hung in the air. Both of us—one a has-been and the other a wannabe—were haunted by our teenage selves. It was sort of tragically poetic when you thought about it.

I stole a glance at her and once again marveled at how beautiful she was. She was older than me, of course, maybe in her mid- to late-twenties, but she still looked young enough to be a college student, with skin like porcelain and thick brows like you saw on runway models these days. Gorgeous didn't even begin to describe her, yet I wondered if she even knew it.

Though *Beauty and the Beast* was exaggerating a bit, I knew that my looks paled in comparison to hers. My hair hung just past my shoulders and was a blah brown color that neither shone in the light nor did anything for my skin. My cheekbones were prominent, but not quite in the right way, and my face was bumpy to the touch thanks to a mild case of keratosis pilaris, a fun little skin condition that ensured I'd never have smooth, model-like skin. I was skinny, but tomboy skinny, and longed for some of the curves that my classmates had. Bottom line: it wasn't like I was ugly, but I wasn't really anyone's idea of pretty, either.

"Well, I hope you get everything you want," Ms. Zia said, sounding like she meant it. Suddenly, she reached down underneath her desk. "And to help those wishes come true, and to make up for what should have been a much better day, I've got a little something for you."

After some shuffling, she popped back up, this time holding a single cupcake with a candle on top.

"Ms. Z.—you didn't have to do that!" I squealed, grateful that no one else was around to hear how excited I was over getting baked goods.

"Happy birthday, Brooklyn," she said with a big smile. I blew out the flame and watched as the smoke swirled up into the air, making designs as it lifted and then disappeared. Ms. Zia took out a plastic knife and cut the cupcake in half, letting me choose my piece first. I reached out and grabbed the chunk closest to me, shoving half of it in my mouth at once. It was chocolate with a peanut butter filling and buttercream frosting. I nearly fainted with delight as I licked the leftovers from my fingers.

Ms. Zia delicately pulled a piece off her own section and popped it into her mouth. How did she manage to make everything look effortless? I made a note to try to be more like her when I was eating.

"So, any plans for the big day?" she asked, changing the subject. "You having a party or just taking a spin now that you're officially a licensed driver?"

"Nah, we're not really doing anything big," I said, waving off the idea.

My parents actually *had* offered to throw me a big party in honor of the occasion, but then I would've had to invite people. And when nobody showed, my parents would've found out that I didn't have any friends, and that was a conversation I really didn't want to have. So I'd said that I just wanted to spend the night with them. They didn't question me about it, since they knew they couldn't give me my birthday present when people were around anyway.

"Do you think there's a set of keys in your future?" Ms. Zia asked, suddenly sounding like a giddy teenager. "Man, when my parents gave me my first car, it was like love at first sight."

I laughed as she got a dreamy look in her eyes. "They might let me take the old Ford around the block once or twice," I said.

"I'm telling you, Brooklyn, you're going to enjoy your freedom," she said. "It's going to change your life."

I nodded, because it was true. My life *was* about to change—but not for the reasons Ms. Z. was thinking.

The truth was, I came from a family of witches, and up until now, I hadn't been allowed to use my powers. But my parents had promised to unbind my gifts the day I turned sixteen. I knew through witching chat rooms that most magically inclined kids learned how to cast around the same time they learned how to walk. My parents, however, were beyond strict about magic. Their reasoning behind binding my powers was that they thought I should be mature enough to handle the responsibility it took to do magic safely. I think that, to them, magic equals freedom and my parents just weren't ready to let go. They probably still weren't ready, but they'd promised me that tonight was the night I would come into my heritage. After so many years of wishing I could use magic, I was itching to take my powers out for a test run.

And I already knew what my first spell was going to be.

"I think you're right, Ms. Z.," I said. "I have a feeling things are about to change around here."

Chapter Two

"Happy birthday to you. Happy birthday to you. Happy biiiirthday, dear Brook-lyn." My parents paused for dramatic effect. "Happy birthday to you!"

They'd insisted on singing, even though I'd pointed out that I was sixteen now and entirely too old for such childish traditions. When they were finished, they both laughed at their inability to sing on key and looked at me expectantly as they waited for what came next. For the second time that day, I blew out my birthday candles, wishing for the same thing I always did: a different life.

"Brilliant, just brilliant," my mom said, clapping, when I'd blown them out. Mom watched a lot of British television and I think she wished she lived there. She thought the accent was so proper, and every once in a while she'd speak like the characters in her favorite shows. It used to bug me and Dad, but after a while we just sort of got used to it.

"I bet I know what you wished for," my dad said, wagging

his finger at me like I was a child misbehaving. He did that all the time. It was like he was in denial about the fact that I was no longer a toddler. It probably stemmed from the fact that he'd always wanted another kid, but Mom had said she was done after it took her thirty-six hours of nonstop pain to have me. She'd said if Dad wanted another child, he'd have to push it out himself.

"Let's have some cake," Mom said, already slicing into the vanilla cake with vanilla frosting. No matter how many times I requested something different, like raspberry filling or double fudge, it was always vanilla. My parents said they didn't like riffraff in their cake.

And that pretty much summed up my family. Vanilla, hold the riffraff.

I waited as patiently as I could as my mom served us, my leg bouncing up and down anxiously below the table. After she handed me my piece, I practically inhaled it.

"Can we do it now?" I asked as I swallowed the last bit of cake.

"Patience, Brooklyn," my dad said as he chewed slowly. "Your mother and I haven't even finished our slices yet."

I held in an aggravated sigh and tried to remind myself that I'd waited sixteen years for what was about to happen, so a few more minutes wouldn't kill me. But it turned out to be the most excruciatingly long ten minutes of my life. And just when I thought I might explode, my parents pushed their plates away and sat back, finally full and happy.

"Here, let me get those," I said, jumping up and clearing the table.

"Well, we should unbind your powers more often." Mom chuckled, watching me go. "Maybe then I'd finally get you to do your chores."

"Sure. Yeah," I said, ignoring her tone. "Can we do it *now*?"
My parents looked at one another.

"Please?" I wanted to add, "You promised." But I didn't
think whining would help my case, since I was trying to get
them to see me as mature now.

My dad stood up and reached out his hand to help my mom
up out of her chair. "Fine. But we'll need a few things," he
said, walking into the living room. I followed after them like
a puppy dog. "First, I need a bucket of water, a rose, cayenne
pepper, peppermint oil, dirt from the backyard, a large candle,
and a glass of milk."

"Got it," I said, disappearing at once to gather everything he
mentioned. After several minutes of rummaging around the
kitchen, I came back into the living room with my arms full.
I placed each item on the coffee table, except for the bucket of
water, which I put on the floor between us. My dad held the
jar of dirt in his hands, which he'd been nice enough to retrieve
for me. No girl should have to go digging around in the dirt,
especially on her birthday.

While I'd been gone, my mom had left the room to retrieve
a few items of her own. In her hands was an oversize leather-
bound book with yellowing papers sticking out of the sides.
I'd read on magicking boards that families like mine often had
spell books. I wondered if this was ours.

"Please, remove your shoes, socks, and any jewelry you may
have on and then step into the water," my dad said.

Suddenly everything seemed so formal; it was a side of my
parents I'd never seen before. I did what they said and hurried
into the water, not worrying when a few splashes came up and
over the bucket's edge.

"First, we'll add the peppermint," Dad said, placing the oil
in the water. The aroma filled the air instantly and I inhaled

the scent deeply. "To enhance your memory as well as soothe your stomach so you can always trust your gut."

I watched him bend down and pick up the bottle of red powder next. "Cayenne," he said, sprinkling just a little near my feet, "to add a touch of heat to your spells when they call for it."

It was more than weird to hear my dad talk about heat in relation to me, but I willed myself to stay silent so that he'd continue with the spell. "Rose petals to remind you to be gentle with yourself and others. The power that comes along with performing magic can harden a person and often sweep them up in the moment. Sometimes you need to stop and smell the roses. Try to find the beauty in life.

"A little dirt from the earth to keep you grounded and make sure you always appreciate the gifts that the universe offers," he said, dumping a fistful of the dark stuff right onto my foot. With a flick of his hand, he ignited a flame and lit the tall candle, placing it down into the bucket and away from my legs. It stood firmly in place, with more than half the pillar sticking out of the water. "And finally, a candle to light your way on all your journeys."

"What's the milk for?" I asked, noticing that it was still sitting on the table and hadn't been added to the mixture yet.

My dad looked at me and then down at the glass. He blinked. "The cake made me thirsty."

I rolled my eyes at him but didn't say anything.

"Okay, so now we're ready," he said. "Mabel, do you have the offering?"

My mom stepped forward and presented him with a piece of string that was tied in a knot. I stared at it, noting that it didn't appear to be anything special.

"Your father and I bound your powers when you were

born, to ensure that you had a chance to grow up as a normal kid, free from the complications that magic can bring. As you know, we don't use our powers much in this house and we hoped that by the time you came of age, you would respect the gifts that you were given and make similar decisions."

In other words, they wanted me to choose to live a low-magic lifestyle. They hadn't exactly been subtle about these desires as I grew up. It's not like they'd hidden our gifts from me, but they'd made it very clear that I could live a normal life without using my powers. But all this did was make me feel like I didn't fit in anywhere. I didn't fit in as a normal teenager and I didn't fit into the witching world.

I was over a decade behind in honing my skills, since my 'rents steered clear of that part of our life.

Thank God for the Internet, because without it, I wouldn't know half the stuff I do about magic and casting. Through special message boards online called the witchboards, I was able to connect with other teen witches—nicknamed twitches on the boards—from around the world, so I wouldn't be totally hopeless when the time came.

"We hope that we've shown you that you don't need to use your powers if you don't want to. It's okay to be a normal teenager. You don't have to stand out. Life's a lot easier that way. And a lot safer, too."

I wanted to scream and say that I was sick of being normal, because normal was boring, and boring people weren't popular, and that being invisible sucked. But I didn't. I kept my mouth clamped shut so they would finish.

"Are you sure you want this life?" my dad asked me.

I tried not to answer too quickly, but it was out of my mouth before I could stop myself. "Yes," I said. Then, a little more calmly, "I'm sure."

"All right."

They took a step toward me. "Hold out your hand." I did as they said, and my mom placed the knotted string in my palm, and then closed my fist around it. Then she put her hand over mine, and Dad put his on top of hers. "Now close your eyes."

It hit me that this was the first spell I'd ever been involved in, and I began to get really nervous as I lowered my lids. I wasn't sure what to expect, but I knew I was ready for *something* to happen. Even if things didn't turn out the way I'd always imagined they would, anything had to be better than the way my life had been going so far.

And with that thought, they started chanting:

> *Born free but quickly reined,*
> *Thy powers were hidden but remained.*
> *Deep inside thy bridled soul,*
> *Discovery of thyself was the ultimate goal.*
> *Here, this string ties thou to us,*
> *Unwind, unfurl, undo thou must.*
> *Though once bound, thy gifts are now free,*
> *We wish thou well on life's journey.*

As they spoke the last words of the spell, I felt a whoosh of cold air flow through the room, whipping my hair around like we were in a wind tunnel. And then it stopped. I could feel that the atmosphere had changed around us and was almost scared to open my eyes. But I did anyway and looked down at my still balled-up fist.

My parents both withdrew their hands. After a few seconds, I hesitantly opened mine. The string was still inside, but now it was straight.

"Congratulations, Brooklyn," my mom said. "You're officially a practicing witch."

"How do you feel this morning, sweetie?" my mom asked as I plopped down onto the kitchen chair the next day.

I yawned in response.

"Like I told you last night, it's normal for a witch's body to need to rest after coming into her powers. Having all of that magic coursing through you at once has a tendency to tap you out. Kind of like when you get a new cell phone and you have to charge it before using it."

"Crap, I forgot to charge my cell phone," I muttered as I snagged a piece of toast from the middle of the table and took a bite.

I was grumpy that morning and I couldn't help it. I'd had so many things planned for the night my powers were released. But immediately following the big unbinding, I'd proceeded to pass out. And not in an "I'm a little tired, I think I'll go to bed early" kind of way. It was more like I'd been slipped a sedative or something, and it was all I could do just to make it to my bed before I collapsed. I hadn't even had the energy to change into pajamas. And even after sleeping like the dead for more than eleven hours, I still felt like I needed a few dozen Red Bulls if I was going to make it through the day.

I was mostly annoyed at the fact that I hadn't been able to do any magic at all. There were so many things I'd wanted to try. Summoning spells, levitation, creating light out of darkness—I had a list I'd been making for the past year and figured I'd be able to get to at least *some* of them before I called it quits for the night. Instead, I'd pulled a snoozer.

What a waste.

There was one spell in particular that I'd been waiting

forever to perform. And it was going to change my life, I just knew it. So when I awoke that morning, unchanged and more than slightly disappointed at how anticlimactic the whole thing had been, I couldn't seem to tame my inner brat.

"Do I have to go to school today?" I asked, bordering on whiney. "I know it's not technically my birthday anymore, but I think considering the circumstances . . ."

"Your exhaustion will wear off the more you get up and move," my mom answered. She didn't have to say no for me to realize that's what she meant. My frown grew deeper. "Pretty soon, you'll go back to feeling like normal again."

"That's what I'm hoping *doesn't* happen," I said as I took another bite of the toast.

My mom stopped bustling around the kitchen and stared at me for a minute as I nibbled on my breakfast. "You do look different, though," she said, almost wistfully.

"I do?" I asked.

"A bit . . . older, maybe. I can't believe how quickly you're growing up, Brooklyn."

"Oh, Mom," I sighed, realizing her comment had nothing to do with my magical abilities. She was just having a parental moment.

Even so, by the time she dropped me off at school, I had to admit, I was beginning to believe her. There was a little extra pep in my step, and a tingling feeling in my fingers that wouldn't go away, sort of like when your arm goes to sleep, only pleasant, not painful. Colors seemed brighter and I could swear that the noise around me was louder. Before long, I began to wonder whether other people could see the change in me too.

My pulse sped up as I caught sight of The Elite heading in my direction. Rhodes and Wheatley were goofing off per usual and Eliza was fully engrossed in something on her phone. Gigi and Camden were walking hand in hand down the hall.

The sensation in my fingertips increased, and instead of letting my head drop to stare at the ground, I straightened my back and continued to walk straight toward them. This would be the moment of truth. If anything had changed at all in me, The Elite would surely notice.

They had to.

I sucked in a breath and held it as we got within feet of each other. I forced my legs to continue into The Elite's path instead of walking around them like I typically would, and I began to panic. What if they didn't notice me and we collided? Or worse, what if they noticed me and decided that I was that weird girl who wouldn't get out of their way? What would that do to my chances of infiltrating the group? And worst of all, what if they recognized me from my milk shake humiliation the day before?

And then it was too late to reconsider. I was practically face-to-face with the most popular kids in school and I had no idea how to handle it. Just when I thought I might faint from whatever was about to happen, Gigi's and Camden's hands separated and the two parted like the Red Sea so I could pass between them. I thought I might have caught a flash of Gigi's eyes looking at me as she passed, but it was all over so quickly that it was quite possible I'd imagined the whole thing.

As soon as I was on the other side of them, I stopped in my tracks and turned around. I couldn't help but stare behind me as they left, and noticed that they didn't bother to do the same. They continued on down the hallway, Clearview's power couple linking back up after a few feet.

I felt myself slowly deflate as I watched them disappear.

Nothing was different. I may have been a year older and,

now, a witch, but anything that I thought I'd felt was clearly perceptible only to me.

Once again I was the only one who knew I existed.

Feeling a whole new level of defeat, I dragged myself over to my locker and leaned into it, touching my forehead against the cool metal door. For a brief moment, I considered banging my head against it. How could I have let myself think things would be different? Instead, I closed my eyes and took a minute to collect myself.

"Do you two want to be left alone?"

I assumed the comment was meant for someone else and ignored it. When it was repeated, my curiosity got the better of me and I cracked one of my eyes open.

What I saw startled me. Just a few feet away, two gorgeous eyes stared back. They crinkled at the sides as if they were smiling at me. And as I looked at the rest of his dark caramel-colored face, I saw that his lips were smiling too.

Keeping my forehead on the locker, I turned my head slightly the other way to see whether he was talking to someone behind me, but to my surprise, there was no one there. I pushed myself slowly away from the locker and looked back at him, almost expecting him to have disappeared.

But he was still there, leaning lazily against the lockers, hands resting in the pockets of his jeans. His smile had changed to a slight smirk as he waited for me to respond.

"Um, yeah. No. I mean . . . what?" I said, totally caught off guard.

He didn't move toward me or away from me, just stared at me curiously. "I had a locker like that once. We were hot and heavy for a while, but then she dumped me for the janitor's closet. And, well, how could I compete with that?"

When I didn't answer right away, he chuckled to himself

and then ran his hand through his jet-black faux-hawk.

"Okay. So, nice talk," he said, and slowly began to move away. "Maybe next time we'll get to the part where you say something back? We'll make it a whole conversation thing."

All I could do was nod as I watched Asher Astley, the boy I'd had a crush on since the beginning of school, walk away from me. After a few feet, he turned his head and threw another glance my way. I felt the tingling start up. It was like my whole body was buzzing.

Were hallucinations a side effect of coming into my powers or had Asher just noticed me? Maybe something had changed after all.

I had trouble concentrating the rest of the day, so by the time the last bell rang, I practically ran all the way home. Between what had happened with Asher and The Elite, I was more than a little overwhelmed. And it wasn't like I was cutting into any of my other plans, since heading home right after school was part of my normal routine. But today, all I wanted to do was escape to my room and spend some quality time alone with my spell book.

Well, it wasn't so much a book as a notebook that I'd collected spells in ever since I'd started trolling the witchboards. I'd met so many witches online who were from different covens all over the world and got to hear all about what it was like to cast spells. It had opened my eyes to all the possibilities that magic could bring.

And the spells. Oh, the spells! There were *millions* of them. And so many different variations, too. It was sort of like how a cooking site might have twenty different recipes for meat loaf. So if I wanted to perform a levitation spell, there were dozens of ways to make it happen. Certain words would make an object take to the air with more force, while others were weaker. I'd cataloged as many as I could over the years and planned to use each and every one if it was possible.

My makeshift spell book sort of acted as a diary, too. I could tell how old I was at the time of each entry by the type and quality of the spell in the book. For instance, at the beginning of the notebook, most of the pages included spells like ones that changed vegetables into candy or gave people hives (I'd wanted to use this one on a kid who'd made fun of me at school). The most recent entries included changing the faces of people in pictures and making objects fly.

I flipped to a random page in the middle and sat down cross-legged on my bed. No one was home, so I knew I wasn't going to be interrupted. The last thing I needed was for my parents to walk in on me performing my first spell. It was embarrassing enough that I was getting such a late start. No, this was something I wanted complete privacy for.

Closing my eyes, I began to breathe in deeply. One of the things I'd learned on the witchboards was that you needed to be as still as possible when casting. Many people suggested learning how to meditate, because it helped you tap in to your powers more quickly. After hearing that, I'd begun studying ways to calm my mind and body, and even started practicing on a daily basis. I figured it would be one less thing I had to worry about when I finally got control of my powers.

Today I began by picturing the ocean, waves crashing against the shore. As each one rolled in, I noticed how it was unique to all the others and followed it until it disappeared into the frothy foam that spread across the beach. The visualization became methodical, and after a few minutes my body had relaxed to the point where I could feel my heartbeat pulsing through it.

I slowly opened my eyes and looked down at the page in

front of me. I read its contents and then thought through what I was about to do. I visualized what I wanted to accomplish and, once I was ready, turned my gaze to the lamp that was illuminated in the corner of the room. The house was completely silent as I took my first step.

Narrowing my eyes and concentrating, I said the words that were written in my notebook with as much force as I could muster.

"Electro-reducto!"

I felt a buzzing sensation move from my toes, up to my torso, through my upper body, and then explode out my fingers. I didn't see the magic burst out of me, but almost immediately the light began to dim. It happened slowly at first, but as seconds passed it seemed to pick up speed. Before it could go out completely, I pulled back on the magic and then closed my hand and drew it in toward my body as if I were reining in a horse.

Blinking through the dim light, I leaned back carefully onto my bed, worried that if I moved too quickly, the spell's effects would be broken. When the light remained low, I decided to give it another try.

On the same page was another enchantment, which I'd memorized earlier. With the same amount of concentration, but this time while lying back against my cushy pillows, I summoned my magic again.

"Electro-lumino!" I said, pointing at the lamp. Just like before, the power of my magic flowed through my body and out my fingertips.

The light began to brighten again, and before I knew it, every corner of my room was glowing unnaturally. Shielding my eyes, I brought the glow back down to normal and then collapsed onto my bed, giddy and satisfied with having cast my first spell.

My thoughts immediately flew to what I was going to perform next. I didn't even stop to think about whether I should be casting more or not, I just kept going. Page after page, I tested out the spells, building up from the easy ones to the more difficult. I moved a piece of paper from one end of the room to the other. I turned the radio on and off. I made an apple materialize in front of me—and then changed it into a peach. I made my nails turn a deep shade of red without having to go through the tedious process of painting them.

Over an hour later, when I felt as if I'd had enough practice, I turned to the last page in my notebook and studied it. At first glance, it looked sort of like I'd created a Frankenstein in Photoshop. One model's head was on top of another's body, with the hair of my favorite star topping it all off. I'd taken all the best parts of some of the most beautiful women in the world and created one person. Though my arts-and-crafts project left much to be desired, what I did have was a blueprint for beauty.

And a wish list for the ultimate makeover.

I bit my lip as I studied the individual pictures in front of me and thought about what it would be like to be *that* gorgeous. Certainly people would notice me then, right? I mean, how could they not, with hair like that and a body that would put a Victoria's Secret model to shame?

"I'll just start out small," I said out loud, as if I was warning the universe what I was about to do. But the reality was that people changed their appearances all the time. Cosmetics were a multibillion-dollar industry, after all.

What I wanted to do required a little more magic than could be found in the aisles of my local drugstore.

Before I could feel weird about what I was doing, I performed the spell that would change my boring brown eyes to a gorgeous sea-green color. It was over so quickly that I had to look in the mirror to see if it had even worked. Studying my new eyes, I was amazed by how much of a difference it made. I almost couldn't stop staring at them. I clapped my hands together in excitement, then set to work on all the other parts of me that I felt needed an upgrade.

I lightened my mousy brown hair to a golden blond, which gave me the appearance that I'd spent most of my life on a beach somewhere tropical. My strands grew about five more inches in length, and the ends took on a natural curl they'd only ever had when I spent hours curling them.

Next I focused on clearing up my skin; the tiny bumps that had plagued almost every part of my body disappeared within minutes. Every surface became smooth, and for the first time I loved the feel of my hand on my cheek. My lips took on a pucker that was just slightly bigger than usual and my brows arched into a sassy angle that I'd never been able to achieve through plucking.

I moved on and gave my height a boost without the need of heels. And just to ensure that no one would consider my body boyish anymore, my butt and hips swelled just the tiniest bit, to give me that little oomph I'd always wanted. I wouldn't be mistaken for Kim Kardashian anytime soon, but there was a curve to me now that hadn't been there before. And because I wanted that sun-kissed glow without a side of melanoma, I threw in a little bronzed sheen for good measure.

Feeling like I was getting a bit carried away, I stepped away from my spell book and walked carefully over to the mirror. Still looking at the ground, I took a few moments to remember what I'd looked like before. I couldn't help but feel like I was on one of those extreme makeover shows and was about to be unveiled to the waiting audience. When I felt like I was finally ready to see the results, I lifted my eyes to my reflection.

And gasped.

There, staring back at me, was a glamazon. I took a hesitant step forward, half expecting the figure not to move along with me. But she did, and the closer I got, the more I could see myself staring back. New hair color, eye color, and body aside, there was enough of the old me shining through that I wasn't a totally new person. The shape of my eyes was still the same, as was my face, though the clear skin and golden hue made me glow like I never had before. I was digging the blond locks, and pushed out my hip to test my new sass-factor.

It was me, but it wasn't me. I was new and improved. Buffed and done up. It was like I'd airbrushed a bad picture of me. Only, I got to be like this all the time!

I turned around in circles, admiring my new self until I got dizzy and then collapsed on the floor. What would the reaction be like at school? Things had to be different now, right? *I* was different. I caught another glance of myself and winked.

Nope, being invisible was no longer an option.

Chapter Three

When I opened my eyes the next morning, I lay in bed thinking about what I'd done to myself the night before. Part of me wondered whether it had all been a dream, and my heart began to sink at the thought. I'd been so blown away by the transformation that had taken place that I couldn't bear to think it wouldn't be there again this morning.

Mustering up all my courage, I launched myself out of bed and walked over to the full-length mirror hanging on the back of my door.

Oh. My. God.

What I saw reflected back at me was even better than I'd remembered. Logically, I knew that I'd been asleep for hours, probably tossing and turning in bed, but you couldn't tell by the way I looked. My hair, though tousled, looked shiny and beautiful, just like a shampoo commercial. And the volume I seemed to have naturally was the bedhead look that people spent hours trying to achieve. My new clear skin was dewy and fresh, and upon closer inspection, I doubted I'd need much makeup today at all.

No need to cover up perfection.

I spent about ten minutes poking and prodding myself, barely able to believe it was all me. And it didn't matter which angle I studied myself, because I loved every bit of my new look.

I spent so much time looking in the mirror, in fact, that I ended up having to rush my morning routine in order to not be late. The time it took me to get ready was cut down considerably, though, now that I had a lot less to worry about. There were no zits to cover, no need for product to tame my wild hair. My eyes popped no matter what I wore, and my clothes just fit better. I looked hot.

I'd been in bed by the time my parents had come home from a dinner they'd been roped into with our neighbors, so I'd managed to avoid the backlash of my makeover. And this morning, I timed my departure perfectly so I could sneak out of the house unseen. It's not that I thought they'd be mad, really, but I knew they'd have questions for me. And the truth was, I still wasn't quite sure what I was going to tell them. Besides, I sort of wanted to see if my makeover was going to have any impact on my social life before I decided whether the confrontation was worth it or not.

Dressed in a skirt that showed off my killer legs—which had always been nice, but until now I hadn't been confident enough to show off—and a sequined tank, I gave myself one final glance in the mirror before heading off to school.

I was so busy thinking about how people were going to react that before I knew it, I was ambling up the steps. With butterflies swarming around inside my stomach, I took ahold of the front doors and pulled them open, feeling like I was about to make my grand entrance.

As I walked inside, I began to worry that no matter what I did, my social standing at school was set in stone. I watched as kids scrambled down the hall, either trying to find their friends or hustling to their lockers before classes started. The smile I'd plastered on my face for the moment that people saw the changes in me slowly began to sag into a frown.

There was no reaction at all.

A guy brushed past me then, knocking me out of his way as he went, and mumbled an unconvincing "sorry." But then something happened. He lifted his eyes long enough to look at me—and continued to stare as he walked away. His mouth fell slightly open, and he completely abandoned the conversation he'd been having with his buddies. This caused them all to turn and look my way, which created a similar reaction.

My smile shot back onto my face as I collected myself and began to try my best to strut down the hallway. As my heels clicked against the floor, I started to get into a rhythm and noticed excitedly that my new curves were lending to a slightly more seductive walk. Not knowing if it was working or not, I dared to place one hand on my hip, à la Ms. Tyra Banks, and walked straight ahead.

People began to whisper, quietly at first, and then I could hear bits and pieces of conversations going on all around me.

"Who's that?"

"I bet she's new."

"Uh, this is a hallway, not a runway."

Even the negative comments couldn't wipe the grin off my face as I soaked up the attention I'd always dreamed about getting.

"Damn, girl. Looking good!" This came from Brad Pinkerton, the same guy who'd bodychecked me just a couple of days ago. I rolled my eyes. He wouldn't apologize then, but he was hitting on me now? Yeah, right.

As one of my teachers walked by, I gave her a little wave. "Hi, Mrs. Garrett," I said.

"Hello, Ms. . . ." she began, but then stopped. She squinted at me as if she was having trouble seeing me.

She didn't recognize me.

"It's me, Brooklyn," I said, smiling.

"Brooklyn! Well, well, look at you," she stammered, before hurrying off to class, confused.

I shrugged and then continued on to my locker. By this time I had the attention of everyone within eyeshot and was uber-aware that my every move was being watched and analyzed. Praying that I wouldn't trip in my heels and remind them all who I really was, I took my time getting in my locker and collecting my books. I tried desperately to act like I didn't notice everyone staring and continued on my way to my first class.

I didn't even realize I'd been holding in my breath until I sat down in first-period history and let it out slowly.

Well, that went well.

Better than expected, actually. And all the attention, albeit exciting, was a little bit odd, too. I was still the same person I was before—only blonder, with better skin and a butt that belonged in a music video.

I was still me.

I was so totally lost in thought that I didn't even notice when Eliza and Wheatley walked in and took their regular seats just a few away from me. When I finally looked up from my desk, I saw them both staring in my direction. It wasn't the same way that the others had been looking at me; this was more like curiosity than awe or heated interest.

I turned to make sure they weren't looking at anyone behind me, but saw that I was the only one in their line of sight. As I turned back around, I knocked my pile of books off my desk and they landed with a clatter on the floor. My face growing hot, I scrambled to retrieve them as subtly as I could.

Oh, why couldn't there be an anti-clumsiness spell?

When I finally got everything back on my desk, I snuck a glance at Eliza and Wheatley, who had gone back to focusing on their own stuff. Still, I noted, a glance from The Elite was better than what I'd gotten before, which was a big, fat nothing. And they *had* been looking at me, so the makeover couldn't have been a total flop.

As others filtered into the room, I got more surprised looks. And when the noise in the class began to rise, I couldn't help but think everyone was talking about me. Whether it was good or bad, I couldn't tell, but one look around and I knew it was true.

Finally, the teacher showed up and quieted everyone down, although that didn't stop people from staring. I tried my best to act like everything was business as usual, but it was hard to do, considering the fact that I'd never had this much attention focused on me in my entire life. Even forcing myself to concentrate on the lecture we were being given on the Roman Empire wasn't working. After a few minutes, I gave up and picked at my nails instead.

My next few classes were just as hopelessly distracting, and I began to develop a new appreciation for celebrities and what they had to go through every time they went out in public. Being stared at was hard to ignore. It sort of made you feel like a monkey in a zoo. Only, I'd put myself in this cage, hadn't I?

By the time the bell rang for lunch, all I could think about was escaping. Instead of sauntering down the hallway and letting my hips sway back and forth like earlier, I found myself power walking beyond the cafeteria, to Ms. Zia's office. I skipped the Monkey Business and headed straight for her door.

Only, when I was about halfway there, my path was blocked.

I stopped short to keep from running straight into them, letting out a little gasp as I did so. There, having appeared just like a mirage, were the last five people I would've ever expected to see in front of me: Gigi, Camden, Wheatley, Rhodes, and Eliza.

The Elite.

I mumbled, "Excuse me," and tried to make my way around them, but as I moved, they moved too, putting us once again face-to-face.

"Hi," Gigi said with the slightest hint of a smile.

I was so caught off guard by the fact that she was speaking to me that I couldn't think of anything to say. Nothing that would be worthy of a conversation with someone like her, at least.

"I'm Gigi," she added, filling the silence. "And you are?"

I knew this one. "Brooklyn," I said quickly. "My name's Brooklyn."

"What an interesting name," she said. Then, as if it was an afterthought, she added, "I visited New York once with my dad and we went to this cute coffee shop in Brooklyn. They had these amazing little cappuccinos. . . . Have you ever been there?"

"No."

Gigi looked at me like she was expecting more to the story, so I obliged. "My parents don't really like to travel. They have this weird thing about needing to know where the closest hospitals are and stuff."

She just nodded. Her expression hadn't changed, so I couldn't tell if I'd given her the response she'd wanted or had utterly failed whatever test she was giving me.

"So, Brooklyn," she said, staring at me intently, "where have you been hiding?"

"Uh . . ."

"Are you new or something?" Eliza cut in perkily.

Her question surprised me. Considering the fact that I'd been sitting just rows behind her in first period for the past few months and had been at the same school as all of them for the past three years, I thought maybe she was kidding. But one look at her face and I knew she wasn't. Was it really possible that she didn't recognize me? That none of them did? Talk about self-absorbed.

"Not new, really," I answered slowly. I didn't want to make them feel stupid for not recognizing me, so I chose my words carefully. "But I *did* sort of just go through some . . . changes." I absently reached up to touch my long, blond locks.

Eliza squinted at me and then took a step back. Looking me up and down, she studied me critically. "Who's your surgeon?"

"Huh?" I asked, totally confused.

"Who did your work? I had my nose done last year and my guy did an okay job, I guess—I told him I wanted Dakota Fanning's nose, but he gave me Kristen Stewart's—anyway, I'm thinking of getting it redone, because nobody takes Kristen Stewart seriously nowadays, and possibly even my boobs. Are yours real? Anyway, I just wanted to know who your doctor is because he obviously did a good job. I don't even *recognize* you."

When Eliza finally stopped to take a breath, everyone stared at me, waiting for a response. Only, what was I supposed to say? I had magical plastic surgery? Nope. Not an option.

"Um, thanks?" I responded, my head still spinning from the bizarro turn the conversation had taken. "But I didn't have any of that done. My boobs are the same ones I've had since I was thirteen. I guess it's just a really great bra?"

Eliza opened her mouth and then closed it again as she processed what I'd told her.

"Please forgive Eliza," Gigi said, reaching out and touching my arm. Inside, my head was screaming, *Gigi is touching me! Gigi is touching me!* but I just smiled at her. "A casting agent just told her that she looked too ethnic to play the girl next door. She's sort of obsessed right now."

"There's nothing wrong with wanting to fix your imperfections," Eliza said to no one in particular. "Like none of you have had anything done."

"So you've been right here all the time, then?" Gigi continued, rolling over Eliza's last comment.

"That can't be right," Rhodes said, giving me a smile that made my heart dip in the way that only a gorgeous guy could. "I would've noticed *you*."

"Down, boy," Gigi said without looking at him. "But seriously, why haven't you been on our radar before now? What's the story?"

Even though I was wearing a tank top, I could feel myself starting to sweat. This was beginning to feel more and more like an interrogation rather than a friendly first meeting. And truthfully, I wasn't sure how to answer their questions without raising suspicions or having them realize who I really was. So I winged it.

"I honestly don't know *why* we haven't crossed paths before," I said, shrugging. "And there's no story, really."

"Or it's just not a story you want us to know about," Camden said.

He said it nonthreateningly, but I could tell he was deadly serious.

"No, really. I'm just a regular kid."

"There's nothing regular about you, girl," Rhodes said, shoving his hands into his back pockets.

I couldn't help but blush at his compliment. Gigi looked from me to Rhodes and then back at me.

"Okay, then. Well, it was nice meeting you, Brooklyn," she said. "I guess we'll be seeing you around. You definitely won't be able to hide from us now."

She and the other Elite stepped to the side, allowing me to continue on down the hallway. As I was walking away I heard Eliza say, "I don't see why it's such a big deal to give me her doctor's number. Hello? Share the wealth."

As I walked away from the most influential kids in the school, I could no longer hide the grin that had been threatening to appear on my face. Had that *actually* just happened? The fact that one of them remotely envied something about me just about made my head explode. Even if Eliza *had* thought I was made up of fake parts, she'd still noticed me. It was all I'd ever wanted.

Well, that, and to be a part of the group myself.

But this was a start.

I began to skip the rest of the way to Ms. Zia's office, but when I nearly tripped over my three-inch heels, I slowed my gait to a slightly awkward power strut. Practically bursting to share my earth-shattering news with someone, I hurried in and sat down in my usual spot.

Ms. Zia was reading something intently on her computer and only looked up briefly to see who'd walked in.

"And how can I help you?" she asked me in the "I'm a responsible adult" voice she usually reserved for people who weren't me.

"Um, you can listen to this crazy story I have to tell you," I answered, too excited to bother giving her a hard time for her less-than-stellar hello.

Ms. Z. looked back up at me from her screen and shook her head as if clearing it. "Brooklyn?"

"Yeah?"

"It's you."

"That is correct—now give the lady a prize!" I said in my best game-show announcer's voice.

"But you're . . . blond."

I rolled my eyes. It was the first time she was seeing me after my magical makeover and she was understandably thrown off by my newfound hotness.

"And my skin cleared up," I added.

"Wait, weren't your eyes brown before?"

"You're very observant, Ms. Z. You know, I've always really liked that about you," I said, feeling extra hyper after my run-in with The Elite. "So, what do you think of my makeover?"

"Makeover?"

"Yeah," I said, standing up and slowly turning around so she could get the full effect.

Ms. Zia swallowed hard and then leaned in closer to study me. "You're like . . . a whole new person."

"I know! Isn't it great?"

But instead of getting the same level of enthusiasm back, my question was met with silence. After a few awkward seconds, Ms. Z. seemed to gather herself and then cleared her throat.

"You look . . . different."

"Good different?" I asked, giving her a chance to react more like I'd been expecting her to.

She hesitated before answering.

"Different different."

When she saw my face fall, she got up from her chair and came around her desk to sit down next to me. "I didn't mean it that way. You look great, Brooklyn, it's just—I thought you looked pretty great the other way too. What's with the extreme makeover? Is everything okay?"

"Everything's pretty freaking awesome," I said, still riding high after my encounter with the upper crust. "I was just tired of being the me that nobody knew. I wanted to look back on my high school experience and actually be able to say that I experienced it. Right now I'm just . . . existing. And I'm over it."

"Brooklyn . . ."

"Look, Ms. Zia, I know what you're going to say. High school isn't everything. And yeah, okay, maybe it's not. Maybe I won't even care about any of this a few years from now. But for once I want proof that I was here. I don't want people to look at my picture in the yearbook and wonder, who is that girl?"

"But do you really want to do that as somebody else?"

Now I was starting to get annoyed. This was possibly one of the most significant experiences in my life so far, and she was taking all the fun out of it. Not that I thought she was doing it on purpose, but still, the line of questioning felt a bit harsh.

"How is this any different from you working out to stay in shape or getting your hair dyed? Why is it okay for everyone else to take steps to improve themselves, but I get the third degree when I do it?"

"Calm down, Brooklyn. I'm not trying to upset you, I just want to make sure you've thought about this. If any other student walked in here having changed their entire appearance, I'd be asking them these questions too. Just because we're closer than I might be with other students doesn't mean I'm going to sugarcoat things for you. In fact, I've always been honest with you."

"Yeah, sometimes a little *too* honest," I muttered.

"It's just, you know about my past. . . . I'm hoping you can learn from my mistakes instead of making your own."

"I know, Ms. Z., but you think you're trying to shield me

from the potential downside of high school? Um, sorry. Been there, experienced that," I retorted. Seeing her face grow serious, I tried to calm down. "Look, I just want to be happy, and I wasn't before. I wish I was. I wish the old me was enough. I wish there were more people in this school who were like you, but there's not."

We'd had this conversation so many times before that I was beginning to feel like a broken record. And because Ms. Z. was the only person in my life who I could confide in like this, she also ended up being the one who was always pushing back and challenging me.

Ms. Zia looked at me and bit her lip as she took in what I was saying. "And you think this will make you happy?"

"It already has," I said, thinking about my run-in with The Elite.

After another long look and an even longer sigh, she patted me on the arm. "Then I'm here to support you," she said. She forced a smile on her pretty face.

"Well, I guess I should head to my locker before lunch is over, then," I said, getting up and gathering my things. "See you tomorrow?"

"Sure, Brooklyn," Ms. Zia answered, watching me move toward the door. "I'll see you tomorrow."

I'd barely gotten my foot out the door when I immediately collided with another body.

"Oh!" I said, looking up. When I saw that it was Asher, I couldn't seem to untangle my feet.

"Whoops," he said, placing his hands on both my arms to steady me. "Sorry about that."

I gave him a half smile, wondering whether he recognized me. Then he blinked in surprise and flashed me a smile of his own. "Wow. You look . . ."

Good? Amazing? Beautiful? Like the kind of girl you'd like to have as a girlfriend?

"Different," he finished after a long pause.

My smile disappeared again.

"Seriously?!" I took one last look at my biggest crush and then stormed off in the opposite direction.

Chapter Four

"Sweetie! Can you come downstairs for a minute?"

My mom's voice drifted into my room as I clicked away on my computer. Given my new look, I decided it was time to update all my photos online so people would be able to find me if they were trying. I sat back and admired the self-portrait I'd taken with my phone.

It was perfect.

I'd pretty much avoided taking pictures of myself before, but now I got excited every time I took a snapshot. Each one seemed to be better than the last, and I wasn't even sitting there overanalyzing all the things I'd need to edit out later. Instead I'd spent the last hour trying to narrow down which shot I liked the best, and then how to crop it.

I was putting the finishing touches on my number one choice when my mom called out to me.

"Right now?" I asked.

"Yes, please," my dad answered.

I sighed and made a few hasty adjustments before hitting the publish button. Closing my laptop, I climbed off my bed and went downstairs. When I walked into the living room, my parents were sitting side by side on the couch, looking unusually serious. My stomach sank as I dreaded the conversation I knew was coming.

"What's wrong?" I asked.

"Why don't you sit down, honey," my mom said, motioning to the love seat across from them.

"Is everything okay? You're kind of freaking me out."

"Brooklyn, we couldn't help but notice that you seem to have made some, er, changes to your appearance," my dad began.

"You're blond," my mom chimed in.

"And, well, we know that you just came into your powers, and while it's natural to want to experiment with things, we think you need to know that there are consequences to every spell that you do," Dad said.

My fear dissolved into relief, and then the relief turned into annoyance.

"This is because I changed my hair?" I asked incredulously.

"It's not just your hair," my mom said. "It's your eyes, your skin, your lips . . . I'm pretty sure you even made yourself taller. I barely recognize you anymore." As she finished, her eyes began to well up with tears.

I instantly felt guilty. I had no idea my parents were going to take the makeover so hard.

"Guys, I just wanted a little change. I'm sixteen now. This is what kids my age do! They change their appearance. They wear makeup. They dye their hair—usually crazier colors than this, I might add. I'm just trying something new. Trying to figure out who I am."

I didn't add that it was also so I could catch the attention of The Elite. I knew my parents wouldn't go for the changes if they were for anyone else but me. Even though *I* liked the new me, too, doing things to please other people was unacceptable in our household.

"Hey, at least I'm not getting tattoos or my tongue pierced," I added, cracking a joke to try and lighten the mood.

"It's not so much the changes you're making that we're worried about. We've read all the parenting books—we knew this would happen one day. It's *how* you're doing it that worries us."

I blinked at them. "What are you talking about?"

"We think you're using too much magic," my mom blurted out.

I glanced from my mom to my dad and then shook my head. "I've only done a few spells," I said, staring straight at them. "Look, you said that when I turned sixteen you would unbind my powers. I just thought that meant I could actually use them."

"And you can," my dad answered. "We just want you to practice responsibly."

"You think I'm irresponsible?" I asked slowly. "Because I did a few beauty spells?"

This was unbelievable.

"We just don't want you to use magic for *everything*. There's so much you can do without using spells and we don't want you to get used to taking shortcuts," he said. "Your magical abilities give you an advantage over nonpracticing people, and capitalizing on those abilities isn't exactly fair to them. It also turns a lot of unneeded attention onto you. We don't want you to start choosing magic over good, old-fashioned hard work and perseverance."

"But don't you think these gifts were given to us for a reason? Why would we have them if we weren't supposed to use them?" I questioned. I felt like we were speaking two different languages.

"Of course you can use them, Brooklyn. We just want you to use them *wisely*," my mom said. "History has shown that the more magic you use, the greater chance you have of people taking notice. And when that happens—well, it can be bad for everyone involved."

"What are you talking about?"

My parents looked at each other and then my mom pulled out the same book that she'd been holding the night of my unbinding and stroked it gently. "Brooklyn, we know we don't talk much about our magical history, but we think it's time you learned about your ancestors and the . . . difficulties . . . that fell upon them."

Mom was right about that. Trying to get my parents to discuss our family and their ties to witchcraft was like pulling teeth. Every time I'd asked a question in the past, they'd either changed the subject or told me I wasn't old enough to hear it. It used to frustrate me to no end, because I thought they were just treating me like a kid. But now it seemed as if their motives might have been more complicated than that.

"How much do you know about the Salem witch trials, Brooklyn?" she asked me.

I wasn't sure where this was going but didn't bother saying so. The Salem witch trials had been too big a topic to ignore while I was growing up, because it was one of the only things my parents *had* shared with me concerning the witching world. Anything my parents had conveniently left out, I'd been able to learn from other twitches online who studied witch history in their coven classes.

"I only know what you've told me and what I've been able to find on the Internet," I said. They nodded for me to continue, and I racked my brain for the details. To placate my parents, I regurgitated what I knew about this infamous time in our history. "Um, sometime in the late 1600s, a whole bunch of people in colonial Massachusetts were accused of practicing witchcraft. In the end, around twenty people were killed for allegedly being witches. Since then they've been exonerated to the nonwitching world, but we know from our own magical history that some of those who were killed actually *were* witches. Several were innocent bystanders."

"Correct. And do you know what caused the hysteria in the first place?" I shook my head no. "Well, it all started when Samuel Parris, a member of the Cleri coven, became hungry for power. He wasn't the most powerful of the group—that was Bridget Bishop—but he had aspirations to make the Cleri the most prominent coven in the witching world. When he realized that Bridget and most of the other Cleri didn't feel the same way, he betrayed them by starting the rumor that they—and several other people in the town—were practicing witchcraft."

"Why would he do that? Especially when it could come back to bite him in the—"

"As far as we know, Samuel Parris targeted the witches in the group that he knew wouldn't fall in line with him. And he knew that if he just got the rumors started, the townspeople would take care of the rest," she said. "You see, sweetie, power can be dangerous if put in the wrong hands."

"Wait—let me get this straight. You think I'm gonna go all power crazy like that jerk-wad Parris and sell other witches out?" I was starting to become a bit hysterical, but could you blame me? From the sound of it, my own parents were comparing me to a murderous, lying psycho. I couldn't help but be hurt. "Geez, I've had my powers for, like, a day, and you've already got me starting the next witch trials? Thanks for the vote of confidence."

"That's not it at all," Dad cut in. "You're missing the point of the story. Samuel wanted the power so badly that he was willing to do *anything* to get it. We're just saying that the more you use your powers, the more attention you'll draw to yourself. And the more attention you draw to yourself, the more dangerous things can get. Not everyone has a heart like yours. And people can still be very afraid of things they don't understand."

"It's been over four hundred years since the Salem witch trials. Don't you think people have evolved a little? I mean, think of how popular vampires, werewolves, and zombies are nowadays. You don't think people would be psyched to find out there are *actual* witches out there? No way would people have the same reaction today that they did back then."

My parents shot each other a look.

"Did Grandma Sparks ever talk to you about her sister Evelyn?" Dad asked. As if on cue, Mom opened the book that was lying on her lap and then passed it over to me. The page was full of photos, all black-and-white and old-looking. The first showed two kids, both in little white dresses, bangs pulled back on top of their heads. The taller of the two was smiling, but the other wore a frown.

The progression of pictures showed the two girls growing up. One captured the younger child making a funny face at the camera while her sister's back was turned. Another showed the two facing each other, arms outstretched and appearing to concentrate. I had a sneaking suspicion the camera had caught them midspell in that one. The last was of both of the girls, just a little bit older, hugging each other tightly.

I shook my head. "I didn't know Grandma had a sister," I said quietly, continuing to study the pages. "Why didn't she say anything?"

My dad cleared his throat and fidgeted in his seat. "Well, I imagine talking about Evelyn made her a bit . . . sad," he said finally. "See, Evelyn was younger than Grandma Sparks by several years, but she was always the more outgoing of the two of them. She had big dreams—plans to go out to Hollywood one day—and she wasn't one to shy away from a challenge."

"She sounds pretty cool," I said, smiling as I turned to a picture of Evelyn blowing a kiss to the camera.

"You're actually like her in a lot of ways," he said. By the tone of his voice, it didn't seem that he was all too happy about this. "Evelyn adored magic. She loved casting and wasn't ashamed of it. She thought spells should be used for just about everything, even if it was something simple she could have done herself. But the ease with which she used magic made her careless, and before long, she was doing spells in public."

"Until finally, one day, someone caught her," he said sadly.

"What happened?" I was almost scared to hear the rest of the story, but at this point, I was totally sucked in.

"She must have thought no one was watching when she did the summoning spell that day, but she was wrong. Someone *was* watching. A reporter, and he wanted to expose Evelyn to the world. When he confronted her, she realized what she'd done and tried to dissuade him. She told him he was seeing things. That he needed a good night's sleep. That it was just a trick of the light. But he wasn't a fool. He knew what he'd seen and he knew that breaking the news that magic actually existed would change his life.

"Evelyn managed to get away from the reporter and fled in her car, but he eventually caught up with her. He pulled up next to her in his car, honking his horn and swerving to try and get her to stop and talk to him, but she refused. Finally, the reporter came up with a plan. He figured that if she really *was* a witch, he could push her off the side of the road and she would have to perform another spell in order to save herself. And when she did that, he would have proof of her abilities and then would have something to go to his editor with.

"So he sideswiped her car. The first time, Evelyn managed to swerve and missed the brunt of the impact, but when he did it again, the road had narrowed and there was nowhere for her to go. This time, the car broke through the guardrail and careened down an embankment before slamming into a tree. The reporter grabbed the bulky video camera that he kept in the trunk of his car at all times and rushed down the hill to the car, slipping and sliding the whole way. When he finally got to the bottom, the car had caught on fire and the flames were spreading quickly. He peered through the fumes and saw Evelyn just waking up. Her head was bleeding and she seemed dazed. She began to panic, realizing what had happened, and pulled at her door and seat belt to no avail. The guy yelled at her to use her magic to get out, but by this time she was too hysterical to listen. Instead, she just kept trying to claw her way out. Finally, the two locked eyes, him behind his camera and her behind the flames and glass. There was a moment on the film where it looked like Evelyn was about to do something. Say something. A spell most likely. But it was too late. As they sat there looking at each other, the car blew up."

Something wet hit my hand and I looked down. I hadn't even realized I'd been crying. I wiped my face hastily and waited on the rest of the story.

"So, she died? All because of some guy's career?" I asked, disgusted.

"Power can drive even the sanest person to do insane things. It's an incredible motivator," my mom said. I saw that her eyes were red and gave her a sympathetic look.

"How do we know all of this?"

"Well, after Evelyn's death, the reporter went on trial for her murder and that's what came out during the case. They even used the footage he'd taken that day as evidence. Grandma Sparks and the rest of the family were there and, based on what they knew about Evelyn, realized their biggest fear had come to fruition."

"What happened to the reporter?" I asked, balling up my fists. "I hope he got what was coming to him."

"Well, considering his whole defense was built on the fact that he claimed Evelyn to be a witch, they found him incompetent to stand trial and sent him away to spend the rest of his life in a mental health facility. From what we know, he stayed there until he died, living with what he did that day and being tormented by the fact that nobody believed him."

We sat there in silence for a few minutes as the story hit each of us differently. Finally I spoke. "Good. I'm glad he suffered. What he did was horrible and irresponsible and—"

"And none of it would have happened if Evelyn hadn't been so careless with her gifts," my dad said gently.

"You're blaming *her* for what happened?!"

"He's not *blaming* her, sweetie. We're just trying to make you see that magicking is a big responsibility. One that shouldn't be taken lightly, or abused. Our history has shown that using your powers too much can become dangerous. That's why we raised you in a low-magic household. We just want you to be safe."

Logically I could see that she and Dad truly believed what they were saying, but as far as I was concerned, they were going overboard. They'd never been comfortable with letting me use my powers, and they were still trying to control me. And despite the horrible story I'd just heard, the way they babied me made me want to scream.

"First off, just because a few people had bad experiences using their gifts doesn't mean I'm going to make the same mistakes," I said, trying my best to keep my voice even. "And second, that was, like, fifty years ago. A lot's changed since then. I think people are more open to different lifestyles. I mean, Harry Potter has his own theme park."

"Harry Potter's not real," my mom reminded me, sounding annoyed. "And even Harry had his enemies. Prejudice and fear are still very much alive today, Brooklyn. Our family isn't prepared to take on that kind of battle."

"Nor do we want to," Dad said firmly. "Look, Brook, the bottom line is this: we're not saying you have to stop using your magic. Though we don't necessarily agree with all the decisions you make in that respect, we promised that you could use your powers once you turned sixteen. And we will keep that promise, unless we think you're endangering yourself or others. We just want you to think about how you're using your gifts and understand that there can be serious consequences to your actions."

"I got it. Restraint good, magic spree bad," I said.

"We're serious about this, Brooklyn," Dad warned.

"So am I. Really. I get what you're saying and I promise I'll be more careful with my spells in the future."

Luckily, being more careful didn't mean I had to quit entirely. I could be careful while still having fun, for sure.

Chapter Five

Walking into school the next day wasn't as much of a shell shock as it had been the day before. I was even getting used to the way people looked at me. It was easier to tune out the whispers and pointing now. Even the little voice in my head that used to tell me that everyone was saying negative things behind my back began to get quieter.

It wasn't like I was *popular* yet by any means, but at least I existed, which was a huge step up from the previous week. People knew my name now, and guys made flirtatious comments as I walked by. The attention I was getting just reinforced to me that my magical makeover had been a good thing—despite the lecture I'd received stating the opposite the night before. I could ease up on the magic for a while, now that I'd gotten what I wanted.

Well, kind of.

As I walked up to my locker, I saw that I already had a visitor. The first thing I noticed was the dark hair that swooped into a point at the top of his head; I didn't even have to see his face to know it was Asher. Despite our last interaction, my heart began to race as I got closer to him.

"Hey," I said, trying not to fumble as I worked my locker combination.

"Hey," Asher responded. I didn't dare look at him, for fear that he'd see how nervous he made me. I could feel his eyes on me anyway. "So, what was that yesterday?"

"What was what?" I asked, even though I knew what he was talking about.

"You sort of took off fast."

"Oh, yeah, well, it was sort of a weird day for me," I said, not wanting him to know that I'd been hurt by his response to my new look.

"Oh. Okay," he said, oblivious to what was really going on in my head. Then, as if it had just dawned on him, he added, "You changed your hair."

"It's a little blonder, I guess," I said, still shocked that he'd noticed me enough before to know that I looked different now. Excitement bubbled up in my chest as I thought about what this might mean.

We both stared at each other for a second and then looked away. This time Asher chuckled and I looked down at the ground.

"You look good," he finally said.

My cheeks burned with heat as I let the compliment wash over me.

"Thanks," I said shyly.

I closed my locker door but wasn't ready for our conversation to end just yet. I began to walk away, and then slowed as I waited for him to catch up with me. Without my having to ask, he joined me and we walked side by side a few steps before starting to talk again.

"So—and please don't take this the wrong way—what's with the new look, anyway?"

I looked down at myself, even though I was well aware of what I would see. Slender legs that were a little longer than before, tucked into jeans that made my butt look rounder— but in a good way. And when he looked at my face, which I could tell he was doing now as we walked, he'd see my kiss-able lips, perfect skin, and beautiful green eyes. We'd already talked about the hair, so he'd obviously noticed the changes there, too.

"I wanted to see if blondes really do have more fun."

"And do they?"

"Jury's still out. I'll have to let you know in a few days," I said with a mischievous smile. As I said it, I wondered if I'd accidentally changed part of my personality when I'd done the other spells. I'd never been this bold with a guy before, let alone with someone I had an enormous crush on. But there I was, flirting with Asher. My biggest crush. A guy who was both mysterious and bold, classically good-looking but one of a kind. He had a motorcycle, but he wasn't a bad boy. He was perfect.

"So, there was no breakup?" he asked.

"Breakup? Why would you think that?"

"Well, girls tend to perform extreme makeovers on two occasions: when they're going through a bad breakup or if they're hiding from the law," he said seriously. "Now, you don't look like a girl who committed a crime in the past few months, so the only logical thing left is a breakup."

I laughed and shook my head. "Neither. You really need to work on your theories of women," I said. "Though, I will admit the breakup thing tends to be right. Where did you learn that little secret?"

"I have a younger sister, Abby. If I'm nice to her, she tells me things."

"Ahhh, gotcha," I said, trying to place the name of his sister with a face. But no one came to mind. About 2,500 kids went to our school, though, so it was possible not to know everyone that walked the halls. "No breakup, just a birthday. Sweet sixteen. And it was time to try something . . . different."

"Well, you look great—not that you didn't before," he said, stammering. "Anyways, I've got to go. I'm meeting Mr. Jacobsen before class to talk about a project. Talk to you later?"

"Sure. Yeah. That would be fun."

He gave me that lazy smile of his before heading off ahead of me.

Yep. The magic was totally worth it.

The bell had just rung, signaling that it was lunchtime, and I headed off on my usual walk down to Ms. Zia's. I was slightly nervous about seeing her after the uncomfortable conversation we'd had the day before, but I figured I'd mumble an apology, she'd probably do the same, and then we'd go back to our regularly scheduled friendship. As long as we didn't get on the subject of my new look or The Elite, I was thinking we'd be safe.

I was running through the apology in my head when all of a sudden something clamped down on my left arm. I turned my head to see what it was, but then the same thing happened to my other arm. I was quickly turned around and dragged against my will in the opposite direction.

"Hey! What are you doing!" I screeched.

"Come with us, please," a familiar girl's voice said to my right.

"And stop making that noise," a guy added to my left. "You're going to make my ears bleed."

I did what he said, and then looked up to see Eliza on one arm and Wheatley on the other.

"Where, uh, exactly are we going?" I asked, still bewildered by the whole situation.

"The caf, duh," Eliza answered.

"Why?"

"Because it's lunch," Wheatley answered, looking at me like I was even dimmer than people assumed he was.

"I just meant . . . why am *I* going? With you guys?" I asked as the two weaved us in and out of the crowd and navigated us toward the double doors ahead.

"We want to talk," Eliza answered. "Get to know you better. You know, what you like, what you do outside of school. We want to know absolutely *everything* about you."

"Yay," I said, trying to fake enthusiasm. Inside, I was panicking at the thought of being given the third degree. There were so many questions they could ask that I didn't have answers for. Well, I had the answers, I just couldn't tell them.

"And maybe once you get a little more comfortable around us, you'll tell me who did your work. I promise I won't tell."

I didn't even bother arguing with her this time, because it obviously hadn't worked the first time. Eliza was just going to have to believe what she believed for the time being, because I had way bigger things to worry about.

Like the fact that I was on my way to meet with The Elite. Again.

Once we were inside the hustle and bustle of the lunchroom, the two ushered me over to the raised table at the back of the cafeteria. I ascended the stairs and took a moment to consider what was happening. Less than a week ago, I'd been staring at this place from afar, and now I was about to experience it for myself. And I'd been invited up there. By The Elite themselves.

It was all I could do to keep from passing out as I climbed my way to the top. When I finally arrived, Gigi, Camden, and Rhodes sat in a row like a panel of *American Idol* judges. And I was sure that, just like on the show, I was already being judged.

"Brooklyn! So glad you could make it," Gigi said, her hands folded on the table in front of her. I must have made a funny face at this because she added, "Why do you look surprised?"

"It's just—I still can't believe you know my name," I said. It was out of my mouth before I could stop it.

Gigi looked at Camden and then laughed. "We know *everyone* who goes to our school," she said. It wasn't lost on me that she'd deemed it "their school," even though everyone knew it was true. I also found it interesting that she was claiming to know me, though she'd had no clue who I was the day before. Guess The Elite knew everyone at school who they deemed worthy of knowing.

She patted the space across from her and smiled her thousand-watt grin. "Now come. Sit."

Wheatley and Eliza joined the rest of their crew, leaving a spot open for me in the middle. I looked around the room for hidden cameras and saw that everyone in the caf was staring at me, appearing to be just as surprised as I was that I was up there. Turning back around, I did what Gigi suggested and sat down.

"Kara," Gigi called out without taking her eyes off me.

One of The Elite's underlings scurried over from the nearest table and stood down below where we were sitting. She was a junior like me and was always just on the outskirts of the popular kids. She was willing to do anything to get into the inner circle, and that seemed to extend mostly to doing their crap work and receiving nothing in return. It was hard to watch someone be so openly used like that, but in the end, she'd chosen to put herself in that position. And if she was okay being a slave to The Elite, who was I to judge?

"Yes, Gigi?" she asked hopefully.

"Brooklyn here needs a drink," Gigi answered. Now to me, she added, "What do you want?"

No way was I uttering the words "Monkey Business" among this crowd, so I looked around for a good alternative. Both Gigi and Eliza were drinking Diet Coke, so I figured I'd join them, even though I wasn't a fan of diet drinks.

"I can get it," I offered, starting to stand.

"Don't be silly," Gigi said, motioning for me to sit. "Kara would be happy to get you something. Right, Kara?"

"Of course!" she said brightly. But when I glanced her way, there was just the tiniest hint of jealousy in her eyes.

"Um, okay," I said unsurely. "I guess a Diet Coke would be nice. Thanks, Kara."

"No problem," she said, and bounded off toward the lunch line.

Once Kara was gone, the attention again turned to me. Growing increasingly uncomfortable under their stares, I began to look around at the view instead.

"Wow. Everything looks so different from up here," I said, trying my best to make small talk.

"It's easier for people to see us this way," Eliza cut in, nodding.

"And for us to see them," Camden added.

"Totally." I nodded.

I could tell that Gigi and the others were still watching me, even though I wasn't looking at any of them directly.

"Which is why we're wondering why we never saw you around here before yesterday," Gigi said slowly. I scrambled to try and find an answer that would satisfy them, but she cut me off before I could say anything. "We know you had some sort of makeover, but why now? Why so obvious?"

"What's your angle?" Camden asked bluntly.

I swallowed the bile that was quickly rising in my throat. This was all too much for my brain to handle. It was one thing to have The Elite notice me; it was another completely to be interrogated by them.

"It was my birthday and I was tired of blending in," I said honestly. If they didn't like my answers, then at least I'd crash and burn on my own terms. "I guess it was just time for a change." The words came out a lot more confident than I felt.

"I see," Gigi said, looking at me thoughtfully. "You know, a lot of people don't like change. It throws the balance of things off. Makes people nervous."

I nodded. I was having a hard time catching my breath at the moment.

"But sometimes change can be good," Eliza added. "It can shake things up."

Kara ran up then and handed me an icy Diet Coke. I told her thank you and Gigi nodded at her to let her know she was dismissed. The girl walked back to her table and sat down, where she'd be ready if The Elite needed her again.

"Are you trying to shake things up, Brooklyn?" Gigi asked.

"Maybe," I said, watching their reactions to my confession. Eliza grinned wickedly, but Gigi and Camden remained unresponsive. I was terrified of saying the wrong thing, but at the same time, I felt like I really had nothing to lose here. "You never know what new blood can do for a group."

"And what would you be able to do for, say, The Elite?" Rhodes asked nonchalantly, like he was asking what I thought of the weather instead of something that could potentially change the course of my high school experience.

"Well . . ." I started, my mind suddenly going blank. I stalled as I waited for it to get up and running again, while surveying the scene in front of us. Most of the students who'd stopped to watch my ascension to the table earlier had gone back to their lunches and the conversations they'd been having with their friends. There were, however, a select few still eyeing us suspiciously, trying hard to figure out what the heck was going on.

To be honest, I was wondering that myself.

"Uh . . . Well, I have many, er, talents that I could bring to The Elite if given the chance," I said, hoping they'd buy my vague answer in lieu of something more precise.

No such luck.

"Like?" Rhodes asked.

"Like, I'm kind of . . . stealthy?" I said finally, seeing the argument building up in my head. "I've been at this school for a few years now, and I was able to get around without anyone noticing me until I wanted them to."

This was only partly a fib, since I *had* gone unnoticed for quite some time around this school. So what if the part about me *wanting* to go unnoticed was untrue? What did my favorite PR idols say? It was all about the spin.

"That's true," Eliza chimed in. "I had no idea Brookie existed until she got her boob job. And then she was like, bam, all up in our faces."

"I didn't get—"

Gigi shook her head at me from across the table, as if telling me to let it go.

"So you can blend in. How else can you be useful to us?" Camden continued.

My head was spinning as I tried to make sense of what was happening. "I'm pretty smart—well, not Rhodes smart, but I've never gotten below a B in any of my classes."

This didn't seem to impress them much, considering Gigi was an A student and Camden ran the student body. And Rhodes—well, he was in a league of his own. No way was I going to bring the intelligence factor to this group. I tried to think of something I could do that the others weren't already contributing in their own ways.

There was the obvious, of course, but how was I supposed to express that without outing myself in the process? Yet magic was my biggest asset. I had to give it a shot.

"I have the uncanny ability to make things happen," I said desperately.

"What do you mean?" Gigi asked curiously.

"I mean, give me a task and it *will* get done. It doesn't matter what it is, I will succeed. That, I can promise," I said. "I'm the person you call when you've tried everything else."

The five of them looked around at each other wordlessly, as if communicating telepathically. I waited silently, willing them to say something, to give me an idea whether they were buying my story or not.

Finally, Gigi nodded. "Okay. We're going to give you a chance to prove that what you say is true."

"Now, we're not *promising* anything," Camden said, leaning back in his seat, like he was posing for a catalog. I could practically hear people taking pictures on their camera phones as he did it. "But if we're impressed, we may just keep you around."

My mouth dropped open. Unless I was reading into things, The Elite were giving me the chance to possibly join their group.

"What do you need me to do?" I asked when I'd regained my composure.

"Nothing big," Gigi said, inspecting her nails critically. "I'm sure we can find a few ways to determine your loyalty, drive, and desire."

"Okay," I said, wondering if they weren't being a bit melodramatic. But given their reputation, I knew they weren't joking. They meant just what they said.

"And if you stick around, it will be like you've won the lottery," she said, gesturing around the room.

"You'll be existing among future politicians," Camden said.

"Nobel Prize winners," Rhodes said.

"Hollywood's next big stars," Eliza delivered dramatically.

"This awesome guy," Wheatley said, pointing at himself between bites of his burger.

"And high-powered attorneys," Gigi said evenly. "If you have what it takes and stick with us, Brooklyn, your life will change. I can guarantee it."

I nodded to let them know that I understood what they were offering me and then waited for them to tell me what they wanted me to do next.

"Well . . ."

"What devious plans are you little Gremlins plotting today?" a voice boomed up to us from the floor, interrupting our discussion. "Getting out of your school-ordered community service because you might get your hands dirty? Intimidating others into thinking you're special? Convincing your mommies and daddies to pay your way out of the problems you create? I can't wait for the day you all mess up and I get to lock you up and throw away the key."

"And you wonder why people think school's a prison," Wheatley said, not even bothering to turn around to look at our principal. I did, however, and was shocked to see him flanked by two security guards, both with their hands on their walkie-talkies as if they might need to use them at any moment. My heart started to race as I wondered what was about to happen and what we'd done to make the principal think he needed police assistance.

"I don't know what you've been hearing about us, Frankie, but we're just sitting here eating lunch," said Eliza innocently. "By the way, did you get the tickets that Daddy sent you last week?"

He sneered at her. "It's *Principal Franklin*, Miss Rivers," he said snidely. "And I'm not a fan of basketball."

"But they were floor seats!" Eliza said, her good-girl act dropping for a second. "I mean . . . well, Daddy has tickets to practically *every* team in LA, so if you let me know what sports you *do* like . . ."

"That won't be necessary, Miss Rivers."

"You seem stressed, Principal Franklin," Gigi cooed. "Is something wrong?"

"Besides having to deal with you kids?"

"Well, I'll be sure to bring up the topic of stress levels on campus in our next student government meeting," Camden said. "Stress can be damaging to your health. And we wouldn't want anything to happen to you, now, would we?"

"No."

"Uh-uh."

"Your health is *so* important to us."

I sat there, completely silent, just listening to the exchange. I'd never actually interacted with Principal Franklin before, so hearing the way he was talking to The Elite was a bit of a shock. Weren't adults supposed to be nice to kids? Or at the very least lead by example? Principal Franklin was just being . . . nasty.

Not that my new friends were being entirely respectful either, but what did he expect after everything he was saying? I was completely dumbfounded by the whole situation and sat there praying I wouldn't be dragged into it.

Too late.

"New minion?" he asked, nodding at me. "How'd you

pull her into your web of evil?" I was too shocked by what he was saying to respond, so I just stared at him instead. I'd never had any interaction with the guy before, so why was he picking on me?

"Of course. You've found one that's to be seen and not heard," he continued, sighing.

"She speaks," Wheatley said out of nowhere. "Maybe she just doesn't want to talk to *you*."

The principal flinched. I looked back and forth between the two, still unable to make my lips move.

"You're skating on thin ice, Mr. Thomas," Principal Franklin warned. When Wheatley didn't respond again, the principal attempted to intimidate us with a glare and then har-rumphed and stormed off.

"What a tool," Camden said when he was out of earshot.

"Are we even sure he finished college? What person in his right mind would allow *him* to work with kids?" Rhodes asked.

"What was with the backup?" I asked, still thoroughly con-fused by the whole thing.

Eliza waved this off. "They go everywhere with him," she said. "He thinks he's the president and needs Secret Service with him at all times."

"Either that or he's scared of what Wheatley will do if he gets mad," Camden said, snickering.

Wheatley just snorted in response.

"Now that *that's* over, I think there's something you *can* do for us," Gigi said, looking at me with one of her eyebrows raised. I waited for her to continue. "How do you feel about TP'ing Principal Franklin's house?"

I nearly laughed at the request. "You want me to toilet paper the principal's house?" I asked, incredulously. When they nodded at me seriously, I realized they weren't joking. I didn't think people still did stuff like that . . . after the age of twelve, at least. "You want me to TP the principal's house," I repeated, this time matter-of-fact.

"Yep. You can show us that you're serious about all of this *and* get back at Principal Franklin at the same time. It's a win-win."

Except for Principal Franklin, of course.

I bit my lower lip and thought about what they were asking me to do. I know I'd said that I could do any task they threw my way, but I hadn't counted on it being so . . . vengeful. And potentially dangerous. And now that I'd seen how vindictive and horrible Principal Franklin could be, I didn't want to do anything to make him my enemy. In this case, having a target on my back was a whole lot worse than being invisible.

"He's just so unfair and treats all the students like they're slugs on the bottom of his shoe," Gigi continued, sensing my hesitation. "It's time he saw that there are consequences to his actions."

That's what I was worried about.

But in a way, she was right. Principal Franklin *had* been awful, and everybody TP'd a house at one point or another, right? I mean, I never had, but there was a first time for everything. And besides, toilet paper eventually disintegrated, which meant it was sort of a crimeless crime.

And if I didn't accept the challenge, I knew that would be the end of my chance to become one of The Elite. And that wasn't an option. It was the whole reason I'd done the make-over. I'd come this far, there was no going back now. And if I was being honest, I didn't even want to.

"I'll do it," I said.

Chapter Six

After I agreed to the terms and conditions The Elite had laid out for me, they let me in on a few other useful bits of information that made it clear that passing their challenge was going to be more difficult than I'd originally anticipated. The first being that Principal Franklin's house was on a rather busy street in town, and it was going to be difficult to pull things off without someone seeing me do it.

And The Elite had made it clear that if I was caught, they didn't know me. Meaning I would be on my own in the blame department.

On top of that, the house itself was supposed to be somewhat of a fortress. Separated from the street by an electric gate that you could only get through via a pass code, Principal Franklin's place also had motion detectors located strategically around the grounds. With heavy gear like that, he was either hiding top-secret experiments inside or was extremely paranoid about trespassers.

Considering what I was planning, maybe he wasn't so paranoid after all.

We'd decided that I should do the job right away—as in, that night. Without the Elite having to say so, I could tell it was to let Principal Franklin know that the toilet paper was payback for his little witch hunt earlier. No time to waste, as they say. So the plan was that I would head to the store after school and pick up no less than twenty-four rolls of toilet paper plus whatever else I needed to get the job done. Then, around 8 p.m., Gigi and the others would meet at the Burger Barn, where they'd stay until I joined them after I was finished. This would ensure that they had a public alibi in the event that Principal Franklin accused them of the TP'ing (and they insisted that he would). They all figured that no one would suspect me, still being relatively unknown and all, so it wouldn't matter if I hadn't been there with them the whole time. When people thought back to that night, they'd either assume I was there the whole time or not have noticed that I was missing.

After I bought the supplies, I was to sneak over to the principal's house around 9 p.m. and wait for him to go to bed before sneaking inside the grounds and making it rain with tissue. When I was done, I had to take pictures of my work as proof that I'd carried out the plan and then rendezvous with the others as soon as I could.

When The Elite asked me if I had any ideas on how I was going to pull it off, I just answered mysteriously that they'd have to wait and see. The truth was, I had no idea how I was going to do it, but I knew that magic would be involved. This was both good and bad in my mind.

After my big makeover, I'd planned on cooling it with the magic for a while, if just to appease my parents, but then The Elite noticed me. And, well, I felt like the only way I could do what they wanted me to, and not get caught, was to get a little help from the universe. Besides, the magic I was planning to do wasn't all that elaborate anyway. Just a flip of my hand here and a little spell there—I'd be in and out within ten minutes, tops.

The more I thought about it, the more I realized that this kind of situation really was the best use of my magic. I'd never done anything like this before, and given my propensity for falling all over myself, I knew if I had to do it on my own, I'd mess it up somehow. By using magic I could cut my chances of getting caught in half. And getting caught wasn't an option. Nope, I definitely *had* to use magic.

After making a quick stop at the store on my way home, I headed up to my room to consult the witchboards. Once I found the spells I needed to pull it off, I got to work on all the other details.

Since the assignment called for serious stealth, I knew I had to find an appropriate outfit to match the occasion. Something black, of course, because I didn't want to stand out. But it couldn't be anything that would tip people off, either. I didn't want anyone thinking I was coming to rob them and then call the cops before I'd even done anything.

I pulled on some black leggings, since those were practically a staple at school, and then paired them with a bright pink tank. Over that I threw on a loosely fitting, dark gray sweatshirt to hide my body shape in case I was spotted. Lastly, I stuffed my blond hair into an old baseball cap of my dad's, giving plenty of coverage to my facial features.

Stepping in front of my full-length mirror, I surveyed my work. Unidentifiable yet still fashionable. Perfect couture for any girl looking to make a quick getaway.

I checked how I was doing on time.

Six thirty p.m.

Now all I had to do was wait.

My car was parked about a block away, and for the last half hour I'd been scoping out Principal Franklin's house from behind the bushes across the street. Thank God, The Elite had let me go on my own, because creeping in the bushes wasn't exactly chic.

It was only nine thirty, but the lights inside the house had been off for about forty minutes with no movement as far as I could tell. Since I couldn't sneak around to the back without setting off any lights, I had to guess that the principal was already in bed, hopefully passed out to the world.

The traffic had died down a bit in the area, and cars seemed to be rushing by only every five minutes or so, which meant that I had a bigger window of opportunity to unleash the TP. There was always the chance that I would be seen, and in that case, I needed to be ready to run for it. Luckily, as a last-minute thought, I'd changed into sneakers to make things easier. Women were always running around in heels in action movies, and I never understood that. Sure, fashion was important, but if I had to run in heels, I was definitely going to end up on the ground.

Shifting my balance from one foot to the other, I knew it was time. I needed to get this done as quickly as possible so I could get back to the others at the Burger Barn and still be home at a reasonable hour.

It was now or never.

Focusing on the street lamp closest to me, I concentrated on slowing my breath until I was completely calm and clear. When I felt I was ready, I whispered, "Electro-reducto!" Immediately I felt the now familiar buzzing in my toes and fingers and knew that the power I was creating was expanding out into the street. Within seconds the lights all around me dimmed until nearly the whole block was black.

Confident that I was now covered in a blanket of darkness, I emerged from my hiding spot and lugged my duffel bag full of toilet paper across the street until I was directly in front of the principal's house. I stayed low to the ground and watched for any sign that someone was awake inside. But the night was silent. I peered through the dark to try and find the motion detectors set up on the grounds. Once I spotted them, I performed the same dimming spell as before and knew that if the sensors were set off, they wouldn't cast a glow on me or anything else.

It was time.

I stepped up to the gate and placed the bag on the ground at my feet. Unzipping it carefully, I leaned down to grab a few rolls. I was still ten feet away from the closest tree, but no way was I going to go inside the gate and get caught. At least out here, I still had a chance of getting away if I needed to. Luckily, I had magic on my side and a plan that would allow me to cover the whole area right from where I stood.

And then there was the time factor. The longer I stayed there, the greater my chance of getting caught—and if that happened, everything would be over. This was the part that had taken me the longest to figure out: how to get twenty-four rolls of paper to cover a yard before anyone caught me. After visiting more than a few message boards, I'd figured it out. And it was quite genius if you asked me.

"Here we go," I said to myself.

I hugged the rolls as tightly as I could and closed my eyes. Concentrating on the energy that I could already feel building inside me, I pictured what was about to happen and then said the magic words.

"Pyronicus mizzle!"

Once the words were out of my mouth, I knew I was holding on to ticking time bombs. Literally. Without hesitating, I took the first roll and tossed it as hard as I could toward the house. Seconds passed.

One.

Two.

Three—

There was a cracking sound as the roll exploded, and then I watched as strands of toilet paper fell down in streams, landing on everything below.

"Cool."

After that, I grabbed roll after roll and tossed it into the darkness, no longer bothering to wait for it to detonate before throwing the next one. It was like watching fireworks on the Fourth of July, and I had to fight against stopping to watch the show I was creating. Within minutes, every inch of the property was covered in white, and I questioned whether I really needed to use the full twenty-four rolls. But that was the number The Elite had given me and I wasn't about to fail on a technicality.

I had to admit, the whole thing was actually sort of fun, and I began to wonder if I could use the same spell to accomplish more productive things. Like decorating the Christmas tree or watering the lawn with exploding water balloons. I was so caught up in what I was doing, in fact, that I didn't even notice I'd gone through my whole supply until I reached in and my hand hit canvas. Slightly disappointed that the fun was over so soon, I looked at my watch.

Nine forty-five p.m.

I'd only been at it for a little over five minutes and I was already finished. I took a step back and looked at the scene in front of me. It was a wonderland of white. The house looked like a monstrous igloo and the trees like little ghosts swaying in the night. It was better than I could have imagined.

"Whoa," I said, admiring my work. I took out my phone and snapped a few quick pics before slipping it back into my pocket. "Now, for the final spell."

Even though I'd tried to tell myself that pulling the prank on Principal Franklin wouldn't really do much damage since the toilet paper would eventually disintegrate anyway, I still sort of felt guilty over the whole situation. So, to balance things out, I decided to do a spell to speed the clean-up process. My hope was that Principal Franklin would wake up the next day with a yard full of white, but that by that weekend, it would all have magically disappeared. That way, The Elite got their revenge and Franklin wouldn't have to spend the rest of the year picking chunks of TP out of his bushes.

I was just about to say the words to the spell when I heard a sound nearby that made my head jerk away from what I was doing. I'd been so focused on the task at hand that I'd forgotten I was also supposed to be concentrating on not getting caught.

I strained my eyes through the dark and looked for anything that might seem out of place. But nothing stood out. Everything was as it had been before. No one was there.

Taking a few more deep breaths to calm my nerves before continuing, I reminded myself that I only had one more thing to do before I could leave and meet the others. I centered myself and prepared to do the last of the spells.

"Velocimous alacrity periomo."

The toilet paper took on the slightest hint of a glow before returning to its natural color. And just like that, everything was done. It was time to flee the scene.

Rushing back across the street, I swung by the bushes I'd

been hiding in before, to pick up my purse and stakeout snacks. After making sure I wasn't leaving behind any evidence that could be tied back to me, I began to walk down the street in the direction of my waiting car.

As I neared the corner, I looked back at the street behind me. "Electro-lumino!" I let the power flow through me to illuminate the lamps that I'd dimmed before. With the streetlights back on in the neighborhood, I could easily see Principal Franklin's house and all the damage I'd done. I couldn't help but be filled with a sense of pride and accomplishment. Not because I'd TP'd the principal's house but because of how much my life had changed. Less than a week ago, my only knowledge of magic was what I'd read on message boards, and now I was pulling off multiple spells in one night. I was so happy, I couldn't stop grinning. I had a feeling that the principal's reaction would be of an entirely different variety.

By the time I got back to my car and made it over to the Burger Barn, the adrenaline from earlier had worn off and all I could think about was passing out. I wondered if my sudden exhaustion wasn't also a side effect of using so much magic. My parents had warned me that first night that coming into my powers would drain me, but they hadn't said whether magical energy also depleted physical energy. It was a question I filed away for later.

Right now, I just wanted to give The Elite the proof they'd asked for, scarf down a burger and fries, and then crash.

I pulled into the parking lot and took a space that was far away from the entrance, so people would be less likely to see me from the windows when I arrived. I pulled off my sweatshirt and tossed it into the backseat, took off my cap to let my hair flow free, and dabbed on a bit of lip gloss to touch up my look. I had a few smudges of dirt on my hands and face but managed to get rid of them with a swipe of a leftover piece of toilet paper that had been ripped off one of the rolls.

When I was ready, I skipped over to the entrance and slipped inside without anyone seeing me, and then headed over to the booth where the others were sitting.

"Hey!" I said, sneaking up behind them.

"Brooklyn!" Camden said, unable to hide his surprise. I smiled and sat down as they scooted over to make room for me.

"Shouldn't you be over there now?" Gigi asked, confused.

"I'm done."

Rhodes looked at his cell. "But it's just after ten."

"Yep."

"Did something happen?" Gigi asked, frowning.

"Nope. Everything went fine," I said cheerily.

"Wait, you're finished?" Eliza asked, shocked.

"No way you covered that place by yourself in less than an hour," Wheatley said, shoving fries into his mouth.

"Um, I have pictures. Want to see?" I asked, taking out my phone. When I'd pulled the pictures up, I handed it over to Gigi, who looked at them, her jaw dropping a bit, before passing it around the table.

"Did you have help?" Camden asked.

"I assumed you guys wanted me to do this on my own," I said.

"This place is trashed!" Rhodes exclaimed when it got around to him. "Dude, Frankie's going to be supremely pissed off when he wakes up tomorrow morning."

"I can't wait to see the look on his face!" Eliza bounced up and down in her seat. "This is awesome, Brookie!"

"How did you do it?" Gigi asked, regaining her composure.

"I told you," I said, shrugging. "I have a way of making things happen."

I was expecting her to push back, to demand to know my secrets, but after a few seconds of mulling this over, Gigi nodded. "Good job," she said, sharing a look with the others before turning back to me. "One down, more to go."

Chapter Seven

"Ms. Z.!" I called out as I saw her walking down the hallway. Ever since that night at Principal Franklin's, I'd been seeing more and more of The Elite at school. There were impromptu conversations in the hallway and short talks with Eliza during the class we shared, and I was even invited to sit with them at lunch a few days that week. I wasn't a part of their group just yet, but after a week, things were progressing better than I'd expected.

But that meant that my regular schedule had sort of taken a backseat to my new mission. And the few times I'd stopped by Ms. Z.'s office, she'd been in with another student or her door was closed. There was so much I wanted to catch her up on, but I was finding myself busier than I'd ever been before.

That's why, when I caught a glimpse of her in the hallway, I called out to her without hesitating. Ms. Zia turned around at the sound of her name and saw me running toward her, a smile growing across her face. "Brooklyn! Where have you been? I feel like you haven't come by in ages," she said, placing her hands on her hips.

"Omigosh, I have so much to tell you. You won't believe what my life has been like lately," I said. I glanced around us, noticing for the first time that people were staring and most likely listening to our whole conversation. It had been this way ever since The Elite had deigned to notice me. Suddenly people cared about what I thought. They analyzed my every move and had even begun to copy my style. The day before, I'd worn a sort of sash around my neck, and the next day I saw at least three other girls at school doing the same thing.

It was so bizarre. And totally awesome.

I gestured for Ms. Z. to walk with me. "So, what's up?" she asked, mirroring my excitement.

"I can't really get into it here," I said, suddenly paranoid that everyone was listening to us. "But do you want to have lunch soon? Maybe Thursday or something?"

"Of course. You know I'm always up for lunch," Ms. Z. answered. She gave me a sidelong glance. "But can you give me a hint?"

I smiled. I could always tell when the counselor in her was coming out. She got this look on her face and her voice became lower. It was nice to know that even though we might argue, she still cared about what happened to me. Just like sisters.

"Let's just say that I'm no longer invisible," I said, pulling her away from the crowded part of the hallway and giving her a little spin before striking a pose. Then I leaned in to whisper to her. "I've sort of been hanging out with The Elite."

When I pulled back, I could see the shock registered on her face.

"Oh, wow. Really?" she asked.

"Yep!" I said, wanting to squeal but holding it in.

"How do you feel about that?"

It was such a therapist thing to ask, but I was in too good a mood to care. "Are you kidding? I feel *incredible* about it. All I ever wanted was to feel like I fit in here, and now the most popular kids in school want to hang out with me. *Me*. The person no one knew existed a month ago."

"Exactly," Ms. Zia said, crossing her arms. "Are you sure you want to be friends with people who only noticed you *after* you had this big makeover? Wouldn't you rather they like you for you? The *real* you?"

"This *is* the real me!" I said, trying not to let what she was saying get to me. She was always fighting with me on the subject of popularity, and for once I wished she'd let it go. "Just with a little better packaging."

"Oh, Brooklyn," she said, shaking her head. "Your packaging was fine before."

"I know," I agreed, not looking to get into another argument. "But this is a huge opportunity for me. I mean, if I'm going to own my own PR firm one day, I need to know what it takes to be one of them. One of the ones everyone wants to know about."

"PR people shape the way people look at that world—they don't live in it," Ms. Zia reminded, but quickly moved on. It seemed like she didn't want to fight anymore either. "I just want you to know that you don't have to change for anyone. You're a pretty cool girl all by yourself."

"Awww, it's like we're in an after-school special," I said jokingly.

She snorted. "Please. If this were an after-school special, you'd be pregnant and I'd be trying to adopt your baby," she said. "This, my dear friend, is lightweight stuff."

"Okay, so lunch, then? Thursday?" I asked.

"You know where to find me," she said as she turned and walked away.

I couldn't stop grinning as I continued on to my next class. Things were still okay between me and Ms. Zia, and even though I thought she worried a little too much, I really did think she was happy for me.

Life with The Elite was better than I ever could've imagined, too. It was taking time for them to warm up to me, but eventually I'd win them over. Most of them, anyway. Wheatley had started to let me see his softer side instead of always scowling at me. Not that we were besties or anything, but I wasn't as scared to be around him anymore. Camden was critical but fair and after I'd done such a kick-butt job at Principal Franklin's house, he'd started treating me less like an outsider. Rhodes was always surprising me with his ability to pull facts out of thin air, and we'd started playing a game where every time I saw him, I'd ask him another obscure trivia question to see if he could answer it—which, of course, he could. Eliza still insisted I'd had plastic surgery, but she didn't seem to be mad anymore that I wouldn't divulge my doctor's name.

And Gigi . . . well, Gigi was a little more difficult to read. Her moods were guarded, and though she was always nice to me, I couldn't help but feel like there was still some resistance to my being around. Not that she said anything outright. It was more of a subtle hint in her voice. Like there was always a hidden "but" at the end of her sentences. "I'm so glad you're here (but we'll just have to see how long it lasts)." Or "I absolutely adore that dress on you (but it would look better on me)." I figured it was just going to take a little longer to get her to trust me, but I was definitely up for the challenge.

And so far, so good.

Yep, right now, life was pretty amazing. And that's why I

couldn't help but smile as I walked down the hallway. Even when I was suddenly pushed into the girls' bathroom and the door slammed behind me, my mind didn't automatically go to worst-case scenarios. Especially when I saw who'd pushed me in there in the first place.

"Asher!" I said, thinking that my day just kept getting better. "What's up?"

"I need to talk to you," he said seriously.

"Well, okay. But you realize we're in the girls' bathroom, right?" I asked, looking around at the pink walls.

"Abby's watching the door," he answered.

I blinked. It was weird that he would corner me in the girls' bathroom and then get his little sister to keep watch. What kind of rendezvous was this?

"Okay," I said slowly. My mind began to wander as I thought of all the things he could possibly be bringing me in here to talk about. I hoped one of them involved him confessing his undying love for me. Then again, we were currently standing around a bunch of toilets—which wasn't how I wanted to remember the moment that our love affair began. On the other hand, pushing me into a bathroom because he just *had* to be alone with me? I had to admit, it was sort of hot.

"I saw you the other night," he said, ripping my daydream in half. "At Principal Franklin's."

That, I hadn't been prepared for. My mouth went dry and my palms started to sweat. How was that even possible? I'd been so careful and hadn't noticed anything odd, except . . . except for the noise I'd heard toward the end of the night. Crap. It'd been him. Hiding in the dark, spying on me.

Oh God, what was I going to do?

"Listen, Asher, you can't tell anyone about this. No one," I said, pleading with him. "Seriously, it could ruin my life."

"I know," he said, starting to pace a little in front of me.

I couldn't believe this was happening. My own crush was about to destroy me. My eyes started to well up. I'd only managed to be semipopular for a little over a week and it was already over. I desperately wanted it *not* to be over.

"I promise, it's not what you think," I said, trying another tactic. "I found this exploding toilet paper online and I just wanted to try it out—"

"You're a witch," he said.

I almost had a meltdown as he said it. I'd never heard anyone outside of my family call me that before and certainly not so accusingly. He looked wary as he paced in front of me, absently running his hands through his dark hair. At this moment, I really wished I had the ability to read other people's thoughts. It would have come in handy for what was about to happen next.

"A witch?" I asked, trying to sound like it was the craziest thing I'd ever heard, but I probably just came off as crazy. "I don't know what you're talking about. Witches don't exist, Asher."

"Yes they do. And after watching you that night, I know for certain that's what you are," he said, walking toward me and grabbing ahold of both my shoulders firmly.

"Asher, I . . ." I didn't know how to finish the sentence, because what was I supposed to say? "You're right"? "I am what you say I am"? And then what? If what my parents said was true, danger would surely follow.

They were going to be *so* mad at me.

"Just stop," he said, his voice quieter now.

His face was inches away from mine and he was still holding me by the shoulders. If I had my way, this would be the part in the movie where he would pull me to him and kiss me passionately before telling me ours was a forbidden love because I was a witch and he was a witch-hunter . . . or something like that. God, I hoped he wasn't a witch-hunter.

Instead, he turned his face to the right, let go of one of my arms, and pointed in the direction of the bathroom stalls.

"Erushee aguaso!"

As soon as he said the words, I heard the sound of water flowing. It was different from the toilet running, though; it sounded like a *gushing*. I could feel Asher's eyes on me as I walked over to the nearest stall. Not sure what I was going to see on the other side, I lightly pushed on the door and then took a step backward.

The door swung open. What I saw made my heart nearly stop. There, coming out of the toilet bowl, just like a fountain, was a gush of water that leaped straight up into the air and then back down in a steady little stream. Moving on to the next stall, I saw that that toilet also had a fountain spraying from its bowl, only this time it was split into three little sprays. As I stepped down the line, I could see that every stall held a similar scene, but each water show was slightly different.

I looked back at Asher incredulously, trying to wrap my head around what he'd just shown me.

"What . . . ?" I started to ask, but stopped. I needed to collect myself, because none of this was making sense.

"Brooklyn, the reason I know that you are a witch," he said as he walked toward me, "is because I'm a witch too."

Holy—

"I need to sit down." And I did. Right there on the disgusting tile floor. I slid down the wall until my butt hit the cold ground and stared at the steady stream of water rushing up out of the toilet in front of me.

"I didn't know you were a witch at first," he said, coming

over and sitting down beside me. "Of course I didn't. Otherwise I would've told you my secret a long time ago. And it's not like I suspected you or anything. I was actually just walking around my neighborhood that night and noticed the lights were out on the street, so I decided to check it out and that's when I saw . . ."

"Me doing magic," I answered for him, still a little shocked.

"Well, yeah. But I wasn't sure you were even casting spells in the beginning, because it just looked like you were pulling a prank. So I snuck up behind you and then I heard you say the spell before you threw the toilet paper into the air. After that, I knew what you were doing," he said, looking straight at me. "But I didn't know how you'd react to me finding out. I mean, I thought my parents knew every witching family in the area and we've never heard about yours. What coven do you belong to, anyway?"

I shook my head. "I have no idea," I said quietly. "My parents don't really use much magic in our house. I've only had my powers a couple weeks, so all of this is pretty new to me."

"You just started using magic *two weeks ago*?" he asked, his eyes growing big. "You're kidding me, right? Well, this explains your sudden makeover at least."

"Is it that bad?" I asked meekly.

"No. Of course not. It's just . . . it makes sense that you would sort of go crazy over the magic if you recently started using it. Me, I grew up with it. Been casting since I was about four."

"That long?" I was suddenly embarrassed. "You must think that I'm such a loser. Being a witch and only coming into my powers now."

"You, Brooklyn, are no loser. You're just new to it all," he said, giving me a little smile and nudging me with his shoulder. The touch let off a spark that coursed through my body like a little electric shock.

"Thanks," I said. Letting out a sigh, I pulled my legs up to my chin and rested my cheek on my knees. I studied Asher's face and couldn't help but be reminded of just how cute he was. His skin was tan, and his eyes were almond-shaped and completely magnetic. If it was appropriate to call a guy beautiful, Asher would be it.

And he was magically inclined, just like me.

"I can't believe you're a witch too," I said, shaking my head.

"Yeah. Small world, huh?"

"The smallest."

We sat there in silence for a few minutes as we both thought about what had just happened. In the course of an afternoon, my life had once again been flipped upside down. My head was spinning. Suddenly I had so many questions. Questions that I didn't feel comfortable asking my parents but might be able to ask Asher.

"Are we the only ones?" I blurted out. "I mean, who are witches. Are there others like us here at Clearview?"

"Well, there's my sister, of course, but other than that, not that I know of. Then again, I only just found out about you, so you never know, I suppose," he said. "There are about a dozen other kids here in town, but they're spread across the other public and private schools."

"I had no idea." There were so many other things I wanted to ask, but I knew this wasn't the time or place for it. For one, we were holed up in the school bathroom, and two, Abby was still hanging around outside guarding the door. "So, what now?" I asked, suddenly feeling shy that he knew my deepest, darkest secret.

"Now," he said, winking at me, "we get to have a little fun."

I started to laugh as he pulled me to my feet. In all the excitement, I hadn't realized how cold the bathroom was, and

I shivered at his touch. The only noise was the constant flowing of the water.

"Mind doing the honors?" Asher asked, motioning toward the stalls. He crossed his arms over his chest and leaned against the wall as if to watch. When I didn't move, he gave me an encouraging look. "Come on. Show me what you can do!"

Scared that I would make a mistake and totally embarrass myself, I began to refuse, but then I realized magic was something that we could do together. Asher and I now had this one thing in common, and if I played my cards right, I could learn a lot while spending some QT with him at the same time.

It was genius.

"Um, okay. I'll try," I said, moving over to the first stall and pushing it open with my foot. "But I've only done a handful of spells, so don't laugh if I mess up."

Asher held his hands up as if in surrender. "I would *never*!"

Turning back to face the flowing water, I took a few seconds to center myself. This was especially difficult considering I had an audience, and a cute one at that. But I forced my eyes to focus on the water, and when I was ready I pointed at the bowl.

"Retro-undular!"

The water instantly began to taper off until nothing was coming out of the bowl. I stepped forward to peer inside and was happy to see that it had settled back to normal. A peek in the other stalls all showed the same thing.

"How was that?" I asked, turning around with a grin on my face. I hadn't been sure it would work, but I was elated that it had.

"Impressive," Asher said, nodding with approval. "It's not what I would've done, but it was good. What was it?"

"Oh, it's a reversal spell. Sort of like hitting the undo button on your computer," I said. "It just reverses whatever you did."

"Interesting. See, you're already teaching me something."

"Well, I'm sure there's a lot you could teach me, too," I said shyly.

"I think that could be arranged," he responded, the slightest hint of flirtatiousness in his voice. I could feel my cheeks fill with heat and I tried hard to hide the evidence of my attraction by looking down at the ground. Now that the water had been turned off, there was only silence. Silence was not something I particularly liked.

Luckily, a few seconds later, the bathroom door opened and a head popped in. The girl was gorgeous: black hair, exotic-looking, olive skin, and amazing eyes. She kind of looked like . . .

"Hey, the natives are starting to get restless out here," she said to Asher. Then she turned her head to me and said, "Hi."

"This is my sister, Abby," Asher explained.

"Hi," I said, smiling.

"So. You're a witch."

"Yep."

"Cool," she said, before turning back to Asher. "We gotta go."

"Okay," he said, leading the way toward the door. "I'll go out first. Why don't you come out in a few minutes so no one gets the wrong idea."

"Definitely wouldn't want *that*," I said under my breath.

Just as he put his hand on the door, he turned to look back at me.

"We should do some magic together sometime."

I took a big gulp and prayed that I didn't pass out.

"I would really like that," I answered.

And with a smile and a nod, Asher slipped out the door.

Chapter Eight

After Asher outed me in the bathroom, things between us changed drastically. He went from popping up every once in a while around school to showing up every morning at my locker. The first time I arrived to see him standing there, I was so surprised I nearly dropped my books. Eventually, it became a part of our morning routine, one that I looked forward to every day. Then we began spending some of our time outside of school together too, going for coffee or walks along the promenade.

It wasn't all as romantic as it sounds, though. Most of the time, Abby joined us. But I was so happy just to have other twitches to hang out with that it didn't even bother me that I wasn't getting more alone time with Asher.

It helped that Abby turned out to be really cool. She was younger than both of us and was practically my opposite, but we got along really well and I instantly felt connected to her. She couldn't have cared less about having a social life and always had her nose in a book, but she was completely interesting. She wasn't a big talker, either, which worked out well, because I gabbed enough for the both of us. When she *did* speak, she always impressed me with what she had to say. I quickly realized that Abby was quiet not because she was shy but because she was so busy paying attention to what was going on around her. She was perceptive for sure. It became clear to me that Abby knew *everything* that was happening around school and was an excellent judge of character. She knew who was dating whom, who was failing gym class, and which athlete hadn't come out of the closet yet. It was like being around a walking, talking encyclopedia of our school—all I had to do was ask.

It was easy to see that Asher adored Abby. To him, she wasn't just his little sister. Abby was, in some ways, his best friend. And after hanging out with her just a few times, I could see why. The girl was wise beyond her years and 100 percent loyal.

On the rare occasions that Asher and I *were* alone, I at first found that I was so nervous just being around him, it was hard to concentrate. As time passed and we began to cast together, I became more comfortable with it all. He still made my stomach do flip-flops every time I saw him, but I was starting to be able to actually hold a conversation with him without getting all tongue-tied and saying something completely stupid. I never stopped smiling when I was around him. Actually, I was pretty much happy whenever I was with either of the Astleys. I felt like I could really be myself.

When the three of us spent time together, we mostly talked about magic and spells. Asher even taught me a few incantations that he'd been using for years. Like the chameleon spell that allowed a person to completely blend into his or her surroundings, until they literally disappeared. He confessed that he'd used this one on several occasions to spy on his parents and even on Abby. I couldn't wait to use it in my own life. Abby showed me a speed-reading spell, which I realized was probably the reason she was able to blow through a dozen books a week. I wasn't exactly a book person, but I figured this could come in handy the next time I had to cram for a test.

"I've been trying to do the blowing-up spell you guys showed me last week, but my accuracy is really bad," I said as I stood at Abby's locker. I was careful to keep my voice low whenever we talked magic in public and kept watch for anyone who might sneak up on us midconversation. "I was aiming for an empty soda can the other day and ended up hitting my mom's fruit bowl. I had to lie and tell her I accidentally knocked it off the counter. She would *not* have been pleased to find out I'm using magic to destroy things around the house."

"Are you concentrating on the object itself? You need to picture it in your mind as well as see it with your eyes," she said, sifting through the enormous pile of books in her locker, most of which weren't school related. "Or maybe your aim is just off. Try moving your hand around to see if it helps you hit your target. You might just naturally lean more one way."

"Yeah, maybe," I said, my mind beginning to wander as I looked around the hallway. A group of football players bumped into each other and trash-talked as they walked by us. One of them caught my eye and winked at me. "Hey, girl," he said, before continuing on his way.

I rolled my eyes and turned away. Stuff like that was so weird to me. I was still trying to get used to the attention I was now getting from everyone, guys in particular. Part of me was like, "Don't bother paying attention to me now if you didn't pay attention to me before." But on the other hand, I couldn't help but enjoy the fact that they were interested.

Wasn't that why I'd wanted popularity in the first place? For people to know and like who I was?

"Why would you want to be popular if that's what happens all the time?" Abby asked, acknowledging the football player who'd just hit on me. I shrugged in response. One of the first conversations Abby and I had was over her confusion about why I was suddenly spending time with The Elite. Since she and Asher were both sort of lone wolves—I think I was only welcomed into their pack because magic bonded us— the popularity quest didn't make sense to her. She thought I was especially crazy to get involved with The Elite, given the rumors and the way they treated people around school, but I'd told her I had my reasons. It didn't stop her from giving me a hard time about it, though.

And she wasn't the only one. The Elite had also noticed that I was suddenly splitting my time between them and the Astleys. I don't know if it was jealousy or if they didn't like me hanging out with people they hadn't approved of, but they ignored me whenever I was around Asher and Abby. As much as I didn't want to, I was getting the hint. It didn't mean I was ready to end the friendship with the only other twitches I knew, though.

I scanned the hallway until my eyes rested on a guy and a girl who were whispering to each other while standing solo across from us. I knew them both, though I'd never talked to them before. The girl was Shayla and the guy she was currently bumping shoulders with was Tucker. Tucker was sort of cool—he played guitar in a band with his older brother and a few of his friends. Apparently, he played gigs at a local hole-in-the-wall and had started to develop quite a following on YouTube. Shayla was a member of the school band and was actually pretty cute, in a slightly dorky way. She had red hair and never went anywhere without her flute.

"What's up with those two?" I asked Abby, nodding in their direction. There was something intriguing about them, though I didn't know why.

Abby turned around and looked. "Shayla and Tucker? They've been friends since third grade," she said, going back to locker diving. "My brother helped hook Tucker up with this guy who was selling his van earlier this year. Needed wheels to cart around his band's equipment. Asher says he's cool. He plays a great set at Water Under the Bridge."

I wanted to ask her how she'd managed to get into a bar at the age of fourteen but was so drawn to the couple that I was having trouble keeping up my end of the conversation.

"Are they dating?" I asked curiously, studying their body language. They were clearly flirting, but neither of them gave off any obvious signs that they were a couple. I felt hypnotized by the flow of their movements and couldn't snap myself out of it. "It seems like there's something there."

"Nah, they're both single. But they've been into each other for years. From what I can tell, both of them are too scared to make the first move," Abby said. "Too bad, too. They'd make a really great couple. They're *exactly* alike."

"They just need a little bit of a push," I said absently.

As I continued to watch them dance around each other, I barely noticed that my body had begun to hum and my hands started to rise from my sides. Before I knew what was happening, my pointer fingers were trained on each of them. I was startled to see my fingers begin to move toward each other without my consciously doing so. The fact that I didn't have control over a part of my body was frightening, but at the same time, something felt right in the motion, like there was a connection I could feel but not see. My fingers drew an imaginary line between Tucker and Shayla until my fingertips touched.

When they did, I felt a surge of power connect in the middle like a little shock to my system. Startled by this, I yelped and took a step back, hitting the lockers behind me.

"You okay?" Abby asked, giving me a funny look.

But I was too busy staring at Shayla and Tucker to respond. They'd gone from joking around to standing stock-still and staring at each other. The way they were looking at each other was different from before. The laughter was gone and their eyes were locked. I furrowed my brow, trying to figure out what had just happened.

Then someone walked by Tucker, bumping into him lightly with his bag. And just like that, the moment was broken. Tucker and Shayla seemed to snap out of whatever daze they were in and resumed the conversation they'd been having. I was too far away to hear what they were saying to each other, but I could see Shayla whisper something to him and then touch his arm softly. He smiled warmly and then took ahold of her hand and held it in his. Shayla looked down at their hands and then back up at him. And instantly you could read it all over their faces.

They were in love.

"No way," I said, incredulous over what I'd just witnessed.

"What?" Abby asked, turning around and following my gaze to Shayla and Tucker. "Whoa. Well, it's about time."

Abby wasn't as surprised as I was to see them holding hands, but I still couldn't believe it. It was too much of a coincidence. "That was so weird."

"Yeah, sort of crazy that we were just talking about them, huh? Maybe you're good luck for couples," she said jokingly. "Like a modern-day Cupid."

Abby laughed to herself, but I couldn't help but wonder if she was right.

★

"Mom, Dad, can I talk to you guys a sec?" I asked later that night.

They both looked up at me as I entered the living room. My mom was watching the BBC, her eyes glued to whatever drama was unfolding on the television in front of her. My dad had the paper open in his lap, his glasses hanging off the end of his nose. They each stopped what they were doing after hearing the tone of my voice.

"What's wrong, dear?" my mom asked, her mind clearly still on her show.

"Um, I was just wondering if I could ask you guys a few questions?"

"Sure," my dad said. "What's up, Buttercup?"

I cringed as he used the nickname he'd given me as a little girl but kept myself from reminding him that I'd since grown up. "Well, I was thinking . . . it was really cool hearing all about our family history the other day, and I wondered if you could tell me a little bit more about our powers?"

My parents glanced at each other and shared a slightly panic-filled look. "What do you want to know?"

"Well, for starters, what coven are we from?" I asked, sitting down on the love seat and folding my legs underneath me. "You mentioned the Cleri the other day, and I'm assuming that we're not related to them, so what *is* our lineage? Where are we in the world of witchcraft?"

My dad cleared his throat. "Well, you're correct, we *aren't* descendants of the Cleri. Our lineage is actually with Wilha, a coven that was based out of New Hampshire at the time of the trials. Wilha was always a passive group; our focus was never on big-time spells or making a name for ourselves in the witching world. We left that up to covens like the Cleri," he said.

"And after seeing what happened to them during that time, you can easily see why we remained that way."

"Our priorities weren't the same as most other covens'," Mom cut in. "Most of us only wanted to raise families, leave behind the danger that spell casting often brought. While other groups were using witchcraft for everything, our coven decided to go back to the basics and try to live low-magic lifestyles.

"Then, after the incident with Evelyn, your grandmother moved out here to try to put a little distance between the coven and her. She refused to use magic except for when it was absolutely necessary.

"The truth is, our line's always laid low."

"So we never did anything big? Anything important?" I asked, unable to hide my disappointment that I didn't come from a long line of warrior princesses or something like that. It was just one more way that I was destined to be ordinary from the start. Even the thing that set me apart from the majority of the rest of the world was slightly vanilla.

"Just because we didn't do anything to land ourselves in the history books doesn't mean that what we've done hasn't been important," Mom said, sounding a bit defensive.

I wasn't sure I agreed with her, but I also wasn't going to argue, either.

"Are there any specific powers our line seems to have that I should know about? You know, like things that we specialize in or anything."

"Hmmm, not really . . ."

"Because this crazy thing happened at school and I'm just trying to figure it out," I said.

"You weren't caught doing magic, were you?" my dad asked, worried.

"It was nothing like that," I answered quickly. "No, see, this thing happened when I was watching these two people at school. My hands started to move by themselves and they sort of drew a line between this guy and girl and . . . well, I swear there was a spark. And not like it sounds. Like, an actual spark of magic . . . between them. Like, because of me."

"What happened after you did that, Brooklyn?" my mom asked.

"Well, they started holding hands," I said, shrugging. "I know it sounds crazy, but it was sort of like I . . . linked them or something. Made them fall for each other. Is that even possible?"

The room was quiet as I waited for my parents to say something. I could hear the ticking of the clock in the corner of the room and counted each second as it went by. I was already up to twenty-four when my mom spoke again.

"It *is* possible, Brooklyn," she finally said, fingers clenched together in her lap. "There's a bit of matchmaking talent in our family."

"What do you mean, matchmaking?" I asked. Then, borrowing a phrase from Abby, I added, "Are we like Cupid?"

"That's certainly an interesting way to put it," Dad said. "Though love's a little bit more complicated than that."

"Love? Is that what I did? Made Shayla and Tucker fall in *love* with each other?" I asked, stunned.

"No, not love, Brooklyn. Nobody has *that* kind of power. Well, that we know of," Mom said. "But lust, interest, a crush, if you will—now that's a different story."

"Are you serious? How could you not tell me about this?"

"It honestly slipped our minds," she said, absently fiddling with her hair. "My gosh, it's been years since I've matched anyone."

"Me too," my dad said. "I never much liked getting involved in anyone else's love life."

I shook my head. What they were saying was crazy. Wasn't it?

"So I can help people find their perfect matches?"

"Sort of. All we have is the power to create a link between two people that will give them the chance to see if there is love there to grow. The lust eventually wears off and at that point it's up to the couple to decide if it's a relationship worth pursuing."

"Oh my gosh . . . is that why so many people start dating someone and then it fizzles? Do all witches have this power?" I asked, wondering if all flings were really just products of a witch's imagination or boredom.

"To my knowledge, it's a gift only our particular line has. And some people are more gifted at it than others. In fact, I've never seen a connection happen without a witch trying to match a couple before. Though it's not entirely impossible. You can certainly tell when two people might be a good fit. You get a tingling from their connection, that tension in the air between them," Mom said.

"So, let me get this straight," I said, still trying to digest what they were telling me. "I have the power to match two people that I think would be a good couple but who maybe are just having a little trouble making the first move?"

"Correct," my mom answered. "And apparently even when you don't realize it. But this is not a gift to be taken lightly, Brooklyn. When you're dealing with matters of the heart, things can get very complicated. And in the end, whether they fall in love isn't up to you. That's for the universe and the real Cupid to decide."

"There's a *real* Cupid?" I asked, my mouth dropping.

"Just be careful, sweetie," Dad said, going back to reading

his paper and ignoring my question. "You're dealing with people's emotions here. In some cases, you may end up doing more damage than good."

"Got it, Dad," I said, still a little dazed. I got up to give them both hugs and then prepared to leave. I needed some alone time to think about this new bit of information.

As I was heading up the stairs, I heard my mom say, "Well, that went better than I'd expected."

I had to agree. I'd definitely gotten exactly what I'd been looking for.

For the next week, I tested out my newfound matching skills, first pairing up two kids in my debate class who were always arguing and trying to one-up each other to win their cases. I figured that if there was a fire between them in class, imagine what they'd be like as a couple. And they'd been hot and heavy ever since.

Then I'd had a feeling about my World Civ teacher and the volleyball coach and decided they could use a little help connecting, too. Older people always seemed to drag their feet when it came to dating and I figured I'd just help speed up the process. Though they hadn't been as outwardly affectionate as the other students I'd matched, I'd seen them meeting up in the cafeteria for coffee on several occasions.

Almost as soon as I'd learned of this new side of myself, the wheels in my head started to spin. I was slightly ashamed to admit it at first, but there was only one potential couple I wanted to test my magic out on—and it wasn't for altruistic reasons. Asher and I had been growing closer and closer over the three weeks since we'd found out about each other's magical abilities and there were times when I thought maybe there was a spark between us. I wanted so badly to match the two of us but couldn't help feeling guilty about it. What if Asher found out and got mad at me for doing it without his permission? Would he be upset or happy that I'd taken the initiative? And even worse, what if it didn't work? What if once the spell wore off, there was nothing there and we had to go back to being just friends? I already knew that I was head over heels for him, and it would mean I'd be left pining for what we'd had. Only it wouldn't have been real. And what would I do then?

The truth was, I hadn't had these particular powers for all that long to begin with and I was still trying to work out the kinks. Because my parents weren't exactly forthcoming with information, I had no idea if I was even doing things right. I thought it best to try things out on those who weren't me first, just to make sure, so I'd turned to other students and my teachers in the meantime. But now a week had gone by and all seemed perfect in the world of love, which made it difficult to hold back on what I wanted to do.

As I drove up to the Burger Barn, I couldn't help but feel nervous and even a little bit excited. Trying to play match-maker was sort of like playing God. Of course, just because I willed it didn't mean it would come true. My parents had made it clear that after the initial spell wore off, there had to be a real connection between the couple in question in order for a relationship to develop. My matching would only get the ball rolling.

After that, I had to hope there was more there.

Shutting off the engine, I checked my appearance in the mirror quickly. I had on a pair of jeans and a tank top. A jade-colored necklace hung low across my front, the bottom of the chunky jewels touching just above my belly button. It was fun but flirty, the perfect mixture of dressed up but not trying too hard. My hair was loose and curls framed my face, which was perfectly done up.

I wanted everything about this night to be perfect.

Taking a deep breath, I made my way over to the restaurant and almost immediately spied who I was looking for.

Asher.

He was sitting in a booth toward the back, pecking away on his cell phone and looking absolutely adorable. His black jacket, fitted white tee, and jeans nearly made me swoon as I watched him through the window. My stomach dropped like it always did when he was around. I'd never felt like this about anyone before, this much was true. Was it possible he felt the same?

Only one way to find out.

I held up one finger and pointed it directly at Asher. Then with my other hand I pointed at myself. While turning my thoughts to what a great couple we would be, I moved my fingers closer and closer together until the tips touched and I felt a jolt.

Right away, my desire to be near him grew. It was like a slow burn that had just been ignited and I was compelled to run inside and let him know how I felt. I had no idea if what I'd done was against any witching rules or even if it was going to work. I only knew that I had to give it a try.

With my eyes trained on Asher, I moved toward the front door of the Burger Barn to see if there was a spark between us after all.

Chapter Nine

I swept into the burger joint and headed straight for Asher, who was sitting at a table in the back. Our eyes locked when I was only halfway there and his face softened into a smile.

My pace quickened as my desire grew and I wondered why I couldn't get to him faster. It was like we were two magnets being pulled together by some unknown force. Only, I knew what that force was.

I slid into the booth across from him and gave him a grin. "Hi."

"Hi," he answered, returning my look.

If anyone was watching us right now, I was sure they would be gagging over our googly-eyed-ness, but I just didn't care. All that mattered was that I was there, with Asher. It was just him and me and a crazy little thing called love.

I mean, lust.

The balloon that had been carrying me along on my high burst as I was reminded that what we were feeling—what

Asher was feeling—right now wasn't true love. We were having a moment, bonding together, but only time would tell if we were truly a match.

Still, it didn't make the feelings I was having seem any less real.

Asher continued to stare at me. "You look amazing."

"Thanks," I answered. "So do you."

We took a break from admiring each other to order some food and then talked about Abby and the different spells we wanted to try out. I ordered french fries even though I was too nervous to eat any of them. But guys didn't really like it when they were the only ones eating, so I forced myself to choke down at least a few as Asher polished off his own meal.

"I had no idea that those two finally got together," Asher said, nodding behind me.

I turned to see Shayla and Tucker walk in. They were holding hands and kept looking over at each other giddily. Sitting down at a booth near us, they wouldn't even give up their hands to look at the menu.

"I sort of got to see it happen the other day," I said, not telling him the whole truth about my involvement in their matchup. "It was so cute to see them make the first move."

Asher looked at them curiously. "Imagine what that must have been like for them. They were friends for, like, ever, yet they both secretly liked the other and never said anything," he said. "Good for them. Tucker's a pretty cool guy—he's the real deal."

"Abby said they were both too afraid to make the first move," I said, looking down at the table shyly.

"I get that. They probably didn't want to ruin the friendship if the other didn't like them back," he said. "But at the same time, think about how many potential couples are single and lonely just because nobody had the nerve to go for it."

"That's so sad."

"Yep."

I knew we weren't just talking about Shayla and Tucker. The fact was, we were in a similar situation. As much as I wanted to believe that the spell had worked—or preferably, that we hadn't needed the spell at all—I felt paralyzed to make that first move. To let Asher know just how much I liked him.

Because if he didn't feel the same . . . well, I might just die of humiliation. Or a broken heart. Either way, it would suck.

"So . . ." I said.

"So."

The air between us was electric, but I knew that nothing was going to happen in a restaurant full of loud teenagers. No, if anything was going to happen, we'd have to leave.

"So, I was telling Abby the other day that I've been having a really tough time with the exploding spell," I said, trying to change the subject.

"Oh, yeah? Your aim is probably just off," Asher said, taking a sip of his soda.

I watched his lips fold around the straw and wondered if they were soft. They looked soft. I was never going to be able to concentrate on anything normal ever again if I was constantly wondering what it would be like to be with Asher!

"That's what Abby said too," I mumbled, still mesmerized by his mouth. When I was finally able to pull my eyes away and focused them again on his, I realized that he knew exactly what I'd been staring at.

"We could get out of here," he suggested, looking at me through a lock of hair that had fallen in his face. "Go somewhere and practice the spell a bit if you want."

My stomach began to buzz with nerves at the prospect of going somewhere we could be alone.

Check, please.

"Sure. Yeah, let's go practice."

Asher paid the bill and we made our way out to the parking lot to our separate vehicles.

"I know where we can go," Asher said as he climbed on the back of his motorcycle. "Follow me?"

"Of course."

I climbed in my car and started the engine, giving myself a moment to take a deep breath. I wanted so badly for something to happen between me and Asher that my chest ached at the thought that it wouldn't. Was it possible that I was just seeing what I wanted to see in this situation, since I knew I'd bound us? Or were we really making a connection?

Pulling out into traffic, I made sure to follow right behind Asher, keeping my eyes trained on his back. As I drove, I imagined what it would be like to sit on the back of his bike, my arms around his waist, feeling his muscles as I gripped him tightly . . .

Suddenly, he made a sharp right and I had to swerve to avoid running into him. We'd pulled onto a dirt road about five minutes outside of the city. Several more minutes went by as we made our way farther down the tree-lined road and finally into a clearing up ahead. We parked and got out, listening to the quiet of the night.

"Where are we?" I asked, looking around and seeing that the place was empty except for us and the trees.

"This is where I like to go sometimes, when I need to get away," he said, walking slowly over to me. "Nobody else knows where this place is. Not even Abby."

"Oh," I said, feeling myself blush as he said it. "Well, what do you do here?"

"Sometimes I practice spells, other times I just think. It's my own secret hideaway."

"It's amazing," I breathed, surveying the scene. I dug the toe of my Converse shoe into the ground to give myself something to do. "So quiet and . . . gravelly."

He crossed the space between us and reached out to grab ahold of my hands. His hands felt soft in mine and fully covered each of my palms. My pulse sped up as we touched, and I began to sweat, suddenly so nervous I could hardly contain myself.

I can't believe this is happening!

"This isn't where I hang out, Brooklyn," he said with a little laugh. He began to pull me toward him, until my feet started to move. And then we were walking, making our way toward the bushes in front of us. When we got up to them, Asher let go of my hand in order to push the branches to the side and let us through. "I want to show you something."

I nodded. At this point, he could've been taking me to some creepy cabin in the woods to make me his personal slave—and not in a good way—but I didn't care. I still would've gone with him.

It was hard to see in the darkness as we navigated through a foresty area, but luckily Asher knew exactly where he was going. After a few minutes, I began to see a light up ahead and before I knew it, we'd broken through the woods and were standing on the shore of a beach.

"I had no idea there was a beach here," I breathed, admiring the way the moonlight danced off the water. The rhythmic sound of the waves lapping onshore was soothing, and I could see why Asher came here to think. Everything was calm and quiet. It was the perfect place to be alone with your thoughts.

Or with the boy you liked.

"Pretty cool, huh?" he asked. "It's great because you can really be alone out here. There's no one to bother you."

"Yeah," I said, thinking about what he was saying.

"We can do as much magic as we want and we don't have to worry about getting caught." He moved to my side and looked out at the water with me. After a few moments, he cleared his throat. "So . . . uh, you want to try that spell again?"

"Huh?" I asked, confused. "Spell?"

"Yeah, you know, the explosion spell? That's why we're out here, right?"

"Oh, sure. Of course," I stammered, bringing myself back down to reality. "The spell."

"Why don't you show me what you've been doing and I'll see if I can figure out what you're doing wrong."

Asher started collecting big shells from the beach and placed them in a row on a nearby log that had washed up onshore. It was nighttime, but the moon was so bright here that I had no problem seeing the targets. Now I just had to make sure I didn't get distracted by what I was doing. Or not doing, I should say.

I took a deep breath and prepared myself to perform the spell. Training my eyes on the first shell in the lineup, I felt the energy building inside me as I raised my hand toward the target and took aim.

"Detonimous vastomia!"

The power flew out of me like a bullet escaping a gun and within seconds the space just below and to the left of the shell exploded in a mass of splintered wood.

Asher walked over to the log and studied the spot before walking back to where I was standing and, now, pouting. "So, you seem to be aiming a little left of center," he said.

"No kidding," I said, annoyed that I still wasn't hitting the mark and even more annoyed that I'd been so off base about Asher's feelings toward me.

"Just aim a little more to your right and try again."

I sighed and took my typical spell-casting stance: feet shoulder-width apart, body relaxed, head held high. Looking exactly at the center of the same shell, I raised my hand again, this time aiming just right of it. Calling on all the power I had, I yelled out the words.

"Detonimous vastomia!"

The wood blew up again, this time to the right of the target. "Are you freaking *kidding* me?" I asked, moaning. I fell to the sand in frustration. "I can't do it. God, you must think I'm such a loser."

Asher walked over and knelt next to me. "You're not a loser, Brooklyn," he said, giving me a sympathetic smile. "You're just losing *today*."

It was really sweet of him to say, but I couldn't help feeling like a failure. All I wanted to do was impress him, and here I was, not even able to hit a stupid shell. And Asher was practically a pro at this magic stuff. No way was he going to want to be with a girl who was magically challenged.

"It's just embarrassing that I'm this bad," I confessed, looking down at my hands like they were somehow failing me.

"Why are you embarrassed?" Asher asked with a laugh. "You're doing great for someone who's *learning*. And besides, it's just me. Who cares what I think?"

"I can't help it . . . I care what everyone thinks," I said. "I mean, maybe not *everyone*, but everyone that *matters*. People at school, The Elite—"

"Yeah, why *is* that?" he asked, cocking his head to the side and looking confused. "They put their pants on one leg at a time like the rest of us. They might be designer pants, but you get the idea. Why do you want to impress them so much?"

"They're like teen royalty at school. Everyone looks up to

them. And if you're one of them, that means you're some-body," I said. "I want to be somebody, Asher."

"You're already somebody to me," he said.

Swoon.

"Really?"

"Of course," he said, his fingers finding mine. I turned to look at him and found that he was already gazing at me. "Now, come on. Let's try this again."

He pulled me up until I was standing in the sand, facing the log lined with shells. But instead of stepping away and let-ting me take aim, he came up behind me and pressed his chest against my back. I felt his hand make its way up my side until it reached my shoulder and then move down the length of my arm. Finally, his hand rested on top of mine and we raised our arms together. I closed my eyes and breathed in his scent. He smelled like clean linen with the slightest hint of something spicy. It was delicious.

"Now look at the target and take aim." I did what he said, but it took everything in me not to just melt into his arms. "Relax your mind and think about what you're doing."

But all I could think about was kissing him.

He moved my hand slowly until it was pointed in the direc-tion of the shell. I shivered as his breath tickled my neck.

"Now say the words," he breathed, barely above a whisper.

"Detonimous vastomia . . ."

I managed to get the words out just before Asher pulled me around and our lips touched. The sound of the shell shattering rang out through the night.

Chapter Ten

There's nothing more magical than the beginning of a relationship.

Well, except when that relationship involves two twitches, in which case it's absolutely spellbinding.

Everything is new and exciting and each moment spent with that special person is amazing and wonderful. It's like being in your very own chick flick starring Rachel McAdams—everything works out in the end and you know you're going to live happily ever after.

That's what life was like after that first kiss between Asher and me. We spent our time outside of school together, casting spells but mostly making out, and every date we had was a new adventure. For the moment, I couldn't think of anything else but us. Even The Elite took a backseat to my newfound love, a fact that they weren't too psyched about, but I figured that if they hadn't fully invited me to join them yet, I didn't owe them anything. And the bottom line was that they hadn't asked me to sit with them again, so I didn't feel bad about my absence of late. It was like I was wearing love blinders and I couldn't remember a time when I'd been more happy or content.

It was like I'd finally gotten everything I'd ever wanted.

Until I inevitably remembered one little thing: it was possible none of it was real. The fact that it had all happened after I'd matched us that night at the Burger Barn meant that we were magically bound but not necessarily meant for each other. And the thought of his feelings just wearing off at any moment—well, frankly, it made me feel like throwing up.

I wanted to ask my parents more about our Cupid powers but was so worried that they might decide I was using too much magic that I let go of that idea. And I would've gone to the witchboards, but given that these powers were unique to our family line, I knew I wouldn't find the answers there. I had no clue how long a match lasted or when real love actually developed. I knew how I felt about Asher; those feelings had been clear before I did anything. But when it came to his feelings, I couldn't tell whether we were still under the throes of the spell or if it was just nature taking its course.

Shayla and Tucker, my first attempts at playing matchmaker, weren't much help to me either since they were still going strong. As far as I knew, the two had liked each other *before* I'd given them the nudge, so I couldn't use them as an accurate gauge of how long the spell could last. And the other two couples I'd paired—the two debate kids and my teachers—still seemed to be enjoying the newness of their relationships.

The only people who might have actually been able to help me figure it all out were the ones I absolutely couldn't tell.

Asher and Abby.

Asher because I was pretty sure he'd freak out that I'd used magic on him—magic that might have caused him to have feelings for me. And Abby because I knew she'd either tell Asher or she'd lecture me on what I'd done. And I couldn't handle anyone telling me that what Asher and I had was a mistake.

No, neither of them could ever find out.

That meant I was on my own and would just have to trust that what we were feeling was real. Still, it was hard sometimes to convince myself, even though I wanted so badly to believe it. Every day I spent with Asher, I had that nagging little fear in the back of my head that said it might be our last.

So in an attempt to make every moment count, I tried to spend as much time with him as possible. Before school. After school. During breaks. At night on the phone. I hadn't even realized that I'd let everything else in my life take a backseat for nearly two weeks until it was pointed out to me at school one day.

"I had fun last night," I said to Asher, swaying back and forth as I stood next to him in the hallway.

"Me too," he said, a dreamy look on his face. "Wanna do something again tonight?"

"You couldn't keep me away."

"Bye," Asher said, leaning in and giving me a soft kiss as people plodded around us to their next class.

"Bye." I sighed as I watched him walk away, already feeling sad that he was gone.

"So *that's* why you've been MIA," a voice said, snapping me out of la-la land.

I turned to see all the members of The Elite coming toward me.

"Hey, guys," I said.

"Looks like somebody's been busy," Eliza said, raising her eyebrows at me. She had a smirk on her face as she looked pointedly at where Asher had been standing just a few seconds before.

"Huh?" I asked, following her gaze and then realizing what she meant. "Oh, yeah. Isn't it great? We sort of hit it off."

I wanted to tell my new friends all about it but wasn't sure where to start.

"We see," Gigi said evenly. "It also explains why you've ditched us."

"I'm sorry, guys. I haven't been trying to avoid you. I guess I kind of got caught up in the love bubble," I said, worrying that my absence may have seemed more malicious than that. Hoping I could get them to understand, I leaned in toward the girls. "You can see why I've been distracted, can't you? I mean, who wouldn't want to hang out with him?"

"That's exactly why we asked him to join The Elite a few months ago," Gigi said, folding her arms across her chest. "He didn't feel the same."

This caught me off guard, and my perma-smile turned into a frown.

"You asked Asher to be a part of The Elite?" I asked.

"Yep. And the dude said thanks but no thanks," Camden said. "Clearly, he had no idea what he was doing."

"He didn't tell me about that," I said quietly to myself. Lately we'd been telling each other everything: about our childhoods, our interests, and all the big things that had happened in our lives. I'd been honest with him, with the exception of the Cupid stuff and my witchy lineage, and I'd thought he'd done the same. We'd even talked about my joining The Elite and how important it was to me, though he still wasn't a fan. He'd never once mentioned that they'd shown an interest in him. And now I was finding out that not only did they ask him to be a part of their crew, but he'd turned them down.

I knew he hadn't exactly lied to me, since I'd never actually asked him about it, but I couldn't help feeling a bit betrayed.

The thought of him keeping things from me made me feel sick.

"Obviously he couldn't handle everything that comes along with popularity," Gigi said. "And now that the two of you are dating, I have to wonder if *you* can. Brooklyn, are you serious about being one of us?"

The question hung in the air, heavy and purposeful. I knew that the answer I gave could change everything. My heart started to race as I realized how close I was to losing my chance of getting into The Elite. This moment reinforced one thing for me: my goal was still the same.

"Definitely."

"I'm curious to know how Asher feels about you spending time with us," Gigi said.

"I bet he talks about us, doesn't he?" Eliza asked.

"He better not talk about us," Wheatley said, crossing his arms over his chest.

The fact that the conversation had somehow turned to Asher threw me off. I fought the instinct to run away. I was still having trouble processing the news that Asher hadn't told me about The Elite's invitation.

"Asher knows how much I want this, and he's supportive of me," I said carefully.

They didn't look like they entirely believed me, but as I confirmed my allegiance to the group, the others seemed to relax just the tiniest bit.

"Well, we need to know you're loyal to us above anyone else," Gigi said.

"I'm a hundred percent in," I said without hesitating.

"Good," Gigi said, twirling her fingers around the strand of pearls she was wearing to match her black-and-white polka-dot dress. The white lace gloves she wore polished off the outfit and made it seem a little like she belonged in a neighborhood full of white picket fences. If I hadn't seen Gigi in action while in debate, I would have thought she was as innocent and sweet as she looked. But I knew better. "Then there's something that you can help us with, now that you're back on track."

"Okay," I said, standing a little straighter to show my resolve. "What do you need me to do?"

"Well, first, you need to start spending more time with us around school," she said. "Lunch, breaks—people need to get used to seeing you with us. You'll start to gain respect from the other students and you'll need that if we let you in. Besides, if you really want to be a part of this group—"

"Which you do," Rhodes interjected.

"—you really need to be a part of this group," Gigi said, looking at me seriously. "And not just part-time. If you're in, you need to be in all the way."

I bit my lip as I tried to think of a way to explain to Asher why I was going to be spending more time with The Elite. Then I remembered that he hadn't bothered to tell me about being invited into The Elite and figured that he couldn't get all that mad at me. Besides, it was just during school. We could still hang out at night.

"And that means spending more quality time outside of school, too," Eliza said as she twirled a piece of her long, dark brown hair. She raised one of her perfectly groomed, thick eyebrows at me while placing a hand on her slender hip. "We need to be able to trust you and that will only come as we get to know you better."

I swallowed hard and thought about what they were asking me to do. I didn't want to lose momentum with Asher, and he'd already made his feelings about The Elite clear. I knew he wasn't going to understand why I needed to hang out with them more than I already was. Then I thought about what I'd lose by refusing. All I'd ever wanted was to be in this exact position, and now that I was, I needed to do what I had to in order to hold on to it. If Asher truly cared about me, he'd understand. I'd figure out a way to do both. I had to.

"Okay," I said, nodding. "Done."

"Now, the other thing," Camden said, looking straight at me.

"I thought that was the thing."

They all laughed at me like I'd just said something cute. I closed my mouth, feeling stupid, and waited for him to continue.

"We need you to use that head of yours to help Eliza and Wheatley ace your upcoming history midterm," Rhodes said, straightening the sweater he was wearing. I couldn't help but notice that he already looked the part of a Harvard student. All buttoned up and properly dressed.

I thought about what he said and then nodded. "Sure. So I'll prep them for this test and we'll be good then?"

Wheatley snorted at the same time that Eliza began to giggle.

"No, silly," Eliza said, punching my arm lightly. "You're going to pass the test *for* us."

"But—but that's cheating," I said. I knew it sounded lame, and I was sure it happened plenty around here, but I still knew it was wrong. "The test isn't until Monday, I'm sure if we started studying now, we could—"

"I have auditions all week after school, and Wheatley, well, you could prep him for the rest of the year and he still wouldn't pass," Eliza said. I looked at him, but he didn't seem upset by what she'd said.

"I don't know."

"Look, every year my parents let us use our beach house to throw this big blowout party. The guest list is like a who's who of everyone important, and trust me, you *want* to know these people. Anything you could possibly ever want or need, these people can get it done for you. And so much of who *we* are is who we know, and this party is very important to us. If Eliza and Wheatley fail this test, their GPAs will drop and that will endanger their chances at getting into the colleges of their choice."

"And that means no beach house and no party," Wheatley said, frowning.

"I'm sorry, I'm just confused. If it's so important that they pass this test, why isn't Rhodes the one helping them out? He's much smarter than I am."

"Well, for one, I'm not in you guys' history class," Rhodes answered. "And two, I'm already a part of this group. You're the one who's still proving herself here."

"It's just another way to test your loyalty to us and show that you really want this," Camden said, looking at me with kind but firm eyes. "And these two have managed to keep their grades up until now. Would it really be fair if their futures were ruined because of one stupid test?"

Wow, he really would make the perfect politician.

I looked at The Elite, feeling totally conflicted about what they were asking me to do. On the one hand, I knew deep down in my gut that by helping them pass, I'd be doing something wrong. I'd never cheated before and I felt like doing what they asked would mean crossing some invisible line that I could never come back from. Sure, cheating wasn't the worst thing I could do in my life, but what would be next?

Then again, they'd made a good point. It *wasn't* fair for

Wheatley and Eliza to be judged based on one test. In the end, it all came down to one question: How badly did I want to be a part of The Elite?

"Look, sweetie, I know this is sort of a big decision, so why don't you think about it a little and get back to us?" Gigi said soothingly. Eliza's jaw dropped and she look at Gigi angrily. Gigi ignored her as she put her arm around my shoulders. "And in the meantime, Eliza's dad is having a little soiree at their house on Thursday. Why don't you come along for a preview of what you'll be missing out on if you don't go to this beach party?"

Eliza's face softened and she clapped her hands together. "Yes, Brookie, you have to come! Daddy's parties are always uh-mazing."

The invitation to a party held by an Oscar-winning actor was impossible to turn down. I could only begin to imagine the kinds of people he spent his free time with. Maybe George, Brangelina, or the Kardashians would all be there. I was getting nervous just thinking about who I might run into.

"Um, yeah, that sounds like fun," I said, managing to sound far less psyched than I actually was. Better to play it cool with this crowd. "Do you think I could bring Asher with me?"

I thought I saw Gigi wince as I mentioned his name, but then a grin spread across her face and I wondered if I'd just been imagining things.

"Sure," she said evenly. "I'd love to pick his brain about a few things."

I nodded, happy to hear that they weren't planning on leaving him out because of what had happened in the past. Going to this party would be so much better if Asher was there. Maybe there was a way that I could have my new friends and my boyfriend at the same time.

I hoped.

"That's great. Thanks so much for inviting me, guys!" I said. "And for being so understanding. I don't want you to think that I'm any less dedicated to you just because I need a little time to think things through."

"Seriously, Brooklyn, it's not a problem. Take your time," Gigi said, staring at me with her huge eyes. "But do remember that we're running against the clock here. The test is on Monday, after all."

"I know," I said. "I'll let you know soon. I promise."

"I'm sure you'll make the right decision."

My chest started to get that tight feeling it always did when I was wrestling with something big.

"Okay, so we've got to get to class, but we'll see you at lunch, Brookie?" Eliza posed it as a question, but I knew it was more of a demand.

"Yep. I'll be there!" I tried to put as much enthusiasm into the words as possible, but I could already feel myself stressing.

I watched them start to walk away, strutting down the hallway like they were moving in slow motion. After a few steps, Gigi looked back around at me, a twinkle in her eyes. "Tell Asher that we're looking forward to seeing him again."

I nodded and they disappeared as they turned the corner.

I took a deep breath and let it out loudly.

"What was that about?"

I turned to see Abby standing behind me, a book open in one hand and her bag in the other.

"That? Oh, nothing," I mumbled.

"Uh-huh . . ." she answered. I could tell by the tone of her voice that she didn't believe me. Anyone else would've taken my response at face value, but Abby was different. She paid attention to everything, even if it seemed like she was fully immersed in her book. If she thought something was wrong, no way was I going to be able to convince her otherwise. Better to just be honest.

"Okay, fine. The Elite are just giving me a hard time because I've been spending so much time with your brother. They're sort of questioning my loyalty to them and want me to prove that they can count on me."

"Sounds like a secret society," Abby said, fixing her eyes back on her book.

Although I'd never looked at it that way before, she wasn't totally wrong. They were focused on succeeding and maintaining their power and social standing no matter the cost. Even if I might not agree with everything they did, I couldn't argue with their results. But Abby was making them sound much worse than they actually were. Right?

"It's not like that," I said, finding myself defending them. "People just don't know them."

Abby shrugged. "Maybe so. Asher had just mentioned something to me a while back," she said nonchalantly. "Made me think they might not be the greatest people."

So Abby had known about The Elite recruiting Asher too, yet he hadn't bothered to let me in on the info? That really wasn't cool.

"What does that mean?" I asked.

"Just that they're sort of sketchy." It wasn't what I'd expected her to say, but I wasn't entirely surprised.

"Gotta head to class," she said, before I could question her more. "Listen, Brooklyn, just be careful, okay?"

I could hear the warning in her voice but didn't want to take it seriously. She had to be overreacting. But the last thing I needed was for her to worry about me being around them too. So I said what I knew she wanted to hear.

"I'll be fine, Abby." And in that moment, I really believed what I said.

Chapter Eleven

"You look amazing," Asher said as we pulled up to the Rivers's estate later that night.

I snuck a glance at him before turning back to the road in front of us. "Thanks. I've never been to something like this before, so I wasn't sure how to dress."

When I'd asked Eliza what a person typically wore to a party her father threw, she said it was casual. Thank God I asked her what she was wearing, because she'd then proceeded to describe the short black-and-white cocktail dress and vintage pair of Jimmy Choos she'd laid out for the evening. Clearly, my idea of casual and her idea of casual were two different things.

Nothing in my closet even came close to that kind of "casual," so I'd hit the mall right after school to try to find something suitable to wear. Do you know how difficult it is to find something that looks like a million bucks but isn't? Damn near impossible. After trying—and failing—to find something designer at a bargain, I settled for just buying something that *looked* designer. Well, it sort of looked like the cheaper cousin of a designer who was big maybe five years ago, but it would do. I was banking on the fact that the celebrities in attendance would be so self-absorbed that they wouldn't even be paying attention to what I was wearing.

In the end, I walked away with a champagne-colored ballerina-style dress that complimented all my new . . . assets. The material was made of a flowy sort of satin and the top came down in drapes across my chest, crisscrossing at my sternum and then wrapping around my midsection in a sort of layered belt. Delicate straps held the dress up, and the skirt section poofed out but hugged my tush enough to show that I had a little something-something going on in the back. The dress was a little shorter than I typically wore, but that might have just been an illusion created by my longer legs. Or the fact that I'd lathered myself up with shimmery body lotion before leaving the house.

I'd pulled my hair up on top of my head in a loose, low bun, with strands framing my face. And since I no longer needed the extra help, my makeup was minimal, except for a smoky hue around my eyes to make them pop.

At the risk of sounding conceited, I had to agree with Asher. I looked good.

He pulled out his phone and held it out in front of us. When I saw our faces reflected in the middle of the screen, I struck a pose and waited for the flash.

"My parents requested a photo," he said. Then, as if to explain, he added, "It's rare for me to go out to things like this and they wanted proof that I wasn't just making it up."

I laughed. If he wasn't there with me, I might not have believed it either. "Parents can be a drag sometimes," I said.

"Aw, I don't mind," he answered, pushing a few buttons on

the phone and sending the photo to his parents. "They're actually pretty cool. Our family's sort of close." His phone made a beeping sound a few seconds later, signaling he had an incoming message. "My mom says your dress is beautiful."

I smiled at the compliment and fingered the fabric of my dress.

"I just hope I made the right choice," I said, smoothing the material for about the hundredth time since we'd gotten into the car. "It would be humiliating to show up and look out of place."

"It's just a party," Asher reminded me.

His tone was light, but there was hidden meaning in it. Considering we almost didn't make it to the party at all, I chose to let the comment go. The truth was, when I'd told Asher about the party at Eliza's, he'd been far less thrilled about going than I was. In fact, he hadn't wanted to go at all.

"Why not?" I asked, both shocked and disappointed by his answer.

"You know that's not my scene, Brooklyn," he said, sounding tired.

"But I don't get it. You like hanging out with me," I said. "And you like music and food, and there are going to be famous people there."

"First off, I don't care whether someone's famous or not. They're all the same to me," he said. "And you're right. I like hanging out with you. Just *you*. Why do we need to hang out with people like them anyway?"

"Asher, I've told you, being friends with The Elite can set me up to do anything I want with my future. If I hang around them, it means I won't be so low on the totem pole anymore. I'll be at the top."

"And that's fine. For *you*," he said. "But that doesn't mean *I* want to be around them."

"You won't have to be. You'll be around me. Stuck by my side," I said, linking my arm with his. I lowered my voice. "You know, Gigi asked how you felt about me hanging around them today and I told her you didn't mind because you supported me."

"I do support you," he said.

"Then please, just go with me. I need you there to help me through it all," I said. And then, to sweeten the deal, I gave him a long, lingering kiss. "If you did, I'd be very appreciative."

After a few seconds and some puppy dog eyes, he'd agreed to come with, and I was a happy girlfriend again. And now that we were here, I was especially happy that he was beside me to experience everything. Starting with the estate.

"Would you look at this house?" I asked as we came to the end of a long, winding driveway that landed us at the top of a small hill. As we turned into the circular part of the drive, we both looked up at the house that loomed in front of us. A man in a tuxedo stepped out in front of our car, motioning for me to slow down, and then came around to my side and opened the door for me.

"I'll be parking your car tonight, miss," the man said, taking my keys and getting into the driver's seat.

I gave Asher a pointed look. "Oh, sure. Just like any other party."

Asher rolled his eyes as he took my hand and we began to make our way to the front door. When we reached the steps, there was a woman in a black dress, holding a tray of colorful drinks.

"Can I interest you in a cocktail?" she asked us.

"Well, that walk from the car definitely left me parched. How about you, sweetie?" Asher asked, his face serious.

I hit him gently on the arm.

"Anything here a virgin?" I asked, realizing how childish it might have sounded.

The waitress didn't even blink before handing me a glass full of pink liquid topped off with a sprig of mint and a slice of watermelon dangling on the edge. "Freshly squeezed watermelon lemonade with a hint of mint. Absolutely refreshing and alcohol free."

"Oh, okay. Thank you," I said, surprised. I took a sip. "Mmmm." It tasted exactly how she'd described it, though I probably would've been just as happy with a Coke.

"No, thanks. I'm good," Asher said as the woman tried to hand him his own glass. She nodded at us before moving on to the couple who was arriving behind us.

"Wow, this place is insane!" I whispered as we passed another set of tuxedo-wearing workers at the door and crossed the threshold. We wandered into the foyer, which opened up into a cavernous atrium with staircases on both sides. A modern-looking chandelier that resembled crystal swords hanging from the ceiling radiated soft lighting on every inch of the space.

We were ushered through the entryway and into a room off to the right that was even grander than the last. My heels clicked over the hardwood floors as we navigated around the chic furniture. Scattered about were all different kinds of seating: couches, chairs, benches, luxurious beanbags, cushy ottomans, even seats that hung down from the ceiling like birdcages. And everything was white. If the lighting had been turned up all the way, I was sure I would have had to wear sunglasses to see anything.

More than thirty people filled every inch of the space; some lounged in chairs, others mingled from one group to the next, doing their due diligence in schmoozing. As we moved deeper inside the room, the numbers grew and I began to recognize people. There was a famous A-list actor talking to one of the girls from the last season of *America's Next Top Model*. I could count at least three people in attendance who had won Grammys within the last two years—one of which had brought her kid with her, who, I might add, was wearing a dress that was probably ten times as expensive as mine.

Eliza's dad was standing in the middle of it all, a group of at least a dozen other industry bigwigs all rapt as he told a story. After a few seconds, everyone burst out laughing.

"Can you believe who's here?" I asked Asher quietly, starting to point out celeb after celeb. "Oh my God, that's Jonah Hill."

"Who's that?" Asher asked blankly.

"Are you serious?" I asked as he shrugged.

It sort of drove me nuts that Asher didn't care about this stuff, but I tried to revel in the company we were keeping. I took mental notes on those in attendance, including what they wore, ate, and drank, so I could share the news with Ms. Z. later. After all, I owed her a lunch after I'd blown off our original date to spend time with Asher. I hoped that the party gossip would begin to make up for it. At least I knew she cared about this stuff and would give me oohs and aahs when appropriate. We were always talking about the latest Hollywood gossip and arguing over which celebs were cheating on each other. Just another reason that it was annoying when she tried to convince me that popularity wasn't important.

"Oh, there they are!" I said, spotting The Elite gathered in the far corner. I grabbed Asher's hand and practically dragged him over with me, excited to talk to people who actually knew me.

As I made my way over to them, I felt the familiar pull that the group seemed to have on me, and I got more excited as we got closer. Gigi, wearing an all-white dress, her lips stained red, sat perched on one of the hanging chairs, a single leg strategically bent at a slight angle, while her upper body snaked toward the side of the egg-shaped contraption. The pose couldn't have been comfortable, but it was sensual and just a bit complicated—the perfect description of Gigi herself.

To her left, Camden leaned with his back against Gigi's chair, hands in his pockets and head tilted down to look at her. On an ottoman off to the side, Eliza sat in the middle, showing more leg than I thought was possible without flashing the crowd her naughty bits. Flanking her were Wheatley and Rhodes, both dressed in similar suits but rocking totally different looks. Per usual, Rhodes's style was more buttoned up, while Wheatley's showed off his muscles.

It was like looking at a freaking *Vanity Fair* cover. And for all I knew, it was entirely possible that there was a shoot going on, since I'd passed Annie Leibovitz on my way across the room.

"Hey, guys!" I said, walking up with Asher in tow, just the tiniest bit worried about what would happen next.

"Brookie!" Eliza said, jumping up to give me a hug and then planting air-kisses on either side of my face. "You made it!"

"Of course I did," I said, smiling at everyone else, who nodded hello but didn't bother getting up. "Thanks again for inviting us. This place is amazing!"

"Really?" she asked, scrunching up her face. "I don't know, we've been living here for like three years now and I keep telling Daddy we need to get something new. I mean, we don't even have a pool house!"

"I can see how that would be a problem," Asher said from behind me.

Eliza looked past me, seeming to notice Asher for the first time. After a slightly awkward silence, she started giggling and pushed me out of the way in order to air-kiss him as well. "You're so funny!" she said, smacking him on the arm. Then to me, "He's funny, Brookie."

"Hilarious," I said, raising my eyebrow at him.

"Well, welcome to my humble abode, anyway. Help yourself to drinks and food—the artichoke tartlets dipped in truffle oil are to die for," she said. "Once you've settled, I'll start taking you around to meet everyone!" We watched her bounce away, her dress barely covering her tiny butt.

"She's . . . peppy," Asher said as he nuzzled my neck. So far it didn't seem like he was having an awful time, so I figured I'd get the next part over with when he was still in a good mood.

"Come and say hi to the rest of the crew," I said, walking over to a love seat near Gigi and Camden and pulling him down next to me. Asher sat reluctantly and then leaned back coolly. "Gigi, you look supergorge tonight! I could never pull off white."

"It's Marchesa," she said, looking at me from head to toe. Then she turned to Asher. "Nice to see you again, Asher."

"You too," he responded, and then nodded at Camden. "This is quite a get-together. It was nice of you guys to invite us."

"I know, right?" Gigi said, looking around. "I was telling Brooklyn the other day that you could've come to these sorts of things all the time, if you hadn't turned down our offer."

This was exactly the topic I'd been hoping to avoid. In fact, I'd been managing to avoid it for the past three days, ever since Gigi had let this fact slip. I was still confused and a little hurt that Asher hadn't told me himself. I mean, it wasn't like he hadn't had opportunities to bring it up. In all the conversations we'd had about The Elite, he'd never once mentioned that they'd recruited him.

But Asher and I were still so new that I was afraid to do anything that would possibly end us in a fight. The truth was, I wasn't sure our burgeoning relationship would survive it. For all I knew, an argument could mess with the spell, and next thing you know, we could be over. So I'd pushed the question to the back of my mind, rather than confront him, all for the good of our relationship.

But now it was coming out, whether I liked it or not. Right in the middle of a high-profile party. It wasn't quite like Gigi was trying to cause a scene, but she was certainly calling him out. Asher glanced over at me, a look on his face that I couldn't quite read. So I just stared at Eliza, who was throwing her arms around her father's neck across the room, and acted as if I hadn't heard what Gigi said.

Asher turned back to Gigi. He gave her a smile, but I could tell he wasn't happy. "Like I said before, I appreciate the offer, but this isn't really my thing."

"What *is* your thing?" Camden asked, turning his whole body to us now. He placed his hand protectively on his girl-friend's shoulder. "I'm just curious, because I see you around school a lot, but you're never really doing anything. You're not involved in sports or clubs. What *do* you do?"

Asher stuck his hands in his pockets and leaned back on the love seat like he didn't even care that he was sitting just feet away from one of the biggest television stars of all time. I had to smile. He was so cool that he didn't even know how cool he was. And he was mine.

"Oh, you know. A little of this. A little of that. I don't really play well with others," he said in a nonthreatening way. Then, to show he wasn't completely self-absorbed, he flipped the conversation back around to Camden. "You're in student govern-ment, though, right? And on the lacrosse team? I heard you guys are having an undefeated season so far. Must be sort of stressful to have to keep up that title when you know it can be taken from you at any time, huh?"

The two stared each other down while managing to keep smiles on their faces. I looked back and forth between them, wondering if I was going to have to step in and send them to their respective corners. Luckily, I didn't have to, because it was Gigi who diffused the situation.

"Now, boys, this is a *party*," she said, smoothing back a few loose strands of hair. "There will be plenty of time to do this dance later."

"Brooklyn! Come over here," Eliza called from across the room. "There are some people you have *got* to meet."

I looked at Asher nervously, trying to decide whether it was okay for me to leave him to duke things out on his own. I'd dragged him here and promised I'd stay by his side. The least I could do was keep my word.

"Go on," Gigi said, waving me off. "I'll take Asher around and introduce him to a few people he may find interesting."

I bit my lip as I considered whether this was a good idea or not. Gigi rolled her eyes and stood up from her seat gracefully. "*Go!* He's in good hands. I promise."

"Go ahead," Asher said, giving me a quick peck on the cheek. "I'll be fine."

After one more glance back at him, I went over to join Eliza. She was standing with a group of people, all of whom were sipping their drinks and seemed to be posing for imaginary cameras at the same time. In the light, I could see that Eliza's dress was even more stunning than I'd thought before. It had a plunging neckline and an even lower cutout in the back that made all eyes gravitate toward her. And every time she moved, the crystal-encrusted heels she wore sparkled like mini disco balls. She was breathtaking and everyone here knew it.

"You guys, this is my good friend Brooklyn," she announced. "She's sort of new in town and doesn't know a whole lot of people yet, but she's definitely on the verge."

I leaned over to her discreetly. "I'm not new, Eliza," I said.

"You're new to this *group*," she answered through clenched teeth. "So just go with it."

I looked over at her like she was crazy, but then turned back to everyone and said hi. Almost immediately, everyone wanted to know all about me. Who I was, where I was from, my measurements (to be fair, this question was from a clothing designer). It was exhausting but also thrilling to have so many important people interested in me and my life. I felt like I was a celebrity being hounded by the paparazzi. And I loved every minute of it.

"Leah, Brooklyn is really interested in PR and publicity," Eliza said to a platinum blonde standing across from us. The woman was wearing a pleated black dress that hung off one shoulder and black stilettos to match. "You should get her information. Maybe she could intern for you over the summer."

"Huh?" I asked, turning back to Eliza, my eyes wide. I'd never told her about my professional aspirations before. In fact, we'd never really had anything more than a surface conversation. "How did you know that?"

"Duh, Facebook. You said you wanted to work with celebrities when you graduated," Eliza said. "Now, Leah here is Daddy's publicist and a senior account executive at Moynaham PR. She knows everything there is to know about publicity and working with celebs. You should totally pick her brain sometime."

"Let's exchange info," Leah said, digging into her purse and pulling out a card. She handed it to me and then left her hand out for mine.

"Oh. Um, I don't have a card to give you."

"Well, no problem. Just e-mail me and we'll set something up," she said, shifting her purse back onto her shoulder. "Any friend of Eliza's . . ."

My mouth dropped open. I couldn't believe it. Moynaham PR was the real deal. If I got an internship there, it would probably turn out to be the beginning of my career. I turned to look at Eliza incredulously as Leah moved on to the next group, continuing to make her rounds.

"I can't believe you just did that," I said quietly to her.

"Oh, get over it, Brookie. So I Google-stalked you, so what?" she said, rolling her eyes at me.

"That's not what I mean. I don't care about that," I said. "Do you realize what you just did? Eliza, that was a *huge freaking deal*. I don't know what to say."

"Say you'll help me and Wheatley on Monday and we'll be solid," she said, smiling at me sweetly.

Before I could answer, she pulled me over to introduce me to a scout at Ford Models, Jerry Weintraub, and two of the *Gossip Girl* actresses. By the time I made it back over to Asher and the others, my head was spinning and I was dying to tell someone everything that had just happened.

"Looks like you were having a good time over there," Gigi said as I collapsed beside Asher on the couch.

"That was *epic*," I said, beaming.

Rhodes leaned back on the ottoman and waved at someone as she walked by. "This is just another Thursday night for us," he said like it wasn't a big deal.

Squeezing Asher's hand excitedly, I paused a moment to take in the scene around me. I could hardly believe this was my life. I never wanted it to end. I had my man beside me, and even if he didn't like being around The Elite, he'd been willing to suffer through it for me. That had to mean something, right? And I was currently surrounded by a roomful of celebrities. I could totally get used to this.

"So, given any thought to what you want to do about the test, Brooklyn?" Gigi asked, breaking into my thoughts.

"What test?" Asher asked.

I hadn't told him about what The Elite had asked me to do, for obvious reasons. He already disliked them and if I told him they wanted me to help them cheat on a test, it would destroy any chance I had of getting him to accept them. And one of the things I'd learned about Asher was that honesty was really important to him. We hadn't talked about it, but I knew he wouldn't approve of me cheating.

I decided to give him a watered-down version of the story instead.

"Gigi and the others asked me if I'd help Eliza and Wheatley pass their history midterm on Monday," I said.

"Like, tutor them?"

"Uh-huh," I answered quickly. I knew that I was lying to him, but I felt like I didn't really have a choice.

"So?" Gigi asked, cutting in.

I turned back to look at her and knew she wanted an answer now. I swallowed and then said the only thing I could.

"I think I could make that work," I said.

Gigi and Camden looked at each other and smiled at me before turning their attention back to the party.

Chapter Twelve

"I can't believe you met the king of daytime television last night!" Ms. Zia squealed as she passed a book to me.

The Best Advice I Ever Got: Lessons From Extraordinary Lives.

Realizing that the book I held was full of celeb stories, I made a mental note to borrow it later and then found its place on the shelf. When Ms. Z. had asked me to help her shelve books, I figured it was a perfect excuse to spend some time with her and to tell her about the party. I'd hoped, as soon as I'd told her about my celeb-sightings, she'd seemed to forgive me for ditching her for lunch that day. And thank gosh, because I had so much I wanted to tell her.

"I'm telling you, Ms. Z., it was like being on the red carpet. And not in a paparazzi-stalkerish kind of way. It was like I actually *belonged* there."

I pushed the book into place and then adjusted it so that all the spines lined up. It was lunchtime at school, and I'd managed to sneak away from The Elite to meet up with Ms. Zia by telling them I'd been called into a mandatory guidance session. Apparently, they'd been victim to these surprise summons themselves, so they didn't question my story.

In reality, I just needed to spend some QT with someone who knew me BTM (before the makeover). And I knew nobody would understand what my experience at the party was like as well as Ms. Zia. Asher had been unaffected and unimpressed by those in attendance, and The Elite—well, like Rhodes had said, that was just another Thursday night for them. They probably couldn't even remember how they'd felt the first time they met a celebrity, let alone the first time they were in a room full of them. How could they possibly get what that had been like for me? Ms. Zia, on the other hand, was as big a celebrity buff as I was, and she just about died when I told her about everyone who had been there.

I took a break from shelving books to pull out my cell and scrolled through the pictures that I'd taken—discreetly, of course—when no one was watching. Climbing down from the chair I'd been standing on, I huddled close and showed her some of the people who'd been there last night.

Ms. Zia shook her head in disbelief. "I'm totally jealous, Brooklyn," she said, flipping through each screen and studying the stars in various states of partying. "This is insane!"

"See? The Elite aren't *all* that bad," I said, bumping our shoulders together.

Ms. Zia kept scrolling through the photos. "Just because they have a few famous friends doesn't make them *good*," she said distractedly. When she was done looking, she handed the phone back to me. "I know it seems like I've been giving you a hard time lately, but I just don't want anyone to derail you from your goals."

"That's just it, Ms. Z., The Elite are helping me with that, too," I said. "I forgot to tell you, but while we were at the party, Eliza introduced me to this woman, Leah, who's her dad's publicist. She works at Moynaham PR, which is only *the biggest* public relations firm in Hollywood. Anyway, Eliza suggested I intern for her and the woman gave me her *card*. Do you have any idea what it would mean for me to intern there?"

"That's *amazing*, Brooklyn!" she said, giving me an excited hug. "I know how much getting into publicity and PR means to you."

"It's, like, all I've ever wanted to do," I said, beaming. "Just being in the same vicinity as The Elite is already starting to pay off. They keep offering to introduce me to people and I'm getting all these opportunities thrown at me that I never would've gotten before. Did I tell you a modeling scout even wants me to consider signing with them?"

Ms. Z. shook her head incredulously. "Lots of great things are happening for you. You deserve them all, Brooklyn," she said. "And maybe you're right about Gigi and the others. But kids like that tend to only look out for themselves. Take it from me . . . I used to be that person."

I melted into a chair as my excitement deflated a little. I really thought everything that had happened would be enough to convince her that The Elite weren't the terrible people she seemed to think they were. Hearing the hesitance in her voice told me it hadn't been.

"But *you* changed, Ms. Z.," I said calmly. "Don't you think it's possible that they could too?"

She stayed quiet as she thought about this. "Anything's possible," she said finally. Picking up another stack of books, she handed them to me and patted the chair I'd been standing on earlier. "Do me a favor and be careful. Popularity always has its price. You just have to find out what it is and if you're willing to pay it."

She was right about that. My mind drifted to what I'd agreed to the night before. And not only that but I'd lied to Asher about what was going on. I felt guilty every time I thought about it, but I really didn't see any other option. As much as I didn't want to cheat, I knew it was my only chance to move forward with the group. I mean, I could say no, stand up for my principles, but then what? A seat at The Elite table would no longer be a reality, and the opportunities coming my way—they'd disappear too. And then I'd go back to being the girl that nobody paid attention to. Back to being invisible.

When I thought of it that way, I really didn't have a choice.

"Change of subject," Ms. Zia said, noticing my silence. "Have I been seeing you walking around school holding hands with Asher Astley?"

Just the thought of him turned my frown into a huge, love-struck grin.

Ms. Z. gasped. "Okay, spill! Are you two dating? How did this happen? When did this happen?"

Sometimes with Ms. Z. it was like I was talking to a girl-friend and not to a school counselor. There were usually only flashes of it before she went back to being the more mature one in the room, but it still made me feel more connected to her than I was to any other adult. I liked to think of her more as a sister. And I think she felt the same way.

"Well, um, we haven't made anything official yet, like, he hasn't asked me to be his girlfriend or anything, but yeah, I think we're sort of dating. And it happened a couple weeks ago. He took me to the beach and I was having trouble . . ." I stopped before I could say "casting a spell." ". . . skipping stones on the water, so Asher taught me how to"—cast the spell—"skip stones, and then he kissed me. We've been hanging out ever since."

"I can't believe you kept this from me for two weeks!" she said, smacking me on my arm.

I giggled. This was my first time having a real talk about boys with anyone. Mostly because there'd never been any boys to talk about before. I'd been wanting to talk to someone about Asher, but it certainly wasn't going to happen with Abby, The Elite, or my parents. Nope. The only one I could talk to was Ms. Z.

"I didn't keep it from you on purpose," I said. "We just haven't seen each other in a while."

"Also unacceptable," she said teasingly.

"Geez, so needy," I said, joking. Then I sighed. "I am sorry for that, though. I guess I got caught up in . . . everything. I like him so much, Ms. Z. We're seriously *perfect* for each other."

"Asher seems like a great guy. Really seems to have his head on his shoulders. Sort of a loner, though, right? Sticks to himself most of the time? In a way, he's your opposite when it comes to wanting a social life. How does he feel about that?"

"I guess he doesn't really get it," I said, finding it hard to explain. "But he *chooses* not to be popular. It's not because he *can't* be."

"What do you mean?"

"Well, I found out that The Elite wanted him to hang out with them, but he turned them down."

"Do you know why?"

"No," I said, biting my lip. "We haven't really talked about it yet."

It wasn't difficult to tell that I was still sort of upset about this fact, and she came over to put her hand on my arm supportively.

"You don't have to like all the same things to be compatible with someone, Brooklyn," she explained. "You just have to connect on some of the bigger fundamentals, and of course, communication is key. And there has to be that spark. It's that spark that separates a friendship from something more."

There was a spark. But considering that I didn't know whether we were still under the throes of my matching spell or if it was good old chemistry that we were feeling, hearing this didn't make me feel any better.

"Well, we definitely have that," I said, smiling at her before reaching up to place more books on the shelf.

When the bell rang signaling the end of lunch, I said good-bye to Ms. Zia and headed out into the hallway.

"Hi, Brooklyn," a guy said as he passed me.

"Hey," I answered, not sure who he was and surprised that he knew my name.

I continued on to my locker. Asher was already there and I smiled at him as I walked up. Wrapping my arms around his neck, I moved in for a kiss. When we pulled away, his eyes darted around us.

"Why do we have an audience?" he asked quietly.

I turned to see what he was talking about. And surprisingly, he was right. People all along the hallway had stopped what they were doing and were watching us. I couldn't figure it out. It's not like we were full-on making out. It was just a kiss. There wasn't even any tongue. Yet almost everyone was staring.

"No clue," I answered, turning back to him and pulling away slightly.

"O-kay," he said slowly. Then he focused on me again. "Listen, I wanted to talk to you about something—"

"Brooklyn?" a voice broke in behind me. A small brunette appeared between Asher and me. She was pretty, dressed in a polo shirt and fitted white jeans. I'd seen her around school but couldn't remember her name.

"Hi . . ." I started, prompting her to identify herself.

"Annette," she answered. "I was wondering if you would be interested in joining the Interact Club."

"We have an Interact Club?" I asked, looking at Asher for confirmation. He shrugged before leaning back against the lockers.

"Yep! It's really great. We come up with all these ways to volunteer in the community and globally. Last year we ran a hair-cutting booth to benefit Locks of Love and collected donations for our local food pantry."

"I don't know if I'm ready to cut off my hair, but yeah. I could probably sign up for some community service," I said. Nobody had ever asked me to join a club at school before. It was nice to be asked. Not to mention that doing some volunteer work might help get everyone off my back about spending time with The Elite. Speaking of, maybe I could even get them to help out too. Wishful thinking, maybe, but would they really say no to helping people?

"That's amazing," Annette said, bouncing up and down slightly and then regaining her composure. "It's going to mean a lot that you're involved."

"Really?" I asked. "Why?"

"Of course," she said, leaving off the implied "duh." "If students know one of The Elite is in Interact, then maybe we'll get more members this year."

"Oh, I'm not . . ." I began to say I wasn't one of The Elite yet but stopped myself. Did people at Clearview think I was a member of The Elite? Even if I hadn't been officially accepted yet, I was already being treated like I had. This was beyond exciting.

Pasting a smile on my face, I tried again. "Just let me know what I need to do, and I'm in."

Asher and I both watched Annette skip away.

"What was that?" Asher asked when she'd disappeared and we were alone again.

"She wanted me to join their club," I said, doing a little dance.

"I saw that," Asher said, laughing at me. "Don't you think it's weird that just because they think you're in The Elite, that you're worth inviting? I'd be a little offended."

"It's not like that, Asher," I said, slightly hurt by what he was suggesting. Deep down I knew that it was possible he was right. "And even if it was because she thought I was one of them, it just proves what I've been saying all along. Being a part of The Elite could be a good thing."

"If you say so," Asher said. "I just think you have all the power you need to change things at this school. You don't need them to tap in to that."

First The Elite and now Asher. Why couldn't Asher—and The Elite—deal with the fact that I wanted to have both in my life. Was it always going to be this way? Me defending my choices to everyone around me? If so, that was going to get old real fast.

Asher studied my face, but I still didn't say anything. He touched my arm and then pulled me in for a hug. "But I don't want to talk about them right now," he said, returning to his normal sweet self. "I actually wanted to ask you something important."

My body began to relax as it pressed up against his and I closed my eyes dreamily. "Yeah?"

"My parents were wondering if you wanted to come over to dinner this weekend. You know, to get to know them and everything," he said.

I stopped breathing as I realized what he was saying. "You want me to meet the fam?" I asked, glad my face was pressed up against his chest. I didn't want him to see the glee I felt over what he was proposing.

"Well, yeah," he said. Now it was his turn to be shy. "It's not a big deal or anything. It's just dinner."

He didn't have to say it for me to know that it wasn't just dinner. I was pretty sure guys didn't ask girls to meet their parents if they weren't planning on keeping them around. This thought made me warm inside.

"I'd love to have dinner with your family," I said, following his lead and trying not to make a big deal out of the whole thing. Even though it was. "You talk about them so much, it'll be nice to see where you get your magic from."

Relief washed over his face as I answered him. It never would've dawned on me that he might be nervous to ask me, but I could tell he was. But really, how could he think I'd say anything but yes?

"Okay, cool," he said.

Asher leaned in toward me at the same time that I took a step forward, and we knocked heads.

"Ooof!" I said as we made impact.

"Ow," Asher said, bringing his hand to his forehead.

I apologized, embarrassed that I'd ruined the moment. "I promise I'll be on my best behavior when I meet your family."

"They're going to think you're adorable," he said, kissing me softly on the forehead. "Just like I do."

I forgot all about the pain in my head as I watched him walk away.

I'd been so excited by the fact that Asher was taking our relationship to the next level that in the heat of the moment I hadn't stopped to think about what it actually meant to have dinner at his house. Based on my total lack of dating experience, I'd never actually met a boyfriend's parents before. And I wanted to make a good impression. Asher was always talking about his family, and not in the embarrassed or annoyed way I often did. So I knew that what they thought of me *would* matter to Asher.

And it wasn't just that I had to impress them as Asher's high school girlfriend; I felt like they were going to be judging my magical abilities too. This thought filled me with dread. How was I supposed to fit in with a family who'd been using magic forever? And what did one wear to do so?

I tried on about a zillion outfits leading up to the dinner: pants, dresses, jeans, skirts—but nothing seemed quite right. I even went to the mall for new clothes but couldn't find anything there that I liked either. Finally, I ended up in a dress that was both respectful and flattering.

I smoothed out my dress, running my hands over the little cherries that decorated it. It had taken me five trips to my closet to finally find something I thought would be parentally suitable. I'd gone girl-next-door demure and chosen a dress that covered the most skin possible without wearing a nun's habit. The final look wasn't exactly my style, but the point was to make a good first impression, not to show them how hot their son's potential girlfriend was.

And now I stood fidgeting on the doorsteps of Asher's house, feeling slightly sick to my stomach. It was an unusually warm night out, which meant that I was sweating like crazy and regretting the fact that I'd worn a dress that covered part of my arms. The cardigan wasn't helping either, but at least it was currently hiding the stains that were no doubt spreading underneath.

One of the first things I'd learned about Asher was how important his family was to him. At first I thought he and Abby just had an unusual bond and got along really well. But then I realized, after listening to him talk, that he was close to his parents, too. Like, they all actually enjoyed spending time together.

I mean, I liked my parents just fine; they were pretty chill about house rules and they'd never shown up at school wearing something embarrassing. But as far as choosing to hang out with them all the time? No, thank you.

But that wasn't how the Astleys were.

So when Asher invited me over for dinner with his folks, I knew it was an even bigger deal than normal. One that I was beginning to question whether I was prepared for.

Before I could start to stress over whether or not they'd like me, I put my hand up and knocked on the door.

Crap, crap, crap, crap . . . the word seemed to reverberate in my head as I knocked.

And then the door swung open, and Asher was standing on the other side wearing his typical outfit of jeans and a plain white tee. And yet he still managed to look delicious. His arms opened up wide and I stepped into them gratefully.

"Hi."

"Hi," he said, breathing into my hair. He closed the door behind us and slid his arm around my shoulders. "Come on in and meet the fam."

We walked into the small but cozy living room. A man was sitting on the couch and poring over a coffee table. When we got closer, I could see that there were hundreds of puzzle pieces spilled out in front of him, waiting to be connected in the right places. As we watched, he pointed at a piece on the table and it rose up into the air and joined a few other pieces I hadn't noticed hovering before. He connected it and then went on to the next piece. Within a few seconds, he had the beginnings of a puzzle floating in the air right in front of his face.

"Dad, this is Brooklyn," Asher said when his dad had finished placing another piece.

His dad turned around and gave me a big smile. "Brooklyn! It's such a pleasure to meet you! We've been hearing about you for a while now. It's so good to finally put a face to the name." He walked over to me and gave me a big bear hug that lifted my feet off the floor.

"Nice to meet you, Mr. Astley," I said, feeling my cheeks turn red at the rather extreme show of affection. I turned to look at Asher. "You've been talking about me, then?"

"Not me," he said, smiling and holding his hands up in the air. "Abby. She's really got a thing for you."

I started to laugh and punched him lightly in the shoulder. When we'd settled down, I turned back to Mr. Astley and pointed at his puzzle.

"I've never seen anything like this before," I said, admiring the work.

"You mean a puzzle?" he asked. "Hon, you've got to get out more."

"No, not a puzzle," I said, embarrassed. I couldn't tell whether he was joking or not and I didn't want Asher's dad to think I was dim. "I've just never seen anyone use magic like that before."

"How does your family do it?"

"Um, the regular way, I guess. Pick up the pieces with our hands and make the puzzle on the table?"

"Wow, so your family is old-school."

"Oh, leave the girl alone, Henry," a voice called out from the other room. Soon enough, a woman dressed in jeans and a loose-fitting top came out and sat down on the corner of one of the chairs. She looked a bit younger than my mom and certainly dressed hipper than my mom, but she had the mom-guilt thing down pat. "Hi, Brooklyn, I'm Cindy. It's so nice to meet you."

"You too, Mrs. Astley," I said, feeling doubly nervous now.

"So, Asher says you came into your powers recently?" she prompted.

I hadn't really wanted them to know I was new to my magicking skills, but there was no use denying it now. I just hoped they wouldn't hold it against me. "Yep. My parents bound my powers until I turned sixteen."

"How are you adjusting?" she asked.

"Pretty well. I'm a little slow sometimes and not quite used to it yet. I think I just need a bit more practice."

"I take it your parents aren't practicing?" she asked.

"Not really. They like to keep a low-magic household," I said, trying to explain. "It's not that they don't like magic or they think no one should use theirs, they're just sort of—careful about it."

"We have some friends who are like that," Mr. Astley said, continuing to levitate puzzle pieces into place. "To each his own."

Feeling the need to explain things better, I cleared my throat and tried my best. "My parents just think that if they use a lot of magic, people are going to find out. And if they find out, then it will eventually lead to another Salem witch trials or something," I said, rolling my eyes. "They're a bit overdramatic, I think."

Asher's parents exchanged a look before going back to what they were doing.

"Well, they're not alone in thinking that," Mrs. Astley said, getting out of her chair. "Now, you want to see something really cool? Then come with me."

Asher gave me a thumbs-up as I followed his mom into the kitchen, the smell of dinner hitting me at once. Then I looked around, in awe of what was happening. I could see several pots on the stove, most of which had ladles or spoons sticking out of them. This wasn't unusual, of course, but the fact that the ladles were moving on their own, stirring the contents in a methodical clockwise motion, was. My eyes swept over to a counter where several knives were suspended in the air, in the middle of chopping up a variety of vegetables.

"No way!" I said, a little louder than I'd intended.

Asher and his mom chuckled as they watched me move around, surveying everything that was being prepared.

"This is so cool!"

"I can teach you how to do it sometime," Mrs. Astley offered.

Thinking about everything that I could learn from her, I turned and gave her an appreciative look. Not just for the offer but for accepting me into their lives.

"I would really love that."

"Mom, I'm going to go and show Brooklyn the rest of the house," Asher said, taking my hand. "How long before we eat?"

"About twenty minutes or so," she said, looking around as dinner made itself.

"Cool," he said, and then pulled me into the hallway and over to the stairs. We took them two at a time, landing at the top a few seconds later. "Sorry about that."

"Are you kidding? This is amazing! My parents never do anything like that at our house."

"Well, you're about to see how a typical witching family works," he said, still holding my hand. "So prepare yourself."

147

First, Asher took me by his bedroom. I'd never seen a boy's room before except on television, so I was surprised by how clean it was. I'd been expecting dirty clothes everywhere, pizza crusts on the floor, and pictures of half-naked girls decorating his walls.

Thanks a lot, TV land. Not all boys are filthy pigs.

Some, like Asher, actually want to live in an area that's not a garbage dump. I felt weird about going inside his room with his parents just downstairs, so I stuck by the door and looked inside instead. His bed was covered with a blue-and-white striped comforter, a couple of pillows decorating the head. His walls were relatively bare, except for a poster of Bruce Lee on one side and a picture of James Bond on another. There was a corkboard above his desk that was probably the busiest part of the room, and I strained to see what he had displayed there.

"So, this is where the magic happens," Asher said, motioning inside his room with a smile.

We started laughing, nervousness escaping from both of us. "Did you just seriously say that to me?" I asked, my cheeks turning red.

"I figured we could use a little something to break the ice," he said, reaching out and grabbing my hand. "I know this is sort of . . . intense. Meeting the parents and all. But I promise, they already love you. Just relax and have fun. I only want them to have the chance to get to know you like I do."

"Okay," I said, even though his words didn't calm me down at all.

"Asher! Can you come and help me with something?" his mom called up the stairs.

He leaned over and gave me a kiss, a little longer than usual for us. "Sure, Mom!" he yelled back, and started to pull away.

"Abby's room is the third one on the left. She'll be pissed if you don't check it out."

"Sure. And then I'll meet you downstairs in a little bit?" I said, starting to follow him out of his room.

As soon as he'd disappeared down the stairs, I took a few tentative steps back into his room. It was weird being in here. Even though he wasn't there, every inch of the place screamed Asher. It smelled like him. The few decorations he had showed off his personality. It was sort of like an Asher shrine.

And if that was the case, I was sure I could learn something about him in here too. It wasn't that I was trying to snoop, but I was curious to see what he kept around. Maybe I could find out how he really felt about me and give myself some peace of mind. I wasn't looking for his diary, and no way was I going to rummage through his stuff, but I figured it wouldn't hurt if I just looked around a bit. After all, he'd been the one who offered to show me his room.

I walked up to his desk, looking back over my shoulder to make sure that I was still alone. When I got there, I had to decide if I was really going to do it. Was I this person? The one who goes looking for clues in someone else's private stuff?

And then something caught my eye. A picture of me tacked up to the corkboard on the wall behind his computer.

I had no idea when it was from or who had taken it. I couldn't even tell where I was in the photo, since the background was completely blurred out. The photo was of BTM me, and despite my terminal averageness back then, the picture actually wasn't all that bad. In it, my head was tilted down, like I was looking at something in my lap or hands. My hair hung into my face and framed the picture perfectly. It was black and white, so it was a little more forgiving, but I was still surprised to see it there.

Asher had a picture of me hanging up in his room.

A quick glance around showed me that besides the pictures of his family, I was the only person he had represented in his sanctuary. And it wasn't a cutout from the yearbook; it was a photo I'd never seen before. Where the heck had he gotten that picture?

"Find what you're looking for?" a voice asked from behind me, startling me back to reality.

Chapter Thirteen

I spun around to see Abby standing in the doorway, her arms crossed and a book in hand. Abby's moods were so even-keeled, I couldn't tell if she was upset that I was in Asher's room or surprised. Not that I'd ever seen her mad, but if she thought I was snooping, she might unleash her inner witch. Or tell Asher about it and that would just be embarrassing.

"Uh, I was just . . . looking around," I said, stammering. "Asher left me up here."

Abby walked over and joined me in front of Asher's desk. Then she leaned forward and pulled down the picture and handed it to me. "I took this, you know," she said. When she saw the shocked look on my face, she explained. "Don't worry, I'm not stalking you or anything. I had a photography class last semester and took this one day when you were in the library. I'd seen you around but didn't know much about you except that you always ate lunch with Ms. Z. in her office. For a while

I just thought you were always in trouble, but then I realized you guys are sort of like friends. Right?"

I nodded but didn't elaborate. It was sort of embarrassing to have to admit that I was basically BFFs with my guidance counselor. Abby and Asher had enough examples of my weirdness, they didn't need another one.

"When I printed out photos for class, Asher saw this one and asked about you. I told him what I knew, and then asked if he wanted it. He said you looked lonely in the picture, but that he could see something behind your eyes. Like there was more to you than you let on. He's had it ever since."

"But he didn't even know me then," I said, whispering.

"He *wanted* to, though," Abby said. "You intrigued him. He liked that you did your own thing and that you didn't seem to care what others thought of you. And then you had that whole makeover and . . ."

"And I started hanging out with The Elite," I said, finishing her thought.

"Yeah," she said, nodding thoughtfully. "They're not his type of crowd, but he knows you're not *fake* like some of them can be. He trusts you to be honest with him."

The words were like knives to my gut as I thought about how that was exactly what I wasn't doing. I hadn't been honest about what I was *really* doing to get in with The Elite, and I was still hiding the fact that I'd matched us. But telling him about either of these things was out of the question now. The last thing I wanted Asher to think was that I was a cheater and someone who would manipulate his feelings—even if it all turned out for the best in the end. I began to worry about what would happen if he found out that I hadn't been as honest as he thought.

"I think everything changed when he found out about your

powers," Abby continued. "As witches, none of us can let civilians know who we really are. What we can do. And that can
be isolating at times. It's hard to make true friends and not be
able to share that part of ourselves. Maybe that's why we're not
exactly daters."

My ears perked up at this. "Really? No crushes?" I asked.
We both knew I was wondering mostly about Asher, but Abby
didn't let on.

"Maybe a crush here or there, but nothing serious," she said,
smiling shyly at me. "Things can get complicated when you're
dealing with emotions like love. Besides, there aren't exactly a
lot of teen witches around here to choose from."

"You only date other witches?" I asked. In all the time I'd
known her, we'd never really talked about boys before. I was
curious to see how she felt on the subject.

Abby shrugged. "Real teenage boys are disappointing," she
answered.

"What about your brother?"

"He's not a normal teenage boy. He's a witch," she said.
"Witches are *extraordinary*. And then there's the fact that when
you date another witch, you can really let them in. I think you
do that for Asher. You get each other."

"I feel the same way," I said honestly. "About both of you,
actually. There's this whole part of my life that nobody else can
understand, except for you two. Abby, you have no idea how
glad I am that I have you guys around."

She nodded and smiled at me. "Okay, what do you say we
get out of here? I'll show you where I live if you're game."

I agreed and took one more look at the picture of myself
before tacking it back to the board in the same spot it had been
before. I hadn't had much of a chance to snoop, but talking
with Abby had given me plenty of insight into Asher anyway.

We went down the hallway and stopped in front of a room with a black-and-white checkered door. It looked like it had been painted that way, but the lines were so precise that I had to wonder. I'd never seen anything like it. Then again, I'd also never met anyone quite like Abby before either.

"Cool door," I said, touching the surface.

"Thanks!" she said, a grin on her face. "It was inspired by the story *Alice in Wonderland*. In fact, my whole room is designed after some of my favorite stories. Watch this."

She leaned forward and put her hand to one of the boxes, and as she moved her hand, the box moved as well. Pretty soon she was mixing all the boxes into new patterns, sort of like a Rubik's Cube. I knew it was magic, and I was dying to know how she did it.

"That's sick!" I said, brushing past her and moving the squares myself. I could have stood there all day playing with patterns, but I could tell Abby wanted to show me the rest of her room. And if this was just her door, I could only imagine what was inside. She waited for me to finish playing and then finally pushed open the door and motioned me into her room.

What I saw blew me away. It was as if we'd stumbled into another world. Starting in the corner and creeping up the wall was a tree. And I mean a full-on tree, not just something that was painted on the wall. The trunk was so big, I doubted I could have wrapped my arms around it, and the branches—complete with leaves spreading across the ceiling—gave the bed that was situated underneath it the illusion of a canopy.

"Is it real?" I asked as I ran my hand over the bark. It felt real: hard, scratchy, like you could break off a chunk if you had enough strength. It even smelled like a tree.

"Kind of. It's a real tree, but it's kept alive by magic," she answered.

"And your parents are cool with it?"

Abby snorted. "They're the ones who did the spell," she said. "I don't have that kind of power yet. But one day, I'll be the one to keep it alive."

"Our houses are so different," I said, shaking my head. "My parents wouldn't even let me have a plant in my room. And if they did, they'd make me water the thing myself."

"It's so weird to think of growing up like that. Magic's such a big part of my life," Abby said.

I moved over to the dual ropes that hung down from the thickest branch above us and touched the wooden seat that was attached. Because of the high ceiling, the tree swing was able to hang down without touching the bed below. I looked up into the leaves above and pulled lightly on the ropes, testing the weight it could bear.

"You can sit on it," Abby said, watching me. "I do it all the time. That's what it's there for."

"Are you kidding me?" I asked her, my eyes bugging out. When she nodded at me, I climbed up onto the edge of her bed and slowly sat down on the seat. I was practically a foot taller than Abby was, so I wasn't entirely sure that a swing that held her weight would also hold mine. So I pulled my legs up into the air one at a time, prepared to catch myself if the ropes broke and I fell. When they didn't, I started to swing.

"This is insane, Ab!" I exclaimed a couple of pumps in. "What book is this from?"

"*Swiss Family Robinson*," she answered. "I liked the whole idea of living in a tree."

As I swung, I noticed that the entire wall across from me was filled with books. Big, small, paperback, hardback—I could only imagine how many there were altogether. Not that I was surprised by any of this.

"You really like to read, don't you," I said.

"Don't you?" she asked.

"I like reading E! Online," I said jokingly. "I mostly just read what the school assigns us. There's not a lot of time for me to do it for fun outside of homework and tests. By the time I do all of that, the last thing I want to do is pick up another book."

"It's not like that when I read," Abby said, moving her fingers over the cover of the novel in her hands. I squinted to make out the title. *Wither.* "It's my *escape*. It brings me to a world so much more fantastical than this one. I feel like it's the only time I'm not bored."

"Bored? How could life possibly be boring when you're a witch?" I asked, shocked. "I'm only beginning to use my magic, but I get a rush every time I do a spell."

"After a while it gets old," she answered. "It's like, if you're born into wealth, money just becomes a part of your identity. Whereas if you don't have it and then suddenly come into it, it's all new and exciting."

"I don't think I could ever get bored of doing spells," I said.

"Come and talk to me in about five years."

I rolled my eyes. "Okay. You love to read . . . so does that mean you write, too?" I asked.

"Nope."

"You don't like it?"

"It's not that I don't like it—actually, it would be a dream to be able to write something as amazing as the books I read—I just feel like I have nothing to say."

"What do you mean?"

"I really think a writer has to have experiences to draw from when creating a world, and I haven't done anything in my life yet," she said, as if this was a given.

"Wait, you think a person has to experience something to

write a book? But it's fiction! Abby, it's supposed to be made up."

"Yeah, I get that part," she said, sitting in her desk chair to give me room as I continued to swing. "It's the emotional part I don't understand. My life hasn't been hard. I have almost everything I want. I get along with my parents. I haven't had my heart broken. How am I supposed to explain any of that if I've never felt it myself?"

She sort of had a point, although I still wondered if she wasn't holding herself back for the wrong reasons.

"Don't worry, Ab, it'll happen," I said, slowing down the swing. "I'm living proof."

A few minutes later we were called to dinner and fifteen minutes later we were back downstairs, gathered around a fully packed kitchen table and eating the feast that Mrs. Astley had made—with a little magical assistance, of course. We were served with ladles and spatulas that moved by themselves. I was so in awe of what was going on around me, I almost didn't want to eat, for fear I'd miss something.

"I was surprised when Asher told us that there was another witching family in town," Mrs. Astley said as she took a sip from her wineglass. "I'm pretty high up on the local witches' council and never knew about you or your parents."

"Like I said, they sort of like to lay low," I answered, hoping we could get off the subject quickly.

"Typically, every coven in the area has a representative on the council," she said, then looked at me curiously. "Since we're independents, I'm the rep for our family. What coven are you affiliated with?"

If I told her about the coven Wilha, it was possible she would find out that they were a passive group who sometimes had the ability to make love matches. What would Asher's parents think of me then? Obviously their family depended on magic quite a bit, so it was possible I wouldn't be good enough for their son. Would they refuse to let Abby and Asher continue to spend time with me? And what if they told Asher about my ancestors' matchmaking abilities? He was a smart guy—he'd eventually figure it out.

"Um, I don't know a whole lot about my family history," I said, shoving a bite into my mouth, trying to buy some time to figure out how I was going to explain this away. "I think some bad stuff happened to some people that my family really cared about and they don't really like to talk about it. All they told me is that we're from someplace in New Hampshire."

"Really? What part?" Mr. Astley asked, brightening at this news.

"Uh, kind of near Massachusetts," I said.

"Our lineage is about a half hour away from Salem," he said.

"Were any of your ancestors in the witch trials?" I asked, and immediately wanted to take it back. How tacky was that? If they were, then clearly it wouldn't be a fun topic to bring up over dinner the first time I was meeting them. And if not . . . well, I'm still bringing up one of the most horrific time periods in our culture's history.

"No, but our coven was friendly with the Cleri," Mrs. Astley said.

"They were like sister covens back then," Asher explained. "That's why it was so hard when everything went down the way it did. For a while everyone in our coven was worried that Samuel Parris would come after them, too."

"So the group disbanded and most of us became independents," Abby said. When I gave her a confused look, she explained further. "A group of witches, smaller than a typical coven, and usually made up of a single family. We still have power; we just don't depend on a coven to take things to the next level."

"Gotcha," I said, starting to understand. "That's what my family is now, I guess. Only, we don't really use our powers this much."

"A lot of people feel it's safer that way," Mrs. Astley said. "We've all heard the rumors that Samuel Parris and his clan didn't die out back then, and that the witch trials were just the beginning. Some witching folk think that the less magic they use, the less likely they are to be a target."

"And you don't feel the same?" I asked.

Asher's dad shook his head. "Nah," he said easily. "There's no proof that anything's happened since then. As far as I'm concerned, it's just an old witch's tale that parents tell their kids to keep them in line."

"Not that keeping a low-magic household is wrong," Mrs. Astley cut in, giving her husband a look before turning back to me. "It can be a good lesson in doing things for yourself."

"Right, right," Mr. Astley echoed before going back to eating.

"Nice save, Mom," Asher said sarcastically.

"Well, we're just so happy to have you here. Magic or no magic," she said, giving me a genuine smile. Even though she was clearly telling me they liked me, I couldn't help but worry that they thought Asher could do better. Maybe date a witch who actually knew how to use her powers. I tried to give her a smile anyway. "Asher and Abby haven't stopped talking about you since they found out about your powers. They seem to think you're something special."

"Believe me," I said, looking straight at Asher, "the feeling's mutual."

Chapter Fourteen

Although I wanted to play the night with Asher's family over and over again in my mind for the rest of the weekend, I only had one day until I had to prove to The Elite that I was worthy of being a part of their group. So when I woke up on Sunday morning, I turned my focus to how I was going to help Eliza and Wheatley pass our history test. They'd already been asking me how I was going to do it, but I'd held them off by asking that they trust me. Given that I'd handled the situation at Principal Franklin's house better than they'd expected, they left me to work out the details on my own.

The truth was, I was still trying to figure out how I was going to do it myself. Not that it was impossible. I was more concerned with getting caught than anything else. If that happened, it would mean trouble for me—both with the administration and with The Elite. If I was caught, I wouldn't pass their test and that would be the end of my rendezvous with popularity. It would be over before it had really begun. So I started to brainstorm.

I debated switching the tests somehow before turning them in, but figured that would be too risky. I thought about getting ahold of the questions ahead of time and then coaching Wheatley and Eliza on the answers so they could pass the test themselves, but they'd made it clear that they didn't want to have to do any of the work to get their As. I even contemplated putting a spell on Mr. Howard's grade system online, so that any mark he placed under Wheatley's and Eliza's names would automatically change to an A. But it wasn't likely that Mr. Howard would forget failing two of Clearview's most popular students.

No, they'd have to ace the test from the very beginning if this was going to work, which meant I had very few options.

So after sleeping in until ten thirty, I dragged my laptop back to bed with me and decided that I had to consult the only people who could help: the witchboards. I posed my question to the online community and then waited for them to respond with different spells that could help me with my task.

As I waited, I opened a new window and checked my Facebook account. I had forty-seven friend requests.

I wondered if my eyes were still adjusting to being awake. When I clicked on the button to show the requests, I saw that there were dozens of students at Clearview who wanted to be friends with me. Well, on Facebook, anyway. I went through each one and accepted them, noting that the first ones were the Elite members. I began to stalk their pages, gawking over who some of their friends were. From heiresses to professional athletes to young Hollywood, their profiles were like the who's who of power players.

I was reading a comment chain on Eliza's wall when an IM window popped up in the corner of my screen.

AshesToAshes518: Whatcha up 2?

I grinned and abandoned my search of Facebook to chat.

LittleMissB: Not much. U?

AshesToAshes518: Chilling.

AshesToAshes518: You made quite an impression on my parents last night.

My heart started to race and I got up and began to do a victory dance on top of my bed. As my arms waved in the air and I shook my booty, I took a step backward and found there was nothing there to support me. I tumbled down onto the ground, landing spastically on my butt.

"Everything okay up there?" my mom called up the stairs.

"I'm fine!"

Scrambling back onto my bed, I went back to the conversation I was having with Asher.

LittleMissB: ☺

LittleMissB: I'm glad!

LittleMissB: I liked them too!

All of a sudden, another window opened up on the other side of my screen.

GGWonderful: Are you ready for tomorrow?

I rolled my eyes.

> LittleMissB: Hello, Gigi.

There was a pause as I waited.

> GGWonderful: Hi, Brooklyn. Are you ready?
>
> GGWonderful: If you want to run your plan by me, I'd be happy to hear it.
>
> LittleMissB: I'm still figuring things out, but don't worry. Everything will be fine.
>
> GGWonderful: Oh, I'm not worried.
>
> GGWonderful: We both know what'll happen if you fail, and I'm sure you'd never let that happen.

Leave it to Gigi to make a stressful situation even more stressful.

> LittleMissB: We're all going to pass that test, Gigi.
>
> LittleMissB: That's a promise.

Thank God the conversation was over IM and not in person, because I was sure she would've been able to tell how nervous I was.

Then I saw that Asher's IM box was blinking, signifying

that he was waiting. I minimized Gigi and went back over to him.

AshesToAshes518: Want to hang out later?

Gigi's message flashed.

GGWonderful: I sure hope so.

I sighed. It pained me to have to do this, but I couldn't get around it.

LittleMissB: Sorry Asher, but I've gotta help Wheatley and Eliza pass our history test.

LittleMissB: Raincheck.

Now it was my turn to wait for him to respond. Finally I saw that he was writing.

AshesToAshes518: ☹

AshesToAshes518: Sure. Have fun.

I closed both IM windows and went back to the witch-boards. None of the other twitches had batted an eye when I brought up the subject of test taking. In fact, the question was met with dozens of suggestions, some of which were incredibly creative. In the end, the answer turned out to be much simpler than I'd originally thought. I spent the rest of the afternoon practicing the spells and preparing for the task at hand.

By the time Monday morning came around, I felt confident about the spell I was going to do. However, the guilt was another story. Even though I could justify my actions by saying that judging a person by one test grade wasn't fair to begin with and that my joining The Elite would allow me to be a positive role model for others, deep down I still knew that what I was doing was wrong.

So to balance things out, I vowed to continue to match more students around school. It had been my biggest contribution to creating a more positive atmosphere at Clearview so far. And after the first few matches I'd done, I started to notice just how many people were wandering around lonely and single. And there were a multitude of excuses: fear of rejection, fear of commitment, fear of what others would think of them. My favorite people to match were the couples I could tell were perfect for each other but who just had *no* idea themselves. Those were the most fun to watch, because it was like a switch was going on in both of them as they looked at each other for the first time. Being witness to that instant love connection was like a high I couldn't quite explain, and I'd taken to going after my fix at least once a day since matching Asher and me.

Now there were dozens of new couples walking around campus hand in hand making googly eyes at each other, all because of me. Knowing how much good I was doing almost made up for what I was about to do in class.

Almost.

"Geez, talk about love being in the air," Abby said as we stood in front of her locker that morning. We surveyed the scene as nearly everyone walked by in various stages of coupledom. You could practically hear the cartoon birdies singing their songs of love as they fluttered overhead.

"Yeah," I said, not being able to hold back my smile. "It's like spring's sprung early."

"This isn't normal," she said, shaking her head.

"What's not normal?" Asher asked as he slid up to us and kissed me on the cheek before placing his arm around my neck.

Abby watched the exchange and rolled her eyes. "This love-fest. It's like suddenly every day is Valentine's Day. I've never seen anything like it."

"Maybe you've just never *noticed* it before," Asher said matter-of-factly. "Is it possible you're ready to join us on the highway of love too?"

"Yeah, right," she snorted. "The only guys I'm interested in are Ron Weasley and Peeta Mellark. If either of them is inter-ested, you can count me in."

"There's really no one around here that you could see your-self liking?" I asked, still unable to believe that there wasn't anyone here she'd ever crushed on. I hadn't thought about matching Abby before, but now that it was in my head, my interest was piqued. She deserved to find love and I was in the unique position to be able to give it to her.

"Are you kidding? Have you seen the male population at this school? They're like one chromosome away from being monkeys. And not the smart kind."

Or not.

"That Phil kid you're always talking to doesn't seem all that bad," Asher said.

"He's not, but it's still *Phil*. I mean, he's a good guy, funny in a self-deprecating kind of way, and not a total jerk-wad, but it would be like dating . . . you," she said, making a face. "Only, it wouldn't be illegal in most states and he has no magical skills whatsoever."

"And we'll end this conversation with a big 'ew,'" Asher said, shaking his head to clear it. He turned to me. "What do you have going on this morning?"

"Mr. Howard's history test."

"Ahhh, so we'll finally see if all the studying will pay off," Asher said. I thought I heard the slightest hint of sarcasm in his voice, but then he smiled. "Are you guys ready?"

"I think so."

"Well, considering you crammed all day yesterday, I'd think you'd have to be," he said.

I just nodded, wanting to change the subject.

"How about this," Asher continued. "If you pass, I'll take you out tonight, just the two of us, to celebrate."

I leaned over and kissed him square on the mouth. "Sounds like a plan."

The bell rang and everyone began to shuffle to their first classes. Asher and Abby said their good-byes before heading in the opposite direction, and I walked down the hallway toward Mr. Howard's.

When I was just a few steps away, an arm linked through mine and I gasped in surprise.

"Why so jumpy?" Eliza asked as she steered us into the classroom. "We're going to rock this test."

"Uh, yeah," I said, nodding. "And I'm not jumpy. Are you jumpy?"

I looked back to see that Wheatley was bringing up the rear like a bodyguard ready to tackle anyone who got close to us. He winked at me when I met his gaze and then his face went blank as we continued on into the classroom.

"Calm down," Eliza said just loudly enough for me to hear her. "You're acting like we're doing something wrong here."

"We *are* doing something wrong."

"Only if you choose to look at it that way," she said. "You know, you really need to learn to be more positive. Negative people tend to be less attractive. There have been studies on it."

I raised my eyebrows. "What studies?"

"I don't know the exact *names*. I just read it somewhere," she said, scooting me toward my seat before sitting down in the one behind me. I watched as Wheatley sat directly behind her. The only thing he had on him was a sad-looking pencil.

The room was still nearly empty, with just a few students seated and ready. Eliza leaned forward in her chair and whispered into my ear.

"What's the plan, captain?"

More students began to fill in now, as we neared the bell, and the noise levels rose around us. Without turning around, I whispered back, "Just fill out the test like usual, I'll take care of the rest later."

"You sure you got this?" I could hear the doubt in her voice, which only caused me more stress. Eliza wasn't one to ever worry. I'm sure it was something her trainer had told her was bad for her waistline. I realized this was the first time she'd ever depended on me for something and that meant I had control over one of the most powerful girls in school. The brief moment of satisfaction I felt gave me a surge of confidence I hadn't had before.

"No problem," I said as Mr. Howard walked in and pulled the stack of tests out of his bag and immediately began passing them out.

"You'll have forty-five minutes to complete the following test," he said as the papers were sent down each row. "Don't forget that the results will be worth thirty percent of your final grade for the semester. Keep your eyes on your own tests and no talking."

I looked down at the packet in front of me and flipped through all the pages quickly. The whole thing was multiple choice. I smiled, knowing this was going to be much easier than I'd expected.

I immediately started to go through the questions, circling the correct letters as I went. In order for my plan to work, I had to ace the test myself, which was only made possible by the fact that I'd studied my butt off all semester long. As I moved from one question to the next, I began to grow surer of the answers I was giving. When I finished, just four minutes before Mr. Howard was to call time, I knew I'd earned my A.

Which meant Wheatley and Eliza would too.

I closed my eyes and concentrated on the spell I'd memorized. Placing both my hands on the papers in front of me, I muttered the words with conviction. The tingling began in my fingertips and started to heat up my palms as the spell did its thing. I knew from the witches who'd shared the incantation online that my hands were acting as a sort of scanner, taking in the answers I'd given and holding on to them until I needed them again.

"All right, pencils down. Please pass your papers forward," Mr. Howard said, stepping out from behind his desk and heading to the far right of the classroom to start collecting.

My hand shot into the air and I reached behind my head for Eliza's and Wheatley's papers. Once I had them, I placed them both on my desk and said the words that would transfer my answers to their tests. Within seconds, I could see that their answers mirrored my own. To make sure Mr. Howard wouldn't become suspicious later, I zapped a few answers on both the papers back to their originals, so it wouldn't be obvious our tests were identical. Mr. Howard had just stepped in front of our row, and I quickly placed the sheets into the hands of the girl in front of me and looked around the classroom innocently.

I watched him take the tests from her and immediately place them back in his bag, snapping the flap into place with a little click. "You'll receive your grades at the beginning of class on Thursday," he said, sitting down behind his desk. "For some of you, this will be your last week of freedom before your parents ground you for the rest of the year. I suggest you enjoy it."

When the bell rang, we all gathered our things and made our way into the hall. Eliza waited a few seconds before pouncing on me.

"*Will* we be enjoying our week?" Eliza asked me slowly as we walked along.

"We're *definitely* enjoying our week," I said, giving her a grin.

She smiled back and then looked over at Wheatley, who grunted.

"How did it go?" Gigi asked as she and the others joined us in our walk toward the cafeteria. "Everything all set?"

"We're all set," I said, relieved to have the whole thing behind me now.

"Are you sure?" she asked me.

"Positive."

"Tell me, Brooklyn," Gigi said, finally stopping in her place and turning to look at me. Her icy blue eyes bored into mine, challenging me. "How are you planning to pull this off?"

I looked around the group, who all suddenly seemed to want to know the same thing. They looked at me expectantly as my mind raced to come up with an answer that would satisfy them.

"Come on, G, she said she's got it handled. Let the girl handle it," Camden said, putting his arm around his girlfriend's waist and pulling her forward. Gigi's mouth spread into a thin line, and she kept quiet. I appreciated Camden sticking up for me, but it wouldn't help me at all if I caused problems between the power couple.

"It's all right," I said, cutting in. "Mr. Howard spends at least a half hour every day after school speed walking around the track. Ms. Z. told me that he's embarrassed to work out in public but that he's determined to lose weight, so he settles for doing laps at school. I figure that will be more than enough time to get in, change the answers, and get out."

"What if he doesn't leave the tests behind or he locks them up?" Gigi asked. "What will you do then?"

I was surprised that she was grilling me so hard, considering that it wasn't even her grades that were in jeopardy. But I knew that if she wanted answers, she was sure as hell going to get them.

"Then I'll do whatever needs to be done," I answered.

Gigi grew quiet as we continued on down the hall. Finally, when she turned around to look at me, her face had softened. "I'm sorry, Brooklyn," she said sweetly. "I don't mean to be a pain, but this isn't just a test to us. . . . We're dealing with Eliza's and Wheatley's futures here. And we'll do whatever *we* need to to ensure that an Elite member gets what they deserve. Because if one of us fails, we all fail."

I nodded, letting her know that I understood.

"Just like when one of us succeeds, we all succeed," she said. "You'll see what I mean when we head up to my parents' house this weekend to celebrate all three of you passing Mr. Howard's history exam."

The others answered with hoots and sounds of excitement. I followed along behind them, glad that for the moment, I seemed to still be in their good graces.

Chapter Fifteen

"So . . . how did you do?" Asher asked as I let my bag fall to the sidewalk and took a seat next to him on the bench.

"Aced it, of course," I said, grinning and handing over my paper. He took a look at the big *A* written in bloodred ink across the top of the page and then gave me a high five.

"That's awesome!" he said. "Not that there was ever any question. I mean, if you know your stuff enough to tutor people, then you're going to pass. Speaking of, how did the others do?"

I was surprised to hear him ask about The Elite, let alone care how they did on the test. I shrugged and busied myself with opening my Diet Coke. After we'd gotten our test scores back in class and took a moment to celebrate our shared victory, I'd convinced The Elite that I needed to find Asher at the break. Especially considering what I needed to talk to him about. I hadn't planned on waiting until the last minute to talk to Asher about the beach, but we'd only just gotten the scores today, and I'd wanted to wait until I knew the trip was a done deal before bringing it up.

"Not as well as me, but they killed it," I said.

And they had. Well, *I* had on their behalf, but as far as everyone else knew, Eliza and Wheatley had passed with solid scores. So far no one had questioned anything, thank God.

"Guess all that studying really paid off, didn't it?" he said, leaning back and placing his arm on the bench behind my shoulders. "Maybe now we can get some alone time."

"Yeah," I said quietly. "Thanks for loaning me to them while we studied."

I leaned in and slowly gave him tiny kisses up the side of his face. He snuggled in closer to me, enjoying the PDA.

"Well, let's not make a habit of it, okay? I don't exactly like sharing you with anyone else, and those two can definitely afford to hire tutors," he said. "Tutors who *aren't* you."

I dropped my mouth open in mock shock. "Asher Astley, are you jealous of The Elite?"

"Not at all," he said. "I just think that your time could be better spent hanging out with me."

"We spend time together," I said defensively, not looking to get into an argument.

"Brooklyn, you're already spending all your time with them here at school," Asher said, sounding frustrated. "You ate lunch with them all this week, you're linked at the hip between classes, and I don't even see you at your locker in the morning anymore."

Hoping to salvage this conversation, I took ahold of his hand. "Well, what if I told you that there was a way we could do both. Hang out with The Elite *and* spend time together?"

He gave me a look that said, "Yeah, right."

"I promise," I said. I made a cross over my heart, kissed my fingers, and then placed them on his lips. "Look, part of the reason it was so important for Wheatley and Eliza to pass this test was because Gigi holds this big beach bash every year at her parents' summer home at the shore. They invite everyone who's anyone—you know, all the influentials—to come and mingle. Anyway, they've invited me to come with them this weekend and said that I could bring you with me! We'll crash at Gigi's house and it would be a great chance for us to be *alone* together for once."

I raised my eyebrows suggestively but only succeeded in making Asher laugh.

"Look, you know I'd jump at the chance to spend some time with you, Brooklyn, but I'd hardly call a party at the beach with dozens of strangers and a group of power-hungry teenagers a chance for us to be alone," he said.

"But it *could* be. We could go off on our own during the day and spend our nights glued to each other's sides," I insisted. "Besides, Gigi said that there won't be any parentals on the premises, which means we could probably have a slumber party."

I leaned in toward him and placed my head on his shoulder. I tried my best to stay cool, even though my heart was beating a million miles a minute. I wasn't used to flirting at this magnitude and had no idea if I was pulling it off. "Don't you want to spend the night with me, Asher?"

It was practically torture as I waited for him to respond. What if he said no? What if the matching I'd done had already worn off and he'd decided that he no longer liked me enough to be stuck with me all weekend long? If he rejected me now, I might actually drop dead of embarrassment and humiliation.

I started to brainstorm ways I could take the offer back without actually sounding like a total loser, when he cleared his throat and began to talk.

"I would like nothing more than to spend the entire weekend with you, Brooklyn," he said, reaching down and tilting my chin up to face him. "But you know I'm not really into The Elite. I'll run it by my parents, though, and I'll see if it's even an option. Can I get back to you?"

My heart sank. Even though he hadn't exactly said no, it felt like it. I figured that bribing him with the possibility of spending the night with me would've been enough to get him to agree. I mean, weren't guys supposed to have tunnel vision when it came to the possibility of sex? And yet he was still only saying maybe.

"Don't look so upset," Asher said, flashing me one of his smiles that never failed to make my heart melt. He quickly looked around to make sure that we were alone, and then with a swipe of his hand and a few choice words, a flower from the nearby walkway pulled away from the earth and floated over to me, hanging in midair until I grabbed it and held it in my hand. "Look, I promise, I'll think about it, okay?"

"Yeah, okay," I said, leaning forward to smell the flower. "But we're leaving tomorrow, so I'll need to know soon." The sweet aroma filled my nose and made me momentarily forget that I didn't get what I'd come there for.

"You sure you're not missing anything in PE?" Ms. Zia asked later that day as she loaded my arms with boxes and bags and then grabbed a handful herself. Pushing open the door with her foot, she waited as I moved through, and then we walked together in the direction of the parking lot.

"Nope. We were supposed to be playing handball, but it's not really my game," I said, trying my best to see through all the stuff Ms. Z. had piled in my arms. I could barely see where I was walking and couldn't help but worry I might run into something at any moment. And that would've been disastrous. "I would much rather be doing manual labor than dodging flying balls any day."

Ms. Z. laughed and led the way to her SUV, which was parked in the first row of the faculty parking lot. I heard her slow down and did the same, and listened to the car beep as the doors were unlocked. I carefully placed everything down on the concrete and stood there slightly out of breath. My arms were burning from the weight of the boxes and my legs were a little quivery. I was instantly grateful that I'd worn flats to school.

"Well, thanks again. There's just so much stuff to take home with me for the community sale," she said. "People really pitched in this year. I think it's going to be our best effort yet."

Each year, Ms. Zia helped to organize the school's contributions to the community-wide garage sale to benefit the Celiac Disease Foundation. Her cousin was diagnosed with the disease when she was only nine years old, and Ms. Z. had become a big supporter of the foundation. She'd gotten me involved during my freshman year and I'd helped out ever since. At the event, volunteers sold donated items. Booths were also set up to give more information on celiac disease and research, and we sold gluten-free treats. Besides it being for a good cause, I always met really interesting and inspiring people, and always had fun doing it.

"We definitely got a ton of stuff," I said, peering inside one of the bags of donated items.

"That's why it's going to be so important to get extra help this year," she said, picking up some boxes and stacking them in the back of her car. "I can't tell you how grateful I am to have you as my right-hand gal. And speaking of wingmen, do you think you could ask Asher to come and help for a few hours this weekend too? The more people, the quicker we'll be able to set up. And volunteering can be sexy."

"Okay, now you're stretching, Ms. Z.—volunteering is *so* not sexy. Satisfying, maybe, but not sexy," I said. Then something she'd said made me stop short. "Wait, did you say this weekend?"

I'd been so completely caught up with The Elite and the stuff going on between Asher and me that I'd forgotten all about the fund-raiser.

"Yep."

"No, no, no, no. It can't be this weekend," I said, pacing around the parking lot. "Is it possible it's actually next weekend instead?"

"Nope," Ms. Zia said, giving me a weird look. "It's definitely this weekend. The weekend's the same every year, Brooklyn. You know that."

And I did. I just hadn't been paying attention and had completely forgotten. I let out a groan and handed her the last box before sitting down on the ground.

"I'm not going to be here this weekend," I said, not believing this was happening to me.

"What?" Ms. Z. asked, and dropped the box she'd been carrying. Something in it broke but she didn't bother looking inside to see what it was.

"I sort of already made plans," I said, avoiding looking her in the eyes. But I knew what I would see. Disappointment and frustration.

"Is it something you can get out of?" she asked hopefully, trying to do damage control. "Maybe if I talked to your parents about it, I could get them to understand how much I need you there—"

"It's not with my parents, Ms. Z."

"Then what is it?"

I looked down at my feet. "I'm going out of town with Gigi and the others," I said, as if I were confessing some big sin. "They sort of have this annual networking thing and it's really important that I be there."

I purposely avoided using the word "party," because I was sure she wouldn't be able to see the importance in my skipping the fund-raiser to go.

"You're kidding me, right?"

"Well . . . no," I stammered. "It's sort of a big deal to be invited and there're going to be a ton of really great opportunities to meet people who can help my future career and stuff."

"Your career?" Ms. Zia asked, raising her eyebrows at me. "Brooklyn, you're a junior in high school. You won't even have a career for another five years at the earliest. It's only a weekend—it's not going to make or break your future."

I blinked as if I'd been smacked. It wasn't like Ms. Z. to be short with me. In fact, as soon as she said it, she immediately looked guilty and crossed over to me. "I'm sorry, Brooklyn. That wasn't fair," she said, collecting herself. "And I shouldn't have just assumed that you were going to help out again."

"You know I would've, but it's just bad timing," I muttered. It wasn't the best excuse, but it was all I had. First off, I'd already told Gigi and the others that I was going for the weekend. There was a chance that Asher might be coming with me. And if I could get him all to myself, maybe I could finally find out where the spell ended and his feelings began. No, I absolutely *had* to go. Ms. Z. was just going to have to survive without me.

"Sure, Brooklyn," she said. "I understand." Then she continued to pack up the car, this time in silence.

The guilt began to creep over me until I couldn't handle it

anymore. "Look, maybe I can try to find someone to help you out on Saturday. Asher's sister, Abby, is really cool. And there are these students that will do anything The Elite tell them to. I bet I can get them to work the event, if you just give me a chance to talk to them—"

"That's not necessary, Brooklyn," Ms. Zia cut in. "I don't want to bully other students into helping."

Um, okay. "It wouldn't be bullying, it would just be *asking*. And I thought you needed volunteers? I'm just trying to help you out."

"By getting others to take over your commitment," she finished.

"But Abby and the others—" I started.

"Look, Abby's great, but she's not you," she said, looking at me sadly.

"Why does it matter whether it's me or someone else help-ing, as long as somebody's there?" I asked, looking at her in confusion. "I'm sorry, but I just don't get why this is such a big deal."

"I know. That's why it's so upsetting," Ms. Z. said, shutting the back door of her car and walking toward the school.

"Ms. Z.! What's going on?"

I really had no idea what had just happened and wondered if I'd missed something important here.

"Look, Brooklyn, it's not like I can't handle things this weekend on my own. I mean, there will be other volunteers there," she said, spinning around to look at me. "It's you I'm worried about."

"What are you talking about?"

"Last year you looked forward to this fund-raiser all year, and now you've forgotten when it is. You cared about celiac disease research and always did whatever you could to raise money to try and find a cure. You used to *want* to spend time together. Don't you see? You've *changed*, Brooklyn. You never would've missed this weekend before. You probably would've reworked your entire schedule around to make sure you could be there. And now, what? A weekend of socializing is more important than finding a cure? This isn't the same Brooklyn I used to know."

Tears welled up in my eyes. I wasn't exactly happy about the idea of missing the fund-raiser, but the way Ms. Z. was describing it, I was just about the most selfish person in the entire world. How could she stand there and say such hurtful things about me when she knew how badly I wanted this? And what about all the good things I'd been doing around school lately? Not that she even noticed.

"That's not fair," I said, not loudly but as forcefully as I could muster. "I do plenty of things to help other people. In fact, that's practically *all* I've been doing the past couple of weeks."

"Really?" she answered, her voice becoming soft again. "Well, I'd love to hear about it, if you wouldn't mind sharing."

Of course she'd ask me to elaborate on the two things that I couldn't really tell her about. I had to answer, though; otherwise she was going to think I was a liar on top of everything else.

"Um, well, I've been tutoring some kids in history in my spare time," I said. "They were having a tough time, so I volunteered to help them with this test we were having."

"You helped them cram, you mean?" she corrected.

"Yeah. Well, anyway, they got As, which means their GPAs are safe for now," I said, crossing my arms in front of my chest.

"Well, that's really good of you, Brooklyn—"

"I've joined the Interact Club," I cut in. "So I'm going to be doing a lot of volunteer work over the next couple of months."

"Just not this weekend," Ms. Z. said under her breath.

"And I've been helping to connect like-minded people, all for the sake of love," I said, pointing out no one in particular. "And what bigger service is there than helping others find love?"

"True, but—"

"Haven't you noticed there are a lot more couples walking around school lately? People holding hands, confessing their feelings, being extra mushy-gushy? I'm the one who helped them find each other."

"I *have* noticed," Ms. Zia said. "And while that's certainly a noble goal, are you sure you're qualified to do so? Coincidentally, I've seen an insurgence of students come through my office lately that are all heartbroken because of failed romances."

"What?" I asked, totally floored by the news. I guess between everything that had been going on, I hadn't been paying close enough attention to the couples I'd matched. Never mind. I was sure I'd still done some good. I had to remember that until I came along with my mojo, no couple had a chance. Now at least they'd been given a shot.

"I don't want to argue with you, Brooklyn," Ms. Zia said, holding open the door to the school. "I just want you to think about the decisions you've been making and see if they're the right ones. Are you really becoming the person you've always wanted to be?"

I didn't answer her. I was annoyed that she was pointing out all my faults—but the truth was, I didn't know the answer myself.

Chapter Sixteen

It was everything I could do not to call or text Asher every minute to try and find out what he'd decided. Only, I didn't want to be *that girl*. The one who hounds her boyfriend for an answer before he's ready to give it. Not only was it annoying, but I'm pretty sure it would give the impression that I'm needy.

Instead, I kept my mouth shut and let my mind run in circles as I analyzed every interaction I had with him. He mentioned that he wants to be around me all the time? That clearly meant he was coming with me. He wasn't at my locker after class? He must want to stay home and lay low. The whole situation was like torture and the only thing I had going for me was that it was Friday, which meant time was running out for him to decide.

Today I was going to know what was up one way or another.

As I dug through my locker, trying to figure out how to bring up the topic to Asher, who was chattering on about something his dad had said at dinner the night before, The Elite showed up out of nowhere, interrupting our conversation.

"Hey, guys!" I said, surprised to see them. I grabbed a few books from my locker and shoved them into my bag, slamming the metal door behind me. "What's up?"

"We were just talking about this weekend," Rhodes said, leaning up against the bed of lockers. "You guys want to grab a ride up with us? We're taking two cars."

"You *are* coming, right, Asher?" Eliza asked, placing her hand on her hip and crossing her legs at the ankles.

Here it was. The moment of truth, and I didn't even have to bring it up. How convenient was it to have nosy friends?

"Um, actually, I think I'm going to sit this one out," he said.

My heart sank. I'd so been hoping Asher would say the opposite. It was hard to hide my total and utter disappointment.

"You aren't going to come?" I asked, looking up at his face. I couldn't help it. It felt like he was rejecting *me*. And on top of that, he was doing it in front of the most popular people in the school. What would they think of the fact that I couldn't even get my own boyfriend to spend time with me?

I bet Gigi had never been rejected before.

"I don't think so," he said.

I looked around at the others, embarrassed that they were finding out at the same time I was.

"Too bad. Well, maybe next time, then," Camden said, completely blasé about Asher not coming. He motioned for the others to follow him. They did as their commander requested, and with one final look at the two of us, the pretty posse disappeared down the hallway.

"You're seriously not coming?" I asked him once they were gone. I couldn't keep the hurt out of my voice anymore. As much as I didn't want him to see me as the nagging, clingy potential girlfriend, I couldn't help it. I was upset.

"I told you I wasn't really all that into the idea, Brooklyn," he said, looking me in the eye.

"Yeah, but I thought maybe you'd do it anyway. For me," I said, pouting. "I mean, if you don't want to hang out with me, then that's fine . . . just be honest."

"You know it's not like that," he said, sighing. "I love spending time with you, and if it was just the two of us, I'd be there in a heartbeat. But it's *them*."

"But you wouldn't have to spend any time with them," I countered. "Just with me. I promise."

"Look, it's not just that," he said, leaning his head back against the lockers. He closed his eyes as he collected his thoughts. "I've got some stuff going on at home."

"What stuff?" I asked, sounding a little more accusatory than I'd intended. But if Asher heard it, he didn't let on.

"My parents have been . . . fighting lately."

"So? Adults fight all the time," I said, still thinking he was looking for an excuse to get out of the weekend.

"Not mine."

I could hear the worry in his voice and took a step closer to him even though I was upset. I placed my hand on his arm, hoping it would give him some comfort.

"You can tell me, Asher," I said quietly.

He looked at me and shook his head. "I don't know," he said. "You met them. They're, like, the perfect couple. They've always been like newlyweds; they joke, finish each other's sentences. They still go out on date nights, for God's sake."

"So, what's the problem?"

"Lately I've been catching them bickering. Like, I'll walk in and they'll be talking in hushed tones and then they stop when they see me. It's like they don't want me to know what they're talking about."

"Maybe they don't. Some stuff is just personal," I said.

"But our family's always been close. My parents don't hide things from Abby and me. Why would they start now, unless it was something big?"

"I don't know, Ash," I said. "They seemed fine when I met them."

"You wouldn't understand," he said, shaking his head and starting to walk off.

"What does that mean?" I asked, following behind him.

"It just means—well, your family is all about the secrets, aren't they? Your parents have kept a lot of your magical side from you over the years, right?" he said. "They won't even tell you what coven they descended from. Our family's not like that. We tell each other *everything*."

"Obviously not."

Asher stopped walking but didn't turn around to face me. I had to skid to a stop in order to keep from running into him. We were both silent for a minute.

"Don't be pissed just because I don't want to hang out with the Clueless Crew all weekend," he said. "Some of us have more important things to do."

"What does that mean?" I asked, getting angry.

"It means, this pursuit of popularity is such a waste of time," he said.

"It's not a waste of time," I argued, upset that he would say such a thing. I didn't need him to understand why I was doing what I was doing. I just wanted him to accept that it was important to me. "And if you cared about me, you would come with me, even if you don't like Gigi and the others."

"Are you hearing yourself? I just told you something's going on with my family and you still want me to ditch them for some stupid party with people I can't stand," he said. "I never thought you could be this selfish."

It was the most hurtful thing Asher had ever said to me, and in that moment I wondered if the matching spell had officially worn off. I took a second to compose myself but felt the tears building and my throat tighten.

"Well, if that's how you feel, why are you with me?" I asked without thinking.

Asher opened his mouth and then closed it again, thinking better of whatever he was going to say. He was silent for a minute. Finally he took a step away from me and spoke.

"I hope you have fun this weekend," he said, and took another step back.

I couldn't ignore the anger and hurt that was emanating from him right now, and my stomach instantly tied itself into knots. I knew I'd crossed the line. I hadn't intended to, I was just so caught off guard by the fact that he wouldn't be going with me to Gigi's that I was trying to do whatever I could to convince him to change his mind.

And now he was mad and practically pushing me to go.

"Asher, I'm sorry . . ."

"It's fine," he said.

But we both knew it wasn't.

"Look, we'll talk when you get back, okay?" He didn't wait for an answer before walking away, his messenger bag slung haphazardly over his shoulder.

My eyes started to fill with tears as I watched him disappear. Not only was I going on this trip with The Elite without the guy I liked, but now I wasn't even sure if he would be there when I got back.

★

After school, I ran home and packed my bags for Gigi's. My parents had been surprisingly cool about me going to stay with my new friends for the weekend. I think it was mostly because I'd pressed upon them the fact that hanging out with civilians was what *normal* teenagers did. They had sleepovers, talked about boys, went to parties. As soon as I told them there would be no magic used that weekend, they'd automatically agreed. They hadn't even asked whether Gigi's parents would be there. Nope, it was all, "None of them are witches? Go ahead! Have fun! Don't get arrested." In their defense, though, this was the first time ever that I'd asked to spend the night at a friend's house, so it was a first for all of us. But still, it appeared as if magic was the only thing they planned on being strict about.

What hadn't been easy was getting packed. I had no idea what to bring with me. I knew there was going to be a party, but I wasn't sure if it was a formal affair or if we'd be wearing shorts and flip-flops. And Eliza was no help either. When I'd asked her about the dress code, she'd just said, "I dunno, bring some nice clothes. Nothing too hoochie." Not like that would've even been a possibility, since I didn't own any hoochie-style clothes. I ended up bringing way too much for just a weekend away, but given how important it was for me to make a good impression, I felt like it was better to be overprepared than underprepared. Based on the size of the girls' suitcases when they came to pick me up, I realized that they must have been thinking the same thing.

"Hey, golden girl!" Eliza called out the window as she and Gigi pulled up to the curb outside my house.

The crew had decided to split up into "hos and bros" cars, the guys taking off first to make sure the place was stocked and ready by the time we got there. Camden had been there so many times before, he knew exactly where they kept the key to the house and would let the guys in. That meant it was just me, Eliza, and Gigi in the other car. Eliza was driving, which was a little scary considering she'd learned to drive from a stunt man on one of her dad's films. And she drove like it too. I'd never been in a car with her before, but after she took the first two turns like she was in the Grand Prix, I learned to close my eyes and hope for the best.

Gigi herself didn't seem to be too concerned either. In fact, she was somehow able to do her nails while on the road, a feat I never would've thought possible in that car. I watched in awe as she applied two coats of light pink polish and then draped her hands out the open window to dry.

"So, what's with Asher?" she asked, looking back at me over the passenger seat.

"What do you mean?" I asked. Asher was the last thing I wanted to talk about.

"Well, he didn't come this weekend and he never seems to be totally comfortable when we invite him places," she said. "And then there's the fact that he refused to join The Elite."

"Yeah, what's up with that?" Eliza asked, her eyes on the road.

"There's nothing up," I said, wishing desperately that they'd change the subject. I still hadn't gotten over the argument we'd had earlier at school and was feeling angry over what he'd said and scared that we wouldn't survive it. "He just couldn't come."

"Seemed like he didn't *want* to come."

I shook my head a little too emphatically. "No, he wanted to hang out with me this weekend, but he's got some stuff to do back home."

"Ahhh, family problems. Gotcha," Eliza said. "That's so normal. You should tell him to go see a therapist. Ours was so helpful after Daddy fired my old nanny Esmerelda when I was eleven."

"He doesn't need a therapist," I said.

"There's nothing wrong with getting some help," Gigi cut in.

"I agree . . . if there *were* a problem," I said, starting to get worked up again.

"Look, Brookie, we're just watching out for you," Eliza said matter-of-factly. "We figured that if it's not family issues, then it's got to be that he just didn't want to come. And that means it's either because he didn't want to be around *us*—in which case, he should have done it for you anyway—or something's going on between *you two*. Either way, it doesn't really look good."

"I don't want to talk about it," I mumbled, and looked out the window.

"Brooklyn," Gigi said evenly. "We really want this weekend to be about getting to know each other better. Especially you. If you're going to be a part of this group, we need to be able to trust you. And we aren't going to be able to do that if you won't open up to us. If you can't do that, I don't see how we're going to all be able to be friends."

What she was saying made sense, but I also knew that I couldn't tell her or Eliza the whole truth about Asher and his family. Not without spilling all of my secrets as well. And being that he was so private with his personal life, I knew I couldn't tell them about his parents fighting. Asher would never want that to get out.

So I gave them the only thing I could. Information on me.

"Okay, the truth is," I started, "Asher had to stay behind for a family thing and I sort of got mad at him for not coming, and then he freaked out. I'm just not sure he likes me as much as I like him."

"Ahhhh, the age-old question: Does he like me or doesn't he?" Gigi said, nodding.

"You'll drive yourself crazy trying to figure that one out," Eliza said.

Even though I knew it wasn't the whole story of why Asher hadn't come that weekend, it still felt really good to be able to talk about it. To people who actually seemed to understand.

"If he liked me, wouldn't he do whatever he had to to come and be with me?" I asked, truly curious to hear their answer.

"How do you know he didn't?" Gigi asked, in a moment very unlike her.

"It just seems like he could have done more to try to come if he really wanted to," I said, crossing my arms over my chest.

"Has he told you he likes you yet?" Eliza asked.

"Well, yeah . . ."

"And you guys haven't gone all the way yet?"

"What are we, in middle school?" I asked, laughing at her choice of words. "And of course not. We've only been seeing each other for a few weeks."

"Then he can't just be trying to get rid of you because he got what he wanted," Eliza said.

"Guys actually *do* that?"

"Most of them do."

"With the exception of a select few—Camden being one of them," Gigi said.

"So he bailed on this weekend," Eliza said with a wave of her hand. "Big whoop. I don't get why you're stressing."

They both seemed so blasé about it that I began to think maybe I was being a bit silly. Like, maybe I'd overreacted.

"I guess I'm still sort of wondering where we stand," I said, picking at my cuticles. "Sure, he may like me now, but will he tomorrow? And why doesn't he want to change his schedule around to be able to spend time with me?"

"You guys just need to have 'the talk,'" Eliza said, honking loudly at the car in front of us, which was going slower than she would have liked. With a quick glance for oncoming traffic, she stepped on the gas and started to speed up. When we were a foot away from hitting the person's back bumper, Eliza jerked the steering wheel to the left and then passed the car.

"You don't think it's a little too early for that?" I asked, pressing my body against the backseat and trying to ignore the panic that was building up inside my stomach.

"Not at all," Gigi said. "Camden and I nailed down what we were to each other in the first two weeks after we met. I think it's important to establish boundaries and rules from the very beginning if you want to maintain control over the situation."

"Don't guys hate talking about that stuff?" I asked.

"Only if it means they won't get what they want," Eliza said. "Like, if by telling them you're looking for a relationship, it's going to mean they no longer have a no-strings-attached makeout buddy, then yeah—they won't want to have that conversation. And the longer they can put off the conversation the better."

"But if they want something more than just fooling around, the convo won't matter," Gigi said.

I grew quiet as I thought about what they were saying. It was true, I was constantly wondering what it was that Asher and I were doing. Were we boyfriend and girlfriend? Were we just hanging out? Or like Gigi was saying, did he want something more? The truth was, because of the matching spell, I had no idea where we stood and I was starting to think it was about time I found out. Then again, all of this could be a moot point considering the fight we'd had before I left.

"Brooklyn, you're hot and smart and if you play your cards right, you'll be one of us one day," Eliza said. "You deserve to know whether he feels the same way about you."

What she was saying made sense and I wanted to believe it was true. But could I actually do it? Could I actually have that conversation with him, even if it meant I might not get the answer I wanted?

"But don't think about any of that this weekend," Gigi said, breaking into my thoughts. "You're a free agent until you two decide otherwise, so just focus on having fun! That's what this whole thing's about. I'm going to introduce you to so many people at the party, you'll be glad Asher stayed home."

I wasn't so sure about that, but I was willing to give it a try.

Chapter Seventeen

The first thing I thought about when I woke up the next day was Asher. I'd had a hard time falling asleep the night before because I was replaying our conversation over and over again. The last time I'd looked at the clock, it was three in the morning. Now I was exhausted and stressed.

I looked down at the cell I'd fallen asleep gripping—just in case Asher decided to text me—and clicked it on to check it. No new messages. No missed phone calls. No voice mails. My stomach felt sick and it wasn't just because of my lack of sleep. I worried that I wouldn't be able to have a fun time with things the way they were with Asher.

I opened a text and started to write, but then stopped and erased it. Sure, I'd said some bad things, but so had he. And he'd been the one who'd said I was selfish. Messaging him now would mean admitting I was wrong about what I'd said to him. And there was no guarantee he'd want to talk to me. My weekend would be really ruined if he didn't respond. Tossing my cell on my bed, I threw the covers back and opened the door to my room.

The house was silent, so I made sure to be quiet as I closed the door again. I pulled on my swimsuit and a pair of shorts and wandered into the bathroom to brush my teeth and get washed up. I had no idea what time it was, but the sun was already beating in through the windows and all I could think about was getting down to the beach.

Padding to the kitchen, I saw that thankfully there was already a pot of coffee brewing on the counter and I poured myself a cup. Too much caffeine made me jittery but I could tell I was going to need the jolt since it was going to be a long day. I filled it to the top and then added some milk and Splenda. I took a sip and sighed loudly, perfectly content.

Hearing voices, I followed them out the back door and onto the porch, where Eliza, Wheatley, and Rhodes were all lounging around, eating breakfast and drinking coffee.

"Ahhh, Sleeping Beauty finally awakes," Eliza said, gesturing widely with her hands.

"What time is it?" I asked

"Almost eleven thirty," Rhodes said, his Ray-Bans shielding his eyes in style. "You damn near slept the whole day."

"I can't believe I slept that long!" I exclaimed, taking another sip and then sitting down in the empty chair beside Eliza.

I looked hungrily at the elaborate spread in front of me. Plates of fruit, pastries, bagels, bacon, salmon, and cream cheese lay in piles across the table. My stomach growled involuntarily.

"Can I?" I asked no one in particular.

"Go for it," Eliza said. "You're going to need the fuel for tonight. You thought last night went late? Our beach parties are epic and you're practically the guest of honor."

"Hope you're ready to drink up," Wheatley said in a rare moment of speech.

I grabbed a blueberry muffin and pulled back the paper lining. Taking a big bite, I chewed thoughtfully as the sugar hit my system. Then I shook my head.

"Oh, I don't drink," I said.

"You will tonight," Rhodes said.

I frowned but didn't respond. It wasn't just that I didn't drink; I'd *never* drank alcohol before. To do that, I would've had to have the opportunity, and that was taken care of by the fact that, until a few weeks ago, I hadn't had any friends my own age and therefore was never invited to parties where people were drinking. For a while, I'd even questioned whether teenagers really partied that much in real life. I sort of thought maybe it was something that TV and movies perpetuated. And it wasn't like my vanilla parents kept booze in the house either.

Even though I wanted to be accepted by The Elite and was eager to do as they did, drinking wasn't at the top of my to-do list.

"Please tell me you're not one of those goody-goodies who doesn't drink, doesn't lie, blah, blah, blah," Eliza said like she was talking about something repulsive.

"I'm not a goody-goody," I said, thinking about what they'd say if they knew I was a witch.

"Oh, good," she said, relieved. "Those people are so *boring*! I totally knew you weren't like that, Brookie!"

"I just don't get the point," I said, looking out at the beach.

Eliza snorted. "Of partying?"

"Um, because it's fun?" Wheatley said. His eyes were closed, but he was clearly not asleep. His shirt was off and his chest was developing a brown sheen. He may have stopped playing sports, but he hadn't lost his athletic build, that was for sure.

"And because *you* become more fun," Eliza said seriously. "I promise. All that uptightness will melt away and you'll be totally awesome to be around."

"You think I'm uptight?" I asked, my face starting to burn with embarrassment.

"You just seem stressed out a lot of the time," she said, sipping orange juice out of a champagne flute. "Like with all that Asher stuff. A little liquid courage will do you some good. Loosen you up. Besides, that's sort of what this crowd does."

"Mmm-hmm," I said, not committing one way or the other.

"Tonight's going to be so much fun!" Eliza said, and started to clap her hands together like a cheerleader at a pep rally.

"Why the standing O?" a voice asked behind us.

I turned to find Gigi and Camden walking up the beach stairs. They were both wearing workout clothes. Camden was in black shorts with the shirt he'd ditched hanging out the back. Gigi looked like she could've been on the cover of *Shape* magazine, sporting a pair of spandex shorts and a bright pink sports bra. Both were glistening with sweat but appeared to be only slightly out of breath.

I bet they worked out every day, while I, on the other hand, preferred to exercise by nontraditional means. Like walking to and from my car or speed-shopping.

"We were just talking about tonight and getting our drink on," Rhodes said.

"Speaking of, I need you two here later to meet the caterers when they come," Gigi said, stretching out her quads.

"There are going to be caterers?" I asked, surprised to hear this. Weren't high school parties all kegs and loud music?

"Of course," Gigi said, laughing. "This isn't a *kegger*, so one can't get by with *normal* accommodations. The people invited have a certain . . . expectation of living. You'll see. But pace yourself, Brooklyn, it's going to be a long night."

"So I've heard," I said.

"Let's go lay out on the beach," Eliza said, smacking me

on the arm before standing up. "I need a little tint for tonight. And you can run lines with me for my next audition."

"Okay," I said, getting up and following her toward the stairs.

"You coming, G?"

Gigi peeled off her spandex to reveal a tiny bikini that barely covered her perfectly smooth butt. Nobody batted an eye as she stripped down and I fought to keep my surprise under control.

"I'm going to jump in first and then I'll meet you back in a few," she said.

"I'll go with," Camden said, raising his eyebrows at her.

They both ran ahead of us, racing toward the crashing waves.

"Disgusting, isn't it?" Eliza asked as we watched them frolic in the water. "It's like watching a music video."

Beside me, Eliza pulled her shirt over her head and stripped down to what was practically a thong before lying down on a lounge chair. She untied the straps to her bikini and seconds later was lying topless beside me.

"Yep," I said. "Just like a music video."

"What time are people getting here?" I asked, swiping gloss across my lips and puckering up in front of the mirror. We'd been up in the master bathroom for nearly ninety minutes and Eliza and Gigi were just putting the finishing touches on their looks. Part of the beauty of my magical makeover was that I didn't have to spend a lot of time getting ready; it had only taken me about a half hour to complete hair and makeup and that was taking my time. The rest of it was spent chatting with the girls about regular stuff: boys, makeup, TV shows, gossip, future careers. It was exactly how I imagined having girlfriends would be. Of course, the conversation turned to which

TV stars Eliza had made out with at acting camp, and career talk bordered on corporate takeovers of billion-dollar companies, so maybe it wasn't so typical after all. But still, for the first time since this had all begun, it seemed like I was actually part of their group. I belonged. And it felt good.

I was still upset that Asher wasn't there with me and had to admit that I'd been checking my phone every five minutes for the text from him apologizing for what he'd said and begging me to forgive him. About a half hour ago, I'd given up, and my feelings gave way to anger. And to add insult to injury, I'd made the mistake of going on Facebook and saw that some students had posted pictures from the celiac disease fund-raiser online. Everyone looked like they were having such a good time, especially Ms. Z. She seemed to be in every photo, grinning from ear to ear. Looks like she didn't need me after all.

Well, I wasn't going to let either of them ruin my weekend. I was going to have fun, whether they liked it or not.

"Oh, people started to arrive a half hour ago," Gigi said, her mouth parted slightly as she applied another coat of mascara.

"Shouldn't we get down there, then?" I asked, standing up and walking toward the door.

"They'll wait," she said with a wave of her hand. "Besides, the guys are down there schmoozing for now. A girl should always be late to a party. It establishes the idea that it hasn't really started until you get there."

I nodded, seeing her point but thinking it was actually a little rude. Oh well. Gigi and Eliza definitely knew this crowd better than I did. I'd rather take my cues from them than make a wrong move on my own.

"Now let us look at you," Eliza said, motioning for me to stand up. I did as I was told and tried to strike a pose like I was on the red carpet. I'm pretty sure I looked ridiculous, but they didn't give me a hard time about it.

However, earlier had been a different story. When I'd taken everything out of my suitcase and laid it on my bed for them to scrutinize, they'd decided nothing I'd brought was suitable for the party. So I'd been lent a pale pink midthigh-length dress from Gigi's mother's closet. Apparently we were the same size and her mom did not dress her age.

It had a delicate top, fitted right underneath my boobs for ultimate cleavage and held up by two of the most frail-looking strings I'd ever seen. I'd asked Gigi what the chances were of a wardrobe malfunction, and she'd said that the dress was Gucci and practically indestructible. Starting at the waist, delicate feathers hung down, giving the illusion of constant movement, almost like the dress was alive. With it on, I couldn't help but feel like a real-life fairy-tale princess.

The two had allowed me to wear the pair of Jessica Simpson heels I'd brought with me on the condition that I kept them on all night and never took them off my feet. The heels gave me a boost of about five inches and I'd never worn them before, so I had no idea if this was a feat I could actually agree to or not. But what choice did I have, really?

My hair had been pulled into a loose side pony, with romantic tendrils escaping to frame my face. My makeup was flawless and I smelled like Chanel. I looked beyond amazing. Possibly even better than Eliza and Gigi, though I never would've told them that.

Whereas I'd gone princess fairy tale with my look, Eliza had decided on biker chic, tucking herself into a leather-looking dress, one shoulder bare and the other held by a stringy strap that tied in the middle of her back. She'd added in thin, glittery hair extensions that made her hair reflect light from every angle.

Gigi was more understated but couldn't have been described as plain in any way. She was wearing a navy blue strapless Marc Jacobs, fitted perfectly to her body. At the sides of her hips were pockets, parts of which were turned out, revealing a silk pin-striped pattern. To pull the look together, she wore a matching necktie around her shoulders, with a collar to give a sort of masculine power vibe to it all. If anyone but her wore it, it would have been questionable, but with Gigi, it was runway ready.

"I approve," Gigi said finally, taking ahold of my hand and twirling me around in a circle. "A little Barbie's Dream House, but it looks good on you."

"Thanks." I think.

"Okay, girls," she said, walking over to the door and pulling it open. "Let's not keep everyone waiting."

"Any longer, at least," Eliza said, giggling, and followed her out.

As soon as we descended the stairs, we got lost in a sea of air-kisses and greetings. Each person was more beautiful and perfect than the last, and every one of them was clamoring to have face time with us. It was clear to me then that The Elite didn't just exist at Clearview; their reach was much wider than I'd realized. Apparently there was a whole social scene they all belonged to—made up of their parents' friends' kids, socialites, wealthy teenagers, and others who were equally important.

And just like at school, they ran this world too.

"Brooklyn, have you met Prince Rajesh?"

"A prince? Like for real?" I asked, thinking it was a joke.

"Yes, although I'd prefer that you call me Raj," the kid said, and put his hand out to shake mine. He was dressed in black linen pants and an airy white button-down shirt. He didn't look at all like what I thought a prince would look like, though

I'd never met one before, so how would I know? How were you even supposed to greet a prince? What was customary? I hadn't been paying attention when Eliza said hello to him, so I couldn't copy her.

"It's nice to meet you, Raj," I said, doing an awkward curtsy and bowing my head at the same time.

"Er . . . to you as well," he said, looking at me funny before walking away to join another group.

"Madeline, this is Brooklyn. She's superfab and has some killer moves," Gigi said, pulling over a petite blonde with pink streaks in her hair. The name and the hair collided in my head and I realized where I recognized her from. "You should really ask her to show you some of them. . . . They could be good for your next tour. Or if another one of your backup dancers heads off to rehab again and you need a stand-in, Brooklyn would totally be good to help."

"Me? Dance? Onstage?" I asked, my voice little more than a squeak. I hadn't danced since the Macarena was popular and certainly didn't have the moves Gigi was inferring I had. And the others hadn't seen me bust any kind of moves. Now there was a pop star looking at me curiously, like I was an *America's Best Dance Crew* member. I had no idea what they were talking about.

"Oh, she's so modest," Eliza said, leaning in to whisper something to her. "We'll have a dance off later if you're lucky."

As Eliza and Gigi walked away, I scurried after them, totally confused and terrified by what was happening.

"What are you guys doing?" I hissed as we walked. Every few steps, people would say hi and look at us enviably. It was weird but also a huge power surge to know they thought I was someone worth envying.

"Just go with it," Eliza said. "These are very important

people, Brookie. They need to know you're important too. Otherwise, why should they waste their time talking to you?"

"But you're *lying* to them," I said. "I can't dance. I'm not related to Marilyn Monroe. And I've never been a stunt woman in the movie industry."

"But wouldn't you want to meet *that* girl?" Gigi asked. "The truth isn't nearly as interesting—no offense. Let them fall in love with the fake you and then they'll learn to like the real you."

"Why do we even have to say anything?"

"Because all people care about is who you know, what you do, what kind of money you have, and what you can influence others to do," Eliza said. "I could do charity work year-round—and I do—and nobody would care. But give me the lead in a CW show and suddenly everyone would believe I could change the world."

"Look, Brooklyn, we know this crowd better than you and we know what they want to hear. And trust us, you *want* to know them," Gigi said. She took two glasses of champagne off a tray from a server who was walking by and handed them to me and Eliza. Before he could leave, she picked another one up for herself and held it in the air. A perfect little raspberry floated in each glass, like a more fabulous version of a cherry on top. "Now relax and let us change your life. Bottoms up."

We clinked glasses and I watched as both Eliza and Gigi took big swigs of their bubbly drinks.

She had a point. They *did* know this world better than me, and if I wanted to be a part of it, I had to play by their rules. And hadn't I changed myself already so that I could fit in with people who were different from me? I didn't like the idea of them lying about *me*, but I figured that if it got my foot in the door, I could always show my true colors later. And to be honest, I was sort of beginning to enjoy the make-believe life they were creating for me.

"Bottoms up," I said before lifting my glass and letting the bubbles dance their way down my throat.

Chapter Eighteen

I opened one eye and had no idea where I was. There was something cold against my cheek and I felt around to try to figure out what I was touching. As I lifted my head and then my body, every part of me ached. If I didn't know any better, I would've thought I'd been hit by a truck.

Had I been hit by a truck?

One look around showed me that I was on the floor of the bathroom, a towel acting as a makeshift blanket covering my body. I pulled away the towel to find that I was wearing pajamas underneath, which meant that at some point I'd had enough sense to take off my dress.

God, I hoped I was alone when I did it.

My head pounded as I grabbed onto the sink and attempted to hoist myself up. My reflection in the mirror swayed back and forth as I tried to survey the damage. Mascara ringed my eyes to the point where I looked like a trashy beauty queen, and my hair was piled on top of my head in a messy bun.

I turned on the water and splashed my face with it, hoping it would stop the room from spinning. It didn't.

Note: never drink that much again. Better yet, never drink again.

The door suddenly opened and Eliza peeked her head in.

"Good, you're awake," she said, scooting in next to me to look at herself in the mirror and apply some gloss to her lips. "Gigi has to be back for a hair appointment this afternoon and we don't want to get stuck in traffic. Pack up. We're leaving in fifteen."

"Minutes?" I asked, feeling slower than usual.

"Yep! Now get moving, rock star!"

"Rock star?"

"Yeah. You know, after you performed your rendition of 'Pour Some Sugar on Me,' you insisted that everyone call you a rock star whenever they talked to you."

"I did *not*."

Eliza stopped what she was doing and stared at me in the mirror. "You're kidding, right? You don't remember that?"

I thought about what she was saying and tried to piece together the details of the night before. Everything was a blur, but it was all there. I remembered taking that first drink with the girls and then having several after that, meeting a bunch of people, and . . . and singing loudly to a rock song while dancing on a coffee table.

"I *did*," I said, horrified. I covered my face with my hands and thought about shriveling up and dying. "Please just kill me now."

"I promised I'd never do that again," she said solemnly before smiling at me deviously. "It takes forever to get the blood out of your hair."

"What else am I not remembering?" I asked, both wanting and not wanting to know. I felt guilty, nervous, embarrassed,

and humiliated. Who drinks to the point of barely remembering the details?

"Guys! Come on! We've got to go!" Gigi screamed from
downstairs.

"We'll fill you in on the ride home," Eliza said, and then
disappeared.

I dragged myself back to my room and haphazardly tossed
all my things into the suitcase, not even bothering to change
out of my pajamas for the trip back. Chances were, I'd already
embarrassed myself enough the night before, so I didn't worry
about looking like crap in front of the girls.

It took everything in me to bring my bags downstairs and
pile them into the back of the car without throwing up. I was
hungover and tired and just wanted to be home already. My
head was throbbing, my mouth was dry, and I was immensely
thirsty. And nauseous. Every little movement seemed to make
my stomach churn. I had no idea how I was going to make it
through the four-hour drive.

"You gonna live?" Gigi asked once we were all in the car.

"Grrrrrmmmmm," I answered, and then snuggled up in
the blanket that I'd taken from the house.

"I know just what you need," she said, and with that, the car
lurched forward—and so did my stomach.

A few minutes later, we were at the drive-through of a fast-
food chain, and Gigi and Eliza were ordering me the greasiest
breakfast sandwich, hash browns, a coffee, and juice. The idea
of eating anything right then was enough to make me consider throwing up, but once the food was in the car, it actually
smelled really good.

"Don't think about it—just eat it," Eliza said as she tore
into a sandwich of her own. "Trust me, you'll feel so much
better afterward."

And believe it or not, she was right. After I'd devoured it all, my stomach began to settle and I was finally able to sit back without worrying about getting sick. It was funny that the least likely solution was the one that worked.

"Okay. Give it to me straight," I said once we'd finally gotten on the road. The radio was on and Eliza was singing along to an old Britney Spears song while Gigi flipped through a magazine. "What *happened* last night?"

"You really don't remember?" Gigi asked.

"That's a sign of a good night!" Eliza added before "woo-hooing" out the open window.

"I remember bits and pieces," I said, ashamed that I'd drank so much. "Please tell me it wasn't horrible?"

"Not horrible, no," said Gigi.

"But you're much crazier than I thought you were," Eliza cut in.

"What do you mean, crazy?" I asked.

"What's the last thing you remember?" Gigi asked.

"Um, drinking that first glass of champagne with you," I said. "And then you took me around to meet people. Oh, and there was the singing on the coffee table. Besides that, everything's a little fuzzy."

Gigi and Eliza looked over at each other briefly and smiled.

"It's always so funny to see how people react when they drink for the first time," Gigi said. "You really get to see a whole other side of them."

"So after that first glass, we did take you around to introduce you to everyone. There were more drinks, of course, and a lot of dancing," Eliza said.

That triggered a memory and I was suddenly reliving the night before.

The music had grown louder and in order for me to talk to anyone, I had to practically scream.

"Brooklyn, this is Bud Larson," Gigi said, introducing me to a short, dark-haired guy. He was dressed in seersucker pants and a blazer and looked like he'd just come from a very expensive prep school.

"Bud's dad owns an international hotel chain," Eliza said, looking at him like he was much more attractive than he was.

"We just opened another one in Abu Dhabi," Bud said.

"That sounds so exotic," I said, gushing.

"We should go sometime," he said, rubbing his finger up and down my arm.

I giggled, partly because this stranger appeared to be hitting on me and partly because the alcohol was really starting to affect me. "We should all go!" I exclaimed. "It would be so much fun! All of us, hanging out together. In *Abu Dhabi*!"

Bud gave me a confused look, but I was already so gone at the time that I didn't notice he'd only invited me. As in us going alone. Not as a group thing.

The music changed then and I climbed up onto a coffee table as one of the most legendary party songs of all time came blaring out of the speakers.

"I *love* this song!" I said. I tried to pull Eliza and Gigi up with me, but neither of them would go. Finally, I gave up and just started to dance. People began to hoot and holler at me, and a tiny crowd developed as I gyrated like those girls in rap videos. At the time, I felt like the moves were sexy, but they were probably ridiculous.

When the song came to an end, Rhodes and Wheatley helped me down from the table and ushered me over to a quieter section of the house where the rest of The Elite were already seated.

"What's up, guys?!" I screamed.

"Looks like someone's having fun," Camden said, a smile spreading across his face.

"Hell yeah, I'm having fun!" I said, throwing my hands up in the air and woo-hooing. "No thanks to Asher and Ms. Z."

"Okay. Whatever," Gigi said. "Well, we thought this would be the perfect time to do some group bonding."

"Bring it on!" I said. My body had gone numb by now and I managed to swipe another couple glasses of champagne as the server passed by.

"Okay, well, to be a part of this group, you have to be able to keep its secrets," Rhodes said seriously. "In order for us to trust you with ours, you're going to have to trust us with yours. So all you have to do is survive a round of Truth or Dare."

"Ooooohhhhh," I said, acting like I was scared.

If I hadn't already drank so much, I would have been. But by now, I was feeling pretty good, and for the first time since I'd gotten my makeover and started on this whole journey with The Elite, I finally felt like I deserved to be there. I felt pretty, like I was possibly the best-looking girl at the party. And people wanted to talk to me. They thought I was interesting, and at that moment, I really thought that I was. It's like everything I'd ever wanted to be, I suddenly was, and I felt like nothing could stop me.

"Truth or dare," Camden said, bringing me back to the game we were about to play.

"Truth," I said, figuring it was the safer of the two.

"What's the most horrible thing you've ever done?" he asked.

Whoa. We were getting right down to it, weren't we? I racked my brain to come up with an answer that would both satisfy them and not get me into too much trouble.

"I lied to my parents about how our family dog got out of the house and then ran away," I said, cringing.

They all stared at me like I was a piece of abstract art they were trying to figure out.

"*That's* the most horrible thing you've ever done? Lied to your parents?" Eliza asked, shaking her head incredulously.

"Well, what were you expecting?" I asked.

"I stole money from my grandma every week and made her believe she was imagining it."

"I made out with my married neighbor."

"Told my sister that she was adopted—and even made a fake birth certificate to make it more believable."

"Threatened to call the IRS on my parents unless they let me have my inheritance early."

"Agreed to emcee a charity auction, but then didn't show up because they wouldn't stock my room with the bottled water I requested."

I might have been drunk, but I just about fell off my chair as I heard the sins of all my new friends, shared so nonchalantly. And the most astonishing thing? None of them seemed remorseful at all. They could've been telling me what they'd eaten for dinner the night before for all that they seemed to care. It was so bizarre.

"Okay . . . well, mine is still lying to my parents," I said lamely.

"Truth or dare?" Eliza asked me again.

"Truth."

"What's one thing no one else knows about you?" she asked, lifting her eyebrow at me.

This was an easy one, of course, but even in my inebriated state, I knew I could never tell them about my magical abilities. I had to give them something, though, and after my last answer, I needed to step it up a notch, otherwise they'd think I was making it all up. Maybe there was a way that I could be honest without outing myself.

"Well, I'm sort of like a modern-day Cupid," I said.

"What do you mean?"

"Oh, you know . . . I'm really good at matching people up," I said. "It's sort of a *gift* I have. You know Debbie and Ryan? I hooked them up. Oh, and Erin and Jeff—I could tell they were perfect for each other too."

"No kidding," Eliza said, thinking over what I'd just said.

"There are about twenty couples at school that owe their relationships to me," I said proudly.

"And why didn't we know this before?" Gigi asked.

"Oh, you know," I said, waving her off and almost falling over in the process. "If people found out, then everyone would want me to match them and who has time for all that?"

"Next," Wheatley said, breaking in. "Truth or dare."

"Dare," I said, sick of all their questions.

They looked at each other until finally someone spoke. "We dare you to . . . kiss that guy," Camden said.

I turned around and looked in the direction they were pointing. When my eyes finally adjusted, I wasn't sure if what I was seeing was real. There, across the room, talking to a gaggle of girls, was a guy so gorgeous he deserved his own underwear commercial. And because his shirt was so tight that I could see every ripple of muscle underneath, it was a serious possibility. He was blond, had longish hair, chiseled cheekbones, and a butt chin. He was the kind of guy I'd normally be embarrassed just to look at, let alone kiss. And he was the opposite of Asher in every way.

Asher.

"But Asher," I said, turning back to The Elite.

"You said the two of you haven't had the talk yet," Eliza said. "So that means you're a free agent."

"I'm not exactly a *free agent*," I argued, frowning.

"Boys? Can you shed some light on this situation?"

"Unless he's said he wants to be exclusive, you're free to see other people," Camden said, putting the beer he was holding up to his lips.

"Besides, chances are, that's exactly what he's doing too," Wheatley said.

I sat there and stared at my feet as it all sank in. I was so sure that Asher and I were together—or if we weren't serious yet, we were at least about to be. My heart ached to think I'd just been making it all up. What if he *was* seeing other girls? Without that acknowledgment of fidelity, there was nothing keeping him from dating around. I knew that I only wanted to be with him, but did he only want to be with me? Was that why he hadn't asked me to be his girlfriend yet? Because he wanted to see other people? What if that was the real reason he didn't want to come this weekend?

"If a dude wants to stake claim, he'll do it," Rhodes said. "You're a free agent."

"Well?" Gigi asked, nodding in the direction of the under-wear model. "Are you going to do it or will we be parting ways?"

"Why do you need me to kiss someone else anyway?" I asked, shaking my head, trying to think of a way to get out of it.

"Simple. You do this and we're all brought closer together because we got to experience it with you," said Camden. "And it shows us that you trust us and that you are loyal to The Elite above all."

"You *do* want to be a part of The Elite, don't you?" said Eliza.

"Of course," I said, trying to get out of my seat and failing miserably. "You know I want to be a part of the group."

"Well, if you're serious, then, you'll go over there and kiss the guy," said Rhodes.

I thought about what it would mean to do what they asked. Regardless of whether we'd had an "official talk" or not, I did believe that Asher and I were together. But he hadn't even bothered to text me all weekend to see how I was doing and he hadn't seemed too excited about seeing me when I got back. Was I willing to kiss another guy if it led to a spot in The Elite? It's not like Asher would ever find out anyway. That part was made clear by the others at least. They wanted it to be kept a secret between the six of us.

I stood up, still a little shaky on my feet, then smoothed out my dress and began to walk determinedly over to the under-wear model. Along the way, I picked up another glass of some-thing sparkling and chugged it. Without pausing to think, and with the help of a little liquid courage, I walked right up to the group of girls, pushed them aside, and planted one right on the guy's lips.

He stopped talking as soon as my lips touched his, and after a few seconds, he sort of melted into me. The whole thing lasted about six seconds, but it felt like longer. When I was finished, I pulled away and gave him a look that told him not to follow me when I walked away.

Heading back over to the group, I saw a few of them put-ting away their cell phones.

"That good enough?" I asked before heading off to enjoy the rest of the party.

After this, there was more dancing, exhaustion, pajamas, and finally, the bathroom floor because I was worried I was going to throw up. I began to shake my head in embarrassment as I sat in the backseat of the car and prayed to forget that the whole thing had happened.

"Did I really do all of that?" I asked, remembering every last detail now.

"Yep," Gigi said. "And we've got the pictures to prove it."

I didn't like the way that sounded.

Chapter Nineteen

The nausea of that night at the beach didn't entirely go away as I sobered up. My stomach was a bundle of nerves and guilt. And I couldn't get over what I'd done. Sure, I could blame it on the alcohol—but doing so didn't make my actions right. I was so desperate to change what had happened before I got home that I started looking on my phone for a spell that would allow me to go back in time and not take that first drink. Unfortunately, time travel isn't an option, even for witches.

I felt horrible every time I thought about seeing Asher at school. And that really sucked because I usually *loved* seeing him. I loved being around him, laughing with him, casting with him. Seeing him should've been the highlight of my day, but instead, I found myself dreading seeing him when I got back to school on Monday, because I felt so bad over what I'd done.

When I'd mentioned this to Gigi and Eliza, they'd brushed it off, reminding me that we weren't exclusive and that until that day came, I could do whatever I wanted. Kiss whomever I wanted. I was a little annoyed with them, though, so none of their reassurances made me feel better. Because the truth is, if they hadn't dared me to kiss the underwear model in the first place, I wouldn't be in this predicament. I'd seen the photo they'd taken, perfectly timed with us locking lips, and it didn't look good. In fact, it looked much more salacious than the moment was, being that the guy's shirt was slightly askew, as if I was about to rip it off.

But it wasn't just the guilt over what I'd done that made me nervous about seeing Asher. It was the fact that the last time we'd seen each other, we'd been fighting. And then he hadn't called or texted me all weekend, which made me think he was still mad at me. As much as I hoped I was blowing things out of proportion, a part of me was worried he was going to break things off. Most of all, I was mad at myself. I finally had what I wanted: a boyfriend who was wonderful and smart and gorgeous, and a group of friends who'd elevated my social status from nonexistent to popularity princess. So why wasn't I totally happy? Was all the drama really worth it in the end?

By the time I got to school on Monday, I was in full-on freak-out mode. I was finding it difficult to breathe and my nerves felt raw. I had no idea what to do—at any moment it felt like my world could implode.

In other words, I was desperate.

I knocked three times on Ms. Zia's door before heading into her office and taking a seat across from her.

"Brooklyn," Ms. Z. said, surprised to see me. She furrowed her brow and then busied herself with something on her computer. I couldn't be sure, but it seemed like she was still upset. Looks like I wasn't the only one avoiding people. "Can I help you? I'm kind of in the middle of something."

Oh yeah, she was definitely still mad. Then again, so was I, but my crisis with Asher trumped my fight with Ms. Z. I'd have to put my ego aside if I was going to get what I came here for.

I swallowed hard. "Things are kind of . . . confusing right now and I don't have anyone to talk to about it."

"What about Gigi and Eliza, or one of the guys? Surely you can talk to your friends about things," she said curtly.

I know that Ms. Z. was an adult, but right now she was acting more like a hurt friend than my guidance counselor.

"Look, I'm really sorry for not being there this past weekend," I blurted out. "Really. I know it was a lame thing to do and I truly wish I had been there to help you, rather than spending the weekend with Gigi and the others. The truth is, I wish I'd been just about anywhere but that party."

She stopped typing and raised her eyebrow at me but still didn't say anything. I took this as a sign that I should keep going.

"It was awful, Ms. Z."

Then I told her everything that had happened. The argument with Asher before going away, the conversations with the others about the status of our relationship, the drinking, and the kiss—I confessed it all and burst into tears when I was done. Midstory, Ms. Zia came out from behind her desk and took the seat next to me, rubbing my back while I blubbered so hard I could barely breathe.

"I'm the most horrible person in the world," I said when my tears had slowed enough for me to get out the words. "And now I'm so scared he's going to break up with me and I guess I don't really blame him."

"You're not a horrible person, Brooklyn," she said gently to me. "Yes, you've made mistakes—some pretty big ones—but that just means you're human. If you were a horrible person, you either wouldn't think you'd done anything wrong, or you wouldn't care. You do. You know that kissing that guy was wrong. And you understand that by asking Asher to go with you, you weren't being very understanding of his feelings. You feel bad about everything and I bet that you won't do it again."

"I won't," I said, my eyes wide.

"So, the bad news is, you made a mistake. The good news is, you can learn from it," she said, smiling. "Now the question is: How do you make this right?"

I shook my head, because I honestly didn't know the answer.

"Well, I think the others did have one good point—I think you and Asher need to talk. Communication is so important to a relationship, and right now, you're confused about where you stand. It's obviously bothering you and that's no way to live."

I nodded, agreeing with her.

"And you're not going to want to hear this, but I think you need to be honest with Asher about what happened. If you tell him the whole story, I think he'll understand that it was a mistake, one that made you realize just how much you care about him. Then you can decide whether you want to be exclusive and only see each other."

"Do I really have to tell him *everything*? I don't want him to break up with me."

"The worst thing you could possibly do, Brooklyn, is to start your relationship built on lies. Honesty is so important and if something like this eventually comes out, it's going to be so much worse because you kept it from him. And since we know that there are pictures—well, nude celebrity photos get leaked all the time. Those things have a way of resurfacing exactly when you don't want them to."

The idea of telling Asher about everything that had happened that weekend made me feel even sicker and I contemplated throwing up in Ms. Z.'s trash can. Instead, I swallowed hard and forced myself to meet her eyes.

"Okay," I said finally, not sure how I was going to do what she was asking me to.

"And, Brooklyn, remember, if people ask you to change for them, they may not actually be your friends," Ms. Zia said. "Think about who The Elite are asking you to be. And don't be afraid to say no. It's not like standing up for what you believe in is going to mean that you can't be a part of the group."

I knew she truly believed what she was saying, but she had no real idea what the situation was like with The Elite. Because that was exactly what it would mean. The challenges were there for a reason: to see if I would pass or fail. And to say no would mean to fail, and that would mean going back to being a nobody.

And that was something I wasn't willing to do.

Now that I actually wanted to run into Asher, I couldn't seem to find him anywhere. He hadn't been at my locker all day, or his for that matter. He wasn't at his usual lunch spot or walking around the grounds like he often did on nice days. I finally ran into Abby and grilled her on his whereabouts.

"He's at home. Has the flu or something," she said.

"Oh. Is he okay?"

"I assume so, but you'll have to ask him yourself," she said. Then she studied my face. "Are *you* okay?"

I shrugged, unable to trust my voice not to give me away.

"Want to talk about it?" Abby asked, dropping her books to her side and taking a step toward me. "I'm a pretty good listener."

I shook my head. "Thanks, but I really just need to talk to your brother."

She didn't ask me anything else, and in that moment I realized just how special Abby was. I hoped what I was about to do wouldn't ruin our friendship. But even I wasn't that naive. I thanked her and continued on to my next class, texting Asher on my way. I told him I was going to stop by after school, and when I didn't hear back, I assumed that he was sleeping. Poor guy. He felt sick and I was supposed to go and give him bad news. How could I possibly do that?

I finished with my classes and then headed right over to Asher's. If I was going to do this, I knew I had to do it now; otherwise I'd definitely lose my nerve. When I got there, I knocked on the door, hoping he was asleep. His mom answered, her face lighting up when she saw me.

"Brooklyn! Come to see Asher, I suspect?" she asked.

"Yeah. Is that okay? I can always come back later if you think that'd be better." I almost prayed that she would say yes, so that for just a little while longer, I'd be off the hook and everything would stay as it was.

"Oh, no, come on in! I'm sure Asher would love to see you. I don't think he's really sick. Just needed a day home, I suspect," she said, winking at me. "I was about to bring him up some soup. Why don't you take it up for me?"

"Sure," I said, accepting the tray that she handed over.

"Thanks, sweetie," she said, going back to cleaning up the kitchen. "Let me know if you two need anything else, okay?"

"I'm sure we'll be fine," I said, although I wasn't sure at all. I had no idea how Asher was going to react to the news I was about to tell him.

I took my time going up the stairs and practiced what I would say as I went. Everything I considered sounded bad.

How was he possibly going to be able to forgive me? But Ms. Zia was right. Starting a relationship built on lies was a bad idea. I had to suck it up and do the right thing, even if I hadn't before.

I stood outside Asher's room and then quietly knocked on the door. I heard him say to come in, and I balanced the tray carefully in one hand as I twisted the knob with the other. Poking my head inside, I made sure I wasn't walking in on a scene that would embarrass either of us.

Once he saw me, he smiled weakly and sat up straighter in bed.

"Brooklyn! What are you doing here?" he asked, looking around his room anxiously.

"Abby told me you went home sick and I wanted to make sure you were okay," I said, walking over to his bed and looking down at him. My stomach lurched with every step, and I was just waiting for him to throw me out. "Your mom asked me to bring this up."

He took the tray from my hands and placed it on the bed next to him but didn't start eating. I looked for the telltale signs of illness—the damp forehead, the swollen eyes, the red nose—but he seemed fine. Adorable even. Only Asher could look better sick than he did normally.

"So, what's the verdict? Cold? Flu?" I asked, keeping the mood light as I sat down on the bed beside him.

"I'm just tired. I haven't been sleeping very well lately," he said.

In my head I added, *because of me.* I just nodded like I understood.

The lights were dimmed in Asher's room and my eyes drifted up for the first time. "Well, I can see why," I said, my mouth dropping open in awe. Above us, the ceiling was black, with stars twinkling like the night sky. Only, they weren't glow-in-the-dark stars like most people had. These were real. Asher had somehow brought the sky into his bedroom. I watched as certain stars shone brighter than others and even saw one shoot across the ceiling. "I could never fall asleep with this above me. I'd never stop looking at it. It's too beautiful."

"Yeah, pretty cool, huh?" he said, grinning as he followed my gaze. "When I was younger, I used to stay up all night just watching it all, but now it's the only way I can fall asleep. I don't know how people do it just staring up at a white ceiling. It seems so weird to me now."

"I'm going to have to ask your mom about the spell," I said, thinking about what it would be like to fall asleep under the stars every night. Then I asked the question that I didn't want to ask. "Why haven't you been sleeping lately?"

Asher sighed and ran his fingers through his hair. "It's a bunch of stuff," he said cryptically. "This whole thing with my parents is starting to get to me for one."

"How did things go this weekend?" I asked, trying to put off talking about my own weekend and show an interest in his family situation.

"Eh, I didn't really find anything out. I asked if anything was going on, and of course they said everything's fine. But there's this vibe around the house now—like, stress or worry—and I just can't figure out why."

"Maybe it's nothing. Sometimes couples just go through bumpy times. It doesn't mean anything's wrong or that things are going to change. You just have to get through it," I said, realizing that what I was saying applied to us as well. "And from what I can tell of your parents, they really love each other. Whatever's going on, they'll figure it out."

"I hope so," Asher said. "Look, Brooklyn, there's something

I wanted to talk to you about." I opened my mouth to speak, but nothing came out.

Here it comes.

My chest began to tighten and I started to panic. I wasn't ready for what we had to be over. I had to do something. And since casting an amnesia spell sounded a little too dangerous, I had to figure out a better way to fix things. I needed to reignite the love I had for Asher before he ended it for good.

As Asher leaned forward to pick up the glass of juice, I quickly brought my hands out in front of me, one finger pointing at him and one at me. Without hesitating, I brought my two hands together until the invisible line had been drawn, and instantly felt the connection. It was like being struck with love. I knew, in that moment, that as long as I was with Asher, everything was going to be all right. It wasn't like the guilt necessarily went away, but my feelings for him outweighed what I'd done.

Asher put down the cup and turned to face me, this time grabbing my hands.

"I missed you," he said, looking straight into my eyes.

Relief washed over me. "I missed you, too," I said honestly. "The weekend would've been so much better if you'd been there."

This was also 100 percent true.

Asher pulled me toward him and kissed me softly on the lips. Five, ten, fifteen seconds went by and we were still engrossed in each other, as if it were the first time our lips had touched.

"So, while you were away, I did some thinking," he said.

"That sort of thing can get you into trouble, you know," I said, laughing.

"This thing we're doing . . . are we still seeing other people?"

My heart sank again. Was he saying that he wanted to see other people? The others must have been right; you're not exclusive until you're exclusive.

I looked down at the bed. "Um, well, I guess if you want to still see other people, that's okay. Just let me know. And I'll, uh, let you know too?"

Asher didn't say anything at first, but I could tell he was looking at me intently.

"I'm sorry. I don't think I was clear," he said. "I'm not saying I *want* to see other people. I'm actually saying that I hope *you* don't want to see anyone else. I had a lot of time to think about things this weekend and . . . I really like you, Brooklyn. Like, a lot."

"Oh!" I said, surprised by what he was saying. "Well, I like you a lot too, Asher."

"That works out well, because I was hoping maybe you'd do me the honor of being my girlfriend?" he asked, his voice sounding shyer than I'd ever heard it before.

I didn't know if it was the rematching that had kicked our romance up a notch or if this really was something he'd wanted to talk to me about. At this point, I didn't care. Asher wanted to be with me, and only me. That wasn't something a spell could fake. Right?

"Of course I would, boyfriend," I said, and then kissed him again.

Chapter Twenty

I'd dreamed of the day I'd have a boyfriend. Wow. Boyfriend. It was such a weird word to say. Even more crazy when it was "my boyfriend." But that's exactly what Asher was to me now. He was my boyfriend.

Things had been good between us before, but being in an official relationship was *so* much better! Everywhere we went, we were attached at the hand. And there was no more questioning whether he wanted to be with me. He was officially mine. And everyone in the school knew it. It was like we were partners in crime, each other's biggest fans. We were like the best couple of all time—at least it felt that way. And I'd never been happier.

That wasn't to say that *everyone* was happy about the matchup. Though they didn't say it straight out, I could tell that The Elite weren't psyched at the news. I purposely hadn't brought it up to them, and so far I'd been able to avoid the topic. Every time I ate lunch with the rest of the gang, I felt nervous that they might bring it up, but so far—nothing. I could feel something brewing, though, and wanted to wait as long as possible before having to deal with the confrontation that I knew was inevitable.

I couldn't hide my elation at home, though, and as soon as my parents recognized the change in me, they wouldn't let me off the hook. When they finally asked me if I was on drugs, I decided I had to tell them the truth.

I was in love.

Of course, this news shocked them nearly as much as if I *had* been on drugs and immediately led to a myriad of questions, which ended with them insisting that I invite Asher over for dinner.

So, I asked him, even though a part of me was hoping somehow it wouldn't happen. I knew what Asher's house was like. His parents used magic for just about everything and were really open about it. Mine were the opposite.

A week later the big night had come, and I was both excited and terrified about them meeting each other.

"Please don't do anything to embarrass me," I said, moving around the living room and lighting candles I'd found in the back of a closet.

"Why would we embarrass you?" my dad asked without looking up from his newspaper.

My mom, however, watched me from the doorway of the kitchen. "Brooklyn, you know those are emergency candles, right? They're not for decoration."

I continued to light each one, placing them carefully around the room. True, they were all white and none of them was scented, but at least it added a little something to our boringly plain decor.

"I'll buy you more emergency candles," I said. "When have we ever needed to use them, anyway?"

"Well, we haven't yet," she answered. "That's why they're *emergency* candles. They're for emergencies *only*."

"This is an interior-decorating emergency," I said.

"So this Asher, he uses magic?" my dad cut in, not realizing Mom and I were in the middle of an argument.

"Yes, Dad. Asher's a witch," I said, rolling my eyes. "We've talked about this a million times."

"I just don't like that he's been trying to get you to do more magic," he said, looking at me over his glasses.

"He's not pushing magic on me, Dad. He's shown me a couple of spells, but we're always careful. His parents are really great, too. They made Abby a tree in her bedroom, and Asher's ceiling is a mirror image of the night sky. It's pretty amazing."

"They use magic for frivolous things like that?" my mom asked, putting her hand to her chest.

I swear, my parents were impossible. I'd tried on several occasions to explain the Astleys' take on living a magical lifestyle, but they hadn't wanted to hear about it. And now suddenly they were all ears—a few minutes before Asher would arrive.

"It's not frivolous, Mom," I said. "It's really cool. They just look at magic differently than you do."

"Well, I don't know if it's such a good idea for you to be spending so much of your time over there, then," she muttered.

"Are you kidding? Mom, it's a great family and they're all really close," I said. "I promise, nothing crazy goes on over there."

A knock interrupted our heated discussion and I silently thanked Asher for having such great timing. I ran around the couch and tugged at my light gray sweatshirt so that it fell off one shoulder and exposed the strap of my tank top. I glanced back at my parents and gave them a warning look before pulling the door open.

"Hi!" I said, excited to see him on the other side.

"You look great," he said, and leaned in to give me a quick peck on the lips.

"Thanks. So do you," I said, noting that he'd dressed up to meet the parents. He was wearing a pair of dark slacks and a white button-down shirt. His hair was crazy as usual, but he still managed to look clean-cut. Realizing that I was staring at him and he was still standing outside, I moved out of the way and motioned for him to come in.

I walked into the living room, Asher following behind. My mom had disappeared into the kitchen to check on things. And even though he'd heard the knock, my dad had gone back to reading the paper.

"Dad, this is Asher," I said. "My boyfriend."

"Good to meet you, sir," Asher said, and walked right over to him and extended his hand. My dad raised an eyebrow and then reached out to shake his hand. He didn't put aside the paper, but at least he let it drop down to his lap.

"Likewise," my dad said.

"Thanks so much for inviting me over," Asher continued, looking around the living room. "I've been wondering when we would finally meet. For a while, I thought Brooklyn didn't want you to know about me."

He looked at Asher curiously. "Why wouldn't she want us to know about you?" he asked seriously. "Is there something we should be concerned about?"

This time Asher laughed nervously. His eyes flickered over to mine before he continued. "No, sir. Of course not."

"Dad! Chill out, will ya?" I asked, giving him a warning look. Then I turned to Asher and mouthed, "I'm sorry."

He just smiled.

"So, Brooklyn says you use a lot of magic in your home," my dad said.

"Dad!"

"No, it's okay, Brooklyn. I think we're your typical magicking household, sir. We don't go crazy or anything, but we do use magic on a daily basis," Asher said, sitting down across from Dad. I sat down next to him, close enough for our legs to touch at the knee. "Brooklyn says you guys are a low-magic household? I think it's so cool that you guys choose to do your own thing. You know, without magic. Sometimes I think about unplugging for the weekend or something, but I'm not sure I could do it."

"No willpower, then?" my dad asked.

I was horrified and sent dagger looks his way. Luckily, Asher knew how to handle himself.

"It's more like, this is what we've grown up with," he said, shrugging. "My parents have taught my sister and me the importance of safe magicking. They've raised us to be independent, responsible, and to use our powers for good. We never use dark magic and try to be as careful as possible about where and when we use our gifts. I know it might seem like we use our magic needlessly, but I can assure you, it's not like that."

Dad paused as he surveyed the guy who was dating his only daughter. Then he tried to force a smile. "I can respect your convictions, I suppose."

"Thank you, sir," Asher said, smiling at him.

My mom came into the room, wiping her hands on her apron, which was already stained with spaghetti sauce. "Mom, this is Asher."

"Asher!" my mom said, brightening but looking slightly shy as she walked over to us and shook his hand. "It's so great to finally meet you!"

"And you, too," he said, pumping her hand enthusiastically. "Dinner smells great!"

"Why, thank you," Mom said, beaming. "It's Brooklyn's favorite."

We all paused for a moment just staring at each other and waiting for someone else to say something. I wondered if it was too late to grab Asher's hand and run out the front door. By the way he kept looking at the door, I figured he was wondering the same thing. Had there ever been a more embarrassing meeting before? I doubted it.

"Well, Asher, tell us about your family. Brooklyn says they're just lovely," my mom said.

"Aw, thanks. Yeah, they're pretty great," he said, smiling. "Like I was telling your husband, our family is your normal witching family. Our lineage goes back to the Nex coven. They were a subset of the Cleri, though we weren't directly related to them. After the witch trials, the group sort of took off and we eventually became independents and settled down here. My mom is on the witches' council in town, but we're not affiliated with any particular coven."

"Aren't you worried you'll be found out? That Parris's coven will find you?" my mom asked, her eyes growing wide.

"Parris? Nobody's seen him in hundreds of years, or his coven either, for that matter. It's sort of an urban legend that they'll come back one day," he said.

"Well, what about the others?" my dad asked. "The more magic you use, the more likely you are to get caught. Our family has certainly had its share of tragedy at the hands of normals. Aren't you scared of being persecuted like your ancestors?"

"Like I said, we're pretty careful," he said. "We typically only use magic when we're at home. It's really rare for us to cast in public. Besides, what kind of a life is that—to constantly be looking over your shoulder for something that might never happen?"

"Well, you're much braver than we are," my mom said quietly. She looked down at her watch and checked the time. "Brooklyn, would you mind setting the table? Dinner will be ready in a few minutes."

"Sure," I said, and got up from the chair reluctantly. There were so many possible land mines in this conversation that I didn't really want to leave Asher alone. But the table wasn't going to set itself. We weren't at Asher's house, after all. So I excused myself and put out plates and silverware as quickly as I could, and then made my way back to the living room.

When I did, I nearly gasped at what I saw. Asher was bent over a book, and my mom was talking to him quietly while pointing at the pages. I couldn't be sure, but I swore I'd seen the book before.

"Crap," I said under my breath, and rushed over to where they were sitting. "Mom, what are you doing?"

They both looked up at me, my mom with pride and Asher with confusion. My mom lifted up our family's book and smiled. "Asher was just asking about our family history, so I thought I'd show him our book," she said. I watched as she turned the pages until she got to a few baby pictures of me. "After Brooklyn's great-aunt was killed, we decided it was safer to live this way. And then Brooklyn was born. Wasn't she a cute baby?"

My eyes were still locked on Asher's and I could tell that I was in trouble. In the few minutes I'd left them alone, my parents had managed to let loose the fact that I'd lied to Asher about not knowing my family history.

"Isn't dinner ready?" I asked my mom. She closed the book as she remembered why we were all here and ushered us into the kitchen.

Asher was gracious all through the meal, answering every

question that my parents lobbed his way. If I hadn't been so worried about the conversation we were going to have when we were alone, I would've been falling even more in love with him for trying so hard to impress them. Instead, I spent the whole time pushing my food around my plate, because I couldn't bring myself to take a bite.

When we were finished, my parents stayed in the kitchen to clean up, while Asher and I headed back into the living room. We didn't say anything until we were out of earshot. As soon as we were alone, Asher turned to me.

"You told me you didn't know anything about your family's history," he said, clearly upset.

"I know. Asher, I'm sorry. It's just that . . . I was so embarrassed by who we were—who we *are*," I said, unable to look him in the eye. "Your family is powerful! You do spells like they're nothing. My family? We're lame. My ancestors contributed nothing to the witching world. We just sat back and let everyone else do the important stuff. We might as well have never existed. Do you know how upsetting that is? To know that you're so insignificant that you could not exist and it wouldn't make a difference to the world? It's awful. I didn't want you to look at me any differently than you did before."

Asher took a few steps toward me and cupped my face in his hands. He lifted my chin until I was looking directly at him. "Do you really think I care about where you came from? News flash, Brooklyn, I'm not dating you for your powers," he said. "I liked you before you ever cast your first spell."

"It really doesn't bother you?" I asked, pulling away from him and sitting down on the couch. I shook my head. "I don't believe that. Power matters. It means you're somebody. It means you have the ability to change this world or make an impact on it in some real way. Don't you see? I can't offer you that."

"You offer plenty now," he said, sitting down beside me. "Your power comes from your love. You care about me. When we connect, I feel that power. Don't you?"

I thought about the power he was talking about and felt guilty because I knew that I'd caused it. "Of course I feel it," I said quietly.

"Then stop worrying about it," he said. "I couldn't care less about your magicking skills, Brooklyn. What I can't stand is you lying to me. *That*, I can't deal with."

"I know and I'm sorry. I was just so scared of losing you," I said.

"The only way you could do that is if you keep lying to me," he said. "If we're going to be together, I need to be able to trust you and I need you to trust me. Can you do that?"

I nodded. Of course I trusted him. He was becoming my world and I knew I could trust him with just about anything.

"Good," he said, and took my hand. "Now, before we forget that any of this happened, is there anything else you need to tell me?"

I have the power to match people.

And I kissed another guy at the beach.

"No," I said with a shaky breath. "That's it."

Because the truth was, as much as I trusted Asher, I didn't trust him to stick around if he knew everything I'd done.

But for now, I just had to hope that what he didn't know wouldn't hurt us.

"Brookie! Wait up!"

I turned to see Eliza strutting quickly toward me, Gigi not far behind her. I smiled as the two caught up to me and gave them both air-kisses.

"What's up, guys?" I asked. Things had been progressing

since we'd gotten back from the beach just over a week ago. Going to that party *had* made us all closer. I knew some of their secrets and they knew some of mine. I wasn't just some wannabe anymore. I think we were actually becoming *friends*. And now that things were clear between Asher and me—and The Elite still hadn't said anything about it—life was pretty perfect.

"We've got your next challenge," Eliza said, looking way too excited for a random Tuesday morning.

Ugh. "I thought we were done with that," I said, unable to hide my disappointment.

Eliza placed her hand on her hip and cocked her head. "Awww, you're the cutest!"

"Brooklyn, if it was that easy to get into The Elite, don't you think we'd have more members?" Gigi asked, toying with the collar on her shirt. "I mean, where would the exclusivity be in that?"

"Don't worry, though," Eliza said seriously. "Nobody's made it this far in a long time."

I felt a perverted sense of pride when she said that, even though I was annoyed they hadn't officially let me in yet. But I'd made it this far and, God help me, I was going to finish every last challenge they threw my way.

Or I'd die trying.

"Okay, fine. What is it?" I asked, folding my arms over my chest.

"I need you to shoot someone," Eliza said, a big grin spreading across her face.

"What?" I asked, feeling like I couldn't have heard her right.

"She means with your arrows," Gigi explained, rolling her eyes. "You said you were like Cupid and she wants you to get someone to fall in love with her."

"Oh," I said, relieved. "Well, let me take a look around and see who might be a good match . . . "

"I already know who I want you to hook me up with," Eliza said, raising her eyebrows suggestively.

"Who?" I asked, intrigued. In the two and a half months I'd been hanging out with her, I'd never heard Eliza talk about any specific guy before, so I was curious who she saw as her perfect match.

"Tucker Harris."

I looked at her, confused. "But, Eliza, Tucker's with Shayla. They've been dating for over a month now," I said, shaking my head.

"Oh, I know," Eliza said, a spark in her eye. "And now I want him to be mine."

Chapter Twenty-One

"I can't break them up, Eliza," I said.

"Why not? People break up all the time," she answered. "Watch."

Eliza motioned to one of the girls who were always following The Elite around. A different one, this time a curvy redhead, came running up, excited to have a chance to show her allegiance to the most popular kids in school.

"If I told you that you could eat lunch with us for a week, but you had to break up with that roly-poly boyfriend of yours, would you do it?" Eliza asked her, not even addressing the girl by name. The wannabe looked from me to Eliza, and then around her to see if anyone was listening.

"If you thought I should, sure," she answered.

My mouth dropped open.

"You'd break up with your boyfriend just because she asked you to?" I asked, appalled. I couldn't believe this girl would let Eliza ruin her relationship just to be popular. For a week.

"Well, I'd do it if *you* asked me too," she answered.

That made my head spin. This girl was looking at me the same as any of the other Elite members. I still couldn't believe people might see me this way, and as cracked as it sounds, I was excited.

"Are you asking me to break up with my boyfriend?" she asked, waiting for us to tell her what to do.

Before Eliza could answer, I shook my head. "No. We're not asking you to do that."

"Thanks. We're done here," Gigi said, waving her away.

"See? Breakups happen," Eliza said, as if that show had made her point. "And it's not like he's even happy with her. Look at them."

I glanced behind us and saw Tucker and Shayla walking our way. They were holding hands, and after a few steps, Shayla leaned her head against Tucker's shoulder sweetly. There was nothing but love in their eyes. Tucker adjusted the books he was carrying for Shayla. He was the ultimate gentleman. And so cute, too. I wasn't surprised that someone was attracted to him but still didn't get why Eliza was. She was more of a what's-on-the-outside-is-what-counts kind of girl.

"Eliza, they're *happy*."

"Well, he'd be happier if he was with me," she said, pouting. "He just doesn't know it yet."

I shook my head. "Isn't there anyone else I can set you up with? There are plenty of guys at this school who would love to go out with you," I tried.

"But I don't *want* to go out with them," she said, frowning. "I want Tucker. He's in a band and he's one of the few guys around here who acts like I don't exist."

"Wait, you want him just because he doesn't want you?" I asked incredulously.

"Why do you care about them, anyway?" Gigi asked curiously. "It's not like they're your *friends*. That would be us, remember?"

I bit my lip. "Yeah, but Asher's sort of friends with Tucker, and he knows how long Tucker and Shayla have liked each other," I said. "I can't do this to them. To him."

"This is about Asher again?" Gigi asked, rolling her eyes. Then she folded her arms. "Look, Brooklyn, I didn't say anything when the two of you became a couple—thanks for letting us know, by the way—but if he's going to constantly get in the way, I just don't know if it will work."

"Are you telling me to break up with Asher?" I asked, horrified by where the conversation was going.

"Not yet. I'm still hoping you'll come to your senses and do what needs to be done. Show us that dating Asher isn't going to be a problem," she said. "Eliza wants Tucker and we always get what we want. Now are you going to do it or not?"

I thought about what they were saying for a few seconds. Then my eyes fell on the girl who'd just offered to break up with her boyfriend if I asked her to. It was so sad that she would be willing to do something like that just for a few stupid lunches. I knew I didn't want that to be me. I wanted popularity, but not at the cost of anyone and everyone.

"No. I'm sorry, guys, but I'm not going to break two people up who clearly care about each other," I said. "But, Eliza, give me anyone else and I'll do it. Anyone. I promise."

Gigi and Eliza shared a look. Then Gigi took a step toward me and hooked her arm in mine. Eliza did the same on the other side, and then the three of us began to walk down the hallway arm in arm, like we were the best of buddies. But based on the tight hold they both had on me, I knew they were feeling anything but friendly toward me right now.

"Listen, Brooklyn," Gigi said just loudly enough for me to hear. She kept a smile on her face as she spoke, so that no one else around us knew what she was up to. "I think you need to reconsider setting up Eliza and Tucker, and here's why. If you recall, you had a certain indiscretion on a recent trip and there's a photo floating around that you wouldn't want to get out. And if Eliza doesn't get Tucker, that picture might just end up being sent to Asher. And how do you think he'll react to that? I'd think this sort of thing would mean the end of your relationship before it even started. But hey, if you think Tucker and Shayla's little crush is more important than what you and Asher have, then by all means, bow out."

My head was pounding. I couldn't believe that Gigi was actually blackmailing me. It had always been a nagging worry of mine since the photo had been taken, but I guess I'd convinced myself that they were my friends and wouldn't use it against me. Was this what they'd planned all along? Was that why they'd dared me to kiss him?

I watched Tucker and Shayla giggle as they walked by. They seemed so happy. How was I supposed to break them up? I was pretty sure I wasn't supposed to use my magic for evil. And this was definitely not a good use of my magic.

But the alternative was for Asher to find out that I'd kissed someone else. Gigi was right about one thing. Our relationship wouldn't survive that. Not only had I cheated on him but I'd lied about it, specifically when he'd asked me if there was anything else I needed to tell him.

There was only one positive about this situation and I had to believe that it was enough to balance out the bad. If I matched Eliza and Tucker, it wouldn't last forever. And if I knew Eliza, she'd grow tired of Tucker in about a week, and then I could reconnect Tucker and Shayla. In fact, the breakup might just make the couple stronger if they realized they truly were each other's perfect match in the end.

Besides, the alternative was too scary to think about.

"Fine," I said between clenched teeth. "I'll do it."

"Yay!" Eliza said, clapping her hands excitedly, having gotten what she wanted. Then she added, "Now that that's out of the way, Daddy's having a big party on Friday. It's the biggest one of the season and I need a sufficient date. So, if you could get this going soon, I'd like to bring him with me."

She wanted to destroy a perfectly happy couple because she needed a date for a Hollywood party. And what was left of my rose-colored glasses was shattered. I realized all the rumors about The Elite were true. They were popular, but it was at the expense of other people's feelings. I'd seen them be nasty to others, but I never thought they'd direct it at me. I was sure that what we had was different.

Did I really want to be a part of that?

"This party is going to be epic, Brooklyn. You definitely don't want to miss it," she said, hinting that I would if I didn't do what they wanted. "If you thought the other two were big, this one will blow them out of the water. Everyone who's anyone will be there. And everyone will get a chance to meet you. Think of it as your coming-out party."

Gigi let go of me and continued on ahead, but then turned her head and stared back at me, a deadly serious look in her eyes. "And, Brooklyn? Be sure to bring Asher, won't you? I have a feeling he won't want to miss this."

I felt sick over what I was about to do, but I couldn't see a way out of it. And I'd tried. I'd spent three class periods coming up with alternatives to matching Eliza and Tucker, but each of them ended with Gigi sending Asher the photo and him breaking up with me. I even debated telling Eliza I'd gone to Tucker and he hadn't been interested, but I knew they wouldn't take no for an answer. I was sure the incriminating picture would still be sent, and the thought of that made me feel even worse than breaking Shayla's heart.

And that's what would happen too. If she was feeling even half the emotions I felt being with Asher, then Tucker was already her world. And according to Asher, they'd felt that way about each other for a long time before I helped them take the leap. This was going to be awful and it would be at my hands.

I could barely stand it.

But my love for Asher was stronger than my need to do what was right. Besides, love had a way of working itself out. Once the spell wore off, I had to believe that Shayla and Tucker would find their way back to each other. And if they didn't, I'd be there to help them get started. So, in the end, no harm would really be done. Right?

I'd passed a note to Eliza during one of the breaks and told her to meet Tucker in the hallway just before lunch. The party was only a few days away. Time was ticking.

I knew this was the only chance to catch Tucker alone. He always walked by himself to the cafeteria and met Shayla there. The last thing I wanted was for Shayla to see the connection happen. There was no need for her to be tortured more than she already would be. No, I wanted this part to be done in private. Well, as private as you could get in school.

I leaned against my locker as my eyes darted back and forth around the hallway, waiting for the two to show up. Eliza was first and she flashed me a smile when she saw me. I nodded back at her to let her know everything was set. I hadn't told her how I'd done it, how I planned to get Tucker to dump Shayla for her. All she knew was that she was supposed to go up to Tucker and start a conversation with him and, when she felt the time was right, ask him to go with her to her dad's party. I promised her that Tucker would say yes.

Tucker appeared at the end of the hallway and began to make his way toward the cafeteria. He had his cell phone out and smiled as he checked it. I imagined him reading a sweet text from Shayla. Only, he didn't have a chance to respond, because just then, Eliza stepped in front of him. He stopped and looked at her, and then tried to walk around her. She blocked his path again, this time placing her hand on his arm. He looked down at it as she began to talk to him. I couldn't hear what she was saying, but I knew it was time.

I lifted my fingers and pointed one at each of them. Then I begrudgingly brought my hands together, feeling the spark at the end. I didn't have to be near them to know something had shifted. Tucker went from trying to get around Eliza to suddenly leaning in to her as she spoke. Abandoning the message on his phone, he placed it back into his pocket and smiled at her. Eliza smiled back, saying something and then giggling loudly.

After a minute, she whispered to him and he nodded and then typed something into her cell phone. I assumed it was his number. She smiled and bit her lip as he walked away, a dazed look in his eyes. He was no longer heading toward the cafeteria, his lunch with Shayla forgotten as quickly as their relationship.

"Abby would've loved this place," Asher said, shaking his head as we looked around. For the blowout party, Mr. Rivers had rented out a castle about forty-five minutes away and appeared to have invited about two hundred of his closest friends. Thousands of candles filled the space. They were the only source of light, which cast an ethereal glow over everything. Mr. Rivers had brought in furniture befitting royalty, and movie stars and pop stars alike sat upon thrones and red cushions lined with gold thread. Drinks were being poured into goblets decorated with rubies and sapphires, which guests then carried around like accessories.

Lining the ceiling were dozens of chandeliers dripping with even more candles, casting shadows along the walls and giving the illusion that there were more guests wandering around than there really were. It was the most elaborate party I'd ever seen and I wasn't even able to enjoy it.

"Are you kidding? Abby would *hate* being around these people," I said. "Almost as much as you do, I suspect."

Asher chuckled. "I'm doing this because it's important to *you*," he said. "And I just meant that Abby would love the fantasy of it all. You know her. She reads her books specifically for things like this."

"Well then, we should take some pictures for her, shouldn't we?" I said, taking out my phone and snapping a few. As a waiter dressed in chain mail like a knight walked by, I grabbed a goblet off the tray and handed it to Asher. "Now give me a royal pose so Abby'll get the full effect."

With one hand on his hip and the other raising the glass to the camera, Asher held still so I could take a picture.

"Well, aren't you two just the cutest," Gigi said, appearing out of nowhere, Camden on her arm. As usual, they looked like a perfume ad. Camden was wearing a tux, with lines as clean-cut as he was. Gigi was breathtaking, which made me even more annoyed to see her. Standing like she was at the end of the runway, she was wearing an iridescent white gown that gently brushed along the floor when she walked. The plunging neckline perfectly displayed the giant sapphire she was wearing, which probably cost more than the average college education. "Taking pictures to preserve the night? There's nothing like capturing a moment in time, is there, Brooklyn?"

I frowned slightly, my mood dampening at the sound of Gigi's voice. I was still upset over what she and Eliza had made me do and it was clear to me now that they weren't above hurting people to get what they wanted. I wasn't sure I was through with The Elite completely yet, but I didn't trust them the way I had before. I wasn't ready to give up on popularity yet and once I was officially a part of the group, I knew I'd have more power.

But for the moment, I was still irritated.

"Nope. Pictures are the best," I said sarcastically.

Asher gave me a sideways glance.

"I agree. We should take one of the two of us! Asher, would you mind doing the honors, please?" Gigi opened her eyes really wide as she handed her phone to him.

I panicked as I thought how easy it would be for her to show him the picture of me and the underwear model. If she wasn't already handing the photo over to him right now, one wrong button push would likely reveal it.

My whole body stiffened as Asher took the camera and then raised it so it was pointed at the two of us. Coming in close to me, Gigi put her arm around my waist and pushed our faces together goofily. "Say 'Long live the queen!'" she said sweetly. I faked a smile as the sound of the cell phone's camera went off.

Gigi took her phone back and showed the picture to Camden. He nodded. "You two look hot."

Then she took it back and began to fiddle with the phone. "Asher, give me your number and I'll text it to you," Gigi said.

"Oh, you can just send it to me and I'll send it to him," I cut in.

"No way. If she sends it to you, I may never get ahold of it," Asher said, quickly giving Gigi his number.

"Thanks, Asher," Gigi said with a smile. "Sending it your way now."

I saw his phone light up and Asher clicked on the incoming message. Then he turned to me.

"What's this?" he asked me questioningly. I began to panic as he started to push a bunch of buttons on his phone and finally stared at me again.

"What's what?" I asked, looking over at Gigi like she was the enemy. She just shrugged.

"What's this photo doing as my new background picture?" he asked. Then he smiled at me before handing the phone over. I sighed with relief as I saw that he'd cropped the photo Gigi had sent him so that I was the only one looking back at him.

"Ha, ha," I said, rolling my eyes at him.

"Like I said, you two are the cutest," Gigi said, shaking her head. "But not quite as cute as those two. They're definitely the royal couple here tonight."

We both looked over and quickly focused on a couple who couldn't seem to keep their hands off each other. I saw Eliza right away—she was the only person I knew who could pull off wearing a corseted dress with a hoop skirt the circumference of a small car. And although I knew who I would find standing next to her, it was still a shock when his face came into view. There was a part of me that had hoped the spell wouldn't work. That love would trump my powers. But alas, I was better at matching people than I'd thought.

"What are they doing?" Asher asked as he recognized Tucker. "I thought Tucker was with Shayla?"

"Not anymore," Camden said, a hint of glee in his voice.

"And now he's with Eliza?" Asher asked. "Just like that? When did they even break up? Like yesterday?"

"Actually, it was a few days ago," Gigi said. "Guess he was just with Shayla until something better came along."

Asher shook his head. "No way. Tucker's not like that. He's been into Shayla since middle school. And no offense, but Eliza's not his type. Neither is this party."

"From what Brooklyn's said, this isn't really your scene either. Yet you're still here," Gigi said.

I gave Gigi a look that said to keep her mouth shut.

"Well, I love Brooklyn, and I know that going to this thing is a big deal for her. Even though I don't care about any of this, I care about *her*. That's why I'm here."

"You *love* me?" I asked quietly, repeating the one thing in the sentence that mattered more than anything else. He'd never told me he loved me before. I'd been thinking it for a while now, but didn't want to be the first to say it.

"Of course," he said. "I thought you knew."

I shrugged shyly and leaned in for a kiss. With our faces just inches from each other, I whispered that I loved him too.

"Well, it looks like you're on a roll tonight, Brooklyn," Gigi said, breaking up our moment. "First those two and now this."

"What are you talking about?" Asher asked, looking at Gigi.

"Oh, just that it was your girlfriend who hooked Tucker and Eliza up in the first place," she said. I watched as Asher's face fell. Gigi looked back and forth between the two of us and then brought her hand to her mouth. "You *did* know that Brooklyn here is, like, a hotter Cupid, right? She's paired up, like, half the school. Your girl here just loves dishing out the love!"

Asher's eyes slid to mine and I could tell right away that he already knew the truth. And he wasn't happy. He shook his head and without saying anything began to walk away from us. Away from me.

"Asher! Please don't go," I said, running after him. He didn't stop until we were both outside, breathing in the night air. I was finally close enough to grab onto his arm and he turned around at my touch. "Asher."

"What did you do, Brooklyn?" he asked me.

I didn't answer. The last thing I wanted was to confirm his fears and have the disappointed way he was looking at me now become permanent.

"Are you using magic to make people fall in love?" he asked. It sounded like he was in physical pain just saying the words.

"It's sort of something that people in my family can do," I answered. "And I was only helping people *find* love."

"And Shayla and Tucker? What about them? Don't try to tell me that breaking them up was supposed to be helping!"

"That was just . . . a mistake," I said.

Asher paced around in front of me, trying to get a handle on what I'd just told him. Suddenly he stopped. He turned his head in my direction and spoke to me slowly.

"Were *we* a mistake?" he asked, the strain obvious in his voice.

My eyes started to tear up and I moved toward him. He took a few steps away from me. Knowing he was still waiting for an answer, I shook my head.

It was all the confirmation Asher needed to realize that I'd matched the two of us. He turned and began to stalk off.

"Please, Asher! It wasn't like that. All I can do is ignite the spark. The rest—the fact that we're still together—that's *real* love. The way we feel about each other is real! You have to believe me."

For a second I thought I'd gotten through to him, but then his eyes dipped to the ground and he headed off into the darkness and out of my life.

Chapter Twenty-Two

I knew Asher couldn't have gotten very far, considering I'd driven the two of us to the party and we were so far from home. It wouldn't have been realistic for him to try and walk it. I raced back inside to retrieve the jacket I'd checked and then asked one of the valets to bring my car around.

One reason why rich wasn't always better: your car was never where you left it.

When I was finally behind the wheel, I sped off in the direction that Asher had gone. As I'd suspected, when I saw his body take shape in the headlights, he'd barely made it off the property. He'd taken off his suit jacket, and the white button-down practically glowed against the dark night. I lowered the passenger window as I drove up beside him. He didn't bother to look over to see who it was. Somehow he knew.

I didn't even hear him say anything, but all of a sudden the window began to close and not by my hand. Asher was using a spell. I reached for the button in the car and forced it down again.

"Asher! Please get in the car," I said, crying. "Let me explain."

"Save it, Brooklyn. I don't want to hear any more of your lies," he said, his eyes straight ahead.

"Fine. Okay. I won't talk, then. But at least let me drive you back to town. You'll be walking all night if you don't," I pleaded.

"Maybe I feel like walking," he said. Now I could tell he was just being stubborn. Not that I could blame him for being mad.

Asher continued to walk, and I settled for driving alongside him for as long as he did so. He must have realized just how far home was and that he was wearing dress shoes, not hiking boots, because he stopped in the street and just stood there, looking straight ahead. Finally he turned and got into the passenger seat. I took a deep breath and put the car into gear.

"Thank you, Asher," I said, glancing his way. "I—"

"You said we didn't have to talk," he interrupted.

It felt a little like a slap, and I abruptly closed my mouth. Instead, I reached out my hand and flipped on the radio. Carrie Underwood was singing a song about getting back at a cheating man, and I quickly did a spell to change the channel. I wasn't interested in listening to angry girl music right then, especially when the subject involved cheating. The stations turned until the tuner landed on an Adele song. I turned the volume up a bit to try and drown out the deafening sound of silence in the car.

Five minutes went by. Ten. And just when I was about to give up hope that the two of us would be able to hash this whole thing out, Asher turned down the radio a few decibels.

"You had no right to do that spell on me," he said, his voice angry. He still wouldn't look at me, but since my eyes were on the road, I couldn't look at him, either. Maybe it was better that way.

"I know that now," I said, surrendering. If I was going to have any chance that he'd forgive me, I'd have to show him that I knew what I'd done was wrong and that I wouldn't do it again.

"Why did you do it, Brooklyn?"

I swallowed. "Because I loved you," I said. "And I wanted to see if we had a chance."

"You couldn't just wait and see like a normal person?"

"You don't get it, Asher. My powers don't force people to fall in love," I said, sighing. "My matching acts as a catalyst to get things going. It's like lust at first sight. After a few days, couples are left with their actual feelings. See, I just set people up."

Asher was quiet as he took in this information. "How long does the spell last?"

"I'm not entirely sure," I said. "But some of the others wore off in a week or so."

"There were others?" he asked, looking over at me. "I mean, besides Tucker and Eliza."

"Well, yeah. In fact, I'm the one who actually matched Tucker and Shayla first. They were just so cute together and you could tell they really liked each other, so . . ."

"And then you broke them up?" Asher asked, the anger sneaking into his voice again. "Why make them happy, only to destroy them later?"

"Because *they* told me they'd tell you the truth if I didn't do what they said!" I shouted, frustrated. This was only partly true, but hopefully it would be enough for him to begin to understand. I couldn't tell him what they were really black-mailing me with. Not without breaking us up for good. And

I knew—even though we hadn't officially been dating at the time—that if he knew I'd kissed someone else, that would be it. We'd be done. That is, if we weren't already breaking up now.

"You shouldn't have hurt anyone else in the process," he said. "You should have had faith that we'd get through this."

His words filled me with hope, even though they were in the past tense.

"I begged Eliza to choose someone else, anyone else who wasn't already in a relationship, but she wouldn't budge. And they made it clear that if I didn't do it, I'd never be a part of The Elite."

"Who cares?" Asher said. "Who cares if you're a part of The Elite? Knowing what they are and what they've done, why would you even want them as friends?"

It was a good question and one that I'd been asking myself the past couple of days. And the truth was, they had the potential to do great things, even if it didn't seem to be the way they were leaning these days. I could only imagine the charities they could get behind and lives they could change with all the advantages they had. I hadn't been lying. The single most important thing to me was to know that I was here on earth for a reason, that I was going to impact lives in a big way. And the only way I knew to do that was with power and influence. The Elite had it, so I saw them as my way to achieve all my goals.

I also believed that if given a little bit of time at the center of the group, I might be able to get them to do things my way. Sort of change them from the inside out. But it was hard to explain that to someone who only saw the bad that was going on.

"I don't know, Asher," I said. "I just felt like it's where I was supposed to be. I know that doesn't make sense, but I was going with my instincts. I thought I could do a lot of good if I could just get in with them. Think of what I could do for this school and the people in it, if I was at their level. I could be the role model so many teens don't have right now. And I was almost there. I was *so* close, Asher."

We drove along in silence for a few more minutes, staring out into the night. It seemed darker than it should have been. Trees whipped past and I tried not to imagine unknown terrors hiding in them.

"I would have been happy for you, you know," Asher said quietly. "Getting your new powers? It's really cool that you can help people find love."

"I know. It feels like I have a hand in making others happy," I said cautiously.

"I suppose I can understand why you did it. I think everyone wants to know they're important to the world in some way. Do something big. Make a difference," he said, looking back over at me. "I might have done the same thing if it was for the greater good. But at some point you have to decide what's more important to you: deciding you're satisfied with the future you have now or giving it up for a possibility of a better one."

"I'm trying to find a way to do both," I said, looking over at him hopefully. "Do you think that could still happen, Asher? I don't want to lose you."

He paused and looked out the window as if he was going to find the answers there. I held my breath as I waited for him to speak, not caring if I passed out in the meantime. "I don't want to lose you either," he said finally. "But you've gotta let me in, Brooklyn. I've got enough lies going on at home, I don't want to have to wonder what yours are too."

"Do you want me to match your parents? Maybe it'll get them to take a break on the fighting a bit."

"No, thanks," he said. "I'm not sure why, but I don't think they're upset with each other. It's got to be something else. It's like they're . . . scared of something. You know, they almost didn't let me come tonight? They wanted me to stay home. They've wanted Abby and I to both stay home lately. It's like they're suddenly overprotective, and that's never been their deal."

"Weird," I said, wondering if my parents had gotten to them somehow.

"That's why I can't deal with this, too," he said. "If we're going to have a chance at making this work, Brooklyn, I need you to tell me the truth. No more lies from here on out or I'm done. Okay?"

"No more lies from here on out," I repeated, noting silently that the kiss had happened in the past and therefore didn't fall under this category.

It took us a couple of days to get back to normal, but soon Asher and I were holding hands again and kissing in the hallways. This might have annoyed other students who had to watch, but as for us, we were happy.

"And then he grabbed the maiden around the waist and pulled her into his arms, promising never to let go," Abby said dramatically.

"Huh?" I asked, moving away from Asher long enough to look at her.

"Oh, I just thought you two were acting out a scene from the book I was reading last week," she said with a smile. "My bad."

"You read romance novels?" I asked, surprised. Abby didn't seem like the bodice-ripping, epic-love-story type.

"Me? No way. All that fighting and then making up? Too

much drama," she said, sticking out her tongue. "That was sort of my point."

We both knew that she was talking about us, and I wasn't at all surprised to learn that Asher had told her what had happened. They were so close that sometimes it was difficult to remember they were even siblings. They were more like friends who told each other everything than brother and sister. And I was grateful that it seemed like Abby wasn't holding a grudge for my misdeeds either.

"Sorry," I said.

"She's just kidding," Asher said, smiling and then giving Abby a warning look. She raised her eyebrow but didn't say anything else. He leaned toward me and gave me another kiss before heading to his next class and leaving the two of us alone.

I looked over at Abby, wondering if I needed to talk to her about what had happened. Her face was neutral, as always, and even though she didn't seem upset, it was hard to read her. I bit my lip and wrestled with how to bring the subject up.

"It's okay, you know," she said, doing it for me. I didn't even think she was paying attention to me, so I was surprised when she spoke. "Asher filled me in, and it's cool. When I first started getting my powers, I didn't want to tell anyone about them, either. I wanted to keep them to myself for a bit. Eventually, though, I realized that it was much more fun having people around me who knew what I was going through and being able to confide in them."

I nodded, understanding what she meant. It *had* been a little lonely not being able to discuss my powers with anyone these last few weeks before Asher found out. Especially with those I cared about most.

"You can trust Asher, you know," she said. "And me, too,

if you want. We won't judge and we won't tell. Your secret's safe with us."

My heart began to fill with love for this girl who was so young yet so wise. It was like how I imagined having a younger sister would be. Minus the fighting and jealousy. I was so happy that she sort of came as a package deal along with Asher.

"I know," I said. "And I'm sorry about . . . everything."

She shot me a smile and then went back to flipping through her latest book, an old beat-up copy of *Little Women*. "Just don't hurt my brother, okay? He's kind of a great guy."

"I know," I said earnestly. "And I'm really going to try not to."

I opened up my locker and placed my history book inside, only to retrieve my math book. Then I pulled out a notebook and my calculator and tried to balance it all in the crook of one arm. With a groan, I kicked the door shut.

"You may be one of *The Elite*, but that doesn't mean you can treat people like this!"

A girl was shouting and I could tell by the sound of her voice that she was seriously upset. Abby and I both turned to see Shayla standing in the middle of the hallway. Her face was bright red and she was shaking slightly. I wasn't close enough to see if she was crying, too, but where there was anger, there often were tears.

When I saw who she was yelling at, my stomach practically took a jump off a cliff.

"You *knew* that we were dating, Eliza," Shayla said, pointing at her accusingly. "Why would you go after him when you knew he was taken?"

I watched as Eliza pulled Tucker in closer to her, so they weren't just holding hands, but their upper bodies were touching as well. This little gesture made Shayla flinch, like it physically hurt her to watch. Despite my better judgment, I found myself gravitating toward the scene. Something the other students still in the hallway were doing as well.

"Look, Shayla," Eliza said sweetly. "I didn't *make* Tucker do anything. Maybe you two weren't as perfect together as you thought. You're a smart girl, so think of this logically. If you two were meant to be, then why is he with me now? And why did everyone else think we should be together too?"

"Nobody thought you two would be a good couple," Shayla spat, crossing her arms over her chest.

"Not true," Eliza said, practically singing the words. "Plenty of people did. In fact, Brooklyn's the one who set us up in the first place. And her boyfriend's friends with Tucker, right? So it sort of looks like you were the only one on the Tucker/Shayla bandwagon."

The crowd around us gasped at what Eliza said. Shayla opened and closed her mouth, suddenly unsure of how to respond. Hearing my name, people started to throw glances my way, which only made me feel like I wanted to run. I turned to see if there was an escape route, but my eyes locked on Abby's and I knew the damage had been done. It was easy to read her face now. She must have been feeling shocked, disgusted, and probably about a dozen other emotions, but the look on her face was sheer disbelief.

I couldn't exactly defend myself, so I turned back to the car wreck of a fight that was unfolding right in front of us.

Shayla had turned to Tucker, tears running down her cheeks. "How could you do this to me, Tuck?" she asked, quieter now. "You're my best friend. You told me you were in love with me. How could you just go off with her after everything we had?"

It was so hard to watch this girl who was perfectly nice pour her heart out to the guy she loved and know that she was hurting because of something I set in motion. I felt someone come up behind me and then heard Abby whisper, "Brooklyn, you've got to do something."

She was right. I'd created this, I had to try and diffuse it. I took a step forward, planning to talk to Eliza and encourage her to walk away, let Shayla and Tucker have their moment in private. And if that didn't work, I'd at least attempt to get Shayla to leave before she could be humiliated more. But before I had a chance to do anything, Eliza's head turned in my direction and she held up her hand to stop me.

I stood still as if she'd somehow put a spell on me that made me unable to continue. Only, I knew I was stopping on my own accord. Her eyes were threatening, and I knew what would happen if I got any closer and pissed her off.

"I'm sorry I hurt you, Shay," Tucker said sadly. I could tell he wasn't happy that Shayla was in pain. Matching him with Eliza had just made it so they would have a chance. It didn't stop Tucker from caring about Shayla as a person. "I don't know what else to say."

"I do." Eliza took a step toward Shayla. In her three-inch heels, she had about half a foot on her. I felt intimidated just watching Eliza, so I couldn't imagine what it must have felt like for Shayla. "Go find someone else."

That was it. Bursting into a fresh bout of tears, Shayla turned and ran down the hall. As she left, someone chased after her.

Ms. Zia.

I hadn't realized she was there too. I wondered if she'd seen the whole thing, or maybe just the end. She looked straight at me, her eyes cold, and I had my answer: She'd seen enough. She shook her head and then continued on down the corridor after Shayla.

Chapter Twenty-Three

I felt awful.

I couldn't imagine how humiliated Shayla must have been to not only have lost her boyfriend to Eliza but then to have it thrown in her face like that. Just watching it all explode had been painful. Experiencing it must have been so much worse.

And then when Eliza had brought me into it, I'd just about died. I hadn't necessarily wanted the student body at large to know that I was playing matchmaker behind the scenes, and I certainly didn't want them thinking that I went around breaking up happy couples.

The school was already divided on who was in the wrong: Tucker or Eliza; I'd heard bits and pieces of conversations as I walked from class to class. Some were Team Shayla and thought that it was wrong of Eliza to go after a guy who was obviously already taken. But surprisingly, even more seemed to be Team Eliza, the idea being that if Tucker was happy in his relationship, he wouldn't have strayed. I would have avoided the whole thing completely if I could have helped it.

What I couldn't avoid was Abby's disappointment that I hadn't done anything to break up the confrontation. As Eliza and Tucker walked away hand in hand and people began to disperse, I turned around to see Abby walking away from me too.

"Abby!"

She turned around. Her face was back to being blank as usual, but there was a sadness in her eyes that wasn't usually there.

"Look, there was nothing I could do," I said.

"There's always something you can do," she answered. "Especially given *your* talents."

She was being unfair. It's not like I could just bust out a spell in a crowded hallway, in front of everyone. Besides, Abby was way more experienced with magic than I was. Why couldn't she have done something? Why did it have to be me?

"This isn't one of your fantasy books, Abby," I said. "This is real life."

The only reaction I got was a hard couple of blinks. She looked down at her book and traced the letters of the title with her finger. "Why do you think I like to get lost in these?" she said, holding it up. "Real life sometimes sucks."

I watched her walk away, not bothering to look back.

Well, great. Asher was definitely going to hear about this.

I tried my best to get through the rest of the day without any more drama. I took random routes to get to class because I knew I'd run into fewer people. I arrived right as the bell rang and left directly after, so I wouldn't have to talk to anyone. I even volunteered to work solo on a science assignment, so I could avoid any questions about what had happened earlier. By last period, I was beginning to feel like I was back to my old self.

Alone and on my own.

I'd just sat down in my seat during sixth period and was taking out my homework when the teacher called me up to the front of the room. Perplexed, I walked quickly to her desk.

"You're wanted down in the guidance counselor's office, Ms. Sparks," she said, writing on a pad of paper and then handing me a pass. "Bring your things with you."

Ms. Zia.

I gathered all my stuff and started the long walk toward the front of the school. I'd been dreading this moment ever since I'd seen her follow after Shayla, and then notice me standing there in the hallway. I knew it looked bad. And to say my relationship with Ms. Zia had been strained lately was an understatement. She never really had forgiven me for skipping the fund-raiser and she'd made it clear she didn't agree with some of the choices I'd been making lately. She wasn't going to understand how I could have had anything to do with this.

Then again, maybe she would. After all, she knew me better than most, so she got that deep down, I was a good person. That I'd never hurt someone unless I didn't have any other choice. Ms. Z. had been my friend when I'd had none.

Maybe it wouldn't be as bad as I thought it would be.

The door was open when I got there, and I knocked lightly as I walked inside. "Hey, Ms. Z.," I said, giving her a friendly smile and sitting down in the chair across from her.

She was looking out the window absently, but then put her face in her hands and rubbed her forehead slowly. My mood dropped a few levels as I saw how stressed she was.

"Everything okay?" I asked, knowing already that it wasn't.

She separated her hands, revealing red eyes, and then cupped her face. Ms. Zia took a deep breath before talking.

When she finally did, her voice was cold and even. "How could you possibly think things are okay, Brooklyn?"

It was what I'd feared. I'd been brought in for another lecture.

"It wasn't my fault—" I started.

Ms. Z. held up her hand to stop me. "I don't care that you didn't start this, Brooklyn. I care that you did nothing to stop it. First when you helped them get together and then out there," she said, motioning outside her office.

I started to say something but thought better of it.

"What? You have nothing to say? There seems to be a lot of that going around lately," she said. "How could you let your friend humiliate Shayla like that? And so publicly, too."

My guilt changed to anger as she put all the blame on me again. I felt my face grow hot and I clenched my fists without even realizing it.

"Wait a second here. It was *Shayla's* bright idea to confront Eliza, not mine. She knew that what she was doing would draw a crowd. I bet she was even counting on it. What she didn't expect was for Eliza to fight back. And *that* was stupid. Eliza's an Elite. Nobody goes up against them."

"Well, maybe somebody should," Ms. Zia said, slamming her hands down on her tabletop.

"And why does that automatically have to be me?" I asked, gesturing wildly.

"Because you're better than this."

"You're right. I *am* better than this," I hissed. "I don't deserve to be lectured about something I had nothing to do with!"

"Brooklyn, Eliza said you were the one that set the two of them up!" she said, throwing her hands up in the air. "Was she lying about that?"

I didn't want to answer her question, because I knew no matter what I said, it would sound bad. But I couldn't just sit there and be silent.

"I let Eliza and Tucker know that they were interested in each other," I said finally. Ms. Zia's face fell. "But I didn't break up him and Shayla."

She shook her head. "I don't even know you anymore," she said. "First the makeover, then the new friends, the lying, and now this? You've changed, Brooklyn. You're not the girl I used to know."

"Good!" I shouted, sick of hearing about how awful I'd become. I was tired of defending myself to her. "I didn't like the old me very much. She was boring and lame and had no friends. She was never going to do anything amazing. This me—the *new* me—people are going to remember her."

"Do you really want them to?" she asked. "Do you want them to remember you for this? As a girl who compromised what she believed in to become someone she wasn't? Someone who hung out with a group of kids who were shallow and conniving and only cared about themselves?"

Tears threatened to fall. "The Elite have made me better. People care what I think now. They listen to me."

"The only problem is, now you have nothing of value to say," Ms. Z. said slowly, emphasizing each word.

It was a major blow. The one person who was supposed to be in my corner no matter what had now become my enemy. I was so upset, I didn't even know how to respond. Instead, I picked up my things and, without saying another word, huffed out of the office, leaving Ms. Zia to stare after me.

The final bell rang just as I was walking out the door, and instead of heading back to class, I stomped straight toward the parking lot. I had to get out of there. My hands started to cramp and I realized that they were still balled up in fists.

I replayed the conversation over and over again in my head as I walked, trying to come up with better comebacks for the things Ms. Zia had said to me. About me. Someone slammed into me and I almost dropped my books.

"Are you blind?" I screeched at whoever it was, and just kept going. The screaming made me feel slightly better and I debated doing it again. Just screaming at the top of my lungs. But I didn't need to give anyone another reason to stare at me like a freak. There'd been enough of that today already.

I needed somebody to talk to, to confide in. Someone who'd see that I'd been backed into a corner and that I didn't deserve to be blamed for all the bad things that were happening around this school. And also, how crazy Ms. Z. had been to say all that to me. How ironic, before, it would have been her that I'd have gone running to for advice and understanding.

With that no longer an option, I pulled out my cell and began to call Asher. But I closed it again without finishing. He hated The Elite even more than Ms. Z. did, if that was possible, so I had a feeling he wasn't going to side with me on this either. And I already knew how he felt about what I'd done to Shayla. We'd probably just end up getting into another fight, and this time it wouldn't end as well.

I settled for taking a drive, maybe heading out to the boon-docks somewhere and screaming my guts out. Maybe I could use a spell to blow things up. Yep, a little physical exertion sounded like a perfect solution.

"Brooklyn, wait up!"

I heard my name but didn't slow my pace. I kept my eyes trained on my car and made a beeline for it, hoping to make a quick escape. It wasn't until my name was called again that I even glanced over my shoulder.

Gigi and Camden were just a few feet behind me, trying their best to catch up, while Rhodes, Wheatley, and Eliza brought up the rear.

"Today's been really shitty, Gigi," I warned, still walking. "You might not want to be around me right now."

I was surprised when a hand closed over my arm and spun me around. They'd closed the space between us much more quickly than I'd thought possible.

"I know. I heard," Gigi said, looking sympathetic.

"We all heard," Camden added. He wasn't even out of breath. Here I was, huffing and puffing after making my hasty exit, and the guy hadn't even broken a sweat. Damn him.

I looked back and forth between the two of them, trying to figure out what they wanted. By this time, the others had caught up too, and were surrounding me.

"Look, guys, I can't take another big blowup, so *please*, just let me go," I said, trying once again to walk away.

"We just wanted to thank you," Gigi said, stopping me in my tracks.

I wondered if I'd gone momentarily crazy, but then she reached out and touched my arm, more gently this time.

"You were really there for Eliza today," she said.

I was going to correct her by saying that I had been one step away from leading her away from the confrontation, but then Eliza cut in.

"I didn't want things to go down like that," she said, appearing sincere. "You saw her, though. Shayla just came up to me, accusing me of taking her boyfriend—as if I had the power to do that."

"Eliza, that's what we did!" I said, the frustration coming out in my voice. "How can you not see that?"

"Brookie, trust me, if I had that power, I would be richer

than Daddy," she said. "We can't make anybody *do* anything."

I couldn't exactly argue with that, because she was right. She didn't have the power to do it, but I did. Only none of them knew that. And in a way, I couldn't totally fault Eliza for this. As far as she knew, she was right.

"We also know you took the hit from Ms. Zia today," Gigi said, surprising me once again.

"How do you know that?" I asked.

She nodded back toward the building. "I left class a little early and saw you storm out of her office," she said, shrugging. "It didn't take a genius to figure it out."

"Oh," I said, looking down at the ground.

"Are you okay?" Rhodes asked, putting his arm around me comfortingly. "I've been in that position before with Z. It isn't fun."

I shook my head. The mention of her name made all my feelings of anger rush back with a vengeance. I wasn't sure why I hadn't thought of it before, but The Elite were sort of the perfect people to talk to about this. I knew from past conversations that there was no way they'd side with Ms. Z. over me. And that's what I really needed right now: someone to back me up. Tell me that I was right, when it all felt so wrong.

"The whole thing is bull!" I exclaimed, letting myself get worked up all over again. "Can you believe she tried blaming everything on me? She said that I should have been able to control Eliza better. That I'd *changed*."

"Well, you *have* changed, Brooklyn," Gigi said, her eyes catching mine. "You're *better* now."

"What do you mean?" I asked. It wasn't the answer I'd been looking for, but I was curious to see where she was going with it.

"You're drop-dead gorgeous, people follow you now, others

look up to you," she said, ticking them off on her fingers one by one. "Before, you were, well . . . and I mean this in the nicest way possible . . . but you were a nobody."

"That's totally not the case now," Eliza said, nodding emphatically.

"Ms. Zia's a bitch," Gigi continued. "She's just a sad, aging woman who used to be popular but couldn't hack it in the real world, so she went back to high school to relive her glory days. She's washed-up, a has-been, and I hate to say it, but, Brooklyn—I think she's jealous of you."

I didn't necessarily agree with everything Gigi was saying, but I was so mad that I couldn't get myself to defend Ms. Z. either.

Gigi turned to me with a sparkle in her eyes. "I think there's a way we can get back at Ms. Zia, but we're going to need your help, Brooklyn."

The last thing I wanted on a day like this was another challenge to prove my loyalty to the group. I sighed and took a step backward.

"How many tests are you guys going to throw my way before you see that I'm loyal to you?" I asked, feeling fed up. "I don't think I can do this anymore."

"And you won't have to," Camden said. "Not after this."

"If you do this, you'll officially be one of us," Gigi said. "Promise."

She drew a cross over her heart and then kissed her finger and held it up to the sky. I thought about what she said. I was *so* ready for this whole thing to be over.

"What do you want to do?" I asked slowly.

They looked at each other hungrily before answering. "We want to break into her office and read our files," Gigi said.

"Why?" I asked, surprised that that's what they wanted. No

vandalizing, no blackmailing. They just wanted to see their files.

"We're all getting ready to apply to colleges, and they'll look at our files before making their decisions," Eliza said. "We want to make sure that what she said about us is correct. And if it's not, then we can make some . . . alterations."

"Don't you want to see what she's said about you in there?" Gigi asked. "Especially after today?"

I thought about this for a few seconds and then realized that I did. I was curious to see what Ms. Z. really thought of me. Even if I ended up not liking what I read.

"I'm in," I said, resolved.

Chapter Twenty-Four

Later that night, when I'd had a chance to calm down a bit and I began to see a little more clearly, I realized that by saying yes to the others, I was actually going to have to break into the office. This wasn't small-time—toilet papering a house or sabotaging a couple—this was breaking and entering. A possible felony if we were caught.

Which meant that we couldn't get caught.

I wasn't the only one worried. Immediately after I'd agreed to make this happen, Gigi started to grill me about how I was going to pull it off. I told her that I would figure it out, that I'd have a plan. Hadn't I already proven that I could get things done? Gigi argued with me a bit, saying that in order to feel comfortable with everything, she'd have to know what the plan was. I asked her to trust me for now and said that I'd have plans to them by the end of the week.

This challenge was going to be the most difficult to pass for several reasons. For one thing, I knew that the others would be watching me closely to see how I pulled it off. This meant that not only was I going to have to make sure I left no evidence of us being in Ms. Z.'s office, but I'd also have to be doubly certain that the rest of The Elite didn't see me using magic. Initially, I tried to convince them to let me break in alone and pull our files myself. It was much more likely we'd get caught as a group than individually. But they insisted on coming along, saying if I was going to be a part of the group, it was time we acted as a group. They also pointed out that with all of us involved, our files could be found much more quickly and we wouldn't have to take them with us. This made my job much harder, but not impossible.

To make things more complicated, I knew from all those times in Ms. Z.'s office that anytime she wasn't there, the door was locked. This was also the case with her student files. And unfortunately, she kept her keys on her at all times and would notice immediately if they were gone. So there was the question of how to get in.

Similarly, the school was always locked up at the end of each day, and all the main entrances were monitored with outdoor surveillance cameras. It was going to be a lot of work to cut the feed for the cameras and then break into the front door and expect no one to get suspicious at the lack of footage during those hours. That left me with the task of figuring out other ways to get inside.

Lastly, the same rent-a-cop security guards that followed Principal Franklin around all day also walked the campus at night. Several years before, a few runaways had broken in hoping to take off with computers and other electronics that they could sell on the streets. Unfortunately, they hadn't expected to run into the guard who'd immediately detained them, hand-cuffed them to a pipe in one of the classrooms, and waited until the police arrived. If we weren't careful, the same thing could happen to us.

Believe me, given the numerous challenges facing us in trying to get ahold of our files, I understood Gigi's desire to be let in on the plan. It wasn't just my future that I held in my hands, it would be all of theirs, too.

Eventually I told her that I'd get copies of all the keys needed to get past the doors and would do some research on the guards. This seemed to satisfy her enough to leave me alone to figure out the rest. Eliza even offered to set up a few video cameras in various places around the school, so that we could get a handle on their patrol patterns. Eliza liked this particular job, saying that it was good practice for her upcoming audition as a badass *Mission: Impossible* type.

After a few days, we had the guards' patterns down and decided it was time to put our plan into action. Luckily, by then I'd figured out my side of things. It certainly wasn't easy, but if it went as planned, we'd be in and out within fifteen minutes. Plenty of time to take a look at the files, make any changes necessary, and head home, our presence in the building going unknown.

I'd gone to bed early the night of "Project E-Files"—this was what Eliza had started to call it, *E* for Elite and the rest because Mr. Rivers was in talks to do an *X-Files* remake. I lay in bed, my stomach churning as I waited for the hours to pass. Time seemed to go by excruciatingly slowly and as I was alone with my thoughts, I continued to go over what I was going to do in my head. My alarm went off at 1 a.m., but I didn't even need it, considering I'd never fallen asleep in the first place. I quietly got up, grabbed the bag of items I'd need for the night off my desk, and tiptoed downstairs and out the front door. Sticking to the shadows, I ran halfway down the block and met up with Eliza, who was driving Rhodes and me over to the school to meet up with the others. We parked a few blocks away and planned to enter from the side, lessening the chances of us being spotted.

When we arrived at the location we'd all agreed on, we got out of our cars and circled up.

"You sure you want to do this?" I asked. I wasn't trying to convince them not to do it; I knew by now that was impossible. But I figured I had to ask, considering the consequences if we got caught.

"You think this will work, right?" Camden asked, throwing the question back to me.

The truth was, it had to. I nodded.

"Then we're in," Gigi said. "And if you can pull this off, that means you're in too."

"No pressure," I said, partly joking but mostly serious.

I knew what I was up against, having them along while I used my powers. And I'd gone over what I was going to do so many times that I had an alternate plan for just about anything that could go wrong. What I didn't have a plan for was what I would do if we didn't make it to Ms. Z's office at all.

That just couldn't happen.

"Okay, let's go. Follow me and I'll show you where we're getting in," I said, motioning them forward.

We stuck to the side of the building, stopping every few feet to listen for any noises. It wasn't just the rent-a-cops we were worried about, it was the wandering teenagers or random passersby we couldn't be sure of, who would see us and then hold the break-in over our heads. When we got to the huge Dumpster around the back, I slowed to a stop and turned to face them.

"Ugh. Let's keep moving," Eliza whispered, covering her face with her sleeve.

"This is where we're going in," I said, gesturing to the top of the Dumpster. We all looked up and saw the window locked tightly above. Eliza began to shake her head.

"No," she said. "No, no, no, no . . . these are not Dumpster-diving clothes. These aren't even trash adjacent clothes."

"This is the only place we're getting in undetected," I insisted, grabbing on to the side of the Dumpster and pulling myself onto the closed bin. This could be the end of our plan before we'd even started. Knowing that I could manage to trip over air if the wind was blowing too hard, I knew my clumsiness could be our biggest saboteur. I was especially careful not to make any noise as I stood up slowly. "Give me a sec while I unlock the window."

This was the first hurdle to pass, and if I could get the rest of them to stay below me, it wouldn't be a problem. I put my bag down and reached inside, pulling out a long, thin object and turning to face away from the prying eyes. I purposely used my body to shield what I was doing, acting as a barrier to give me some privacy to do my work.

I took a few deep breaths to get my already rapidly beating heart down to a calmer pace and said the first spell I'd memorized for tonight.

"Releechio boltum," I breathed, barely above a whisper.

I heard the sound of the lock click and watched as the latch slid away so that I'd be free to open the window.

One down, three to go.

I smiled and started to turn around to tell the others to join me, when I nearly ran right into someone. I stifled a scream as I saw that it was just Gigi. She must have jumped up on top of the Dumpster when I was in the middle of casting and snuck up beside me. How she'd managed to be so quiet, I didn't know, but I instantly began to worry that she'd seen the whole thing.

"Oh!" I said. "I didn't know you were there."

"I thought you might need some help," she said. "What's that you've got?"

She was talking about the thing I'd taken out of the bag and now had in my hands. I looked down at the object again, already forgetting that I'd had it to begin with. Then I shook my head and offered it to her.

"Metal hanger," I said. She squinted while looking at it in the dark and saw the mangled piece of metal I'd formed before leaving my house. "Perfect for getting into cars and unlocking windows with latches."

I reached out and pulled the windows apart and touched the latch I was talking about. Of course, I hadn't actually used the tool to get inside, but after Gigi had been on my ass about every aspect of the plan, I figured it was smarter to have an explanation ready for everything.

Gigi ran her hands along the length of the metal hanger and then cocked her head to the side quizzically. I worried for a second about the hint of suspicion that was in her eyes as I waited for her to respond.

"You'll have to show me how to do it sometime," she said finally. "It could turn out to be a very useful skill to have. I'm always locking myself out of my car and something like this could be so much easier than waiting for Triple A."

Relief washed over me and I nodded. "Of course. Just let me know when you want that tutorial," I agreed nervously. After we successfully got out of our current predicament, that is.

The others climbed up after us, Camden giving Eliza a boost and her trying desperately not to touch anything. Watching Eliza scramble up and then nearly gag at the smell was almost worth the whole trip. Camden and Rhodes popped up next, just as easily and noiselessly as Gigi and I had. Wheatley, on the other hand, took a running start and hit the garbage bin like it was another football player. There was a loud jangling as the metal Dumpster hit the wall, and we fought to stay standing as it lurched forward.

"My bad," Wheatley said as he struggled to get up.

I looked around us, half expecting to see lights from the guards running toward us, but as I listened, there was nothing. Satisfied we were safe for the moment, I turned back to the matter at hand.

"Let's get inside quickly," I said. I swung open the window as far as it would go and pulled my body up onto the sill. Finally, I kicked my legs over the side. The light from the moon shone in through the space and gave me a peek at what was below us. Right underneath my dangling feet was a counter in the science room. It was about two and a half feet wide and ran along the whole wall. Still holding on to the window frame, I pushed off and landed with a quiet thud on the counter's surface. I continued down until my feet were firmly on the ground again.

Looking up, I saw that Gigi was already on her way through, followed by Eliza and then the guys. This time Wheatley took the drop like a champ, making almost no noise at all.

We quietly made our way across the room and let ourselves out, being sure to peek into the hallway before doing so. A quick check of my cell phone showed that it was one forty-five. This was perfect, because from our surveillance, I knew that the guards wouldn't come around again for another half hour, when they'd start at the opposite side of school and make their way over to where we were.

Walking down the hallway at school at night was eerily creepy. Probably because it wasn't the way a school was meant to be seen. Dark, quiet, empty. I couldn't stop thinking that it would be the perfect scene for a horror film. Considering that for most people, high school was a nightmare to begin with, it didn't seem like much of a stretch. As the others stuck close to me, I wondered if they were thinking the same thing.

When we got to Ms. Z.'s office, I motioned for the others to head across the hall and hide just around the corner of the L-shaped hallway.

Gigi gave me an inquiring look. "If the guards come early, they're going to see me trying to get into the office. And if that happens, I'm done. But they won't see you, so you can all still get away," I explained. "There's no sense in everyone getting caught, but if you really want to help me . . ."

"No, it's all right," Camden said, pulling Gigi toward him and the others, who had already stepped out of sight. I watched Gigi go too, not totally willingly, it seemed. She looked around the hallway, her eyes resting on a space just above the lockers. Then she took one last look down the hallway before she hid behind Camden.

What a control freak.

I took a key out of my pocket and gave them a smile as I held it up to show them. Convinced they'd gotten the hint, I turned toward the door and, making sure my body was cheated away from them, pushed my arm forward like I was unlocking it. Instead, I let my hand hover over the knob and said the spell that would let us in. I felt my hand tingle and then heat up, causing the handle to glow the faintest bit before going dark again.

Just as I was about to reach out and open the door, I heard something that made me freeze in my spot. It was faint, but it was there. A whirring sound. At first I couldn't be sure whether it was the roaring in my head or if it was something out there. I started to look around, trying to find anything in the darkness that could have been the culprit. Finally, my eyes fell on Gigi, who had her phone out and was typing something into it. I gave her a look and mouthed, "Really?" She made a face and then put her phone away quickly to show me that she was done.

I took another look down the hallway and then reached for the handle. Grabbing ahold of it, I twisted and then pushed the door open. It was still warm to the touch.

Disappearing inside, I performed the same spell on the cabinets where the student files were kept. Then, heading back to the door, I gestured for the others to join me. A few seconds later, the six of us were inside the room, the door closed behind us to give the illusion that nothing was amiss.

Camden and Gigi went right over to the cabinets and began pulling files. They passed one out to each of us, our names written in black permanent ink on the tabs. I recognized Ms. Zia's handwriting and I felt a tugging in my chest over what we were doing.

I'd had plenty of time over the last couple of days to think about the last argument we'd had in her office. And although my anger had died down from a blazing fireball to a lit match, I was still heated. It was hard to explain what I was feeling. In fact, I'd tried my best to tell Asher about it, but he just kept saying to give it time and that we'd both cool down eventually. He didn't seem to understand how much I valued Ms. Z.'s friendship and opinion, and that I'd never felt more betrayed.

Then again, Asher's mind was elsewhere right now. Over the past week, his parents had begun holding family meetings and making him and Abby go over all their family spells. He'd said it was like they were going through some sort of midlife crisis, only they were choosing to focus on their children rather than getting a new car or having an affair. I knew he was having a tough time with it, but all the time he was spending at home had allowed me to concentrate on what we were doing here. It had also given him zero time to focus on what had gone down between Tucker and Shayla.

I flipped open my file and used the flashlight application on my phone to see what she'd written. I settled down on the floor to read what my former confidant really thought of me.

The first thing I noticed was that the file wasn't all that thick. As I leafed through it, I caught glimpses of my past report cards, notes from teachers, attendance records, awards I'd been given. But toward the back, apart from everything else, were several loose papers written in Ms. Zia's handwriting. I turned to the most recent one, which was labeled the same day as the blow-up between Shayla and Eliza. I could only imagine what it said.

Brooklyn Sparks, though she's been an exceptional student over the past few years at Clearview, appears to be struggling recently. Her quest for acceptance and her obsession with popularity can sometimes manifest itself in negative ways and I have witnessed physical as well as emotional changes as a result. She recently began to spend time with a particular group of students her classmates call

"The Elite," in order to attempt to gain popularity. I fear that this is a fellowship that might be dangerous for her and have encouraged her to find another group that might be more fitting.

This said, I have spent a lot of time with Brooklyn over the years and have found her to be a responsible, talented, caring, and loyal young woman. Though her desire to be popular is puzzling and might lead her into difficult situations, I have no doubt that she will find a balance between who she is and who she wants to be.

In the meantime I will continue to try and guide her to make good decisions and have all the faith in the world in her passion and abilities.

I finished reading her latest notes about me and let the file fall into my lap. I'd been sure that she was going to rip into me about the Shayla thing. Say that I was a horrible, irresponsible, selfish brat. But all she'd expressed was that she was worried. That, I had to admit, was sort of understandable. Looking at the situation through her eyes, I *had* changed. And all she saw was me pulling away from the person I'd been and hanging out with a group of kids she'd had some personal experience with. She could have brought up what I'd done to Shayla, said that I'd terrorized or manipulated other students, put it all down in the file so it would've been on my permanent record, but she didn't.

She was trying to protect me.

The realization hit me like a tidal wave. I hadn't had any reason to be mad at Ms. Z. She was just doing her job, both as my counselor and as my friend. It was me I was mad at. My life had gotten so much more complicated the last couple of months and I was blaming all my circumstances on the wrong people.

And now I'd helped the people Ms. Zia was trying to save me from—allowed them to break into her office to do God knows what. I looked up and saw that Gigi had moved on from reading her own file and was shuffling through others.

I needed to get us out of here before anything happened.

I started to get up and was going to try and push everyone to leave when Rhodes hit the ground a few feet away from me.

"Get down!" he whispered. "Flashlight at the end of the hallway!"

We all followed suit and got down below the windows. Everyone in the group was looking at me, like I was supposed to come up with a plan. I scanned my head for a spell, any spell that would be able to get us out of this situation. But my mind had gone blank.

How was I possibly going to cast without The Elite seeing me do it? Was there any way to get us out of this without getting caught?

Chapter Twenty-Five

Once my adrenaline started pumping, it seemed to kick my brain into high gear. It didn't take long before I knew what to do.

"Close the file cabinets and hide," I said. "Nothing behind the desk is visible from the window."

"Are you sure?" Eliza asked, scrambling to get behind the big structure.

"Positive."

This was, in fact, a total lie, as I knew that you could see anything in the room from the window in Ms. Z.'s office that peeked out into the hallway, and even if you couldn't see behind the desk, there was no way everyone would be able to fit back there. But they didn't need to know that for my idea to work. I pushed myself up against the door in a crouched position, so I was far away from the others and completely out of their view.

"What are you doing?" Gigi hissed at me when I didn't join them.

"The door's a blind spot too," I said, hoping she'd buy it. I needed to be alone in order to cast the spell. And with the rest of them behind the desk and the lights off in the room, no one would know what I was about to do.

The glare of a light was getting closer and closer, until I knew the guard was only a few feet away. I quickly cleared my mind and then mumbled a few words, feeling the electricity move through my hands and then spread into the air all around me. I hoped the others were too frazzled to notice the change in the atmosphere.

We could hear footsteps now as someone walked slowly past Ms. Z.'s office. A single beam of light moved around the room, illuminating the tops of everyone's heads as they ducked behind the desk. I held my breath as I willed the spell to work and prayed for the guard to keep moving. After a few excruciatingly long seconds, the light started to fade and I could hear the steps move away from us. When I knew he was gone, I stood back up.

"That was close," I said, breaking the silence. And it had been. If I hadn't performed the spell on the guard to make it so he couldn't see anyone human inside the room, we would've been caught for sure. I quickly said the counter spell, and then crossed over to the desk.

"You guys, we have to go," I said. "We got what we came here for. Let's not press our luck."

I turned to collect the files everyone had in their hands, but the others pulled back when I tried to take theirs. I looked at them quizzically.

"Seriously, guys, we have to move. Put the files back and let's go!"

When they still didn't do what I asked, I brushed past them and put my own file away. "If you take your files, they're going to know it was you that broke in," I said, hoping this would scare them into doing what I wanted. "And if you want to get caught, fine. I'm getting out of here."

I turned my back on them and then heard shuffling and papers rustling noisily. Finally, the drawers snapped shut and after a few seconds I felt them join me at the door.

The hallway was dark and quiet as I stepped outside. I waited as everyone moved past me, and began to run quietly down the hallway toward the science room, fifty feet away. I just needed to lock up and then we'd be out of there, the mess of the night behind us. I'd worry later about how I'd make this up to Ms. Zia.

Wheatley was the last to leave, and I watched him shuffle toward the others, who were all gathered at the door to the science classroom, waiting anxiously. This time I didn't stop when I heard a noise in the darkness, wanting so badly to get out of there that I was willing to ignore whatever it was.

I put my hand over Ms. Zia's door handle again, saying the words that would lock the door. The warm glow appeared and I waited for the unmistakable clank of the lock falling into place and then turned around to run.

Only, when I turned, I saw a person standing at the other end of the L-shaped hallway. The hallway that had been empty just a few moments before. I wanted to scream, but the sound got caught in my throat. In that moment, it felt like all the wind had been knocked out of me and I wondered if maybe I was imagining things. It was a *him*, that much I could tell. For a second, I wished for the man to be a psycho killer, because that would probably cause less damage than getting caught.

"Stay where you are," the man shouted, beginning to raise his arm. He had something in his hand. A gun, maybe? Oh God, he was going to shoot me and I was going to die inside this school. I couldn't think of anything worse. And so I did the only thing I could think of to do.

I ran.

The hallway illuminated in front of me and I realized what had been in his hand was a flashlight. This was both good and bad, because on the one hand I could see where I was going, but on the other, it would make it easier for the guard to spot us.

"Go!" I screamed at the others. They hadn't seen the man, but they'd heard him and immediately scrambled inside the room to the still open window.

Gigi, however, remained at the door, encouraging me to run faster, her eyes growing wide as she watched the figure turn the corner and then chase me down the hallway. I appreciated the fact that she was sticking around to make sure I got out, but at the same time, she was making it difficult for me to cast any spells to diffuse the situation.

Even if the guard never got a look at our faces, he'd still know someone had broken in, and the chances of us getting caught were amped. I had to do something to stop him from blowing the whistle on us.

Thinking quickly, I turned to face him while still running backward and lifted my cell in his direction. I'd been squeezing it so hard that my hand hurt. Ignoring my pain for the moment, I pressed a button that activated my camera flash, to try and blind him long enough to slow him down. The white light exploded through the darkness and illuminated the man, who I could see now was wearing a navy blue outfit and was carrying the flashlight in one hand and a radio in the other. He lifted his hand to his face to try to shield the glare. I was happy when he began to slow down, and I thought I might actually be able to get away.

And then my feet tangled and I started to fall.

No, no, no, no, no! Not now!

I cried out as my body hit the ground and I slid across the floor. It was like being on a Slip 'n Slide. I wondered if I would be able to make it all the way to the science room before stopping.

In the fall I lost my grip on my phone and it skittered out of my hands, slamming into the lockers a few feet away. I watched the guard recover his eyesight. He was gaining on me. He was only twenty feet away now and I knew he would catch up with me before I'd be able to grab my phone and get out of there.

I glanced back at Gigi, who was screaming for me to move my ass. She was so close that I knew it would be virtually impossible for her not to see me cast if I did. But looking back at the guard, who was now only ten feet away, I didn't have a choice.

I had to either cast or get caught.

So I hastily sat up and faced my attacker.

"Flatismo bolistic!" I tried to keep my voice down because I knew Gigi was still watching. As soon as the words were out of my mouth, the guy tumbled to the ground beside me before passing out on the smooth floor. I leaned over to see if he was breathing and make sure I hadn't mistakenly killed him.

"Are you crazy? Leave him there and let's go," Gigi hissed.

I ignored her and felt for a pulse. Finding one quickly, I watched his pudgy belly move up and down in a deep rhythm as if he were asleep. The exact intention of my spell.

He was going to be okay. Groggy when he woke up, and probably a bit embarrassed for falling asleep on the job, but he wouldn't remember finding a bunch of kids breaking into one of the offices.

For now we were safe.

I scrambled over to my phone and snatched it from the floor

before joining Gigi at the door. She grabbed ahold of my hand and dragged me toward the window, where we scrambled out into the night.

After reading what Ms. Z. had written in my file and then almost getting caught at school, I was ready for life to settle down. Go back to normal. Avoid the drama. In fact, now that I was officially a member of The Elite, I was looking forward to reaping all the benefits of being popular at Clearview. Maybe it was naive of me to think it would be that easy, but after everything I'd been through, all the hurdles I'd crossed, I really thought everything was about to pay off.

It had to. Right?

I woke up the next day feeling like a weight had been lifted from my shoulders. It was sketchy for a minute there when the security guard showed up, and I saw my life flash before my eyes. It wasn't pretty. I didn't want to think of what would have happened if I didn't have magic on my side.

Now, walking into school the next morning, I could finally concentrate on the life ahead of me. No more living in the shadows of other students at school. I was dating a majorly hot guy, who, despite everything we'd been through, seemed to really care about me. I was a freaking witch, for God's sake, and was starting to get the hang of the powers that were my birthright. And now I was going to try my best to patch things up with the one person who'd always been there for me.

Once that was done, all would be right in the world.

I strutted down the hallway, my baby doll dress grazing my toned thighs. My four-inch wedges made me taller than most of the students I passed, and I had to admit, I kind of liked the view from the top. For the first time, I felt powerful—like I belonged. Something had changed in me. I'd gone from wanting to have people respect and admire me to actually believing that I deserved it.

The thought made me smile, which caused others to look at me curiously. They were doing what I'd always done. They were trying to figure out what I was thinking and, quite possibly, why I'd been chosen for teen royalty.

And the answer was that I hadn't been chosen—I'd made it happen.

Unable to stop grinning, I turned the corner at the front office and headed straight for Ms. Zia's. I wanted to tell her she didn't have to worry about me, that everything was going to be okay and that I was still the responsible girl who cared about other people. And that from here on out, my actions were going to prove it. But as I approached her door, I saw that it was closed. Inside, a girl appeared to be in the middle of a meltdown. Her head was in her hands and her shoulders were shaking. It took me a second to realize that she was crying. Ms. Z. was sitting next to her, comforting her, her back turned to me.

Two other students sat outside the office door, both looking miserable. I recognized the girl as the captain of the women's basketball team, and the guy next to her had the second highest GPA in school. It was clear that something was wrong, but I didn't know either of them well enough to ask them.

Just then, Ms. Z.'s door opened and Shayla came walking out, eyes bloodshot. She looked at me before I could avoid her stare and I instantly felt awful. I would make it up to her. From here on out, I would focus on doing good things for others. No more blurring the lines of good and evil.

I was half expecting Shayla to start yelling at me the way she had at Eliza earlier that week, but she was either too tired or too fed up to fight. She just walked past me and headed for the doors that led to the parking lot.

Even though I knew the other kids were there before me, I slipped inside Ms. Zia's office before they could get up from their seats. I could tell by the look on her face that she was surprised to see me.

"What do you need, Brooklyn?" she asked, sounding tired even though her day was just beginning. "Look, I don't know if you could tell, but I've got a lot to deal with here."

"What's going on?"

"You know I can't discuss the details . . ."

"I don't need the details, just the CliffsNotes," I said, hoping she could tell I was being sincere.

She looked at me and then sighed, realizing that I wasn't going to go away.

"Someone's been terrorizing students. They've somehow found out personal information about certain students and have begun to leak it to the rest of the student body. Some kids have even received anonymous notes saying this information will be divulged if they don't follow certain orders."

"They're being blackmailed?"

As soon as the words left my lips, I got a sick feeling in the pit of my stomach that began to grow until I had to sit down.

"And it's serious, Brooklyn. One student was outed on a website for being gay and he hadn't even come out to his parents yet. Another student's mom was sent an e-mail telling her that her husband had been cheating on her and that the kid knew about it. Someone's sent anonymous letters to the admissions offices of the schools that our most promising students have applied to, divulging personal issues the students don't want the world to know, endangering their chances of getting in. We don't know who's doing all of this, but I've got six students so far who are devastated by these attacks."

"I can't believe this is happening," I said. Any happiness I felt before had drained out of me.

"Brooklyn?" she asked. I looked up at her, still thinking about what she'd told me. "Do me a favor and be really careful who you trust right now. Okay?"

"Got it, Ms. Z.," I said, a little dazed by everything. I got up from the seat and threw my bag over my shoulder. Before I reached the door, I turned back to her. "And for what it's worth . . . I'm really sorry for everything."

She smiled and nodded. I wasn't sure if she fully believed me, but it was a start.

She called the basketball player into her office as I walked out and I could hear her begin to cry before the door was even closed.

In the hallway I looked around and saw that nearly everyone looked upset. Those who hadn't been affected yet were worried that someone would come after them next. Some students consoled their friends as others stood around in tiny circles, whispering about what was going on. As I turned to leave, I noticed that someone had taken the place just vacated by the basketball player.

"Abby," I said, surprised to see her sitting there. Even more shocking was that her hands were empty. I'd never seen her without a book to read and it was a really odd sight. Like a doctor without a lab coat, a football player without a helmet. "What are you doing here?"

She looked up at me, her eyes sad. "You don't know?" she answered.

"Know what? I just got here."

"Someone put these up all over school," she said, and thrust a sheet of paper at me. It was a xeroxed copy of what looked like a letter. Upon closer examination, I saw that it had Abby's name at the top. "It's a project I had to do for creative writing class. We were supposed to write something that made us uncomfortable. The type of topic that we'd never gravitate toward in real life. It was supposed to push our limits."

I scanned the page and my eye caught a line halfway down that made my mouth drop open.

> I leaned over him, pressing my chest against his, feeling the heat between us. He was going to be my first and I couldn't wait to know what it felt like to be with a man.

My cheeks began to flush. It wasn't quite Danielle Steel, but it was pretty darn close. Who knew Abby had it in her?

"Um, it's . . . descriptive," I said, trying not to offend her or make her any more embarrassed than she already was.

Abby let her head tilt back until it touched the wall behind her. "People think I wrote it about *myself*," she said finally. "Like it was a diary entry or something. Everyone thinks I'm this freaky girl now. Guys keep catcalling me. Girls are calling me a slut. All I want is to go back to people not knowing who I am."

I crumpled up the paper and tossed it into the trash. "I'm so sorry about this, Abby," I said.

"It's not your fault," she muttered, looking hopeless.

I wasn't about to correct her, but deep down I knew that it was. And I had to do something about it.

"I'm going to stop whoever's doing this, Ab," I said, the anger building inside of me. "I promise."

Without waiting for a response, I took one step, and then

another, and another, until I was power walking down the hallway toward the cafeteria. I knew they were in there. It's where they were whenever they weren't in class. I narrowed my eyes and continued straight for them, not slowing as I stomped my way up the stairs to their raised table.

"Hey, Brookie . . ." Eliza began. But I didn't let her finish. I reached straight for Gigi's bag and started to rifle through it. I pulled out a few books, several tubes of lip gloss, a Kate Spade wallet, and her cell phone. Starting to really get pissed, I moved to grab Eliza's bag next. She lunged for it before I could, and held it to her body protectively. "What are you doing, you freak?"

"Where are they?" I hissed.

Throughout the whole display, Gigi had remained calm. In fact, she hadn't moved at all. Her face was set with a smile and her arms were delicately crossed over her chest.

"Where are what?" she asked.

"The files," I answered. "I know you took them, Gigi."

"I don't know what you're talking about. We put our files back just like you."

"Not *your* files. The ones you *stole*. The ones that belonged to the other students."

They were all silent.

"I never would've helped you guys get in there last night if I thought this was what you were going to do. I want it to stop *now*," I said, the anger causing my voice to crack.

Gigi leaned forward on her elbows and entwined her fingers before resting her chin on them.

"That's not going to happen," she said, challenging me.

I'd really thought that they were people to aspire to be like, that they were going to open doors for me, that the group would let me in, but clearly I'd been mental. They were only out for themselves, each of them making their decisions based on selfishness. It was clear that they were only going to continue their reign of terror on the other students at the school; they'd already proven this by torturing the students they didn't like or had grudges with by using their files against them. And it was just going to get worse.

Unless I stopped them.

I placed my hands on the table and leaned down so that I was looking Gigi right in the eyes. Her eyes grew wide as I did this, but she didn't move away from me. That was something that had always impressed me about her. She had this ability to stand her ground in any situation. Of course, now that I was trying to intimidate her, the quality was just annoying.

"If you don't stop going after students at this school, I will tell everyone what you've done," I said, knowing that I was crossing a line I'd never be able to come back from. I was hoping that the threat of getting caught would be enough to get them to concede. Our friendship would be over, of course, but that was going to happen anyway. I could see that now. At least this way, the rest of the kids at school would be safe.

"You'll get in trouble too," she said, calling my bluff. "We'll destroy you."

"I don't care anymore," I said. And I realized that I didn't. I was sick of worrying about my world falling apart around me. In fact, I almost welcomed it. It would be a relief not to have to try and control everything anymore. Whatever the consequences, it was time to do what was right.

The Elite looked at each other, all of them waiting for Gigi to answer. My dress was soaked with sweat and my body was growing cold as the adrenaline began to wear off. Finally, Gigi sat back calmly in her chair and folded her hands in her lap as she stared at me.

"Fine," she said.

I wasn't sure I'd heard her correctly, but I was afraid of getting a different answer if I asked her to repeat herself. A wave of relief washed over me and I fought back a smile.

"Okay," I said, taking a step backward, still staring at them. When I neared the edge, I finally turned away and started to walk down the steps.

"Oh, and, Brooklyn," Gigi called out behind me.

"Yeah?" I asked, looking up at her from my place on the ground.

"You should probably go find Asher. He's going to want to talk to you," she said, holding up her phone and showing me the picture of me kissing the underwear model.

And then I watched with horror as she hit send.

Chapter Twenty-Six

I searched for Asher, thinking that if I could just find him, maybe I could fix things somehow. There was a part of me that held out hope that the photo hadn't actually made it to him; texts went missing in the cell-iverse all the time, right? Another hope was that he just hadn't seen it yet. If there was a possibility that I could get to the photo before he did, then that would at least buy me some time. Of course, even if I was that lucky, it still meant that I'd have to somehow get rid of the original picture, which was on Gigi's phone.

I could tell the odds were stacked against me, but I had to at least try. The alternative was just too devastating not to.

A peek into his first class showed me that either he hadn't come to school today or he'd left class early—a bad sign either way—and after ditching and driving past his house, I still had no clue where he was. His bike was gone, which meant he could be anywhere. And I wasn't about to knock on his family's door and ask them if they'd seen him. I wasn't sure I'd ever be able to face them again, considering all the lies I'd told Asher. They'd probably feel just as betrayed as Asher did by my actions, and how could I blame them? I'd hurt their son and, indirectly, Abby. Considering how close they all were, I doubted they'd forgive me anytime soon.

So I just began to drive, thinking maybe he was doing the same thing. I scanned the opposite lane, looking for a motorcycle like his, but every time I saw one, I was disappointed to see that he wasn't the one riding. I was getting desperate and contemplated giving up on my search, but my heart wouldn't let me. I pictured kissing him and what it felt like to be in his arms and I knew I had to at least try to make things right.

Kissing.

Something clicked, and I had a total eureka moment. Nearly flipping my car as I turned it around, I headed in the opposite direction, knowing in my gut that my instincts were right.

I only hoped I could remember how to get there.

A half hour and a few wrong turns later, I was headed down a dirt road and toward the wooded area a quarter mile ahead. As I drove up, I saw him standing there, his back to me. I knew he'd heard me pull up, so I was surprised when he didn't turn to see who was there.

At first my heart soared to see him, but then it lurched as I noticed the woods around him. Nearly every tree in the clearing had a hole in it. Some had fallen down; others looked like Swiss cheese. The wood around the holes was charred black and I knew why, even before I saw it happen for myself. Asher raised his hand and shouted the words to the exploding spell and another hole appeared in a tree nearby. I winced at the noise and the anger he must be feeling to create such a blast.

He had perfect aim.

I turned off the engine and got out of the car, my hands

shaking as I pushed the door closed behind me. He knew it was me; he wouldn't have risked doing a spell if it wasn't someone who knew he had powers. That much I was sure of. What I wasn't sure of was whether we were going to be okay.

"Asher?" I asked, my voice quavering. I was scared. Not of him—I knew he'd never hurt me—but of the possibility of this being the end.

He kept his back to me and I watched it rise and fall like he was breathing hard. The silence was worse than having him yell at me. Anger I could deal with. Him never talking to me again? That, I had no chance of surviving.

I started to walk over to him, hoping that if I could just hold him in my arms, it would somehow show him how much I cared about him. How sorry I was. But I only made it a few steps before he spun around to face me.

"You lied to me," he said, the words dripping with venom. "Again."

I stopped in my tracks. I'd expected him to be upset, but the way he was looking at me was shocking. His eyes were wild, his hair, which usually fell perfectly in place, was disheveled. Only parts of him resembled the guy I loved, the rest belonged to someone else entirely.

"I know," I said, looking down at the ground. "I'm sorry. I never wanted to hurt you, but The Elite dared me—"

"The Elite? Jesus Christ, Brooklyn, get a mind of your own for once," he said, throwing his arms up in the air and starting to pace in front of me.

His words stung. "I *do* have a mind of my own," I said, though I couldn't blame him for thinking I didn't.

"Oh, really? So kissing some guy while you were with me was all *your* idea?" he asked. I could tell that just saying the words was torture.

"No. It was theirs. But they got me drunk and it didn't mean anything. It was just a stupid dare," I said. "And we weren't even together yet. I mean, we were hanging out, but you hadn't asked me to be your girlfriend. For all I knew you could have been seeing other girls too."

I hadn't meant to turn things around on him like that, but I felt like I'd been backed into a corner. And everything in me was telling me to fight. Fight for myself and fight for him. Everything felt like it was crumbling around me and I was trying desperately to get a handle on it all.

"So you think what you did was okay due to a *technicality?*" he asked, shaking his head incredulously. "You're a piece of work. And, Brooklyn, you know I wasn't seeing anyone else."

"You could have been . . ."

"Stop with the lies!"

His words echoed in the air around us. When he first showed me this place, he said it was where he liked to go to be completely alone. That no one was around for miles, so there was no threat of anyone seeing him do magic. I could tell by the silence that followed that it was true. I wondered if this experience was going to ruin the secret sanctuary for him, and felt bad that I was hurting him yet again.

"Okay."

It was all I could say. I was tired. Tired of keeping up appearances. Keeping things from the people I loved. Pretending I was someone I wasn't. I knew the only chance I had of holding on to Asher and what we had was to finally come clean. On everything.

"A few months ago, I was no one," I said quietly. "People walked by me in the hallway like I didn't even exist. My only friend was Ms. Zia and I spent every day at lunch eating with her in her office. I've never been invited to another person's birthday party before. I don't know what it's like to have a best friend, let alone a BFF. It was like I didn't have a role in the movie of my life. I wasn't even an extra. Getting up in the morning was excruciating for me, Asher. I was so lonely I wanted to die.

"When I got my powers, I thought my life was going to change. But it didn't. Until I became this." I gestured to my new-and-improved self. "And suddenly people paid attention to me. I became a part of this world, finally. Strangers began to talk to me. The Elite invited me to join them. Other kids knew my name. They even started to copy me. *You* finally noticed me."

Asher winced at this. At least I knew he was still listening to me.

"All I ever wanted was to *be* someone, Asher. Do you know what it's like to walk around feeling like you don't exist? It's awful. I wanted to prove I was here for a reason. That all of this wasn't just pointless. I needed to feel something other than sadness. So, yeah, I started to change to make myself into what everyone else wanted. But I swear, I did it because I wanted to get to a place where I could do something positive with myself. I couldn't do that being who I was before.

"I've done things I'm not proud of. Things that hurt people. Last night I helped the others break into the school and they stole files that they're using to destroy other students' lives." I didn't feel like now was the time to let him know that Abby'd been caught in the crossfire. One crisis at a time. "I had no idea they were going to do that, but it was me that made it possible. When I found out, I told them that I was going to confess what we'd done. Gigi sent that picture to you as a warning to me. A warning to back off. She knew that if I lost you, I wouldn't have the strength to do what was right."

Asher slowly sank to the ground, sitting down on the wide trunk of one of the fallen trees. His face had relaxed and he was no longer shaking. I knew I was dumping a lot on him all at once and I had no idea what he was feeling, but I kept going.

"I know I've hurt you, and for that I'm truly sorry. It was never my intention. It was never my intention to hurt anyone. I've lied to you in the past, but I'm telling you that it will all stop here. You know everything about me now. Every last dirty detail. And I can understand if you don't want to be with me, now that you know the *real* me. But if anyone can help me find the best me, it's you. You're the power behind my magic. Please give me the chance to change—this time into someone *better*."

Asher stared at the ground as I finished spilling my guts to him. I was surprised at how relieved I felt, now that I'd confessed all my sins. I had no idea what his reaction was going to be, but I knew deep down that it had to be done. In that moment, I also came to another realization: no matter what happened between Asher and me, I had to stop The Elite once and for all.

Asher stood up. For the first time, I noticed that he looked exhausted. His arms hung limply by his sides and he could barely lift his head. Seeing him like this created an ache in my chest that I'd never felt before. All I wanted to do was rush over to him and hold him to me and comfort him until he could be himself again. But I held myself back, knowing it was ridiculous of me to assume I was the answer to his problems when I'd created most of them in the first place.

Finally, Asher spoke, his voice so quiet that I had to strain to hear it at first.

"I had no idea life was like that for you. It would be awful not to have anyone to support you and love you and convince you that the world needs you. I'm *so sorry* that you had to go through that, Brooklyn," he said. "And I'm sorry that I didn't come to you sooner and let you know that you existed to me. Because you did. I'd been admiring you for months before I finally came up to you and said something. I suppose it was my fault for dragging my feet."

My heart swelled.

"And I wish you would've told me all of this from the very beginning, because it would have explained a lot. I could've been there for you, showed you another side of this world we live in. But you never even gave me a chance."

My eyes began to tear up. He was right.

"Instead, you decided to lie to me. Repeatedly. If you'd given me the benefit of the doubt, I would've shown you that I'd love you no matter who you were before. I could've gotten over just about everything, Brooklyn. Everything except not being able to trust you."

I was fully crying now. I wanted to beg him to stop. Ask him not to say the words that I knew were coming, but I was having trouble breathing and couldn't get it out.

He ran his hands through his hair and then shoved them in his pockets. "This stuff that's going on with my parents right now—it's heavy. I can't explain it, but it's not good and it's making me reevaluate who I can trust. And with everything that's happened," he said, motioning around us, "I just don't know if I can trust you anymore."

"You can!" I said, suddenly finding my voice. I rushed over to him and grabbed onto his shirt tightly. "You know everything now. I promise you can trust me. I will never lie to you again."

"I don't know, Brooklyn . . ." He began to back away from me.

"I'll help you with whatever's going on at your house. I want to be there for you. Please let me help you," I begged him.

"It's so much more serious than I thought," he said, turning to look off into the woods. "People could get hurt. *You* could get hurt."

I had no idea what he was talking about, but I needed to prove to him that I would do anything if it meant I could be with him.

"I don't care," I said. "I want to help. I'm going to come over right after school, okay? Let me show you that you can trust me again."

We were quiet for a moment as I waited for his response. Finally, he nodded. It was practically imperceptible, but it was there. And that was enough to give me hope.

He turned to me. "This doesn't mean we're back together," he said quietly. "So many things have to change before that could ever happen."

"I know," I said, nodding. "And they will. I will. I promise, from here on out, I'll be everything you fell in love with."

We stood there, me still hanging on to his shirt and him looking off into the distance. When he began to pull away, I let him go and watched as he went over to his bike.

As he drove away from me, I thought about everything I needed to do in order to win him back. I'd caused so much wreckage and it was going to take a while to clear it all. But I had a feeling I knew just where to start.

Chapter Twenty-Seven

Since there was nothing I could do about Asher's and my relationship until after school, I turned my focus to taking down The Elite. There was no way that just telling the administration about the break-in was going to be enough to destroy them. Gigi had proven that before. First of all, they had enough resources that I knew they'd somehow get off. With money and power came lawyers, influential parents, and unlimited resources, which meant that they'd most likely get a slap on the wrist. And since I didn't have access to any of that, I'd be the one to take the brunt of the blow.

I also knew that Gigi had something else up her sleeve. I had no idea what it was, but if she'd been willing to get rid of her only means of blackmailing me, it meant she had something even bigger in her arsenal, just waiting to be used. I couldn't imagine anything worse than the photo she'd sent Asher, but it had to be more serious than that. And that was a scary thought.

That brought me to the realization that if I was going to hurt The Elite, I had to do something *huge*.

And so I began to plan. As I made my way back to school from the woods, I ran through all the spells I'd ever read or written down in my notebook. An idea began to take shape, and I wondered if I'd be able to take care of it all myself. I debated asking Abby for help but knew that Asher wouldn't want me getting her involved. Besides, she'd probably be so mad at me after finding out I had something to do with her essay getting out that I'd be the last one she'd want to do any favors for. Nope, this was a problem I'd created alone, so I had to take care of it alone. I couldn't afford any more collateral damage.

By the time I got back to school, it was lunchtime and my plan was fully formed. I walked into the building, this time confident for entirely different reasons. It was just after eleven, which meant that lunch was in full swing. I ignored the stares that came my way as I passed people in the hallways. Whatever they were thinking about me didn't matter. Not anymore, at least.

As I walked, Tucker turned the corner up ahead of me and headed toward the cafeteria. My pulse began to speed up as I had a thought. I quickened my pace until I was just a few people behind him and then stopped just inside the cafeteria doors. He walked over to the food line and grabbed a tray.

Scanning the room, I quickly found Shayla sitting alone at a table in the corner. She had her head down and her hair was covering her face, but I could tell that it was her. The misery rolled off her in waves. Taking a second to clear my mind, I lifted my hands nonchalantly, pointed a finger at each of them, and then brought my hands together until they sparked in the middle.

Shayla's head slowly raised and then Tucker turned to look in Shayla's direction. Their eyes met and I knew it had worked. I wanted to watch them reunite, bask in the afterglow of them getting back together. I couldn't begin to explain how it felt to pair two people so perfectly suited for each other. It made my heart ache in a way that was both gratifying and slightly jealous.

But instead of sticking around to admire my handiwork, I moved on. I had things to do, plans to set in motion. I turned to look at The Elite, who were all gathered at their usual table at the back of the room. They sat there feasting while looking down at their kingdom below.

It was time for their tyranny to be over.

Eliza was sitting at one end of the table, checking out her reflection in a small gold compact. She'd been holding it since I walked in, clearly enamored with her own good looks. I briefly debated matching her with her own reflection so that she'd fall in love with herself but figured that might already be the case. I had to think bigger picture.

Sticking to my original plan, I let my gaze turn to Camden, who was popping grapes into his mouth and listening to something Wheatley and Rhodes were saying. His arm hung across the back of Gigi's chair protectively.

Satisfied that I was doing the right thing, I placed one finger on Camden and the other on Eliza. The electric shock I got when my fingers met was so big that I could actually see the spark.

If you hadn't been looking for it, you wouldn't have noticed. But I did. It was the slightest of glances, but Eliza slowly shifted her mirror so she could see Camden in it. His eyes darted almost imperceptibly away from Gigi.

I smiled.

Next I said a few words under my breath while focusing on Tweedledee and Tweedledum, casting a spell on each of them. There was no physical change in the two—I'd have to get closer to be sure it had worked—but I wasn't worried about that.

Right now I had a thing or two I needed to talk with The Elite about.

I walked over to the stairs, praying with every step I took that I wouldn't trip. Hopefully I looked more poised than I felt—because in actuality, I felt like the ultimate fraud—but I had to play the part if this was all going to work. So I placed one hand on my hip and let my other sway back and forth as I walked. My chin was tipped slightly in the air, and I wore a smile that implied that I had a secret and it was delicious.

Gigi saw me first. And though her head didn't turn in my direction, she studied me as I made my way across the room. She was wondering what I was going to do. Would I yell? Would I make a scene? Would I walk right by and claim a table in the corner and eat by myself like Shayla had? Her face didn't betray her, though. It stayed stony and strong. She even smiled at me as I approached the bottom of the stairs and then ascended them confidently.

Others in the cafeteria were watching now and I was happy about that. I wanted an audience for this. If everything worked like I'd planned, people would be witnessing the beginning of the end for The Elite.

"Brooklyn," Gigi said as I pulled out the chair across from her and sat down, crossing my legs slowly and looking into her face. The others stopped whatever conversations they were having and turned their attention to me, stunned to see that I was back.

"Gigi," I answered. Then, nodding to the others, I added, "Guys."

Eliza put down her compact and Wheatley dropped the sandwich he'd been chowing on. I had their complete attention now.

"How did things go with Asher?" Gigi asked, sticking out her bottom lip. "I hope he wasn't too mad."

I couldn't believe how callous she was being and wondered why I'd never fully seen it before. "We broke up," I said, trying not to let my emotions show. "And I wanted to thank you for that."

Gigi blinked, her face breaking momentarily by the news. "What?" she asked.

"Well, you know, Asher was getting a bit . . . clingy," I lied. "And now that I'm one of The Elite, I figured it was time I traded up. I'd been looking for a way to break up with him myself, but the picture actually took care of things for me. So, thanks for that."

This wasn't what she'd been expecting and she looked at the others uncomfortably before answering slowly. "Well, good," she said, not sounding like she actually meant it. "Glad I could help."

I smiled as sweetly as I could, thoroughly enjoying watching her squirm. Then I leaned forward and whispered, "I was hoping I could return the favor one day."

"Um, no need," she answered, matching my faux politeness.

"Oh, I *insist*," I said. "Maybe I can help you with whatever you're working on now. Who are you planning to destroy next?"

I looked straight at Wheatley as I asked this, testing out whether the spell had worked, while getting my answers at the same time. He leaned back in his chair, no doubt planning to keep his mouth shut and stare me down, but instead started to talk.

"That kid Tisch. We found out that he's seeing a therapist because he's bipolar," Wheatley said. "People will think he's crazy if they find out he's seeing a shrink."

The others shot Wheatley a look. His eyes grew big. I knew he was wondering why he was telling me all that. He'd had no plan to divulge the information, but he'd been compelled to.

The spell, which acted like a truth serum, was working.

"Cool," I said, acting like I didn't think it was horrible that they were planning on humiliating another kid because he needed someone to talk to. "Well, I just wanted to stop by and tell you no hard feelings. Things have a way of working themselves out for the best."

"What are you doing, Brooklyn?" Gigi asked me as I pushed away from the table and stood up.

"What you guys taught me to do," I said sweetly. "Live up to my full potential."

Then I gave them a little wave before turning my back on them. I knew they were watching me walk away, stunned at what had just happened.

All I'd done was plant the seeds. The rest I was leaving up to them to do themselves. I thought it might take a few days for things to get under way, but I'd grossly underestimated how quickly things could snowball out of control. It started with a few conversations here and there. Whispers that something was going on as people walked the hallways. I overheard one girl say that Rhodes had told a teacher that he thought he could teach the class better than she could. This was shocking for many reasons, but mostly because he was every teacher's pet. He was the one student they could count on to always know the answer and he brought up the whole school's average. He'd never had an attitude problem before, so at first the teacher had thought he was joking. When he said it again a few minutes later, followed by a rant about how he was surrounded by idiots, he was sent down to Mr. Franklin's office.

But it didn't stop there. Word was that Camden had been walking around school sans Gigi, something that *never* happened. The two were always attached at the hip, and the fact that they were walking around solo had everyone buzzing. Nobody knew what was going on exactly, only that it appeared there was trouble in paradise.

And Wheatley had practically been on a rampage all day. The fact that he couldn't seem to keep his mouth shut had clearly pissed him off because he'd gone ballistic on the lockers in the boys' changing room, denting a few before Coach was able to get him to calm down. According to a kid in my econ class, when the coach had asked him what his problem was, he'd responded, "I can't stop!" before running out of the room, hands covering his mouth.

Yes, things were progressing much faster than I thought they would, and I figured it was all going to come to a head very soon. The only problem was that I had somewhere to be. As the day wound down, I hoped that the finale would hold off until the next day so that I could meet Asher as planned.

As soon as the bell rang, I headed straight for the door that would bring me to the lot where my car was parked.

I was so preoccupied with what I was going to say to Asher when I met up with him at his house—the first being what I had done to The Elite—that I didn't even see Ms. Zia walk out of her office and make a beeline for me. In fact, I didn't even notice her until she was already blocking my way.

"Ms. Z.," I said, surprised to see her. I peeked around her and looked at the door that would assure my escape, and then back at her.

"Brooklyn, I know what happened," she said evenly. "And I think you know it too."

I did know, and I fully intended to tell her everything—just not now. Right now I had to get over to Asher's like I'd promised.

"I can't really talk about this now," I said, trying to step around her.

"They broke into my office, didn't they?" she asked, stopping me in my tracks. We both knew who the "they" were that she was talking about. I figured she'd suspect The Elite at some point, but not this soon. "I don't know how they did it. My office is always locked and so are the cabinets. And the guards didn't see anything. But I can't find any of the files of the students I've seen today and I know that *they* did it. I just don't know how to prove it."

I didn't know what to do. I wanted to say something, but it would mean that we'd be here for hours. And as much as I wanted to help, I needed to get to Asher.

I stood there feeling torn in two different directions.

"Well?" Ms. Zia asked, looking at me like I was the only one who could help her. There was no more anger toward me, just a desperate plea. "Please don't tell me you're going to cover for them, Brooklyn. You know, eventually they're going to get caught, and if you're there when they do, it's going to be bad."

Students were walking around us, and whenever they'd disappear out the doors, I'd catch glimpses of my car. I needed to get to that car. It was a long shot that Asher would forgive me as it was, but I knew that if I didn't show at all, it would be over for good.

"I'm not going to cover for them anymore," I said. "But I really have to—"

"What the hell are you two doing?"

It was Gigi's voice. I'd never heard her raise it before, but there was no mistaking that it was her. Ms. Zia and I turned to see her standing in front of Rhodes and Wheatley, her expression dark. None of them looked happy.

"It's not us," Rhodes hissed. For someone who always looked so together, it was weird to see him bothered. Nervous even.

"How can it not be you, if you're the ones saying it?" she asked, growing more annoyed by the second. "Come on, Rhodes. You're not the dumb one here."

Wheatley scowled at her not-so-subtle dig. "It's like, when we open our mouths, we can't control what comes out," Wheatley said, so low that I could barely hear him.

I smiled despite myself. When I'd cast the truth serum spell, I couldn't have envisioned it working so well. They seemed so confused as to why they were spilling their guts. It must have made them feel helpless having something specific in mind to say and then something else entirely coming out. Ms. Zia caught me staring. She leaned toward me and whispered, "What's going on?"

By now we weren't the only ones watching the show unfolding in front of us. People were starting to gather in the hallway, slowing down to see what was going to happen next. Gigi noticed the crowd and instantly put a smile on her face to give the illusion that everything was fine.

Of course, nothing was fine, but to fight in public would give the impression that they were weak. And the Fab Five were fab because they stuck together.

Wheatley and Rhodes took her cue and tried to appear calm, though Wheatley still looked as if he was about to erupt. Gigi motioned for them to follow her and they started to walk in our direction. Almost immediately, she saw me standing there with Ms. Zia and her face became icy. She continued our way, her eyes set on me and the guys walking behind her like they were her bodyguards.

Just when I thought she was coming for me, Gigi's gaze shifted to a place behind me and her demeanor completely changed. It was like watching a statue crumble. I was totally confused by what was happening, but then I turned around.

There, walking toward us, were Camden and Eliza. He had his hand on her lower back and they were leaning in toward each other, Eliza seeming to fit perfectly in the crook of his arm. She laughed softly as he whispered something in her ear. They weren't doing anything that would be considered cheating, but the intimacy of the moment was clear.

They looked like a young couple in love and Gigi had seen it all.

Gigi marched right in between me and Ms. Zia and yanked Eliza away from Camden. Eliza looked as shocked as the rest of us and took a step back to put space between her and Gigi.

Gigi was practically breathing fire. "What are you doing?" she demanded.

"Calm down, G," Camden said, shoving his hands into his pants.

"Don't tell me to calm down. What the hell was that?" she said, gesturing between the two of them.

The crowd was growing around us now; everyone wanted the chance to see the drama go down. For me, it was the perfect time to sneak out and meet Asher. Only, if I left now, I might miss my only chance to stop The Elite. And if that happened, their reign over Clearview would continue and I wasn't sure how many more lives would be ruined because of my inaction.

It felt like an impossible decision to make, yet I knew what Asher would want me to do.

I took a few steps toward Gigi and the others, pulling Ms. Zia along with me. "Here's your chance to find out," I told her.

"It was nothing," Camden muttered.

"It didn't *look* like nothing. It looks like my *boyfriend* is hooking up with my *best friend*."

"We're not hooking up," Eliza cut in.

"Like I'd believe *you*," Gigi spat.

"What's that supposed to mean?" Eliza said, taking a step toward her, hands on her hips defensively.

"Can we just go somewhere and talk . . . ?" Camden asked, glancing over at Eliza.

"We can explain," Eliza said.

Gigi looked from one of them to the other, her face genuinely shocked. "I can't believe I didn't see this before now," she said, turning to Eliza. "You're not even a good actress!"

"What?" Eliza shrieked. She stomped over to Gigi and pointed a finger in her face. "I'm a *great* actress. I've been *acting* like your friend for the last three years, haven't I?"

"Please. Your nose has been so far up my butt, I'm surprised you even have time to go for auditions," Gigi said, crossing her arms. "Then again, if my mom had ditched me when I was a kid, maybe I'd be a kiss-up too."

"I can't believe you read my file!"

This was what I'd been waiting for. I leaned in toward Ms. Zia and elbowed her. "Go in now, and ask about the files."

Her forehead crinkled up and she looked like she was about to ask me more. I shook my head to let her know there was no time. She hesitated just another second before stepping into the middle of the escalating fight and placing her hand on Eliza's arm.

"What files are you talking about, Eliza?" she asked.

Noticing Ms. Zia for the first time, Eliza opened her mouth

and then shut it again, thinking better of divulging the information. She may have been mad at Gigi, but she wasn't stupid enough to admit anything yet.

Frustrated by her silence, Ms. Zia turned to face the guys, who were standing quietly behind her.

"What files are they talking about, Rhodes?" she asked.

Rhodes licked his lips and I could tell he was struggling. Finally, his mouth fell open and he began to talk. "The student files we took from your office," he said.

There was an audible gasp around us, and Rhodes began to sweat. Ms. Zia's eyebrows raised and she glanced over at me before turning back to them.

"Who's we?"

"Me, Wheatley, Camden, Eliza, and Gigi."

I was surprised when he didn't name me as one of the culprits, but then I remembered that I hadn't actually stolen any of the files, so technically this was the truth. Ms. Zia smiled triumphantly.

"Wheatley, why did you want the files?" she asked, enjoying their game of truth.

His face looked pained, but he spoke again. "We wanted to find out things about the other students, use it against them for our own purposes," he said. "It's important that they know we can hurt them if they step out of line. And then there are the ones who just deserve it."

"You son of a bitch!" Camden yelled, and lunged for him. Rhodes stepped in between them and held him back. "Shut up!"

"Whose idea was it?" Ms. Z. asked no one in particular.

But it was Gigi who answered. "It was Brooklyn's," she said, pointing at me. "All of this was her idea."

The Queen B walked over to me angrily. Everyone who

was standing near me moved away like I was contagious. Nobody wanted to fall victim to Gigi's wrath. Truth be told, neither did I.

"This is all your fault," she said, just inches away from my face. "You don't think we're the only ones who are going to go down for this, do you?"

Ms. Zia briefly stopped talking when she heard what Gigi said. After catching my eye and holding it a beat, Ms. Zia turned back to interrogating the others. I got ready to square against my nemesis one last time.

"I don't care if I get in trouble," I said as evenly as I could. "What we did was wrong. I can't watch you hurt anyone else. And if I get suspended or even go to jail for it, then so be it. I won't let you control me anymore, Gigi."

"I don't think you have a choice about that," she said, a flash of defiance in her eyes. "I think you're going to take the fall for all of this."

I snorted. "That's not going to happen."

"I think it will," she said. "Because I have proof of who you *really* are." I had no idea what she was talking about but I could tell she was serious.

Ms. Z. started to herd all of us into her office, and the crowd was beginning to break up. Eliza and Camden had somehow found their way back to each other and were talking quietly and giggling despite the circumstances. Rhodes continued to spill his guts and Wheatley simply looked defeated.

It was just a matter of time before the whole group imploded. And then everything would be okay. There was no way of stopping the momentum now.

"What are you talking about?" I asked Gigi, not really caring about the answer.

"I'm talking about you, *witch*."

My mouth went dry and every inch of me felt numb. I was sure I hadn't heard her correctly. She couldn't have possibly said what I thought she said.

"What did you say?"

She smiled then, and what I saw scared the crap out of me. Underneath the prim-and-proper exterior lay an evil bitch, so much more deadly than I ever thought possible.

"I taped you the night we broke into the school. We hid a cell in the same spot we used for surveillance and Rhodes rigged it to start taping when I texted it," she said. I suddenly remembered hearing the whirring sounds and then seeing Gigi on her phone just before going into Ms. Zia's office. "I knew you were hiding something. And you can only imagine what I found when I watched it. You didn't open that door with a key, Brooklyn. You used something else."

"I don't know what you're talking about . . ." I said, fear creeping inside me.

"I think you do, and if you don't take the fall for this now, everyone else will know your secret too," she said. "Witch."

I watched with terror as she walked into the office and joined the others. I had no choice but to follow.

Chapter Twenty - Eight

My life may have not been ending, but in the seconds after Gigi confessed what she had against me, memories began to flash through my mind. Vacations with my family, the time we went to Disneyland and Dad threw up on the teacups, the first spell I ever cast, my first kiss with Asher. But the one thing that I couldn't stop thinking about was the story my parents had told me about my great-aunt Evelyn. She hadn't been careful while doing her magic and she'd paid for her mistakes with her life. I'd promised my parents that I'd be careful, and here I was, practically in the same position as Evelyn. I suppose the saying was right. History had a way of repeating itself.

"I can't tell you how much trouble you're all in," Ms. Zia said as she closed the door behind her and took her place behind her desk. "Breaking into my office, blackmail—these are all serious offenses. Suspension doesn't even begin to cover what's going to happen if this is true."

Gigi had her gaze locked on me and seemed to be barely

listening to Ms. Z. She took the strap of her hobo bag, adjusted it on her shoulder, and then placed her hand over it protectively. I knew from searching her earlier that she wasn't carrying the files. But considering how Eliza had refused to let me see what was in hers, I had a feeling I knew where they were.

Was I willing to put myself in danger just to stop a few selfish, spoiled brats?

Self-preservation told me to run. And it was certainly what my parents would have wanted me to do. But my gut was telling me differently. And then something dawned on me. All I'd ever wanted to do was impact the lives around me, and here was my chance to do it. All I had to do was put myself in the line of fire.

Taking everything into consideration, I made my decision.

Searching my memory for the right spell, I said the words that I knew would switch the contents of Gigi's and Eliza's bags. "Alterago fila."

"What was that, Brooklyn?" Ms. Zia said, not quite catching what I'd said.

"I said, 'I'll tell you about the files.'"

Gigi's face relaxed as she realized she'd won the fight. Ms. Zia, however, frowned. I don't think she'd ever really suspected that I was involved. Deep down, she'd still been holding out hope that I was the girl she'd befriended years ago. Well, she was about to find out exactly who I was. I only hoped I was doing the right thing.

"I'm the one who broke into your office, Ms. Zia," I said, keeping my focus on my feet. "I knew that you kept the files here in your cabinets and figured no one would get hurt if I just took a look."

I looked up and saw Ms. Zia's face fall as I confessed. It felt horrible to know I was causing her anguish, but I had to keep my main goal at the forefront of my mind. Swallowing hard, I pushed forward.

"It's true," I said quietly. "All of this is my fault."

"I guess that means you don't need us anymore," Gigi said, straightening and heading toward the door.

Ms. Zia started to say something to Gigi, but then gave up.

"But," I cut in, "I wasn't alone."

Gigi stopped, her hand on the doorknob. She didn't dare turn around, because she would've seen the defiance in my face.

"They told me they just wanted to read their own files. Only theirs. I had no idea they were going to take the others and use them in the way they did," I said, shaking my head. "If I had, I never would've agreed to it."

"Shut up, you liar!" Gigi screeched, turning around to face me now.

"I'm not keeping your secrets any longer," I said.

"Then I'm not keeping yours," she answered bitingly. "Ms. Zia, there's something Brooklyn's been keeping from you. From all of us. And I have proof. Ask her how she broke into your office. Ask her!"

Ms. Zia turned to me but couldn't seem to get the question out.

"Fine, I'll tell you," Gigi said, bordering on hysterics. "She used *magic*. Brooklyn's a witch."

Ms. Zia studied me, eyes wide and mouth open. Then she took a step toward us. "You're kidding, right?" Ms. Zia said, not amused by Gigi's joke and definitely believing that's what it was. "Gigi, you've got to come up with something better than that."

"I'm telling you the truth!" she yelled, reaching into the pocket of her jacket for the proof she knew she had. My heart began to race. If Gigi had the video with her and it showed what I thought it did, I'd have so much more explaining to do. My life—and my family's life—would never be the same. But it'd be worth it if it meant everyone else would finally be free to live without fear of what The Elite would do to them.

However, when I looked around the room, I saw that the others were staring at Gigi as if she'd gone crazy. Good. That meant that she'd been the only one to see the video. So far, at least. Maybe it was still possible to contain it. I didn't know how I would do it, but I'd have to come up with something.

Gigi started to rummage through her purse. As she did so, I saw her eyes bug out and she closed it up quickly before turning to me.

"What did you do?"

"I don't know what you're talking about," I said, breathing for the first time since she'd said the *W* word out loud.

"How did you get them into my bag?" she asked. "Did you do a spell? Was that what you were doing before?"

Ms. Zia grabbed Gigi's bag and emptied its contents onto her desk. Dozens of file folders fell out, along with Eliza's compact and other assorted items.

"Hey! How did you get those?" Eliza asked, noticing her stuff and looking at her former friend accusingly. "Did you go through my bag?"

"I didn't go through your bag, you dimwit. I told you, Brooklyn is a *witch*! Why won't you people believe me?"

"Because it's insane," Camden said, scooting closer to Eliza without even noticing it. Gigi did, however, and narrowed her eyes at them. "What's your angle here, Gigi?" It was clear that she hadn't bothered to tell anyone else about her little witch hunt, so the others were just as in the dark as I was about what was happening.

"I'm not insane, *Camden*, and when I find my phone, I'll prove it," she said, putting her hands back into her pockets only to come up empty again.

"I think it's time to go see Principal Franklin," Ms. Zia said, picking up her phone and calling ahead to make sure they knew we were on our way.

We were each taken into separate rooms and interrogated individually. I tried to be as honest as possible without letting Principal Franklin know about my witchy ways. I told him everything I knew about The Elite and what they'd done— recently and in the past. I confessed to my own part in everything. I was sincerely sorry.

In the end, my parents were called and I was suspended for two weeks. What I'd done would go down on my permanent record, but the school wouldn't be pressing charges against me. I was lucky and I knew I had Ms. Zia to thank for the reason I wasn't in as much trouble as the others. I don't know all the details yet, but I could imagine they wouldn't be coming back to school. As for them, the truth spell I'd put on Wheatley and Rhodes had lasted much longer than I'd thought it would, and they'd both ended up spilling every last secret The Elite had. And apparently there were a lot.

By the time my parents and I left school, it was after six and all I wanted to do was go to bed and forget all about the last couple of months.

"I don't understand why you'd do this, Brooklyn," my mom said, her disappointment clear. We were in the car on our way home, so I had nowhere to escape to. I was stuck listening to everything my parents wanted to say to me. It was torture. And not just because I was about to get a major lecture. I couldn't believe I had let down everyone I cared about:

my parents, Ms. Zia, Asher. I felt lower than I'd ever been before and wondered who it was that I'd become. My only hope was that eventually, everyone would forgive me.

I stared out the window as houses zipped past. I hadn't told Mom and Dad about Gigi taping me while I used magic, and thankfully, none of the other adults mentioned Gigi's accusations. But the more worrisome thing was that we had no idea what had happened to the tape—not even Gigi knew—and that could prove more problematic than any of us could imagine.

"I hope it was all worth it," my dad said. "Because you won't be doing anything for the next several months. You'll go to school—when they let you back in, of course—and then you'll come home. No phone calls, no boyfriend, no magic. It's all off-limits."

The mention of Asher caused a flutter in my chest.

And then I remembered that I'd promised to meet him after school.

"I understand," I said. "Can we stop by the Astleys' so I can at least tell him that? Please? After that, it'll all be radio silence, I promise."

My parents looked at each other. I could tell they wanted to say no, but they were hopeless romantics. Maybe they figured that if I said good-bye to him now, it would cut down on the chances of me sneaking out to do it later.

"Fine. But make it fast," my mom said, turning the car in the direction of Asher's house. "This isn't a social call."

We pulled up in front of his place ten minutes later. A light was on in the kitchen, but other than that, the house was dark. It was too early for them to have gone to bed and I hoped that they were home. And that Asher would agree to speak to me.

"I'll be quick," I promised as I jumped out of the car and ran up the sidewalk. I knocked on the door, and as I did, it swung open a few inches.

Weird.

Pushing it the rest of the way open, I took a step inside.

"Hello? Anyone here? Asher? Abby? Sorry to bother you guys, but the door was open!"

No one responded. There was a silence I'd never experienced in the Astley house before. I walked through the living room and into the bright kitchen. There were pots on the stove, steam still rising off them, though there was no sign that any of it had been eaten.

Taking the stairs two at a time, I made my way to Asher's room first. It was empty. Walking over to his bed, I sat down on it and then lay back and closed my eyes. The comforter smelled like him. I took a deep breath and imagined he was there with me and that things were right again between us.

When I finally opened my eyes, I stared at the ceiling and noticed that something was off. The starry night that was always twinkling above the bed was no longer there. In its place was plaster and paint. I blinked at the plainness of it and sat up, confused. Leaving Asher's room, I headed down the hallway and into Abby's. When I turned on the light, I gasped at what I saw. The tree that had been so green and lush before had turned brown. Leaves covered the bed like they did the ground in the fall.

The tree was dying.

Abby had told me her parents controlled the spell that kept the tree alive, so where were they? Where were any of them? Had they left? Was it all because of me?

I heard a honking outside, my parents' way of letting me know it was time to go. Stunned, I made my way back downstairs and out the door. This time, I closed it behind me, listening for the click of the lock to tell me it was secure.

Two weeks passed much faster than I thought they would, and by the time I was allowed back into school, I felt like a new person. Not that my nerves weren't going a little crazy; I had no idea how the other students were going to react to me. I knew how quickly rumors could make their way around school, so I figured word would already be out about my part in the scandal. The question would be whether everyone would view me the same way they did The Elite.

One thing was sure: I was no longer invisible. Whether that was good or bad, I'd have to wait and see.

"How does it feel to be back?" Ms. Zia asked me as I sat down across from her on my first day back after my suspension.

"A little weird, I guess," I said. "It's sort of like it was before, but different, you know?"

This was true. Now that the rest of The Elite were gone, I was back to spending my days wandering the hallways alone. While I'd been stuck at home I'd discovered that after Rhodes and Wheatley had sold the others out, Gigi, Camden, and Eliza had followed suit. Pretty soon everyone had turned on each other and every bad thing they'd ever done was out in the open. The specifics were confidential, but I'd heard the rumors. Ms. Zia, being the professional she was, wasn't telling me what had come to light behind closed doors and I respected her enough not to ask.

What I *had* been able to find out was that all the members of The Elite had been suspended indefinitely and would not be graduating from Clearview. The most popular gossip included cheating on their SATs, harassing a freshman girl on Facebook until she transferred schools, and illegal gambling. I already knew they weren't above blackmail and breaking and entering, so I could only imagine what else they'd done.

I'd been prepared to go back to being invisible, but apparently the universe had other plans. In fact, word was I'd single-handedly brought down The Elite. And as much as everyone had put them up on a pedestal around school, it seemed that they were equally hated. Now that they were gone, nobody had to worry about being victimized next. That made me sort of a hero in the eyes of my fellow students. When people began to say hello to me in the hallways and step out of the way when I walked by, I realized that although The Elite were gone, my quest for popularity hadn't exactly disappeared with them.

But I was once again without friends. With Abby and Asher gone, I was left with no one I could be myself around. But I was hopeful that would change. Some of the followers of The Elite had already approached me, ready to do for me what they'd been willing to do for them. I had no need for personal assistants and no desire to treat people the way The Elite had, so instead, I invited them to sit with me at The Elite table. I hoped it would begin to make up for what they'd endured over the years.

And I'd decided to follow through with the Interact Club I'd joined on a whim. I'd started to attend meetings and even helped choose some of the activities we were going to do for the rest of the year. It felt good to take the focus off myself for a bit and be able to give back. Sort of like I was making amends for all that had happened.

"And how are you dealing with the Asher situation?" Ms. Zia asked carefully.

I winced as she mentioned his name. The truth was, I wasn't dealing. By now I was just trying to forget.

I'd snuck over to Asher's house every day for a week after that first night and nothing had changed. It was like the Astleys had just disappeared. Ms. Zia finally told me that someone had notified the school that Asher and Abby would be visiting relatives out of town for the remainder of the year and finishing up their classes there. She couldn't tell me where they'd gone, and I'd tried more than a dozen times to call Asher but always got his voice mail.

So a few days before my suspension ended, I'd decided to let it go. If Asher could just give up on what we had and leave without even bothering to say good-bye, then our relationship obviously hadn't meant much to him after all. It hurt at first, his leaving, but eventually the pain gave way to anger and then eventually, to accepting what happened. Soon I stopped thinking about him every second of every day and began to think about my future at Clearview.

"I'm dealing," I said, shrugging noncommittally. "He won't return my calls, I have no idea where he is, and he obviously thinks he's better off without me. And maybe he's right."

"From what you've told me, Brooklyn, it sounds like whatever's going on with him has nothing to do with you," Ms. Zia said.

"Yeah, I guess," I said. "I just want to move on."

"Well, it looks like you're certainly doing that," she said, gesturing to my outfit. I'd started to put time and energy into my outfits again lately, as a way of getting myself out of my funk. It was hard to feel bad when you had on a great dress.

"Yeah," I said, smiling. "I'm starting to refocus on the important things."

Like my magic and making the most of this second chance. Since I'd come so close to losing it all, I'd made a promise to myself that I wouldn't let it happen again. And that meant never letting another Gigi into my life. From here on out, I was going to be the person people followed. It was finally my turn to be on top.

And when it came to magic, this whole experience had taught me that I had a lot to learn. About casting and spells and practicing safely. Knowledge equals power, and the only way I was going to be able to hone that power was by learning from those who knew more than I did. I wasn't sure how to bring it up to my parents yet, but I was working on it.

"Well, that's good to hear, Brooklyn," she said, smiling at me. "I really think things are going to be better around here now."

"Me too, Ms. Z,," I said, standing up from the chair to leave. "See you after school, then? We'll go through all the donations for the school drive?"

She nodded and I walked out the door, swinging my purse as I went.

I was only a few steps away when I heard my phone beep, signaling that I had a message. I pulled out my cell and looked at the screen. There was a text from a blocked number. I clicked on the message, and the screen filled with a video that began to play immediately. My breath caught as I recognized what I was seeing.

It was me standing outside Ms. Z.'s office, my hands hovering over the handle. Looking closely, I watched as a rosy glow appeared underneath my hands. A few seconds later, I opened the door. It was obvious from the angle of the video that I'd never used a key to open the lock.

This was the video that Gigi had talked about. Only, I had no idea why it was being sent to me now.

My phone beeped again and I opened a new message, this time just a basic text.

Enjoy the show? I know I did. We'll be in touch soon.

I looked around the hallway as if I was suddenly going to see the person behind the text, but it was useless. I knew it wasn't from Gigi, because if it was, she wouldn't have texted it to me. She probably would've sent it to everyone in school for maximum collateral damage. And the person who *did* send it wasn't threatening to show it to anyone; they obviously just wanted me to know that they had it. But who was it?

I had a feeling I wasn't going to find out until the person wanted me to. And when they did, I'd be ready for it. After all, what did I have to lose? I'd already fallen once and survived. I thought I could probably handle this. I shoved my phone back in my purse and began to walk toward the cafeteria, forcing myself to think about what I *could* control—my standing at this school and taking the throne that was now mine. With The Elite gone, there was a serious hole in the social hierarchy, and I figured I was the only one able to fill it. And I planned to be the leader that the students needed. Someone who wouldn't abuse her power and would work to build others up instead of tearing them down. It wasn't going to be easy. With power came drama—I'd learned that the hard way. But it's the sacrifice you have to make to be at the top.

It's like they say: life's a witch.

Acknowledgments

How can I possibly thank all the people who've changed my life forever? Well, I can't, but here's my valiant effort. First, a world of thanks to everyone at Simon & Schuster Books for Young Readers for fighting for this series and being just as excited about it as I am. Alexandra Cooper, editor extraordinaire, for really "getting" these characters and making the revision process a truly enjoyable experience. You took this book and made it *magical*. Justin Chanda, for giving me a chance to make this the year of the witch. Amy Rosenbaum, for being just as punny as I am. Siena Koncsol, for sharing in my love of everything Whedonesque. And, of course, Paul Crichton, Krista Vossen, Jenica Nasworthy, Dorothy Gribbin, Chava Wolin, Bernadette Cruz, Elke Villa, Chrissy Noh, Lucille Rettino, and Anne Zafian, for working their magic on a daily basis.

Love and thanks to my phenomenal agent, Kevan Lyon, for being my guide through this crazy world of publishing, yet never telling me what to do. You're cool, smart, and such a great teacher. Taryn Fagerness, for getting my books out to the rest of the world—you were one of the first phone calls I got and you set me up with the best agenting team in the world. Brandy Rivers . . . I can't begin to describe what a *dream* it is to work with you! I can't wait to see this witchy world on the screen. Oh, and thank you for letting me borrow your last name for Eliza's character!

I have so much gratitude for those who've had a hand in my success (but might not know it): To everyone at Wattpad, thank you for giving me an amazing platform to tell my stories before anyone knew who I was. And for all my fans on Wattpad . . . it's because of you that my dreams are coming true. I can't underplay those who've inspired me with their ability to tell great stories: Joss Whedon, Meg Cabot, Christopher Pike, John Carpenter, Jessica Bendinger, Wes Craven, Tori Spelling, and Rob Thomas. Thank you for letting your imaginations run wild and sharing it with the rest of us. Without the incredible gluten-free muffins from Pip's Place, in NYC, I never would've made it through revisions. Thanks to Denise and the rest of the staff for keeping me happy, healthy, and full. Calvin Reid, thank you for taking this underdog and making her a top dog. You're a class act with a huge heart.

No girl can survive without her crew, so I have to give shout-outs to Amanda Healy, Tammy West, Kate Chapman, Jessica Grant, Alicia and Sue Chouinard, and Zachary Booth. You were there for me when I was just an "aspiring" writer and always indulged me in my crazy dreams. You're all rock stars in my book!

Lastly, I've been beyond lucky to have such a loving and supporting family. Mom, Dad, Jacey, and Amy, I have so much gratitude for the fact that you never set limits for what I could accomplish. I've loved being on this journey with you. To the Gielens, thanks for treating me like one of the family. And Matt . . . thank you for challenging me while being my number-one fan. I'm excited to conquer the world with you.

To the powers that be: Thank you for finding me worthy of telling your stories.